THE CARTOGRAPHERS

ALSO BY PENG SHEPHERD

The Book of M

THE CARTOGRAPHERS

peng shepherd

ORION

First published in Great Britain in 2022 by Orion Fiction,
an imprint of The Orion Publishing Group Ltd.,
Carmelite House, 50 Victoria Embankment
London EC4Y 0DZ

An Hachette UK Company

1 3 5 7 9 10 8 6 4 2

Compass by AlenaO/Adobe Stock

A CIP catalogue record for this book is
available from the British Library.

ISBN (Hardback) 9781398705425
ISBN (Trade Paperback) 9781398705432
ISBN (eBook) 9781398705456

Printed in Great Britain by Clays Ltd, Elcograf S.p.A.

www.orionbooks.co.uk

Author's Note

We tend to think of maps as perfectly accurate—after all, that's the point of them. What good would a map that lied be? But in fact, many maps do just that. Unbeknownst to almost everyone who unfolds one and trusts it to take them to where they want to go, there's a long-standing secret practice among cartographers of hiding intentional errors—*phantom settlements*—in their works.

Most of the time, these intentional errors are so small and well disguised, they're never found. But every once in a while, a phantom settlement doesn't stay a phantom.

Sometimes, something magical happens.

The Cartographers is a work of fiction, but its inspiration is rooted in truth. This story is for anyone who's ever opened a map and gotten lost in it.

THE CARTOGRAPHERS

I

The Library

I

In the dim light of her desk's single bulb lamp, the map nearly glowed.

Fra Mauro, it was called. It had been created in 1450 A.D. by a Camaldolese monk of the same name, who had designed it in his small cartography studio in the Monastery of St. Michael, in that glittering, floating city of Venice. Fra Mauro had researched his map by interviewing merchants traveling through the area from afar, which allowed him to depict the known world of the time with far greater accuracy than those cartographers who had come before him. Even to this day, the Fra Mauro map was considered one of the finest pieces of medieval cartography in existence.

Gently, Nell traced her gaze over the painted gold circular frame, looking for blemishes, inconsistencies in color, errant lines. The Fra Mauro map was also unique in that it was drawn opposite to most other world maps—it oriented the south at the top of its design, rather than the north.

Simply put, it was nothing short of a masterpiece.

If she'd been at a workstation in the conservation lab of the New York Public Library, with the map carefully installed onto a drafting table and her personal assortment of custom restoration tools laid out beside her, she would have chosen her graphic knife edge to gently cut away a frayed edge of the vellum or faintly scrape back a layer of too-boldly restored ink. She would have delicately touched the leg of the repainted *T* in the *ANTARTICVS* of the map's lower right legend, to nick the most minuscule width away, so that it matched the original letter beneath it more perfectly.

Instead, she simply pressed print, and went to go retrieve another copy of the map from the clunky machine.

The Fra Mauro map—the *real* Fra Mauro map—was on permanent exhibit in the city of its creation, in Venice's Biblioteca Nazionale

Marciana. The diagrams before her were no more than a stack of cheap facsimiles.

What she was doing was not what she had trained her entire life to do: conservation and research on priceless, ancient pieces of art in a hermetically sealed museum laboratory. She was adding flourish—nonsense weathering marks and fading—to budget scans of those masterpieces at a cramped, sagging desk in Crown Heights, Brooklyn, and then printing them out by the batch to be sold to casual enthusiasts to add a bit of academic flair to their decor.

Nell Young was not a scholar of cartography anymore. She was a design technician at CLASSIC MAPS AND ATLASES™, WE CAN MAKE ANY MAP!

Classic, as her boss called it for short, was the antithesis of conservation. Thousands upon thousands of reproductions of real ancient or rare works of art, mass printed onto modern, acid-free paper, then mass crinkled, or mass aged, or mass hand-decorated with anachronistic symbols, all able to be ordered with two-day shipping direct to a doorstep and hung in a living room that same afternoon.

It was also Nell's only paycheck.

It hadn't always been this way. Once, she'd been staring at a bright future ahead of her. She'd attended the best schools, successfully defended her Ph.D. dissertation, and landed an internship at none other than the awe-inspiring main branch of the New York Public Library, in its prestigious conservation department. She was on her way to someday matching, perhaps even surpassing, the illustrious reputation of her father, one of the NYPL's most celebrated scholars. People had even started to whisper about "the new Dr. Young" in the halls as she passed. Once, for a brief moment, she had been just a little bit famous in that tiny, overhead-fluorescent-lit, cluttered world of endless stacks and musty archive drawers.

Then the Junk Box Incident had happened.

Nell put her thumb on the right bottom corner of the Fra Mauro reproduction she'd just printed, to cover the small, unobtrusive logo. Seven letters in a faux-ancient font: *CLASSIC*. Every one of their products had the little word somewhere, to indicate that the map was indeed a known copy of the original and not attempting to pass itself off as the real thing. She didn't know how anyone could mistake an ancient work somehow printed onto matte-sheen finish poster paper for the real thing, but she ensured the logo was on every printout just the same. It was her only way of apologizing to the priceless originals.

"I don't know how you get here so early with the trains like this," a booming voice cried, preceding its owner. A moment later, Humphrey trudged around the corner into the office. "Do you just sleep here?"

"Obviously," Nell shot back, without looking up. She could tell by the rustle of fabric that Humphrey was still in his coat, his face probably pink from the walk from the subway station in the crisp spring weather.

They were an artist's perfect study of opposites. Nell was young, short even in heels, and in desperate need of some sun, topped off with a mop of mousy brown hair and tiny enough to completely disappear into an oversize cardigan, leaving only her glasses behind; and even though tall, bearded, warmly tanned Humphrey had to be in his sixties at least, everything was still huge about him—his voice, his build, his energy—and also his patience with her.

"So, what do you have for me today?" Humphrey was asking, leaning over Nell's desk.

"The Fra Mauro," she said. She spun it around and held it up by its corners. "I fixed the frame so the crackle will look perfectly accurate now, even under the matte finish and a layer of glass."

Next to her mouse on the desk, her mobile phone lit up suddenly as a call came through. The glow caught her eye—*a job, perhaps?*—but she resisted looking in front of Humphrey just in case. That was always her first, most hopeful thought when she got a call at work. But she hadn't applied for anything lately, not that she could remember, although after the first few hundred attempts, the applications all started to run together. The cartography field was small, and it always ended the same way. Once a potential employer realized who she was, and that none other than the elder Dr. Young himself had banished her from the industry all those years ago, she always stalled out at the next stage in the process.

"It's good," Humphrey nodded thoughtfully.

For a moment, Nell started to smile.

But then he said what he always did. "But we need it to look older." He curled his meaty hands into claws as if to indicate—something. A crumpled pirate treasure map, or ancient sand running through his fingers, or trash. "Like much older. Gimme another hundred years, plus storm damage or something. I want it to look like it went on a dangerous voyage, then was smuggled to us in a sunken treasure chest." He laughed. "You know?"

"That doesn't make any sense," Nell argued. Her phone lit up and buzzed again, a second call, but she continued to ignore it. "First of all, the Fra Mauro map was drawn on vellum, which lasts much longer than paper, and second of all, it wasn't a pirate map. It was created by a monk in the personal offices of his monastery, and stored there for the entirety of its existence until it moved to the Biblioteca Nazionale Marciana, making it one of the best-preserved specimens we have from the fifteenth century—"

"Nell, Nell, *Nellllll*." Humphrey sighed over her, gesticulating dramatically. "Historical accuracy, due respect to the original work, the code of conservation, a cartographer's honor. Spare me for once. It's not even nine o'clock in the morning yet. This isn't the Smithsonian. Our customers don't want perfectly accurate reproductions. They want old, mysterious, antique-looking things." He plopped the draft down on her desk, where she watched it halfway unfurl and come to a rest against her keyboard. He spread it out a little more, and caressed its minimally tarnished, historically accurate surface. "It's more romantic that way."

The phone screen went dark again, for the third or fourth time, and stayed that way at last. Whoever had been trying to reach her must have finally settled for voicemail.

Nell sighed, deflated. Humphrey was right, and she hated it.

"I get it," she finally said.

"Look, I get it, too," Humphrey replied, his voice gentler now. Even with her refusing to ever talk about the past, he'd been able to glean over the years just how passionate Nell had been about the work she used to do and the maps she used to curate. "I know this is not your dream career."

"Humphrey, I'm sorry," Nell started. Most of the time, Humphrey found their blue-collar boss versus uptight academic back-and-forth entertaining, but she knew she should be more grateful. After the Junk Box Incident, Humphrey was the only employer even just barely associated with the cartography industry that would take her in. Classic was hardly map work, but it was better than nothing at all. "Like you said, it's not even nine A.M.—"

"Hey, all forgiven." He rapped his knuckles on her desk, and then fished a twenty-dollar bill out of his wallet. "How about some coffee? My treat. You want one of those fancy caramel-mocha-swirly-whipped-cappuccino things?"

Nell forced a smile at his generosity. She was his head design technician, but the office was small. She was also the head accountant. She knew how tight money was, and how badly the office was falling apart. "Just black with some cream."

Humphrey smiled back and pressed the bill into her palm. "See you soon, then."

"You are *insufferable,*" she laughed, reaching for her purse with her other hand.

"Those stairs are insufferable!" he called after her over the slam of the office door.

Outside, the air was brisk and biting. Nell wrapped her cardigan tighter around her and set off, shivering. There was an artsy coffee shop across the street that would serve the kind of adjective-laden drink Humphrey had described, but she turned right and headed down the sidewalk for the bodega on the corner, where they bought their morning coffee most days. The owner was an old woman from Bangladesh, and Nell liked that no matter the weather or day, for as long as she'd known her, Farah always wore orange. There was at least some item of clothing on her that was bursting with that bright citrus hue. It made the whole shop warmer, somehow.

The bell on the door jangled sharply as she pushed her way in, and Farah—unfailingly, in orange—glanced up from her crossword puzzle and tipped her head. Nell made her way to the back of the bodega, where she poured two cups of coffee from the stainless-steel thermos, and then brought them to the counter.

"'Something lines,'" Farah muttered, brow furrowed. She and Nell never chitchatted, just nodded at each other and occasionally traded puzzle hints, which made Nell like her even more. "Only three letters."

"Try 'ley,'" she replied as she held out Humphrey's money.

"What?"

"Ley. L-E-Y." *Ley lines.* She smiled. It was a mapmaking term.

The old woman studied the crossword, and then nodded briskly. It fit.

The cash register clicked, the drawer shot open, and Farah handed Nell her change. Nell grabbed a coffee with each hand and ducked into the cold morning again. She almost made it back to their building in one breath, but had to suffer one more lungful of biting air before she scrambled inside and up the stairs.

"Nell." Humphrey's voice echoed from the other side of the office as soon as she opened the door.

"I got the coffee," she replied, but trailed off as she rounded the corner and saw the expression on his face.

"Did you take your phone with you?" he asked. He wasn't in his office, but by her desk.

"No. What's wrong?"

In response, his gaze slid over to where her phone sat, screen dark and silent.

"Someone's been trying to reach you all morning. They just called the main line, in my room," Humphrey finally said.

"Who was it?" she asked. "Humphrey. Who was it?"

He hesitated, but her warning glare forced him to continue. "You should check your messages," he said. "Someone from the library needs to talk to you urgently."

The library.

Nell went to her desk and set the coffees down, then gently picked up her mobile as if it were a small, not quite tame animal. Humphrey was still there, but was staring awkwardly at the pile of junk papers on the desk they used for dumping old mail instead of at her. Trying to give her support and privacy, but in fact just making everything more awkward. She wouldn't have expected such a big, loud man to become so meek in a crisis. *Was this a crisis?* She knew she was stalling. Before she could think about it anymore, Nell swiped the screen to unlock the phone and poked the green icon to pull up her calls.

"Are you okay?" he finally asked.

"Yeah," Nell said.

But she wasn't. Not at all.

The one she'd missed, several times now, was from someone who wasn't stored in her contacts anymore and so displayed only as a number rather than a name, but she still recognized it immediately. It was not a number she'd seen in almost a decade, since her unceremonious firing from the NYPL, and never expected to see again, because she'd sworn never to speak to him again for it.

But it was not her father who had made the call from his office phone.

Nell, Swann's voice was frantic and hushed after the beep. It startled her to hear him, after all this time. *I'm sorry to call you like this after so long, but there's been an emergency. Call me back as soon as you get this.*

As soon as the message ended, the phone rang again in her hand, startling her. This time it was the police.

Less than an hour later, she'd gathered her things, assured Humphrey she'd text him if she needed anything, and scrambled through the morning rush hour subways to find herself standing in front of the main branch of the New York Public Library. It was a Tuesday, but the entrance was still teeming with visitors. Children on school trips to the city clamored up and down the stairs, teenagers flirted, and elderly regulars edged slowly forward, book bags and lists for the day's research tucked under their elbows. Behind them, taxis honked as they jostled for space at the curb. Somewhere, a busker was playing a fast, nervous violin.

Nell could hardly remember the last time she'd come to this part of town. How many years had her life been only her small, dingy apartment, endless subway rides, and the cramped offices of Classic? Everything on Fifth Avenue was three times brighter and louder, as if someone had turned up a dial on every surface.

Just before the towering wooden doors of the library, however, all sound fell away. As she passed between the thick marble pillars and beneath the arches that carved the entryway, Nell felt a familiar shiver of wonder. This had always been what she imagined when she'd dreamed of her future. Echoing hallways, vaulted ceilings, grand old academic buildings. Not rickety staircases, crammed cubicles, and the faint smell of mold.

The lobby was quietly bustling, seemingly full despite its vastness. As she pushed through the clusters of visitors, Nell caught a flash of a familiar face across the huge space, kind but sharp eyes scanning beneath a navy-blue hat. Henry Fong, one of the library's longest-serving security guards, was on shift today. He'd been with the NYPL almost as long as her father had.

She ducked her head on instinct—she was already inches from losing her nerve, and to be spotted by someone she knew before she could find Swann would make her turn and flee for certain—and edged through the milling crowd for the room at the end of the lobby's northern hallway, above which the words *The Lionel Pincus and Princess Firyal Map Division* were carved in gold. Through there, she could reach the back offices, where Swann, and answers, would be.

A jolt of electricity went through her as she entered the Map Division. It was like resurfacing from a dark, cold lake into life. The air became warmer, the colors brighter, the sounds sharper. The reading tables waited, waxed wooden surfaces gleaming, and the shelves around the walls beckoned, bursting with relics. Sunlight, nearly blinding, streamed in through the huge windows. It took a moment for Nell to get ahold of herself.

It was so strange to be back again, after so many years. She had almost managed to block it out. To stop missing it so acutely. Every detail, every moment.

Just beyond the main reference desk, the unobtrusive side door marked Staff Only waited. She paused with her hand on the knob.

Just do it, she admonished herself. Her hand wavered. *Get it over with.*

Nell didn't really know what to prepare herself for, but the scene on the other side of the threshold was not it. She'd been bracing for chaos and shouting, like the day of the Junk Box Incident, she realized as she waited awkwardly in the quiet, half in and half out of the door.

It wasn't just quiet, it was utterly silent, she thought. She'd never seen the back offices *this* deserted.

After a few seconds, the door started to slowly close on her before she snapped back to life and leapt clear.

"Hello?" she called softly.

"Oh," another voice answered. "Just a moment!" A librarian not much older than Nell poked her head out of the first office, surprised.

"I'm sorry, I didn't mean to disturb you. I'm trying to find Swann," Nell said. She didn't recognize the woman, which meant she must have been hired after Nell had left. "Do you know what's going on?" The police hadn't told her anything on the phone, just ordered her to come.

"There's been—" the woman paused. "Well, we don't quite know yet. But it looks bad."

"Ma'am?" Nell looked up to see a police officer appear out of the conference room partway down the hall, and his partner behind him. "Are you an employee here?"

The librarian was staring at Nell more intently now. "Oh my," she said. "You . . . you're Dr. Young's daughter, aren't you?"

"I am," Nell admitted. "Helen Young. Nell."

Her face darkened. "I'm so sorry, but all this"—she gestured to the stillness—"this is about Dr. Young."

Nell stared for what felt like an eternity, trying to discern the answer in the woman's face.

What had he done now?

Her father had always been an uncompromising, unstoppable force. It was what made him the best at what he did while also making him impossible to love. Had he attacked a colleague's work? Disagreed over the provenance of a new specimen? Quarreled with the board, even?

"Whose life did he ruin this time?" she finally managed.

"If you could come with me," the first officer replied.

From within the conference room, a familiar figure burst into the hall behind the other policeman. "Nell!"

"Swann!" she cried.

Her heart clenched. She had missed him! He'd been the director of the Map Division for decades, but he had been so much more than that to her, too. An uncle, a mentor, a friend. And he looked the same, even seven years later—tall, impossibly slender, wispy white hair—just like an actual swan. The sight of him brought tears to her eyes.

"Ma'am, please—" the officer near him started, but Swann had crossed the hall in three steps on his long legs and swept her up into a bony hug before she could move.

"I'm so, so sorry," he said as he released her, his hands still on her shoulders. "I was hoping to pull you aside before you got here and tell you privately."

The first officer beckoned, and they fell into step behind him, past the conference room, to where her father's office waited. Nell tried to stay calm, but her heart was racing. She hadn't set foot in that place since the day she'd run out, pathetically cliché cardboard box full of her things in hand, her life ruined, because of that man. And now not only did she have to go back in, but she didn't know what waited there.

"Tell me now, then," she whispered. "Fast."

She could see that Swann wanted to say more than he was going to, to soften the blow of the news, but he knew her well and knew that she would just want it straight. She finally noticed, with a flutter of panic, just how red and puffy his eyes were, and how hoarse his voice seemed.

"I'm so sorry to say this," Swann said shakily. "Your father passed away at his desk early this morning."

What?

Nell blinked, not understanding at first.

"He's—he's dead, Nell."

II

A long time ago, the room in which Nell was now standing had been her favorite place in the whole city. The public areas of the library were breathtaking—she could not deny the almost otherworldly beauty of the rich wood-paneled walls, the gleaming chandeliers overhead, the old windows that loomed from floor to ceiling—but it was the simple, endless archives of the back offices of the Map Division that had secretly kept her heart. The library had been built in 1898, a year that had seemed impossibly long ago when Nell had learned the fact as a child, and contained tens of thousands of books and atlases, and almost half a *million* sheet maps, in its vast archives. If she had ever believed in magic, here would have been the place where she would have gone looking for it. Even now, it was hard not to imagine that there could be some secret tucked between the pages of an unassuming text, as she ran her hands over the back of her father's leather office chair and breathed in the musty scent of ancient paper and wood. Every time he'd brought her with him to work in her youth, he'd sat her on its well-worn cushion and promised her in his deep, solemn voice that this office would be hers one day.

She had believed him.

"Heart attack," the officer said, to draw her attention back. "Or stroke, maybe. It looks like he fell and hit his head on the way down."

It was an open-and-shut case, they'd determined. Dr. Young had been alone—the security cameras in the Map Division didn't turn on until the last employee in the department had clocked out, but they had already been running in the lobby since closing time the night before. The only reported movement was from the security guard on patrol, who had been the one to find him when he'd peeked in on his last loop around the library, sometime in the early hours of dawn.

"Age catches up to us all, unfortunately," the officer concluded.

"Sixty-five?" Swann replied beside her, his voice hitching for a moment. As the director of the Map Division, he'd been not just her father's boss, but his closest friend as well.

"Pardon?"

"He was sixty-five, I think."

Nell tried to summon the will to do the calculation. Her father had been thirty when she'd been born, and her own thirty-fifth birthday was just months away. "Yes," she finally confirmed. Swann squeezed her arm gently.

"Oh. Well." The officer frowned. It wasn't old, but it wasn't so young that tragic accidents like this couldn't happen either. It could have been any number of things. He had been at his desk late, probably tired, and he'd been having a little Scotch while he worked. He might have lost his balance when he went to stand. Or maybe it had been a stroke or heart attack, like the officer had suggested. He was smiling sympathetically at Nell now, as if waiting for her to burst into tears. Lieutenant Cabe, his name tag said. His utility belt jingled with all of his tools—handcuffs, radio, flashlight, holstered pistol.

"But where"—Nell hesitated—"where is he?"

"Heavens, Nell," Swann cried. "Did you think you were going to have to identify him here at his desk?"

She shrugged and cleared her throat awkwardly. "I guess I did. I didn't really know what to expect."

"We wouldn't make you do that," Lieutenant Cabe said. "We try to prepare the remains first. Lay him comfortably, fix his clothes."

Nell nodded, not knowing what else to say. All she could think was, *It's not like he cares. Or I do, either.* She was grateful he hadn't passed violently, she guessed, but now that he was gone, she didn't think it would be any more traumatic to have seen him for the first time in nearly a decade slumped next to his desk than laid out on a cold, stainless-steel table. In fact, the desk probably would have been better. More natural. How many times had she peeked into his office and seen him napping in nearly the same way, leaned over in his chair, with his forehead against the polished wooden surface? She thought he would have preferred it, too.

Or would he? She hadn't been back to the library in a long time, but this was not the way she remembered the esteemed Dr. Young's office. Her father thought of himself as an artist, but not in the chaotic, inconsistent way of tormented painters and musicians. The study and making of maps demanded an organization and precision in line with the most technical of fields: the meticulous record keeping, the endless research, the calculations to ensure absolute accuracy. He had always kept his space so pristine, it sometimes reminded Nell more of a science lab than a museum curator's office.

Today, however, it looked like the ruins of a building ravaged by a tornado.

Dr. Young had always kept his records filed neatly in the cabinet behind his leather chair, but they were open now, their contents dumped around the room. Aside from the corner of his heavy oak desk where the police had stacked their evidence bags, every surface was covered in papers—flying loose, wadded up, torn apart, scattered out of order—so much so that it was impossible to walk through the room without stepping on one. The texts in the bookcase had been similarly yanked from their shelves and strewn about with a carelessness that stunned Nell. For her father to treat an atlas like this, especially ones as old and rare as these, was unthinkable.

"You're also in the field?" Lieutenant Cabe interrupted her quiet study of the office at last.

Nell tore her eyes away and turned to him. "I work as . . ." She paused. "I reproduce maps." It was as far into it as she wanted to go.

He smiled. "Like father, like daughter."

She tried to smile back and failed. *Nothing like that at all.* If one had been able to ask him, Dr. Young would have said that nothing could have been further from cartography than Classic. It pained Nell that she had to agree.

But now whose fault was that, that she'd ended up there, after such a promising start to her short-lived career?

"We were hoping to ask you some background questions," Lieutenant Cabe continued, oblivious. "Just for the official file."

"I won't be much help," she mumbled.

"Sure you will," he replied encouragingly. "You're family."

"I haven't seen him for seven years."

"Oh," he said. "I see." But the notepad was still out in his hand, the pen still poised. She heard the implication in what he'd said. *You're family. His* only *family.*

Nell sighed.

If there was anything more tragic than the disgraceful demise of Nell's career, it had been the untimely end to her mother's: Dr. Tamara Jasper-Young.

She had died when Nell was no more than a toddler, and it had been Nell and her father ever since. Nell did not remember her, not beyond just a flickering moment or two, but she hardly needed to— Dr. Tamara Jasper-Young had been even *more* famous than her father in their world, and had done it in such a short time. Words like *visionary* and *peerless* were always placed before her name in articles about her, and the list of awards and honors bestowed upon her, and the places where her work continued to be cited, even so long after her death, was dizzying.

It had been an accident, Nell knew. There had been a fire in the house where they were living in upstate New York when she was just a baby, and her mother died rescuing her from the blaze. She didn't remember that either, but knew it was true. There had been a short obituary in the local paper she'd once found using the library's old microfilm machines, with accompanying news headlines like "Tragedy Strikes Visiting Scholar Family" and "Mother Heroically Gives Her Life to Save Daughter from Fire." Her own left arm even bore the faint ghost of that night. The scars were no trouble at all, and most days she forgot about them—but she felt herself absently rubbing the flesh through the fabric of her sleeve now, as she sat there in her father's office.

Nell had always planned to ask her father more about her mother at some point, but every time even the hint of her came up, she could see the pain in his eyes, still just as raw as it must have been the first day. There had always been a gulf between them—he had been a protective, doting father when she was a child, but the older she grew, the wider the gap became, Dr. Young growing more gruffly formal and more distant, until he treated her more like one of his junior researchers than his daughter. Nell hadn't wanted to do even more damage to what was left of their relationship by causing him more agony. She could always talk to him about it later, she'd reasoned. Maybe after she'd proven herself, when she was an equal to him, another distinguished Dr. Young in her own right, and not just a bright, potential promise.

That secretly had become her life's goal, as soon as she was old enough to realize how passionate about maps she also was. Other than her mother, who also had been a cartographer, there was nothing Dr. Young loved more than maps, and so Nell had always hoped that if she could only impress him as a cartographer in her own right, that gulf might somehow be bridged, and they might finally, finally be able to open up to each other.

She had been well on the way to someday accomplishing that.

Until the Junk Box Incident, anyway.

Nell glanced around again, listening to the buzz and jabber of the police walkie-talkies as the other officer moved about the room. She wasn't getting out of the interview, she knew. "I'll try my best," she finally said.

"Do you know what he was working on lately? Any special projects or a new focus?" Lieutenant Cabe asked.

Nell shook her head. They hadn't spoken even once since the day she left the NYPL—she had no idea.

"I can answer that, if that's okay," Swann replied, to which the officer nodded. "Daniel worked primarily in early American colonial and post–Revolutionary War maps of the East Coast. We have an extensive collection of Dutch, French, *and* English naval maps, but Daniel . . ."

Lieutenant Cabe bravely tried to appreciate the extraneous details of Swann's explanation. Swann had always been like that—even at a time like this, he simply couldn't contain his passion for the field. He loved his work so much, and did his job with such dedication, that Nell sometimes wondered if he didn't also secretly live in the department's back rooms. Once, during one of her many summer internships as a teenager, she and her father had sneakily moved something small in a rare moment of levity between them—one of the antique green glass lamps in the main reading hall, no more than a few feet—just to see if Swann would catch it when he next came into the room.

The old man rushed so desperately to correct the error, it was as if it had caused him physical pain. In his panic, he'd nearly tripped over himself and gone sailing into one of the glass display cases. Nell and her father had laughed so hard they cried, but she never pulled something like that again. Pranks were much funnier without blood.

"Are early American colonial and post-Revolutionary War maps a . . ." Lieutenant Cabe paused. "A controversial area of study?"

Nell snorted, despite the grim setting.

"Sorry," Swann said. "Sometimes I just . . . I get carried away."

"It's all right. We're interested in any information that might be relevant."

Nell looked at Lieutenant Cabe again, and the realization hit her all of a sudden, a cold knife through the fog of her shock.

Oh.

Was that why she was there? Because the police were considering her father's death suspicious?

She could hardly fathom it. This was academia, for crying out loud. Rivals wrote counterarguments and published rebuttal papers. They didn't *kill*.

"Do you think there was foul play?" she asked.

Swann gasped. "You mean because of the angle of the questions?"

"And the mess," she said.

"Is Dr. Young ordinarily very tidy?" Lieutenant Cabe asked, his gaze landing on each pile of papers with much more focus now.

"Yes," Nell said, at the same time that Swann said, "No."

"Which is it?" Lieutenant Cabe asked.

Swann sighed. "I'm sorry, my dear. I don't mean to contradict you. He really was much tidier, back when you were here," he said to her, and then looked at Lieutenant Cabe. "But these last few years, he became less and less so. He was working on something lately that took all of his time." He turned to Nell again. "You remember how he used to get with his big projects. Distracted, secretive. Obsessive."

"*Consumed,*" she replied, disdainful. At least that hadn't changed about him, even if his organizational habits had.

"We think it's unlikely there was foul play," Lieutenant Cabe continued, apparently mollified. "He wasn't that young, and other than the mess here, which it sounds like he may have created himself, there's no suspicious evidence. And he was clearly alone last night. The guard said he was the only employee still in the building after eleven P.M. Everyone else had checked out, and the front doors were locked. We just have to cover every possibility, even if it's a formality. Part of the job."

"Dr. Young was outspoken," Swann offered diplomatically. "He was very passionate about his work, and that sometimes got him into arguments with other researchers, or even the board. But these arguments, they were academic. Theory and dissection of sources, debates over paper types and ink composition and salt levels from various oceans. Reputation means a lot in this field, but I can't imagine someone would actually *hurt* him over it."

Nell couldn't really either, even given what he'd done to her career. If anyone had a reason to murder him, it would have been her, and her father had still been blustering around the department and hogging the archives until just last night. The whole thing was unbelievable.

But then seeing his office like this, his things, even if Swann had said he'd become less tidy . . .

"Ma'am?"

"I just . . ." Nell sighed. Despite everything—the chasm between them, the damage they'd both done to each other—tears were threatening. She pinched the bridge of her nose to stop them from falling.

"Why don't we give her a minute?" Swann asked Lieutenant Cabe, who said he'd go check with his partner and circle back. "Are you all right, my dear?" he asked once they were alone.

"Yes," she said. She didn't know.

Swann scooted closer to her, using his slim frame to block her view of the rest of the room, to give her a little privacy.

"I'm sorry, Swann," she said, looking down. "It was wrong of me to avoid you for so long. And especially after everything you did to try to help, in the beginning." She put a hand up to stop his protests. "I know about all the calls you made, the interviews you tried to get me at smaller branches, the old colleagues you begged—"

"Please," he replied. "I'm just sorry I couldn't have done more."

"You did far more than anyone else." She sighed. "I was just so angry, I needed to block it all out. But later, I didn't want to put you in that position. Having to choose between me or him."

"I wouldn't have chosen," Swann said. "I loved you both."

"My father would have made you choose. We both know that."

Swann sighed sadly. Nell knew that he knew she was right, although it didn't make all the years she'd shunned him along with Dr. Young and the rest of the library any better.

"All that is in the past," he said. "You're here now. That's all that matters."

She swallowed the lump that had formed in her throat and nodded.

"Let me get you a tissue." He patted her shoulder. "I'll be right back."

Nell smiled gratefully. "Thank you."

The library's back offices swirled quietly around her as she sat huddled on the edge of her father's desk, next to the mess strewn across it. Researchers were finally getting to work in their cubicles, turning on their computers and shuffling through their mail. And past the staff door, patrons were browsing the stacks and choosing seats at reading tables, clicking on lamps and pulling out notebooks and flipping pages. Children were running through aisles and sneaking around the lobby. Taxis were pulling up and dropping off passengers outside. Nell tried to think about all of it out there, and nothing in here.

Gradually, she realized her hand was resting on the corner of the desk where the hidden lock was.

Ever dramatic, her father long ago had a secret compartment built into his desk that only he, she, and perhaps Swann knew about. He kept especially valuable maps inside while working on them for security's sake, he'd said, even though the NYPL had never been robbed in the history of its existence. But when Nell was young, and he'd been a slightly gentler version of himself, he had hidden little notes to her there as well, and she would reply with childish drawings of maps she'd copied or created herself.

All she had to do was push her index finger forward a little bit. The dullest, quietest thud told her the compartment had opened.

Slowly, without moving anything but her hand, she reached inside.

There was just one thing there this time: a slim, leather-bound shape. Not a book, but a leather portfolio, for carrying around important documents or maps. She moved her fingers another subtle inch, feeling the familiar texture.

It was *the* leather portfolio, she was certain. Hovering near the top, three embossed letters would be clinging to the last flecks of gold leaf: TJY.

Tamara Jasper-Young.

It originally had belonged to her mother. After she died, Nell's father took to using it, as a way to remember her. That was another thing he'd promised—that one day this portfolio, the only keepsake of her mother, would also be lovingly passed to her.

As a child, it had held almost magical power to Nell. She used to watch him slip it into and out of his briefcase when he went to work or came home in the evening, trying to imagine what beautiful work could lie inside. There were other maps he brought home too, but those came in clear plastic sleeves or cardboard folders. Only the most valuable, the most rare, of them were carried in the leather portfolio. Nell always begged to see what was inside when she spied it, because she knew it would be something special. She wondered at all of the priceless maps she must have laid eyes on as a small girl that she couldn't even remember now. The things she'd seen every day over breakfast or before her evening bath that adults would have had to devote years of research to in order to gain access. Long after they'd stopped talking, she had sometimes thought of the portfolio, about the things he still carried inside it.

And now here it was. Hidden in the mess.

Lieutenant Cabe was still at the door beside his partner, the two of them giving instructions to the rest of the employees in the corridor, and Swann was over at the bookcase, plucking tissues gently out of a box to bring back to Nell.

For a split second, no one was looking at her.

Before she could think about what a huge mistake it would be, how much trouble it could get her into, Nell slipped the portfolio out from the compartment and into her already stuffed tote bag in one smooth motion and returned her hand to the top of the desk.

"Everything all right?" Swann asked when he turned back around.

"As all right as it can be," she replied.

III

By the time Nell had clamored up the old, creaking staircase to the fifth floor and wedged herself through the door into her apartment, it was after ten o'clock at night. Her stomach was growling, having missed both lunch and dinner, but she ignored it. She kicked the door closed and turned the lock, then collapsed in a heap onto the kitchen table with all of her belongings.

The rest of the day had been nothing short of torture. Nell had spent hours answering Lieutenant Cabe's endless questions and accepting Swann's comfort, the whole time not daring to open her bag to take out her spare granola bar, or phone, or even her lip balm, lest she draw attention to what was also inside. After Lieutenant Cabe had finally let her go, she'd had to return to Classic, where Humphrey had told her she was now on bereavement leave for the rest of the week. She'd argued that she didn't need it, but family was family, he'd said, and refused to believe she was fine. He was from a gigantic one, several generations all crammed together in the same ancient house on Long Island.

Even after boarding the subway home, she still hadn't dared to take out the portfolio, not yet. When she'd slipped it from the desk into her tote bag, she'd been able to tell by the feel and weight of it that there was only one thing inside: a single medium-thick folded paper—which of course meant a map.

It was the famous Young portfolio. It could be nothing else.

Nell's cheeks flushed with embarrassment as she finally opened her tote bag and reached in. She couldn't believe she'd actually taken it from his desk. Never had she been so brazen, and possibly slightly criminal. Whatever was inside was probably library property.

She tried not to think about that part as she wriggled her hands into a pair of clean dish gloves from under the sink. She'd grown up with the man, known his passion and his work too intimately to have ignored such an important artifact hidden among the mess. Had he located a rare, previously unknown copy of a historical set? Had he convinced a billionaire to donate a priceless piece to the NYPL? Whatever it was, it would be incredible. Even if she could replay the day, she'd still have snatched the portfolio all over again, to see what was inside.

And now she was about to find out.

With a thrill, Nell eased open the leather cover.

She stared for several seconds.

"What?" she finally managed.

Nell had been imagining something old, or astoundingly rare, and most likely controversial. A disputed maritime routes map or an early diagram of Brooklyn, prebridge. Something worthy of a place inside the leather case.

This, she didn't understand.

It was technically a map, yes. But not any kind of map she would ever expect to see here.

"It's a . . . a . . . ," she stammered. "A gas station highway map?"

Why on earth did her father have an old, cheap, fold-out road map in his prized portfolio?

And most of all, why on earth was it the *same* old, cheap, fold-out road map that he'd fired her for over seven years ago?

"Why do you have the *Junk Box map* in your portfolio?"

Nell got up and went into the kitchen, and returned with a generous glass of wine.

Why had he kept it, all this time? She took a long, nervous sip. *And* especially *after what had happened because of it?*

The map stared back at her, silent, unhelpful.

It looked the same as the last time she'd seen it, no more faded or weathered, or even opened up since then. The art on the covers of these types of old driving maps was always some kind of Americana: a family smiling and waving outside their American-brand car, a field of bison, sometimes the American flag, midripple in an imaginary breeze. This one had a cabin or lodge of some sort—a simple brown wood building in the middle of a lush valley, framed by a river that ran behind it. Cheap, out of date, and unremarkable.

What on earth could one of the NYPL's most revered scholars be doing with a worthless piece of paper like this?

She had to calm down. She had to think.

This was no Vespucci, or Mercator, or Ptolemy mural—it was a little eight-fold on cheap paper that condensed to fit into a glove compartment—but it was still a map, as far removed from those works of art as it was.

This was her father. He had to have a reason.

And she would figure it out. There was a system to figuring out things like this—she had trained her whole life to do it.

Nell set the wineglass aside, adjusted her dish gloves, and picked up the map again.

General Drafting Corporation. 1930 edition. New York State Road and Highway Map.

Carefully, hesitantly, she unfolded it into its full form.

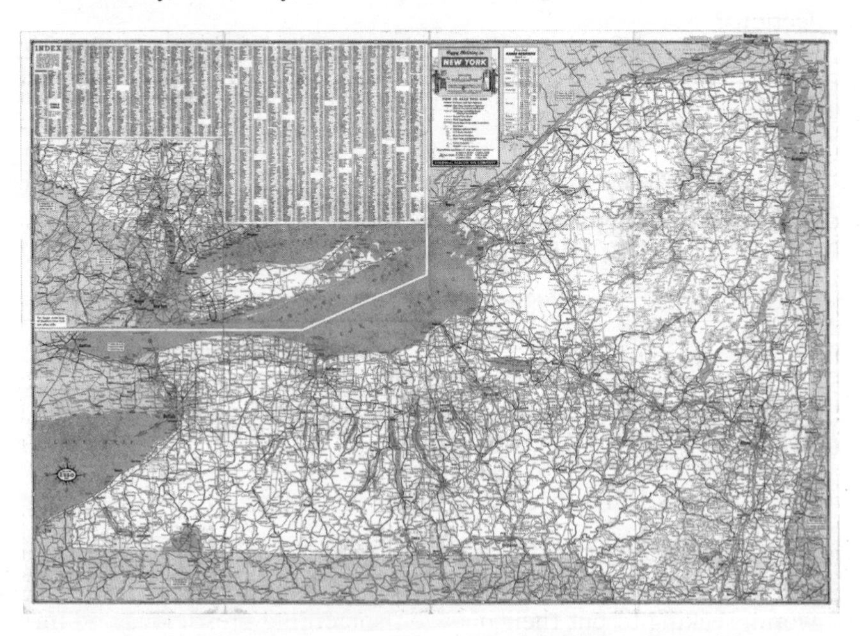

New York City & vicinity, 1930: General Drafting Corporation, prepared for Esso Standard

The vastness of New York State spread out across her kitchen table in pale greens and yellows. The sight brought memories rushing back.

That day seven years ago had started so perfectly. The morning of the Junk Box Incident, Nell and Swann had gone to breakfast, where she'd asked about the chance there might be a permanent position for her after her internship. Swann couldn't say it outright, but his grin was so big that Nell knew it was for certain. She was going to be a full-time junior researcher at the NYPL.

This was her dream, and she was *in.* Everything she'd ever hoped for was within arm's reach, at last.

Too excited to go home before her afternoon shift, Nell swiped her card at the back entrance and went downstairs into the basement archives. Swann was already impressed, but why not make an even greater splash? What if in addition to performing her duties perfectly, she also brought in a specimen of her own to add to one of the collections?

The lights flickered weakly. Nell brushed aside the cobwebs on the railing and tried not to trip on the way down. The uncatalogued archives were a world away from the pristine white marble upper levels, where rich oak bookcases towered and gilded chandeliers twinkled beneath ceilings painted with murals of the sky. The place had always reminded her more of a medieval dungeon. And not just because of the gloom and darkness.

There was an entire lifetime's worth of maps down there, moldering away in the clammy stillness. More, even. Whenever Nell snuck down to this forgotten level, she got chills of excitement just trying to imagine what she might find.

Since the NYPL's inception, it had survived not only on funding from the government, but also on the generous donations of its patrons. Wealthy families from all over the United States, and later the world, seeking to put their mark on something prestigious and immortal, often gifted the NYPL books or maps to be held as a public collection in their names. It was how the library had acquired some of its most treasured pieces, and still did. There were just some maps too rare to ever find on the market again—those historical pieces drawn only once or a handful of times, all bought centuries ago and kept in private offices of generals, royalty, warlords, and business tycoons.

Nell could not imagine receiving a box from a prospective donor and *not* opening it immediately, but after so many years with its illustrious reputation, that's exactly what had begun happening at the NYPL. Examining a map to ensure it was authentic before allowing it to be displayed took weeks, if not months. Sometimes, there would be an entire library in and of itself inside a donation box. There was simply not enough time. And so, the uncatalogued basement had been born. It was supposed to be a stopgap, but as time went on, more and more deliveries arrived, faster and faster, too many to keep pace with. There were just not enough librarians to care for the NYPL and also go through every single box of the now thousands that were down there. Each one was simply marked on an inventory sheet, then filed away under the ever-optimistic promise that "your donation will be examined soon."

Well, Nell was going to finally make good on that promise.

She dug through eighty boxes and inhaled at least a lungful of dust by the afternoon. Almost everything had been underwhelming so far, but she was nothing if not a Young—stubborn to the end. She would not give up until she'd found something incredible.

Finally, near the back and buried under a handful of much older arrivals, she stumbled across an intriguing container. It was a simple banker box, like one could get from a university, smaller than most of the others.

On the side, someone had written *junk* in permanent marker before donating it—but that was not what was inside at all.

Nell peeled the brittle tape free and peered in. The items had been put into polyethylene sleeves to help preserve them from the humidity—whoever had packed it had known a little bit about what to do. Her pulse quickened. Was this her big break? Discovering the needle in the haystack beneath them all this time and being catapulted to full researcher, or even some kind of specialist?

"Wow," she'd gasped to herself at that moment, and then gave an embarrassed yelp as the soft echo came back from the corners to startle her. "What the . . ."

In her hands was a small pile of treasure. An immaculate 1700s Franklin of New York City, a Calisteri of its early docks and harbor, what looked like a Dutch-style Visscher draft of the same—and the very same 1930 gas station highway map of New York State she would find again in her father's portfolio.

Nell stared in stunned silence at what she'd uncovered. The focus of her Ph.D. had been on ancient cartography, so she didn't know exactly what these three specimens were worth—or why the gas station highway map had been tossed in with them—but the Franklin and Calisteri were famous enough that she recognized them on sight. The box was clearly a gold mine.

Her father was going to be *thrilled*.

It might even be the first step toward finally breaking through his armor. To someday becoming what she'd always dreamed they could be. The two esteemed Drs. Young together, working side by side, curating the world's most priceless maps, in one of the world's most respected institutions.

She was up the stairs and sprinting toward the Map Division offices before she could think. Everyone was coming back from lunch, and she managed to show a handful of senior researchers what she'd found on the way, including Swann, who was so excited he hugged her. She thought she'd never reach her father's office for all the interested calls from offices she'd had to duck into to show her findings, but at last, she sat bouncing impatiently in one of his guest chairs, waiting for him to return. The accolades this would bring her! She could hardly contain her excitement at imagining how surprised—and maybe even how proud?—he would be.

At last, Nell heard his heavy, purposeful footsteps. She was on him nearly before he could even open the door.

"Dad!" she'd shouted. "I was down in the basement, and I found this box—it's got a perfectly preserved partial collection of rare eighteenth-century American maps—you have to see this!"

She described her findings at blinding speed, rattling off early guesses as to their provenance, her ideas for how they could fit into the library collection, and how to go about finding the donors to give them proper credit.

"And what about this gas station highway map?" she'd also asked, holding it up. She begged him for permission to examine it in greater detail. Obviously, it was worthless compared to the other specimens, but perhaps it had something to do with a route to where even *more* valuable maps could be located? It was nothing short of the greatest adventure a cartographer could ask for.

But to her surprise, her father had the exact opposite reaction to what she'd been expecting.

"Why were you wasting your time in the uncatalogued archives?" he asked.

She tried to explain how much extra time she had as an intern, that she hadn't been shirking her duties, but rather giving more. Her father didn't seem convinced. He took the box, glanced through the maps—and then tossed the bundle dismissively back in.

"Nell. These are not authentic."

The words struck her like lightning.

"Not a single one."

"How—"

He tilted the box slightly, caught sight of the word *junk* scrawled on the side, and smirked, as though it was evidence in his favor.

"Come on, the donor could have just reused a box. Why would someone purposefully donate junk to the NYPL?" Nell said, frantic, but he just shook his head. It only made her angrier.

"Plenty of reasons. Fame. Money. Attention from a scandal."

"But these are—"

"Enough," he said, with a coldness that startled her. "They're nothing more than cheap reproductions. Not worthy of the library's time."

She was stunned to silence. Her father was renowned for his expertise, his abilities incomparable, but still. The speed with which he'd rejected her discovery was shocking.

If she hadn't already shown half the department what she'd found, she would have just run out of his office, sobbed in the bathroom, and never brought it up again. But this time, she couldn't just accept his assessment lying down. Nothing would be more humiliating than to have to crawl back to everyone, especially Swann, *especially* just after he'd all but promised her a position at the NYPL, and admit she'd been nothing but an overeager intern who didn't know what she was doing. She *did* know what she was doing! She was sure the maps were authentic. This was her professional reputation on the line, and she would not let her father bulldoze her the way he did everyone else.

The ensuing argument was the worst they'd ever had. And what happened after . . .

The elder Dr. Young was well known for his temper when he didn't get his way with a certain project or his portion of the research budget, but she'd never experienced the full brunt of his anger until that day. Their debate escalated to a shouting match, but Nell refused to back down. In the end, she didn't even know what they were screaming about.

But she would never forget what happened next.

There was a whole crowd watching them by then. Swann and several other researchers were crammed into the office, trying to defuse the situation—and one more.

As the chair of the NYPL herself, steely, regal Irene Pérez Montilla, came running into Dr. Young's room, shouting that the library's patrons could hear them in the main hall, her father snatched the box from the ground and demanded Nell's immediate firing. Or else he—the Map Division's most acclaimed scholar, the famous, invaluable Dr. Young—would *quit*.

Nell had argued. She had begged.

She had even cried, in front of everyone.

An hour later, she was standing at the corner of Fifth Avenue, holding another cardboard box—this one containing everything that had been at her desk.

• • • •

Nell shook her head sharply, throwing off the reverie, and folded the map back up so she didn't have to look at it.

She didn't know what had happened to the rest of them, but out of everything that had been in that box, this map was the one in his portfolio. This was the single one he kept from that day.

Why on earth would her father have insisted to the point of destroying her life that the Junk Box Incident maps were worthless, but then secretly have kept clearly the *most worthless one* of them all for over seven years?

She cast about, looking for something to distract her from the churn of emotions inside. Across the kitchen table, her eyes settled on her laptop in its battered case.

According to NYPL procedures, Nell knew the next step after the initial survey of a new specimen to a collection was to log it into the vast interinstitutional artifact database.

But . . . this *one?*

The map lay there mutely, offering no answers.

Nell sighed.

She was disappointed that her father had hidden such an underwhelming map in the portfolio as his last possession, confused as to why he'd kept it all these years despite knowing it was so worthless, and yes, a little upset at his sudden death, even if she was still too angry at him to figure out how to grieve yet. Mostly though, she was just bitter and exhausted.

You know what, she thought. *Serves you right.*

Dr. Daniel Young's last ever entry into the database, and it would be for this useless thing. Logging the map would make a nice goodbye ritual, perhaps. And that it would be a little bit of a screw you to him as well didn't hurt.

It was definitely not enough to make up for it all, but it was something. At least a little funny.

She edged her chair closer to the table and popped the screen up to rouse the machine from its slumber. It was old, very old, and Nell knew the program would still be installed, even though she hadn't used it in years. As she waited for the database to load, she picked up the map again, and turned it over and over in her hands absently. On the back panel, near the bottom corner, something caught her eye.

A little hand-drawn symbol: a simple eight-point compass rose set in a circle, with the letter *C* in the center.

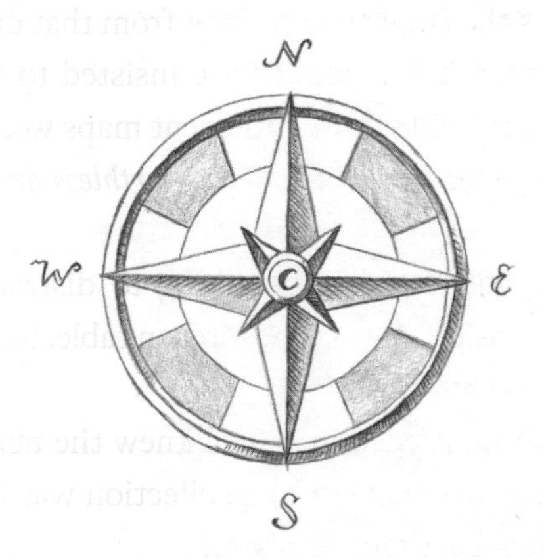

She had forgotten about that little mark on it. She'd noticed it that day in the library as she'd been proudly showing off the contents of the Junk Box to everyone, and had meant to look into it further once her father had given his approval.

But of course, that was not how the day had gone.

After, it hadn't mattered. She'd been fired—her life wrecked and the map lost to her, she'd assumed thrown back into the uncatalogued archives or perhaps even submitted with paperwork for disposal. She'd wanted nothing to do with it anymore anyway.

But now, she studied the little mark with renewed interest.

Was it just an errant doodle from an old owner, or was it actually important? What did it mean?

The program finally sprang to life on the screen with a happy ding, drawing her back.

The interinstitution database was massive. It had been in wide use since the 1980s, back when the internet was still the domain of scientists and academic institutions, and had only grown from there. Books, relics, maps, manuscripts, statues, tools, art—anything and everything that had ever been in any museum, library, or university in almost any country—was in the database. Nell had loved seeing how many copies of each specimen existed elsewhere, who had them, and what condition they were in. She couldn't imagine the amount of work it had taken to create it. To date, she'd never once come across an item for which there wasn't at least a rudimentary entry.

Nell selected the option to search for an existing log and entered as much information as she could glean from her father's odd map. After a moment, the screen spit back several rows of information. There were 212 similar entries in total. About average for an item of this caliber—it was very commonly available, but also of very little value. She clicked on the first one.

Log Identifier: G77089257435

Specimen Name: Esso 1930 Highway Map, New York State

Date of production: 1930

Description: Mass produced foldable map depicting major highway routes of New York State by mapping company General Drafting Corporation for distribution at major gas station retailers in the relevant geographic area.

Attachments: [COVER.jpg] [COVER2.jpg] [LEGEND]

Date of log entry: 24 July 1987

Location: Americana Exhibit, Rochester County Public Library, Rochester, New York, USA.

Status: MISSING

"Oof," Nell muttered to herself at the last line. It was an old superstition, but she never liked to make an entry from a lost item. But it was going on midnight, and she was utterly exhausted. Taking an extra half hour to enter all the data manually for such an insignificant specimen would be a waste of time.

She checked the images to be sure it was the same map and nodded to herself. She clicked replicate to create a new entry, snapped two quick pictures of her copy's cover and legend with her phone, and then tweaked the details so it was accurate to her father's piece. For *Location,* she put the NYPL. She'd take the map back to Swann tomorrow.

Log Identifier: [PENDING]

Specimen Name: Esso 1930 Highway Map, New York State

Date of production: 1930

Description: Mass produced foldable map depicting major highway routes of New York State by mapping company General Drafting Corporation for distribution at major gas station retailers in the relevant geographic area.

Attachments: [COVER.jpg] [LEGEND.jpg]

Date of log entry: 15 March 2022

Location: New York Public Library, Map Division Collection, Room 117 New York, New York, USA.

Status: In collection

Nell let out a long breath, her finger hesitating on the trackpad.

This would be it. Entering the final thing he was working on, its nonsensical worth aside, and closing the database out. The last goodbye.

Her eyes drifted over to the map.

She felt a tightness in her chest as she tried not to think about her father sitting at his desk in his sixties, years after that horrible fight, pulling this map out of the secret compartment in his desk to look at it.

Why? Just to remind himself of how alone he'd made himself?

Why to all of it. Why had he been, if not a good father when she was young, then at least possibly a proud mentor and colleague when she was an adult? Why had he let her work so hard her whole life, and then ruined it all in one moment? And why did he regret it afterward—enough to save this cursed piece of paper that had caused it all?

Why, Dad?

Nell stifled a hiccup before it turned into tears.

Enough.

She clicked submit, and the screen blinked as her entry was uploaded into the database. A moment later, a confirmation box popped up with her map's log identifier number and a link to the entry. It was done.

"Hope the maps are good wherever you are now, Dad," Nell finally said. "Better than this one, anyway."

She closed the program.

In the darkness, Nell tossed the covers off and sat up in bed. The red numbers on her clock glowed in the dark, displaying a ghastly time.

She tried to blame it on the wine, but she knew it wasn't that. It was the log, and her own superstitions about copying a bad entry for her own. It was silly, but so what? Even if her father didn't deserve it, at least she'd sleep better.

Nell dragged herself to her laptop again. She reopened the database, squinting at the burst of light from the screen, and ran the same search, pulling up 213 entries this time—the same as before plus her newly created one. She clicked on the second entry in the list, to borrow that data instead.

Log Identifier: G77089257332

Specimen Name: Esso 1930 Highway Map, New York State

Date of production: 1930

Description: Mass produced foldable map depicting major highway routes of New York State by mapping company General Drafting Corporation for distribution at major gas station retailers in the relevant geographic area.

Attachments: [COVER_LEGEND.jpg]

Date of log entry: 13 May 1985

Location: Stamford County Public Library, Stamford, Connecticut, USA.

Status: MISSING

But it was missing, as well.

Nell frowned. These smaller libraries needed to take better care of their artifacts, no matter how minor. She clicked on the next one, her eyes jumping immediately to the bottom of the entry to check its status.

DESTROYED.

She backed out of that entry and clicked on the one after it.

MISSING.

What was going on?

STOLEN.

She scrolled faster, hopping quickly into and out of each entry in the list.

It had to be a coincidence. These were old, nearly worthless maps. Why would any of them be *stolen*? Who would risk so much to break in to a museum or library only to take something so small, when works worth thousands more lined the walls around it?

Surely these first few were flukes, she told herself. Surely if she kept going, *surely*, they would begin turning up safe in their archives. Frantically, she clicked again.

STOLEN.

How was this *possible*?

DESTROYED.

STOLEN.

MISSING.

MISSING.

STOLEN.

DESTROYED.

STOLEN.

Nell sat back in her chair, confused. Her skin prickled at some invisible chill.

All 212 copies of the same map were missing from every collection. Not a single one remained.

And she had just entered their own into the public record.

IV

Nell paced, counting the rings impatiently.

"Swann, it's me," she said as soon as his voicemail beeped. "Call me back as soon as you can. It's about something from my father's . . ." She paused. As next of kin, she probably now owned all of his belongings, but this map wasn't his. It was the library's. "It's something I found while going through his things," she finally said. "I need your advice. Call me as soon as you can."

From the table, the folded-up map stared back at her. With a huff, Nell slid into the chair and picked it up again.

"What the heck would cause over two hundred of you to be missing or stolen?" she muttered.

The map said nothing.

Nell glanced over at her laptop nervously. She had no idea what was going on, but the longer she thought about it, the worse the idea of leaving her own listing up seemed. She couldn't think of the last time she'd *deleted* something from the database—the thought seemed almost sacrilegious—but she also couldn't think of the last time, *any* time, she'd come across something this strange.

She reached for the keyboard. The screen refreshed, and her entry was gone.

"There." Nell sighed. At least that was taken care of, until she had a chance to talk to Swann.

Speaking of that. The clock on the wall now read 6:45 A.M. It was odd he had not called her back. She knew the man had risen at five o'clock every morning since before she'd been born. He was likely on his way to the NYPL or already at his desk. He definitely should have heard her message by now.

But his line just rang uselessly a second time and went to voicemail.

Nell sat there for a moment, confused. They hadn't spoken since she'd been fired, but that had been all her doing. Even years later, Swann had still sent her a birthday card every spring, still mailed a little gift every holiday, to remind her that he was always there and would always welcome her back with open arms, if she ever wanted.

It was very unlike him not to call her back—especially right now.

Her eyes drifted back to the table, where the map sat.

Then she jumped up and made for the shower. If Swann would not call her back, she would go to him.

The subway was a crush of bodies, strollers, backpacks, and buskers somehow managing to sing and dance in the cars even though there was hardly any room to breathe. Once the train passed beneath the river and clattered into Manhattan, Nell escaped a stop early at Thirty-Third Street to walk the last half mile to the library. She needed time to rehearse what she would say to Swann.

The breeze was still chilly, but the sun was out, bright and strong. At each red light, she tried to come up with a speech, but every time it turned green again, she had no more than a few rambling sentences about the mess in her father's office and the strange database logs. Nothing that would convince Swann it was a map whose origins were worth pursuing.

As she rounded the corner, however, Nell stopped dead in the middle of the sidewalk.

Something was wrong. Again.

Across the street, parked all along the front of the New York Public Library, was an entire *squad* of police cars.

Inside, the lobby was chaos. Reporters jostled amid a sea of uniforms and librarians, cameras held over their heads. Nell pushed her way through the mass, trying to figure out what was going on. A protest? A fight? A fire? There was no way it could be about her father again. Within those halls he was a legend, but outside them, she doubted a random patron could name even one of the researchers or curators.

As she edged forward, elbow by elbow, the crowd seemed to thicken toward the right side of the building. *Please don't let it be the Map Division,* she prayed. *Let it be some other collection.* But the farther she pushed, the more decisively the clamor in that direction heightened, until there was no other doorway for which she could be aiming but that very exhibit.

And that was when she saw the blood.

Beside the deep crimson stain in the middle of the tile floor, a well-worn navy hat lay on its side. Nell knew there would be golden letters that spelled out *SECURITY* on the front.

"Henry," she finally managed.

The crackle of police radios burst louder as a handful of officers turned toward her. "Excuse me, ma'am?" the nearest to her said. She felt hands on her shoulders, moving her away. "Nell, right? It's Lieutenant Cabe. We met yesterday."

Nell nodded numbly. The Map Division slowly came back into focus, like a lens shifting. There had been only the two officers when her father had died, but now, it seemed like every cop in the city was there in the room. Detectives were on phones, and forensic specialists were crouching, placing tiny plastic markers or taking pictures. Behind her, a double strip of yellow police tape had been fastened to either side of the doorway to prevent gawkers and journalists from wandering in, but they still clustered right up against it, a big, swarming mass, dispersing slightly only when one of the officers stationed there shouted for them to back off.

Lieutenant Cabe sat her at one of the reading tables. "I'm very sorry about Mr. Fong," he said. "The hospital said they did everything they could."

Nell didn't realize she was clutching his sleeve until he gently patted her hand. "He's . . ."

"I'm sorry. He made it to the ER, but he passed away on the table."

She tried to say something, but her throat was clamped tight. Not even air would come out.

Henry was dead. Kind, funny, patient Henry, who always let her skip in the hallway even though it wasn't allowed, or take more books off the shelves to read than she should, or interrupt him anytime at the front desk and ask where in the building Dr. Young or Swann was—and he always knew—was *dead.*

And only a day after her father.

"You knew him well?"

She had to find her voice. "Yes," she croaked. "He worked here since I was a kid."

Then a horrible thought.

"Was Henry the only—"

"Dr. Swann's all right," the officer replied. "He wasn't here at the time of the robbery. We're estimating it took place around midnight, after he'd left for the night."

"Thank God," Nell said, so overwhelmed with relief she worried she would faint.

Robbery.

Lieutenant Cabe had said "robbery," she realized.

The magnitude of the situation, what all of this chaos and Henry's death meant, finally cut through her shock. She spun around, the next most important question after Swann's safety repeating frantically in her mind.

What did the thieves take?

Her eyes rose to the gallery wall, where the pride and joy of the NYPL's collection, Abel Buell's *New and Correct Map of the United States of North America,* 1784, had hung for years. Nell had been there, just nine years old, filing paperwork for pocket money from her father, when the crate came in from the Chathams, some of the library's most generous benefactors. There were only seven copies of the Buell map still in existence, and they all had been housed at museums or hanging in private collections for generations—including this one from the Chathams, which they had purchased from another family several decades ago for a million dollars. At the time, Nell had wondered why they were willing to lend such a rare, precious piece to the NYPL, tax break or not. She had been terrified it would be stolen. And now it had been.

Except it was still there on the wall.

"I don't understand," she finally said.

"What do you mean?" Lieutenant Cabe asked.

"The Buell map," she murmured. "It's still there."

"It is," he agreed. He was studying her closely. "Why are you surprised?"

"It's the most valuable piece in the Map Division," she replied. "If someone broke in, I don't know what else they could have been searching for but that. Even if they were after something else, to walk right by and not take it . . ." She turned to Lieutenant Cabe. "What *did* they steal?" she asked desperately.

She could not read his face except to know that he was telling the truth when he finally spoke.

"They didn't steal anything."

"What?"

"Not a single thing."

Nell couldn't make sense of it. "You're saying that thieves broke into the most historic library in New York, didn't trigger the alarm, killed Henry, had free run of the entire collection, and then just . . . *left*?"

Lieutenant Cabe opened his hands to indicate he didn't understand it either. "As far as we can tell, yes. Either they were spooked by something, or maybe what they were looking for wasn't in the library."

Nell's blood ran cold.

It couldn't be.

There was no way that what the burglars had been after was her father's map.

"What do you know, Nell?" Lieutenant Cabe asked.

Nell blinked, surprised. "Nothing! I had no idea anything was wrong until I saw all the police cars out front."

He nodded placatingly. "I'm not accusing you of anything. We just have to cover all our bases, like I said before. First your father's death, then the same library where he passed away was violently burgled, and I find you in the lobby—"

"Before yesterday, I hadn't been to this library in years," Nell said. "And the only reason I came was because you ordered me to meet you here. I returned today to check on Swann, to make sure he's holding up all right. And then I saw the sirens, and the blood, and . . ."

"That's the truth," another voice said, and Nell whirled around to see a woman looking at them from her place among another cluster of police officers. She was a few years younger than Swann and her father but wore her age far better than either of them. The silver hue of her chin-length bob combined with the impeccable lines of her black blazer and pencil skirt gave her the air of a retired fashion model, or perhaps assassin.

Nell gaped. It had been years, but she easily recognized her. "Ms. Pérez Montilla," she finally managed. The chair of the board of the entire New York Public Library.

"Nell, call me Irene," she said as she approached. "I can vouch for her. Until yesterday, she hasn't been back to the library in many years—to our great misfortune."

"Thank you, Irene," Nell finally managed, as Lieutenant Cabe noted Irene's statement in his notepad. Nell wondered if the years had been so long, Irene had forgotten she was the reason for the misfortune—she was the one who had fired Nell, after all. Even if she hadn't had much of a choice, either.

"I'm very sorry about your father," Irene was saying to her, as if reading her expression. "He was a great man, his complicated history aside."

"Yes. Complicated," Nell agreed.

"Our captain would like a word, when you have a minute," Lieutenant Cabe said to Irene, and then went to help push back the crowd of reporters at the door.

"Another interview." Irene sighed. She was still as composed as ever, but Nell could sense a flicker of strain beneath the steely veneer. "With Dr. Young's passing yesterday, and now the break-in last night, the media has whipped itself into a frenzy. There's never a right time for tragedy, but this *truly* is a terrible blow to the library."

"Swann told me yesterday how much trouble the city's been causing with the revised budget," Nell said. "He said it's worse than ever."

Irene shook her head. "It is. And now with this, I'm afraid we might be in danger of losing the bumper funding we'd been promised altogether."

"That's terrible!" Nell cried. "What would that mean for the library?"

"I don't want to speculate, and I'm not going to give up." Irene grimaced. "But without it, I'm not sure we could . . ."

"That can't happen," Nell replied. "The NYPL is a cultural institution. The heart of the city."

"I agree. But this main branch, with all its galleries, right on Fifth Avenue . . ."

"There has to be something," Nell said.

"I'd hoped," Irene sighed. She looked haunted. "I actually think your father, rest in peace, was working on some kind of secret project before he passed. He kept requesting funding and wouldn't disclose the purpose, and was skipping our monthly meetings. I let it go on, because half the board assured me that whenever he got like that, it was because he was on the verge of a huge breakthrough. I thought we were going to see the fruits of it any day. Increased publicity from the press announcing our discovery, increased memberships, a windfall from being able to loan the item out on temporary exhibits—the kind of prestige and buzz that would leave the city no choice but to honor its original budgetary promises. But then . . ." She sighed. "I only wish he'd told someone about what he was working on."

Nell swallowed hard and tried not to cower. Before, when she'd been an intern, she'd been able to bluff her way through project updates, argue her case to senior researchers, even step in and take a meeting for one of her superiors who was late on a paper to shield them from the chastisement. Now, it was hard to even look Irene in the eye. Had her confidence really been so shaken seven years ago that anything related to maps still turned her into a mouse?

"I'm sorry," she finally said. "I wish I knew. We really didn't speak again after I left the library."

"Oh no, it's me who's sorry," Irene replied quickly. "I didn't mean it like that. I shouldn't have said anything at all. You just lost your father, and I'm complaining about business. Forgive me."

Nell tried to smile. In the back of her mind, the gears were already turning. *A secret project.* She thought of the portfolio, and what she'd found inside.

She had absolutely no idea how that map could be the subject of a secret project, but after the strange missing copies in the catalog and today's robbery, she was going to stop at nothing to find out. If it really could somehow help fix the NYPL's budget crisis, if *she* were the one to be able to figure out why . . .

Suddenly, Nell spotted Swann as he emerged from the back offices, flanked by police still asking questions. He looked even more haggard than yesterday, like he might faint at any moment.

"Please excuse me . . ." She was already moving toward him even before she realized it, arms outstretched as if to catch him.

"Of course," Irene replied. "He needs you right now."

The tea mug was hot to the point of pain, but Nell cradled it in her hands instead of holding it by its handle anyway, feeling the prickling, stinging heat on her palms. It felt good. Or rather, it didn't feel good, but it was so intense it was numbing everything else in her body, and that was good.

They were huddled in Swann's office, struggling through their shell shock, for the second time in two days. In the chair on the other side of his desk, Swann looked devastated. He'd just lost his friend, and now this violation. The Map Division was his career, his passion, his home. His *life*. She didn't have to imagine the depth of his grief, because she felt it, too.

"I'd forgotten all about that silly little secret compartment," Swann finally said, wiping his eyes, after she'd finished telling him everything she'd discovered so far. "You have the map with you now?"

"No," she admitted. "I was going to bring it, but I couldn't find the safety sleeve." It was true, she hadn't brought the map, but the excuse was a lie. The plastic slip had been sitting right next to it on the table, beside the portfolio. She'd been afraid that if she brought it with her, she would have to hand it over to Swann immediately, and she wanted more time with it. Especially now.

Swann sat back and massaged his temples, a gesture she had long ago learned meant that what he was about to say was nothing good.

"Do you *really* think this is what the burglars broke in for?" she asked. "It just makes no sense."

This was the New York Public Library's exclusive historical cartographic collection. An archive assembled over centuries of careful curation and research. There were *thousands* of pieces far more rare and valuable than the map in question. It would be like breaking in to a bank vault of diamonds to take the light fixtures.

"I know, but I can't think of any other explanation that *does* make sense," Swann said, pointing to his computer. "Look."

On his screen was a checkerboard of all the security camera live feeds in the Map Division. Nell crouched beside his chair and surveyed each one, eyes combing every chaotic surface, until she'd examined them all.

Every glass case. Every display. Every cabinet that had been opened, every drawer that had been pulled out, every frame that had been pulled down from the walls and sat crookedly on the floor.

All of it—they really had looked through *all* of the maps and taken nothing.

"I have my assistants triple-checking the inventory, but so far it seems true—that what the burglars were looking for wasn't here," Swann said. "Because it must have been the map that you took out of your father's office yesterday. They must have been searching the database during the few hours last night that the entry existed or set an alert for any new entries with similar keywords. When they saw your addition, they struck."

It sounded ludicrous. Who would set keywords for such a useless item? But then again, *something* had happened to the other 212 of them.

Nell stood up and began pacing. "Okay. Fine. Say it's true. *Why?*"

Swann gasped. "We need to tell the police!"

"Wait," she said, before he could pick up his phone. "They'll just take the map into evidence, and we'll never see it again."

"Nell," Swann began.

"This is the last thing my father worked on. The thing that ruined my life, and that he kept for years after, for some inexplicable reason. I can't just let it go like that, without knowing why."

The old man hesitated. "I understand, I do. But I really think . . ."

"Just for a little bit," she begged. "Just give me a little time to see if I can figure out what's going on. If I can't, we'll go right to Lieutenant Cabe. I promise."

Swann glanced at the phone, then back at her, chewing on his lip.

"Please, Swann," she said. "I ran into Irene out there. I let slip that I knew about the library's financial situation, and she told me she thought my father might have been obsessively working on something just before he died. Something she hoped could save the library. Maybe it was this."

"What?" Swann choked. "I can't even imagine—"

"It *has* to be this map," she insisted. "It all adds up. The big fight, all those years ago. Then the secrecy—he didn't even tell you he still had it. And the robbery last night. And maybe, even . . ." Suddenly, it was much more real to entertain this theory than it had been before. "What if he didn't die of natural causes?"

Nell watched Swann try to reject what she'd just said, but she could tell from his expression he was finding the idea hard to dismiss completely.

She pushed on, encouraged. "I just . . . I want to try to make things right. This is my only chance. At the very least, it might help me understand him, since I clearly didn't before. And if I also could help the library . . ." She hesitated, almost too nervous to say the words out loud. "Maybe Irene would even consider overturning my old file. Wouldn't that be worth it?"

Swann frowned, but Nell could see the hope flare in his old eyes at the idea. "But even if this map could be what Irene's after . . ." He paused. "The danger, Nell. I don't want you to do this on your own."

She leaned closer, desperate. "I have to. It's my only chance."

Swann looked down at his wrinkled knuckles. "What's the purpose of a map?" he asked softly.

Nell sighed. She knew the question well. Her father used to ask it all the time when she was too caught up in the academic minutiae of a specimen, to the point of accidentally offending other researchers she was supposed to be cooperating with as she forced a project off course to follow her own vision. The answer was "to bring people together," but the older she'd gotten, she'd found his saying more and more odd, considering that he could never learn his own lesson. After a while, she'd begun to suspect that perhaps it was really her mother's old saying, and he'd adopted it more as a way to remember her than to actually abide by the words' advice.

"I know, I know," Swann said, seeing her exasperated expression. "But he was right, even if he could never put it into practice himself. I just want you to be careful. To do this for the right reason." He looked at her. "This place isn't everything."

Nell managed a smile. He would never understand. "It's not everything."

It was more than everything.

Swann stared at her for a long moment. Finally, he sighed, surrendering. "All right. I'll get started on the job part—if anyone can convince Irene to set aside your record and hire you again, it's me. You get to work figuring out what on earth your father might have been doing with this map after so long."

Nell reached over the desk and squeezed his hand gratefully. "Thank you, Swann. You're the best."

"Anything for you, my dear," he said. "Now, we need somewhere safe to keep it in the meantime. Bring the map back here, and—"

"No!" she cried. "The library is the *least* safe place for it."

"But security will be double for weeks!"

"Yes, double. Which means just barely inadequate instead of woefully inadequate," Nell said. "And now the burglars will be watching like hawks for any change. The minute I bring you the map, they'll strike again."

"So, you want to keep it . . . at your apartment? In a completely unsecure location, with no security whatsoever?" Swann fretted.

"I want to keep it in a place the burglars would never think to search, because they have no idea it's there," she replied.

"Are you not the most logical assumption though?" Swann asked.

"'Dr. Daniel Young' entered the item into the NYPL database, and now he's dead, and you're his daughter . . ."

"It actually might be the perfect cover," she said. "Anyone who knew my father well enough to know he had a daughter also knows about the Junk Box Incident. Knows that the two of us hadn't spoken a single word to each other since."

And now we never will, she thought.

Swann frowned. "You do have a point," he admitted. "It might be a good hiding place for now. But if the burglars *do* figure out you have the map . . ."

"We better work quickly, then," Nell said.

II

The Map

V

It was almost too dark to see, but Nell kept the curtains drawn and all the lamps turned off anyway, hoping to hide the fact that she was home.

She triple-checked the door lock, and then returned to where the map was spread across her coffee table. Outside, on the street below, she could hear the faint sound of a kid on a skateboard rattling by. The clock read seven thirty in the evening.

After finishing her discussion with Swann, Nell had wandered out of the NYPL in a daze, nearly bumping into a black Audi sedan oddly parked along the same curb where taxis pulled up to let passengers out for the library. It stuck out darkly in a river of yellow, pristine except for the paint slightly rusting around the edges of the wheel wells, an odd blemish given the luxury brand of the car.

On her way home, anyone who had stepped too close or paused too long as she passed sent a bolt of fear through her—followed by an equal bolt of embarrassment. She was not in danger. No one was following her. No one knew she had the map. Despite the coincidences so far, she technically didn't even know for sure if that was *really* the reason for the NYPL break-in. In the moment, standing amid the chaos, seeing the librarians huddled nervously together and hearing the chatter and blare from police radios, everything had seemed so dangerous, so urgent. But in the fresh evening air, kicking stray leaves on the sidewalk as she made her way to her apartment, it all seemed less certain and more circumstantial, at best.

Then Nell had seen another black Audi, idling at a stop sign on the street before her own. She had no idea if it was the same one—could that be rust on the wheel wells, if she squinted?—but it didn't matter. The next thing she knew, she was upstairs in the dark, trying to figure out if her landlord would evict her for prying up a floorboard to hide her map beneath.

Her map. She was thinking of it as hers already.

Nell turned on the flashlight in her phone to see it better. Cold light crept across the pale, weathered paper, seeming to make the roads come alive. The thin lines danced, shifting one way and then another.

If the burglars had taken the Buell, or the Bingham Early Brooklyn map, which hung on the adjacent wall above the colonial artifacts, or even one of the atlases from the rare books shelf collection, Nell would have understood. The last time one of the Buell's seven other precious copies had come up for auction at Christie's upon the death of its private owner, generating a bidding war so frenzied it had come to blows in the gallery, was twenty years ago. The Chatham family's copy hanging in the NYPL could be worth almost two million on the market, now. Maybe even a little more.

And rare maps were different from famous paintings in that if stolen, they actually *could* be resold. There could only be one Van Gogh *The Starry Night,* but the purpose of maps had always been exactly the opposite of paintings—after all, what good would a map of a place be if only one person had it? Thus, even for the rarest specimens, like the Buell, there was never just *one* of them out there. And as a result, it was that much harder to prove a map came from a dirty source—or not.

If the burglars had taken the Buell, within a few years and after a miraculous discovery of an eighth copy, they might be several million dollars richer than they were tonight.

Which is why Nell couldn't understand why they'd done exactly the opposite.

What on earth could it be about this little, worthless map that could cause so much trouble?

What would drive someone to break in to a museum for it?

She shivered as a chill crept through her.

To kill?

A sudden burst of sound at the door made her jump.

"Nell?" a voice called through the wood. There was a pause. "It's me."

Nell peeked through the peephole, and then yanked open the door. "Why didn't you buzz at the lobby?" she cried, her heart still pounding.

"I followed someone in," Felix said, his voice rising defensively. "It's after seven. Steady stream of people returning home from work."

They stared at each other for several seconds, the adrenaline wearing off.

Seven years.

Seven years since they'd last seen each other.

Before she'd messaged him, it had seemed twice that long had passed, but now it felt like no time at all. He'd cropped his grad school afro into a modern cut, and the first fine line had started to thread itself across his deep brown brow, but otherwise, Felix Kimble looked exactly the same, the tall, dark, lean shape of him standing there in the doorway just as she remembered. He was still working out, clearly, and had traded his old student sweater and sneakers for a tailored charcoal blazer and warm brown Oxford shoes, polished to a shine.

Felix looked good.

Really good.

Nell was suddenly very aware that he was probably studying her in the same way. She wondered if she'd grown more tired or frumpy looking over the years. She resisted the urge to pull her stretched-out cardigan tighter around her like a protective shield.

Gradually, Felix's eyes drifted down to her hands, and Nell realized that she was holding the half-empty wine bottle from the night before, its cork awkwardly jammed in.

"Hitting it hard already," Felix said, and stepped past her into the apartment.

Nell let the comment go as she followed him. She didn't want to tell him that she'd grabbed the bottle when his knock had startled her because it was the nearest thing to a weapon she could find in the moment. She winced in the sudden brightness as he flicked the lights in the kitchen on, giving her a strange look in the process.

This was such a bad idea, she thought. But it was too late now. She still could hardly believe she'd actually messaged him—even for Swann.

<It's me. I know it's been a long time,> she had written and deleted about fifty times. Finally, she just sent:

<Dr. Young died.>

Then:

<Swann asked me for help. I know I have no right, but it's in your specialty. Just one last favor.>

She didn't even know for sure if he had the same number. But a few long minutes later, her phone buzzed.

<I can stop by tonight.> Then: <For Swann.>

She thanked him and promised the bare minimum in one more message: there was a map in her father's things, and all she needed was some context, nothing more. No arguments, no scandals, and especially, no professional reputations further destroyed.

Because that was another thing Nell's father had done. In addition to ruining her own career in the Junk Box Incident, he'd also ruined Felix's—and their relationship.

She and Felix had met in grad school at UCLA. He'd asked her out by drawing a map leading to a restaurant he'd chosen. It was so unbelievably corny, but until then, Nell had never met anyone who loved cartography as much as she did, except her father and Swann. But Felix was better with computers than all of them. The data, the modeling, the algorithms. Her specialty was ancient maps, and Felix's was contemporary. They were a perfect team—opposites in everything, from their backgrounds to their work to their personalities, but somehow it worked. After graduation, when the NYPL's call for interns went out, she fought as hard to get him a spot as she had for herself, but she hadn't needed to. His application stood out just as strongly as hers. It was a dream come true for them both, everything they'd ever wanted. Nell couldn't wait to tell her father after they had published to critical acclaim that not only was Felix brilliant, but he was also in love with her, and she with him. That his maybe future son-in-law was also a cartographer. Their family was going to be insufferably cute.

But then the Junk Box Incident happened.

Felix had been sucked into the argument once it reached shouting levels, and defended her against her father like he thought a good boyfriend should. He'd dared to suggest that the great Dr. Young could be wrong about the contents of the box and offered to run the maps through electronic analysis for him—and brought down the man's infamous wrath on himself as well. Nell's father had demanded Irene Pérez Montilla fire Nell in one breath, and Felix in the next.

After that, there had been no point in telling him about her and Felix. Firstly, because Nell had vowed never to speak to Dr. Young again for what he'd done, and secondly, because Felix seemed to feel the same way about her. She came home from the library for the last time cradling the remains of her desk to find that all of Felix's things were gone. There was a letter for her on the table in his handwriting. But there was no map inside that time—just an apology.

"You have got to be kidding me," Felix said suddenly, startling her back to the present. "What is *that* doing here?"

Nell looked up to see him already in the living room, staring at the coffee table in shock. At the map upon it, back again like a bad ghost.

This was already going *so* well.

"I can explain," she started, but he interrupted, furious.

"That is what you called me here for, after seven years? Is this a joke? Did you secretly keep it all this time?"

"No!" she insisted. "I'm as surprised as you. This is what I found in Dr. Young's things." She paused. "In his portfolio."

Felix glared back at her. "*The* portfolio?" He clearly remembered the significance of the leather case as well. "Why would he keep something like this in there?"

"I don't know," she said. "And I thought, since your focus was modern era and urban maps, maybe over the years since, you'd come across something that—"

He laughed. "I had been talking about the other maps in the box that day, Nell. The Franklin, the Calisteri. *Actual* maps—not this piece of crap! Maybe the years have been a little long for you at Classic, but map curation is a science, not—"

"Okay, that's enough!" Nell snapped. "You come into my home after years of not speaking, and then start insulting me—"

"Are you serious? I didn't just show up here, Nell! You asked *me* for a favor—even after everything that happened. I'm not the one who owes you anything. And here I still am," he growled.

They squared off for a long moment, the air crackling, electric with anger.

There was a perverse comfort in the fact that they were already yelling at each other, still just as angry as the day they'd broken up. She'd been nervous that their meeting was going to go badly, but she'd been even *more* nervous that it might go well—she'd spent so many years desperately missing Felix, then so many more trying to forget him, she didn't think she could have handled it if there had been a spark again after all this time.

Because there definitely had not been a spark when she'd first opened the door and seen him.

Right?

She pushed the thought roughly from her mind.

Felix finally sighed. "I'm sorry about your father," he said, quieter this time.

Nell massaged her eyelids. "Are you going to help or not?"

In response, Felix threw up his hands, giving in. He took the map from the coffee table and moved back to the kitchen, where the light was better. She watched him study the unremarkable design, the plain colors and simple lines that wound their way across the state between dots whose names sounded like places from a movie, not real life. Sullivan, Ferndale, Howell, Cold Spring.

A few months after their banishment from the NYPL, Nell had heard Felix had gotten a job at the giant tech company Haberson Global, in their mapping division. Money enough to live on, and at a respectable company, for which she knew he was grateful, but not happy. It wasn't cartography. It was data mining and navigation algorithms. The day she finally got an offer from Classic, she understood how he felt. But as had happened to Nell, no other museum or library would touch Felix after Dr. Young had declared them personae non gratae—even with Swann's behind-the-scenes attempts to help.

But seeing Felix now, older, more confident, she couldn't help but wonder if maybe he *was* happy again. Haberson was so gigantic and profitable, it made companies like Amazon and Google look small. It was practically a country unto itself. She couldn't imagine what it was like there.

After a few seconds, Felix folded the map back up again. "Well, your father was right the first time—it seems like a regular old piece of junk. I don't know why he would still have it after all these years."

Nell let out a sigh. "It's ridiculous. These were worth less than pennies when they were actually *in use*. Why would anyone risk breaking in to the library to try to steal it?"

Felix looked up sharply. "What?"

"The NYPL was burgled last night," she whispered, as if saying it too loud might make it happen again. "You'll probably start seeing the news stories anytime. That's why I messaged you."

His face was incredulous. "And you and Swann think this map, *this* gas station pamphlet map, was the target. That's what you're telling me."

She shrugged nervously. "It's all just speculation at this point—"

"Do you think this map *also* has something to do with your father's death?"

"I don't know—"

"What is *really* going on, Nell? If you want me to actually be able to help Swann, you have to tell me!"

"Look, Dr. Young died, and there was this map, this inexplicable piece of junk map, hidden in his portfolio," she cried. "And then a day later, the break-in happened, but Swann's assistants swear they've triple-checked the inventory, and *nothing* was taken."

Felix was still looking at her, but the intensity of his suspicion had cooled slightly, so she no longer felt like she was being burned through. "Why go to all the trouble of breaking into a place as revered as the NYPL only to not take anything?" he muttered to himself. "Unless . . ."

She nodded. "What they were looking for wasn't there. This was the only thing not on display or in the back collections last night."

Felix studied the map again with renewed, hesitant interest.

"I don't know if they're connected. But I want to find out—for Swann." She picked up her father's portfolio from the counter and handed it to Felix. "He made a copy of the library's security footage from the break-in. He said the police found it inconclusive. He was hoping that you could look at the video, maybe using some of Haberson's fancy tech, and tell him what you see."

Felix opened the portfolio, and his gaze jumped to the bottom, to a little rectangular shape pressing against the inner pocket where she'd hastily shoved it—the USB drive Swann had given Nell before she left the library.

"Inconclusive how?" he asked, as he went to pry it free.

"I'm not sure," she said. "He didn't tell me. I think he doesn't want to influence you before you view it."

"Does this go with it?"

Nell looked up. "What?"

"There's something else here." Felix was working something else out of the same pocket, where it had been jammed so deep Nell hadn't noticed it. "I think when you stuffed the USB drive in, it helped dislodge it a little." He finally yanked it free and held it out to her—a little piece of paper.

A note from her father?

"It's a business card," she said. It was faded and creased from where it had been stuck for years. There was a scribble on the back, a hastily sketched map of some city streets downtown in the Chinatown area, she guessed, perhaps done by her father as a way to remind himself of where the business the card advertised was located.

She turned it over.

RW Rare Maps
By Appointment Only

They both gasped at the same time as they read the words.

"No way," she choked.

"Your father . . ." Felix rubbed his face in amazement. "Your father was doing business with *Ramona Wu?*"

Nell shuddered at hearing the name out loud. She'd never met Ramona Wu in person, back when she was still moving in industry circles, but she didn't have to—Ramona's reputation far preceded her. And it was not a good one.

Ramona was technically a private rare and antique maps dealer, a consultant who worked with wealthy clients to help them build their personal collections, but *dealer* was not what her father and Swann called Ramona on the rare occasions she came up in conversation.

Deceitful was the word they used.

There were plenty of dealers they did like. They often even worked with them to convince clients to loan or donate some of their most historically significant pieces to the Map Division for temporary exhibits. But throughout the industry, Ramona was known to operate on the more slippery side of the line. It seemed she could find *any* map a collector wanted—the provenance papers just didn't necessarily follow.

For anyone as scrupulous as Nell's father or Swann, and for most of the amateur collectors who knew even a little about the field, that alone would have been enough to convince them that the maps Ramona acquired were stolen or fakes. For anyone with any kind of standing to maintain, they would never be caught dead dealing with Ramona. Nell's distinguished father most of all.

But then why did he have Ramona's business card tucked away? And in his special *portfolio,* no less?

"Folding . . . gas station . . . highway . . . map," Felix mumbled. He had pulled out his phone and was typing the words into the Hab-Search browser open on his screen. The device's sleekness bordered on obscene, like some kind of a sci-fi gadget. "You didn't happen to already Hab this, did you?"

Nell rolled her eyes. "No, Felix, I haven't Habbed it yet. I've been a little busy with my father dying and the library getting robbed and worrying about Swann. Besides, if the map really was that significant, don't you think *we* already would have heard about it somewhere? It's not like we did this for a living or anything."

He held up a hand in surrender before they spiraled into another argument, then went back to typing. "I was just asking because Haberson is testing a new search algorithm. Still in the beta phase, but it's way better than the general HabSearch, because it can cloak to trawl the dark web at the same time."

"I thought you were in navigation," Nell said.

"I am, but it's all related." He shrugged. "I was thinking, if a black-market dealer like Ramona Wu is involved, then maybe . . ."

His thumb punctuated the search with a lazy poke.

"I'm sure there's no demand for these old gas station maps," Nell continued. "Now, or back then. They were a dime a dozen. They literally gave them away for free next to the cash registers for decades when we were kids, until GPS and smartphones came along. Now they're even *more* worthless."

Nell finally realized that Felix was still staring at his phone. He hadn't said anything for a long time.

"What?" she asked.

Finally, Felix turned the screen toward her. "They don't seem so worthless."

Nell gaped.

He'd skipped the first few pages of the search results. Once casual browsers would have gotten bored—or perhaps this was the dark web?—the results were a list of incomprehensible figures.

Felix chose a link at random, an old forum post, and handed the phone to her.

Seeking vintage gas station highway map ($100,000)

By *GRB2477*, Dec 14, 2011 in ART/BOOKS

Joined: Dec 14, 2011

That's a real offer. I'm looking for a foldable gas station highway map of New York State from 1930. Has to be from the mapmaker General Drafting Corporation. Will pay for overnight shipping. Serious sellers only. Please send photographs.

At the end of the post, the comments exploded into an endless web, some attacking GRB2477 directly, some looping back on themselves, others in their own conversations with previous replies.

First came the baffled ones:

Why the [*redacted, explicit*] would someone pay this much for a piece of [*redacted, explicit*] mass-produced map? Anyone can be a "collector" these days.

This is a rare and antique editions forum, OP. Your time might be better spent on Craigslist, or perhaps scouting local garage sales.

The sarcastic ones:

Photographs of the map or of me?
| I want photographs of you.
| | No you don't.

| Are you a serious seller?
| | VERY SERIOUS

And finally, hidden among the rest, the ones who seemed to know why GRB2477 was after the map:

@GRB2477 you're going to need a lot more money than that. I saw one go years ago for over ten times your offer. My suggestion? Find a new hobby.

wrong place to post this, check your private messages

Hoping you're just a rich old idiot who doesn't understand how the internet works rather than a casual hobbyist. You're going to get the Cartographers on your tail.

Friendly advice: beware, dude.

"The Cartographers?" Nell murmured. "Who is that?"

"I don't know. A collector's group, maybe?" Felix guessed.

Nell followed the next link. It was a listing for a rumored copy at a charity raffle that had sold for a figure that could have been a mortgage for a New York condominium. The next was another desperate forum post asking for help identifying if any of the pictures contained therein were of the right map or a near miss. And there was an old Christie's auction log, with a listing for another possible copy of the same map. Their eyes both bugged at the winning bid: $5,000,000.

More than double what the NYPL's most prized map, the Buell, was worth.

Just what exactly could make a gas station driving map sell for *five million dollars*?

"How on earth is this possible?" Nell whispered.

And in over half of the cases where the map came up, whether it was a sale, a collector trying to track down a possible copy, or a warning, so too did that same name—the Cartographers.

"Okay, there's something really weird going on," Felix said, sounding just as stunned as she felt. "I think you should show this to the police."

"No!" Nell cried. "I can't!"

"You definitely can," he said. "The portfolio is a personal item. You can just say you didn't realize anything from the library was inside at first. You won't be in trouble."

"That's not what I mean," she replied. She didn't want to tell him what Irene had confided in her at the library—that the NYPL was in trouble and she might be able to help—he'd think she was pathetic. Still clinging to a dead dream. He'd moved on and seemed content at Haberson. He wouldn't understand how stuck she was at Classic. How much she still missed the library. How much she missed real maps.

"It's like closure, okay?" she said instead. "I just want some closure. Both about the whole Junk Box thing, and about Dr. Young. I just want to figure out why the map *is* so valuable—so I can know why he lied about its worth and ruined us for it all those years ago. As soon as I get that, I promise Swann and I will explain everything to the police. They can swab and dust this map, stare at it with even less understanding than we do, and then lock it up in their evidence vault, behind miles of red tape, to their heart's content. I just want to know first."

Felix fretted for a few moments. "Fine." He sighed, relenting. He had always been the more cautious of the two of them, but she knew that he remembered how complicated her relationship with her father had been, even before he'd destroyed their lives. "What's your next move?"

"Well, if the map really would fetch prices like these, I suppose my father would have needed help to find a buyer . . ." Nell looked down at the business card still in her hands.

"No way!" Felix exclaimed. "Ramona Wu is shady. Crooked. Can you imagine, if anyone saw you together? I wouldn't be caught dead—"

But Nell shrugged. "I don't have a reputation to lose anymore, remember?"

Felix fell silent, abashed. He glanced around the tiny, dingy apartment, as if realizing for the first time just how solidly on his feet he'd landed after the scandal—and just how far Nell had fallen.

"Well, just be careful," he finally said.

"I will, Felix," she replied. "I promise."

They stood there awkwardly for a few moments, unsure of what else to say. Nell desperately wanted him to leave, so she could let out the metaphorical breath she'd been holding since he'd arrived, but she also suddenly . . . didn't want him to go?

"It was good to see you again, I guess," Felix added.

"You, too," she replied. She went to open the door for him, before the moment could get more embarrassing. "Thank you for your help."

"No problem," he said after he'd stepped through.

See you later, she wanted to add as she slowly closed the door, but that wasn't how it worked anymore. There had been too much damage done, and too much time lost. He would probably email Swann directly after he watched the tape if there was anything noteworthy, and that would be the end of it.

They'd likely never see each other again.

Nell pulled the door back open to see Felix at the stairs, about to descend.

"Dr. Young's funeral is the day after tomorrow, if you wanted to come," she blurted out.

VI

Onscreen, a swarm of dots spread themselves across the black backdrop, shifting from green to orange to red. They undulated, alive, just slowly enough that Felix could track one if he didn't blink, but one shudder of his eyelids and his target would be gone, flickering to another color and racing away.

"Let the variable go," Naomi said.

Felix pressed a key on his keyboard. "Variable is a go."

To the right of the screen, another dot, this one purple, joined the swirling tapestry—but at half speed and moving at right angles instead of smoothly like the rest. Instantly, beautifully, the rest of the dots adjusted. They began to move around the purple one, changing colors and parting in ripples that automatically evened themselves out. It wasn't about cars, it was all conceptual, but Felix couldn't help but think that ecosystem shifts still looked a little like afternoon Manhattan traffic. Chaotic harmony.

"So far, so good," he observed, but Naomi held up a hand as if to say *Just wait.*

On the other side of the desk, Priya stared at the same view on her own monitor. They were all holding their breath. The dots kept adjusting, and adjusting, the balance kept . . .

Then the scenario crashed.

"This is worthless," Priya groaned, flopping back in her chair.

The field had become a tangle of chaos. Green dots backed up everywhere, smashing into each other, flashing straight to red. The purple dot, its mission completed, ran away off screen.

Felix pulled off his headphones. "This can't be done with our current data. It just can't."

Naomi poked her keyboard dejectedly. The dots disappeared from all of their monitors, remaining only on the giant, spaceship-like flatscreen overhead.

"Why did we think we could predict future endangered species? Half of those dots were for insects that haven't even been discovered yet!" Priya grumbled. "Three months of work, down the drain."

If they went back to the very beginning, it was even longer than that. Their team, handpicked by the founder of the company himself—the brilliant, mysterious William Haberson—had been working for almost a year now on his equally mysterious mission.

For all its hundreds, possibly thousands, of different departments, Haberson Global was at its heart a logistics and navigation company, dedicated to finding things. Missing persons, lost pets, ancestry records, old friends who had fallen out of touch, distant branches of a family waiting to be reconnected—the list went on and on. The idea was, if they could amalgamate enough data to trace something on the company's central creation—the ever-evolving, ever-growing Haberson Map—they could find it.

And they almost always did. Felix's team had become so good at tracking things down that the FBI often ended up asking them to consult on especially difficult or time-sensitive cases. Just last month, they had even managed to use the Haberson Map to determine that based on all the traffic data they'd ever processed, there was a 92 percent chance that a man in Phoenix, Arizona, who had carjacked a vehicle with a baby still strapped into her car seat would head west on Interstate 10, not east. And they'd been right. Local law enforcement had scrambled squad cars onto the freeway at the next westward exit and saved the child before the driver had made it three miles.

It was awe-inspiring, the might of the Haberson Map's computing power.

But William Haberson always wanted more. More than percentages, no matter how high.

He wanted perfection.

And that was why Felix, Naomi, and Priya had been placed onto this top secret team by none other than the man himself. To perfect the Haberson Map's algorithm, so it could operate on a scale the world had never seen.

It would be not just unfathomably gigantic, but also graceful, each piece of information so well integrated into the whole that the map would be like music. A symphony. A geographical program capable of containing in one massive depiction every single stream of data from every single arm of the company. Haberson Global had medical consultancies, urban planning teams, mass transit tracking, interior design apps, weather charts, internet search programs, social media, food and grocery delivery, sleep monitoring, flower bloom patterns, endangered species migration routes—all of it would feed into the map, more information from more sources than ever possible before, through the algorithm Felix's team was designing.

A refined code that would, somehow, take the Haberson Map from incredible to *perfect*.

They just had to figure out how to do it.

Impossible or not, Felix loved every minute. He hadn't expected to ever feel like he belonged anywhere again after the NYPL, and he certainly hadn't expected to ever feel like his work was his passion again, but he really did. His teammates were just as obsessed with their jobs as he was, and dizzyingly brilliant: Naomi had a background in programming, and Priya in urban design and UX. When Felix, chosen for his education in cartography and geography, had been brought in to fill the last knowledge gap, he spent the first few days living in terror of not being able to pull his own weight.

He got in early, ate lunch at his computer, and left late, and barely said a word to either of them that wasn't strictly project related. It wasn't until the end of that first week that he finally realized how fun they were, too. During an afternoon lull, when Naomi stepped out of their sleek, metal and glass office into the equally sleek, metal and glass hallway to make a phone call to her wife, Priya scrambled over to her desk as fast as she could, and to Felix's horror and amazement, popped off all of her keyboard keys, rearranged them into a nonsensical pattern, popped them back on, and leapt back into her chair, hissing *Shhhh!* dramatically at him, before Naomi returned.

They all laughed so hard at Naomi's confusion, Felix could hardly breathe by the end.

Back at the NYPL, he could not have imagined ever playing a prank like that on any of those stuffy, pretentious academics. But at Haberson, everything was so different, and so wonderful.

Especially his boss.

William Haberson was a legend in the industry, full of contradictions that made him even more intriguing than being the head of the biggest tech company in the world already did. He was old compared to most Silicon Valley executives, but his ideas seemed to grow only more visionary every year. He employed thousands of people, but would answer any email, at any hour, from even the lowliest of interns. He'd even been the one to personally interview Felix over the phone during his hiring process all those years ago, something Felix could still hardly believe. And his company had created some of the most important innovations in the last several decades, Haberson a household name everywhere—but almost no one knew what he looked like.

The media called William reclusive, but that was a vast understatement.

According to the official company biography, when William had formed Haberson Global, he struck a deal with Ainsley Simmons, his CEO: she would be the face of the company, and he would be, essentially, a ghost. Since the very first day, Ainsley and her team had given every interview, announced every product launch, and handled every negotiation and made every business deal, freeing William to go on creating behind the scenes, his genius safe from even the slightest hint of fame.

And he guarded that anonymity fiercely. Despite being the mastermind behind a corporation worth trillions, to this very day, only Ainsley—and now Felix, Naomi, and Priya—had ever seen him in the flesh.

At first, it had seemed impossible to Felix that, somehow, no one in the company had ever been able to figure out William's real identity, or even tried to sneak into his office on the secure floor to take his picture, but after he was hired, after he'd seen the truly incredible things they were working on, the more believable it became.

But even more than that, William had hired Felix at a time when no one else in the industry would touch him, thanks to Dr. Young, and then given him a place on a project that not only was revolutionary, but also was being used to do real good in the world. For that alone, the man had earned his loyalty forever.

"Well, I think that was our worst attempt yet." Priya sighed, to a round of dejected chuckles.

"There's value in every failure," a voice behind them said then, as if on cue. "It shows us what doesn't work, and gets us that much closer to understanding what *will*."

They all looked up from their monitors to see William Haberson himself standing at the entrance to their office, thoughtfully studying the mess on the big overhead screen.

"William! I didn't know you were there," Naomi said, surprised.

William smiled. "You know me," he replied.

They all laughed, and Felix tried not to be starstruck, the way he was every time he was in the same room with William.

"Well, yikes," Naomi continued, and pointed up. "You saw all of that?"

He shrugged, unperturbed. "I was young once too, you know. I remember how messy the early stages of a new project can be."

"That one wasn't the best, but we've been making progress," Priya tried, but they all knew it was mostly an exaggeration. It was one thing to achieve perfection in a closed environment, but whenever they tried to force it in an open setting, using data from the real world, the scenario always ended up the way it had moments ago. A disaster.

William pushed off from the doorway where he'd been leaning to enter the room. "The failures don't concern me. A hundred, a thousand, a million, doesn't matter. We'll get there."

Felix found that he was nodding, despite the grim state of their project. He always found William's calm, unshakable determination comforting.

"We will," Naomi agreed. "We just need more data."

"Tell me."

"Weather, a plug-in for current events, or maybe even shareable sleep patterns from HabRest," she mused. "I'll know more after the workup."

"Whatever it is, we'll get it," William said. "We'll keep adding until everything is mapped. In fact, I have some good news on that front."

"Oh?" Priya asked.

William crossed his arms and smiled. "Haberson is taking over database and inventory security for the New York Public Library."

"What!" the three of them cried at the same moment.

Felix gaped, his mind racing. *Did he know about the attempted robbery that had just happened?*

"The library board actually voted in favor by a slim majority years ago," William continued, gently waving down Naomi's and Priya's congratulations. "But Ainsley's team has been stalled in talks over the actual implementation ever since. There's been a lot of resistance from the Map Division."

"Ah," Priya said. "They see our own products as a threat?"

"Exactly." William sighed. "Ainsley has tried to explain that this is about protecting their artifacts, not competing—I don't think we can call ourselves a mapping company if we don't do everything we can to help protect *all* maps, not just our own—but some of their scholars are quite old-fashioned. She finally managed to convince the library's chair, Irene Pérez Montilla, to let us go ahead with the work just last week—but someone in the Map Division threw a huge fit and shut it down again. Didn't want Haberson poking around their archives, copying and backing it all up on our servers."

Felix could almost hear those exact words in Dr. Young's voice as William spoke. He was certain the man had been one of the staunchest opposers to the offer.

But was there more to the stubborn scholar's intransigence than just his distaste for technology? Had Dr. Young been afraid that Haberson Global would find the old, uncatalogued map he'd been secretly keeping all this time if they were allowed into the library?

It seemed absurd. And yet . . .

"What changed their minds, then, after years of disagreement?" Naomi asked.

"Last night," William said, somber.

So, William had heard about the break-in, Felix sighed.

"Irene called Ainsley this morning to say she'd held a unanimous vote. They want us in there as soon as possible. There was a break-in."

"At the NYPL?" Naomi asked, incredulous. "What were the burglars after?"

"We're still waiting for the police report," William replied. "But in the meantime, we're going to secure everything, as quickly as possible. Scan and back up every specimen in every department, and tag all physical maps, books, computers, and art with micro RFID. We're installing tracking devices in every room, so the instant anything is moved, we'll be able to follow it right on our own Haberson Map. Something like this will never happen again."

"That's great," Felix said, comforted. He knew it would be a rocky start, but once the NYPL's scholars saw how much care Haberson put into its work, they'd come to appreciate the company.

"I'm glad we're able to help," Naomi agreed. "Their Map Division must have thousands of maps in its archives."

William was grinning now—a jolt of excitement rushed through Felix as he realized why. "And after we finish, so will your algorithm," he said.

They were going to have *so much more* data. It would add an entirely new historical dimension to the Haberson Map. And the tracking tags on the physical copies would provide yet another type of map—a real-time, constantly updating view of how everything moved in the library, and when, and by whom. Soon, Haberson would know the NYPL better than it did itself.

"How many do you think they have? A hundred thousand?" Naomi asked.

"Half a million," Felix clarified.

"That's right, I forgot you worked there," she replied.

"A lifetime ago," he said. "I actually heard about the break-in last night. I would have said something earlier if I'd known we were taking over security."

"How? It's not even on the news yet," William asked.

"Long story," he said. "An old ex stopped by to tell me. She used to work there, too."

"Reigniting an old office romance, are we?" Priya winked.

"She got me fired," he said.

"Oh." Priya winced. "Sorry."

"Water under the bridge now." Felix shrugged. "The visit was just unexpected."

It *had* been unexpected. When he'd grabbed his phone yesterday to see who had texted him, the last person he ever would have imagined it to be was Nell.

"I'm much happier here," he finished. But it irritated him that even now, as he recalled the moment he first saw her name on the screen, he felt a thrill of nervous excitement all over again.

"Well, I'm glad," William said. "Plus, having someone familiar with the NYPL's archives should make getting us up to speed go even faster. And I want this to move fast. We're announcing in half an hour in the main auditorium."

A faint ding echoed through the office then—their calendars all chimed with the meeting alert at once.

William nodded to the big screen, where their team calendar had appeared, the event highlighted. A live video of the rapidly filling auditorium was streaming in the corner, Ainsley Simmons already at the podium, going through her notes. "The two of you can head over as soon as you're ready," he said to Naomi and Priya. "Felix, before you do, I want you to set the Haberson Map to search for the NYPL burglars."

"Now?" Felix asked. "But we hardly have any data."

"It'll start coming in soon enough," William said. "I don't want us to waste any time. Mark it as top priority." He turned to make for the elevators, and Naomi and Priya set off after him. They would go down to the auditorium, but William would go up, back to his private office, where he would watch Ainsley make the public announcement through his tablet screen, like always.

"Bring coffee, we'll save you a seat!" Priya called over her shoulder as the glass doors slid shut behind them, leaving Felix alone in the office.

"Be right there," he said softly. But instead of reaching for his mouse, he stayed motionless in his chair.

In the silence, his gaze drifted over to his messenger bag. Inside the outer pocket was the USB drive Nell had given him the night before.

Seven years.

She was practically a stranger to him now, he told himself. This was just a favor for Swann. That was all.

But then why had he paced the sidewalk outside her building for ten minutes before heading upstairs? Why had he been as nervous as he had when she opened the door and he saw her again, after all this time?

So nervous that the only thing he could do was immediately start an argument, because bickering over the past was so much easier than having to have a real, mature conversation?

Felix sighed.

Well, he'd said he would help. And if he was going to aim the mighty power of the Haberson Map at finding the burglars, maybe this security video was a good first piece of data to give it.

He had to admit, he was curious to see what the Haberson Map could do with such a vague target and so little background information. Just how creative it could get.

It was definitely not because—since he wasn't going to accept Nell's invitation to the funeral of the man who had ruined his life—being able to find something on the tape would give him an excuse to talk to her again.

Who was he kidding?

Felix inserted the drive into his computer.

After a brief load, a folder of video files popped up. The first was a grid with feeds from every camera both inside and outside the building.

Felix clicked his tongue, impressed. Most library and museum security was significantly behind compared to other industries, but it looked like in the last seven years, the NYPL had done at least a little upgrading. He could tell from the model information that the new cameras and speakers were motion sensitive, designed to alert for glass breaks, paper tearing, or wood cracking, so they would turn on automatically under those stimuli, rather than simply wastefully recording all day and night.

Inconclusive, Nell had said.

He clicked play.

The file began at exactly midnight, according to the time stamp. At first, all the screens were completely black. Felix let the scene unfold naturally rather than scrolling through on fast-forward. At 12:02 A.M., the main lobby camera suddenly flared to life—the security guard, starting his midnight rounds, was moving.

For several minutes, Felix followed the guard from the front desk into the DeWitt Wallace Periodical Room, then the Dorot Jewish Division and the Wachenheim Gallery, watching as various areas blinked on and went dark again one at a time in his wake.

Then the Map Division suddenly also lit up as something there quickly moved across the room.

Felix hit pause, and his eyes went to the Celeste Bartos Education Center auditorium, on the other side of the first floor. The security guard was still there, halfway through his rounds. And the burglars were now in the Map Division.

But the lobby hadn't been triggered first.

It didn't make any sense. The burglars were now in their target exhibit, but how did they get *in* there without being caught by the lobby recorders?

Felix checked the records. After the upgrades, there were now two cameras in the Map Division: the first one in a corner of the ceiling, looking out across the entire room, in case anyone tried to tamper with or steal a map or atlas while reading it. The second camera was stationed outside the Map Division just above the doorway, pointing outward toward the lobby, so that any suspected thief could be followed as they exited the Map Division and merged back into the main library population, where they'd then appear on the lobby cameras.

He clicked the first interior camera and skipped back a few seconds before hitting play again.

Suddenly, a lone figure dressed all in black was in the center of the room—a single man, not a group, unusual among art or museum heists—crossing quickly from one side to another, then back again, apparently searching for something on the shelves and in the glass display cases.

"Gotcha," Felix hissed, surprised at how unsettled he felt. He couldn't see the burglar's face, because he had on a mask, but that only made it worse. It had been seven years since he'd been able to call that room his, but his heart was racing all the same, his mouth dry and palms sweaty. It was like watching a burglary of his own home.

He zoomed back out and watched tensely as the security guard made his way toward the burglar, one square at a time. Then suddenly, the only room that was lit up was the Map Division.

He gasped when the guard's head hit the tile floor and he went still.

The Map Division's camera remained on for several more minutes as the intruder continued searching for his target. On the camera feed, he crossed the room several more times, double-checking every case and shelf, growing increasingly frustrated.

It was true. Whatever he was looking for wasn't there.

Because Nell had it on her coffee table.

The thought sent a shiver down Felix's spine.

At last, the burglar looked as though he was about to flee—but then noticed the security camera in the ceiling.

The burglar climbed onto a wheeled book ladder, and then knocked the camera. He didn't manage to break it, but he did dislodge it slightly, so that instead of giving a view of the full room, it angled sharply, looking straight down at the far reading table. Several more seconds passed, with glimpses of the burglar as he moved in and out of what remained of the frame. Then, suddenly, the video feed went dark—all cameras off.

"Wait," Felix muttered, hitting pause.

How was that possible?

The cameras needed motion or sound to continue recording, and since the guard was now out cold on the floor, unconscious or worse, he wouldn't trigger the sensors in the Map Division—but the burglar still should have been caught by the main lobby cameras upon his exit. Except he wasn't.

Felix sped through the rest of the recording, but there was no other stimulus until after dawn, when the first arriving NYPL employees, Swann probably among them, came in through the front doors, saw the guard, and called the police.

Confused, he scrolled back to just before the damaged camera blinked off—when the burglar was leaving the Map Division—and hit play again.

He sat in silence for a full minute, his eyes glued to the screen, waiting for the moment the overhead Map Division camera went dark. When it did, his gaze jumped to the second camera outside the Map Division door, pointing back toward the lobby, to watch the actual footage of the burglar's exit from the room.

But nothing was there.

It stayed black the whole time.

"That doesn't make any sense," Felix finally muttered, confused.

The only explanation was that the burglar hadn't gone out that way—but there wasn't any other way to get out. Felix remembered the Map Division well. There wasn't even a separate entrance for employees. The only way into and out of the entire exhibit and its back offices was through the main door he'd just watched on the feed.

He played the video grid at least ten more times, then went back and watched every single camera in the library, listened to every single speaker, and scanned every line of data, but there was nothing useful. No matter what he tried, there was no recorded footage for the lobby for the entire night, aside from the guard during his routine rounds. The burglar tripped only the camera inside the Map Division, and no others.

Felix went through the police notes, looking for mentions of damage, but they had confirmed that the lobby cameras hadn't been tampered with—only the one in the ceiling of the Map Division. And they were all on the same system, so any attempts to hack them before the break-in would have brought the whole network offline, which clearly hadn't happened, because Felix had been able to watch the burglar prowl the Map Division.

The only explanation he could come up with was that somehow, the burglar hadn't gone into the lobby at all. But then how had they gotten into an exhibit room whose only entrance and exit was a single door directly off the lobby hallway? Felix double-checked the notes again, but there had been no glass broken in the windows or drill holes found in the walls either.

It just didn't make any sense. How could a burglar break in to a building without actually breaking in to a building?

VII

Ramona Wu's shop sat on the edge of Chinatown, at the border where the neighborhood blended into Little Italy. Dim sum restaurants gave way to wine shops and Italian eateries, languages mingled. The Bowery was a blur of rain puddles, puffs of smoke, and the intoxicating scents wafting from inside each restaurant every time the doors opened. Nell's mouth watered for the roast duck she passed, strung up and glistening in the window. She'd been in such a rush this morning, eager to get started on her investigation into her father's map, that she'd forgotten to eat breakfast before she left her apartment, she realized. Barely slept, either. She'd startled awake at the table at one point in the early hours of the morning, still hovering over the map, a pencil in her right hand—of course. She'd been sketching little bits of the map by instinct before she'd dozed off, unable to help herself. It was how she made sense of things. Perhaps it did make a little bit of sense that she'd ended up at Classic after the library.

After that, Nell had dragged herself to bed, where she'd lain for some number of hours, but it had done no good. She couldn't stop thinking about the map. When her alarm finally went off, she was already up, showered, and dressed, impatient to get started.

Pushing her hunger away, Nell broke off from the chaos of Bowery onto narrow Doyers Street, where the honk of cars and screech of tires suddenly dropped away. She could hear the quiet conversations of couples walking up and down the sidewalk, the clink and clang of pans being moved about the stainless-steel stoves inside kitchens. There was a delivery truck unloading fresh vegetables into Nom Wah Tea Parlor, and a few people in line outside the small post office across the lane.

Nell looked down at the business card in her hands as she walked, checking the little sketch her father had drawn on the back to make sure she was in the right place. She'd realized as she'd set out that morning why he'd done it—the front of the card had Ramona's name and the title of her shop, but didn't actually contain an address or phone number. She didn't know how her father had originally found his way there, but she was glad he'd doodled a little street map on the back of the card to remind himself—and to allow her to follow.

Sure enough, a few steps past Nom Wah Tea Parlor, an old glass front proclaimed in delicate gold lettering: RW Rare Maps.

Nell looked at the business card again and chewed on her lip.

She still couldn't believe her father would have anything to do with someone with a reputation as shady as Ramona's. But then again, she also couldn't believe that one of the most respected scholars in the field of cartography had anything to do with a gas station highway map, either. And she hadn't managed to dig up anything more—beyond the map's inexplicable, eye-watering value and its apparent penchant for being stolen—after Felix had left her apartment.

Before heading over to Ramona's, she'd spent several hours that morning in the Brooklyn Library branch just off Grand Army Plaza, looking into General Drafting Corporation, the company that had made the maps from which this Junk Box specimen came, hoping some clue might jump out at her. But as far as she could tell, it was a small company that focused mostly on highway driving maps, producing them for nearly every state—none of which went for the same kind of prices that hers did—until they were eventually squeezed out of the market when the larger corporations caught up. At some point in the early 1990s, what was left of General Drafting was absorbed by some German media conglomerate and then fizzled out completely.

For a time, though, it seemed General Drafting had been quite the enterprising underdog in the field. The founder, a man named Otto G. Lindberg, had come over to the United States from Finland in the early 1900s with just a few hundred dollars in his pocket and set himself up in New York City as a draftsman. Even though American cartography was dominated at that time by two gigantic mapmakers, Rand McNally and H.M. Gousha—names Nell easily recognized, despite her exclusive focus on antique maps—Otto and his assistant, Ernest Alpers, were the first to invent and produce this type of cheap folding map and gained their own small foothold in the industry for it.

But that was almost all there was. She did find some evidence that there had been a controversy of some sort, and a lawsuit, around the same time that this 1930 edition of her map had been published, but she couldn't find the outcome of the case, or any information thereafter. And employees who had been working at General Drafting at the time of the suit were all long gone, having died decades before, so there was no one to ask. There weren't even business records to go through. For a time, there had been physical copies archived in an old historical building in New Jersey, where the company had moved after Manhattan real estate prices soared, but the place had burned down in an accident decades ago, everything lost.

Nell had also called a few of the other libraries and museums that the interinstitution database showed had once owned copies of the same map, but they all had been lost so long ago that almost no one at those places could tell her anything useful, either. There was only one librarian, a now elderly woman who had been working part-time at her local branch in southern Connecticut for decades, who remembered the insignificant little map in question.

It had been the most peculiar thing, she'd said to Nell. The robbery had occurred in 1989 or 1990, she recalled, but the thief was never caught, because the police couldn't actually prove there had been a break-in at all. None of the doors or windows had been damaged and were all still locked when the librarian had entered the building the next morning. And their simple alarm system, which was set to go off if any of the doors were opened before it was disarmed, had not been triggered.

But it had rained all night, and when she went into the history section, she found muddy footprints on the carpet.

She and the other librarians checked and double-checked everything that day, going through the entire catalog by hand. Only that map was gone—nothing else.

Nell sighed. The more she looked into it, the fewer answers, and more questions, she had.

Ramona was her only lead. She had no choice.

She just hoped the dealer might know something more about the map than just its price—or maybe could even tell her who her father's potential buyers for it were.

The bell on the door dinged as Nell pushed it cautiously open and stepped inside. A darkness fell over her immediately, the shop being so much dimmer than the bright morning outside. As her eyes adjusted, a small, involuntary gasp escaped her lips.

It looked as though she'd left Chinatown and stepped into a secret world.

The interior of RW Rare Maps was made of wood and painted black, giving the place an ancient, solemn feel more like a magician's workshop than the dry, stuffy map dealers' offices Nell was used to. Instead of typical overhead lights in the ceiling, lantern-like sconces dotted the walls, casting a soft, yellow glow over everything. And every inch of available space—the display tables, the shelves, the sales counter, even empty spots on the floor—had books and maps stacked everywhere.

As she stood there taking it all in, Nell realized what it reminded her of. The kingdom of buried treasure in the uncatalogued basement of the NYPL.

Where had Ramona gotten all of these maps? It was far, far more than any dealer had. It was more than some small archives had, even.

Her fingers itched with curiosity. She wanted to open every atlas, turn every single page, to see what treasures were hidden inside.

"We're closed," a voice said from behind, startling her.

Nell jumped and spun around, her heart pounding. In the shadows of the corner stood a woman, her arms crossed. She was dressed in dark colors and had been waiting with such stillness, Nell had failed to notice her when she'd entered.

"Ramona Wu?" she asked once she thought her voice would be steady.

The woman stepped forward. She was about the same age as Nell's father, or perhaps just a little younger. Short, though not quite as short as Nell, with dark straight hair pulled into a simple bun. Everything about her was the way Nell would expect an unscrupulous dealer with possible connections to the underworld of stolen texts and art to be, a sharpness bordering on flinty—except her eyes. They looked . . . almost afraid.

"Yes," Ramona said at last. "And you're Daniel Young's daughter."

"I am," Nell confirmed. "How did you know?"

She studied Nell for a few more moments. "You look just like him."

"I'll take your word for it," Nell replied. "Didn't see him much these last few years."

Ramona nodded faintly. Nell knew that even on the periphery of the industry, Ramona would have been told about the Junk Box Incident by some client or another.

"I heard the news of his passing. I'm sorry for your loss," Ramona said. She turned toward the counter. "But you shouldn't be here."

"Wait, please," Nell said, surprised. She had expected Ramona to be happy, eager—not cagey. "Did the Cartographers contact you?"

Ramona looked up at her slowly, as if she'd been struck. She withdrew even further, shrinking in on herself, the effect so unsettling that Nell was afraid she was about to disappear into thin air. "How do you know about the Cartographers?" she asked.

"They're . . . collectors?" Nell faltered.

In truth, she didn't really know what they were. The internet seemed to think the group was either a bogeyman or a joke, academic literature made no mention of them at all, and Swann recalled having heard of them somewhere a long time ago, but believed they were more fiction than fact. A manufactured scapegoat over the years for frustrated collectors or lazy researchers to blame for losing a bid or a source. Nell herself wasn't sure what she believed yet. But their name came up too many times in connection with her map—and in too sinister a way—to ignore.

"I thought perhaps you were selling something for my father," she said, trying a different approach.

She could see in the dealer's expression that of all the possibilities Nell could have guessed for how the two things were connected, that was the wrong one. The woman took another step back and crossed her arms.

"I don't have any dealings with them," Ramona replied. "I can't help you."

"Just tell me wh—" Nell began, but Ramona cut her off.

"I'm very sorry about your father. But you need to leave now."

"But he must have had your card hidden in his portfolio for a reason," Nell pressed, ignoring her.

"Please leave," Ramona said.

Nell frowned, confused. If Ramona was indeed her father's dealer, she must have been disappointed that he'd died before a sale went through. Why wasn't she now thrilled that she still potentially had a shot at the commission? Had the Cartographers, if they were even real, threatened her? But if they were buyers, why would they do that, if she was trying to sell them the map anyway?

"I'm not going to ask again," Ramona said, her voice growing sharper.

But Nell refused to give up. "You're telling me that my father had your card for *no* reason, and you were *not* trying to broker a sale for a folding gas station road map made by General Drafting Corporation," she said defiantly.

The last bit of the sentence had an immediate effect. Instead of another icy comeback, Ramona stopped in her tracks.

I was *right,* Nell thought triumphantly.

Ramona continued to stare at Nell in silence for a long moment, collecting her thoughts. "So, he *did* tell you about it after all," she eventually said.

Not exactly true, but Ramona's assumption was close enough. "Just a little," she replied.

"You're still wrong, though."

"How so?" Nell asked.

"He didn't want me to sell it for him. No one can sell it—it doesn't exist anymore. It was destroyed, a long time ago. And thank goodness it was."

Nell paused. She couldn't tell if Ramona believed that herself or was simply trying to get her to believe it. Was this one of her tactics? Feigning ignorance to trick an unsuspecting mark into admitting something?

To prompt Nell to reveal that the map wasn't destroyed, and that she secretly had it?

"He didn't tell me that part," Nell finally said. Until she figured out what was going on, she figured it was better to give Ramona as little information as possible. "How do you know about it, then? If it was destroyed a long time ago?"

"That's not your concern."

"Isn't it? He's gone now, and I'm the one who has to settle his affairs. I need to know why he had your card. I won't leave until I do."

Ramona studied her again for a long, hard second. "You're just like him," she muttered. "Never, ever give up, on anything."

She had the same expression that Nell had seen so many times on the faces of her colleagues when they were trapped in academic debates with her—that fear and admiration of the infamous Young determination that ran in their family.

But seeing that familiar look here, in this strange place, and after her father's passing, made Nell's throat pinch suddenly, catching her by surprise.

The older woman sighed again. "I suppose I owe it to you." Her eyes went to the door, and back to Nell. "If I tell you, will you go? Will you let that be the end of it?"

"Yes," Nell said. "That's all I want to know."

Ramona nodded at last. "First, my card."

"What?"

"My business card," Ramona repeated. "You must have it with you, if you came here."

"Oh yes." Nell took it from her pocket, where she'd slipped it after she'd entered, and handed it to Ramona.

Ramona turned it over to glance at the little scribble on the back, and then slid it quickly into her own pocket.

"Your father didn't want me to sell something for him. He wanted me to *find* something for him," she said. "Quietly, out of the public eye."

Her father had been trying to *buy* something through Ramona?

Nell was even more confused than before.

"What was it?" she asked.

"Insurance, of a sort," Ramona said. "Only it was too late."

Nell tried to make sense of it, how something a black-market middleman like Ramona could find would be any kind of insurance, but the older woman looked down at her hands before she spoke, as if she were afraid again, or perhaps, ashamed. They were small, the fingers still long and beautiful, just starting to gnarl from age.

"You don't remember me, do you?" Ramona asked. "But why would you."

Nell blinked. "Remember you?" She was sure that in all her time at the NYPL, Ramona Wu had never once entered those hallowed halls, as a dealer, colleague, or simple patron. Swann and her father would have staged a mutiny at the insult.

"It was a long time ago. You were just a child. A baby, really."

A baby?

"I don't understand," Nell said. "You're saying . . . you're saying that you were old friends with my father?"

Ramona shook her head. "Not just with your father. With your mother, too."

Romi

There were so many secrets between the seven of us, but at the time, none of us knew that. We had no idea how much was hidden. We never could have guessed what was to come.

We all met during undergrad, at the University of Wisconsin. Well, not all of us. Your mother and Wally had known each other since childhood. They were inseparable—more like siblings than friends. They'd applied to all the same schools and chosen Wisconsin together. They were the core of our group, the original two who brought everyone else in, and the most brilliant of all of us. The start, and the end, of everything.

I was the first one they found.

Most freshmen had already been on campus at the University of Wisconsin for a week, preparing for the start of the semester, but I'd been helping take care of my grandmother, who was in the late stages of cancer, and didn't leave until the day before classes started. The cheapest flight I could get from Los Angeles landed in Milwaukee, and I'd had to huddle with my suitcases for an hour and a half on an intercity bus with a broken window, shivering as the frigid breeze streamed in off the highway. I dumped my things at dormitory reception and ran, still shivering, to the freshman welcome mixer in the science building, where the geography department was housed.

The door banged as I pushed it open, and the room went quiet as everyone turned to me. I stared back at the sea of faces peeking out from beneath wool hats and thick down jackets, and shifted awkwardly in my thin windbreaker.

"Hi," I managed to mumble. "I'm Ramona Wu."

"Everyone, let's welcome Fiona Chu!" a voice proclaimed, having misheard my mumbling, and a junior professor began to clap.

"Ramona," I said, but I was drowned out by the applause. Mercifully, the room went back to ignoring me, swelling with laughs and chatter. I squeezed through the crowd toward the snack table, hoping for something warm to drink.

"Hot chocolate? Tea? Anything?" I asked desperately, and the overworked sophomore shook his head. The main door kept opening as more people came or left, each time throwing in another gust of arctic air that chilled me to my bones.

The whole plan seemed more foolish by the minute. My parents had wanted me to go to school in California, where I would be closer, but I'd insisted on Wisconsin, on this program. My great-grandfather had drawn tactical maps for the army in World War II, and his work had saved his fellow soldiers many times over. Before he died, he showed me the few he'd saved—these old, yellowing, tissue-thin things. There were so many stories bound up in them, so many lives. To me, nothing had sounded more thrilling than to follow in his footsteps. And it had taken so many arguments with my parents, and finally the solemn support of my ailing grandmother, to convince them to let me, that by the time I finally got to Wisconsin, I'd built the whole thing up to be impossibly perfect. In my head, it would not have been so bitterly cold, and I would not have been so sheltered and innocent, and would have known exactly what to do and say.

There was no way it could have lived up to the dream.

I was about to give up and go back to my dorm room—where I could pretend to be asleep before my new roommate came back, pushing off reality until the next morning—when someone tapped me on the shoulder.

I turned to see a short girl with a curly brown ponytail smiling at me, and a tall, thin boy with pale, grayish eyes and hair that was somewhere between blond and brown, so indecisive it almost seemed gray as well, behind her.

"Are you okay?" she asked.

I started to say so, making excuses, but as we shook hands, she gasped at how cold mine was.

"You're freezing!" she cried. In a flurry of motion, she'd ripped off her own coat and scarf. "Here, put these on. No, don't worry! I'm from New Hampshire, I'll be fine."

My teeth were still chattering so much, I could barely muster a polite refusal before she'd wrapped me up in her clothes. "Thank you," I finally managed, sinking into the comfort. "My name's Ramona, but everyone calls me Romi."

The girl's eyes lit up. "Romi, I love it!" She reached over to her coat on me and pulled a paper out of the pocket—her dormitory check-in form. "Is your last name Wu, by any chance?" she asked. Her grin grew even larger when I nodded, and she put her hand out again, as if to redo the greeting. "I'm Tamara Jasper. I think I'm your roommate." She turned and gestured to the boy behind her. "And this is Wally."

He seemed to cower as I turned to him, as if not wanting to meet me, as if not returning my gaze or the greeting would mean it didn't have to happen.

"Wally can be shy, but I guess all geniuses are," Tam continued, and elbowed him playfully. "You'll never meet a better geometer. He's saved our group projects a million times."

At that, Wally finally came out of his shell enough to shake my hand. "Hi," he said quietly.

And just like that, we were three.

Tam's coat was heavenly, warmer than anything I'd ever owned, and the thrill of having come under her wing so suddenly gave me a burst of friendly courage. We moved through the party as a unit, Tam's arm looped through mine, and Wally clinging to her so as not to be swept away by the crowd. She smiled and introduced herself and Wally to everyone, and me too, as if she'd known me as long as she'd known him. We each had our strengths, and if Wally was our cautious one, our rule follower and detail checker for every research article and grant proposal we tackled thereafter, Tam was our engine. If she was ever in the room, no one could avoid her. She was like the sun. Students, professors, even strangers would gravitate to her, powerless to resist her excitement, her passion.

The three of us already made a strong team—Tam and I were both artists, my realistic style complementing her experimental, interpretive one, and Wally able to analyze both our works from his much more scientific perspective—but it was not enough for Tam. She was always hungry for more minds, more ideas.

Over the next two weeks, as we settled into our classes, we also found studious, solemn Francis, Tam luring him away from a dry conversation about the history of geography as an academic subject and instantly into an intense discussion with her about accuracy versus beauty in classical maps—and also your father.

Every one of us worked incredibly hard for every one of those years in Wisconsin, all through our undergrad, graduate, and doctoral programs. The dean used to say that he'd never seen even one such dedicated student, let alone a whole group of them. But if our circle did have a goof, it was your father.

Daniel was just so *happy*, all the time. So open and joyful, and utterly unguarded. So different from now.

And the sparks flew almost the instant they saw each other.

That second week, it was a Thursday near the end of our morning class, and we were all milling around near the front of the room as we waited for our instructor, Professor Johansson, to finish passing back our first assignments. Tam and I had fidgeted with boredom through the whole lecture—Wally and Francis had been rapt with attention, because it was all numbers and science and math—and we were so impatient to escape that Tam didn't notice Professor Johansson had accidentally handed her the wrong essay until another student near us called out, "Well, if Tamara Jasper gets grades this good, I guess I'm happy to be Tamara Jasper!"

"What?" I asked, at the same moment that Tam looked down at the paper in her hands, and said, "You're . . . Daniel Young?"

"No, that's you," Daniel said, grinning broadly.

Tam snorted, and her eyes dropped to his assignment again. After a long, surprised pause, she looked back up at him, mystified. "You wrote about fake maps?"

"Imaginary!" he crowed joyfully. "Not fake."

We all glanced over at that. His essay was titled "Geography and Cartography in The Chronicles of Narnia."

"You turned in an essay about maps in a children's fantasy novel?" I asked, laughing.

Francis looked utterly bored with the entire conversation, and Wally looked miserable, as he always did every time it was clear someone else was about to join our friend group.

Daniel shrugged, still smiling, not at all embarrassed at how silly we clearly thought his essay was. "They're as real as real maps. Just in a different way."

"Well, you did get a B+," Tam said, holding up his paper for him to see. "Not bad, considering."

"Not bad at all, I do have to say," Professor Johansson joined in then, offering rare praise. "A bit sloppy, but your arguments were very fresh, and very interesting."

That got the attention of all of us. Professor Johansson was a legend in the department, the professor everyone wanted to impress, the mentor everyone wanted to have. And each one of us did end up impressing him, in the end—he read all of our papers and advised every one of our dissertations. We all grew close to him, but Daniel especially so. I didn't know if it was because his own father had been somewhat absent growing up, or because they thought about things so differently, one a cartography traditionalist and one always pushing boundaries, but it was plain to see how much they enjoyed each other's company. Later, it worked to our immense advantage, as well. Whatever we needed from Professor Johansson—an extension on a group project, support for a small travel grant, late admission to a conference, or, most of all, approval for our *Dreamer's Atlas* idea—we just sent Daniel to beg him for permission. And we always got it.

Tam looked at the essay in her hands again and pursed her lips, intrigued. I could practically see the gears turning in her head. His ideas were clearly strange, but creative, and different from any of ours. Having him with us would only make us all smarter, better. I realized that I was already thinking the same thing, too. And Tam did like science fiction and fantasy—our dorm room bookshelf was stuffed with her cheap old paperbacks. She'd tried to foist several of her favorites on me, having already made Wally work through the entire collection years ago.

"Can I read it?" she asked him, holding up the essay.

"Sure," Daniel said. "Want some lunch, though?"

"It's ten thirty in the morning," Francis objected, scandalized.

"I'm not hungry," Wally murmured, but it was so quiet, I think I was the only one who heard him.

"I could eat," Tam said, smiling.

By the end of that week, they were dating. So many furtive glances, and the sneaky ways they tried to sit or stand next to each other whenever we were all hanging out, so they could secretly hold hands. I don't know who they thought they were fooling.

"I'm just concerned about our midterm project," Wally complained to me morosely once during the early months of their relationship as we sat in the empty classroom we'd booked as a late-night study hall, waiting for the rest of the group to arrive. "She's so distracted."

"I know," I agreed, even though it was a lie. Tam was never distracted about anything. I'd seen a draft of her part of the research on her desk in our room, and it was as brilliant as always. It was just that I wasn't ready to admit that I was a little bit jealous. Tam and Daniel were both so outgoing, it would have been impossible for them to have languished in romantic angst for long—but Francis was just as awkward and nervous underneath his formal posturing as I was.

Eventually, Wally came around, of course—it was impossible to dislike Daniel, even for someone as cautious and quiet as Wally—and eventually, Francis finally worked up the courage to ask me out on a date, too. I'm convinced it's because Daniel figured it out and told him to get off his ass before he lost his chance.

By the end of our second year, our group had become a darling among the professors. We were such an eclectic mix of minds, half of us concerned with the beauty and artistry of maps and the other half with the math and precision of them, so that every project we tackled became an electrified debate between the two philosophies, pushing all of our studies even further.

In fact, it was this very drive to always explore every idea from both angles that gave Tam and Daniel the very first inklings of inspiration that would ultimately turn into our grand project—what we believed would be our crowning achievement, a creation that would change the cartography industry forever. Our *Dreamer's Atlas.*

But I'm getting ahead of myself.

Professor Johansson encouraged us to consider graduate school there at the University of Wisconsin, and the dean sent us to conferences and competitions on scholarship, whetting our appetites even more. In our third year, Tam found our sixth member, a big, loud, lovable boy everyone called Bear, who had transferred from New York earlier that spring on scholarship, and then in our fourth year, just before graduating, we met Eve, who would be joining the geography department the following fall with us as a fellow graduate student.

Eve was, at that point in my life, the most glamorous person I'd ever met, even being as young as we were. I was short, plain, and hopeless with makeup, and she was tall and beautiful, with dark skin like Francis's and perfect hair, always. She was from Washington, D.C., where her father worked as a diplomat, and there was a sophistication to her that I had never seen in California or throughout the rest of our grubby undergraduate dorms. I was nervous around her for weeks, until I relaxed enough to realize that her elegance was just a cover—she was as shy as me, or even Wally, in her own way.

There was a lot of her I didn't see. A lot of *me* I didn't see either, until it was too late.

In contrast, even though Bear wasn't the last friend to become part of our little family, he constantly worried about his place in it, in a way that Eve didn't seem to quite as much. I think he needed us the most, is what it was. He was just like a cartoon bear: giant, cuddly, outgoing, sensitive, always wanting to be with us, like we were his cubs—and happy to let others have the glory. Bear was also an incredible artist; his restoration work in the practice studio was almost as good as Tam's, but he lacked her brilliance. Everyone did really, even as smart as we all were. But it always felt to me that Bear was worried he didn't quite measure up—his grades not quite as good, his history with most of us not quite as old, even his family not quite as well-off as the rest of ours, although none of our families' wealth compared to Wally's—and it made him ferociously protective of all of us, of our friendship.

He was the heart of our group, even if Tam and Wally were the start of it. He was the one who always managed to keep us together. Who pushed hardest for our *Dreamer's Atlas* project, that final year of our Ph.D. program.

We were so young then, so ambitious. We believed we were going to revolutionize the field of cartography with our big idea. We were going to *change maps*.

It was uncommon for so many dissertations to be linked like ours were, but there also wasn't a friendship like the one our group had. Since the very beginning of undergrad, all the way through our Ph.D.s, we all purposefully had chosen the same topics from different angles for term papers, all done the research together, and all written our conclusions together, after endless exploration. We even had started publishing together in small university journals, as joint authors. Some of us were more famous than others already, but we all were beginning to make a name for ourselves. That final year of our doctoral program, Professor Johansson, who had read Wally's proposal for the *Dreamer's Atlas* idea and then sat through Daniel's impassioned speech to convince him why he should approve it, wholeheartedly agreed to sign off on it after we each passed our individual oral defenses. He was so proud of us, I thought I saw tears sparkling in his old, kindly eyes as we all burst into cheers and hugged Daniel, and then him.

The *Dreamer's Atlas* is what we'd decided to call it. After all, that was what it was going to be. A creation to bring wonder back to cartography.

You see, over the course of our studies, we had come to believe that even more important than the differences between art and science in cartography were the *similarities* between them. We'd debated the ideas endlessly, the same way that every student and scholar in our field constantly did—but for us, we weren't trying to figure out which aspect was more important. Our goal was not for one side to win over the other. It was for both sides to win. To marry the two concepts irrevocably, to show that one could not exist without the other.

It started with Tam and Daniel, as I said. We'd all been brainstorming for years already over what our next big project would be—our first after graduating with our Ph.D.s. It had to be something incredible, something that would catch the attention of not only the academic world, but the greater outside world as well. We wanted to make something that would remind people of the wonder and power of maps, rather than just their dry utility.

We were in Tam and Daniel's off-campus apartment that night, going through our old articles, searching for inspiration, when Daniel began laughing.

"Remember this?" he asked. He turned the paper he was holding toward the rest of us. It was the very first essay he'd written at the University of Wisconsin. The one about fantasy maps in books.

"You kept it?" Tam chuckled, taking it from him.

He smiled. "It's how we met."

"That is so adorable. Tell me you're that sentimental too, Francis," I cooed at him, teasing, and we all laughed.

"I wonder what Narnia would look like if it was a *real* real place," Daniel said. "Like New York."

"Or what New York would look like as Narnia," Tam replied.

We all laughed again, but I could already see the first flickers of curiosity in their eyes.

It didn't take long for the idea to take shape, or for them to tell us about it.

"The *Dreamer's Atlas*," Tam said a few weeks later, all of us gathered back in their living room again, wineglasses in hand.

The grand idea was an atlas. A collection of maps, both of real places and of imagined ones, but reversed. She and Daniel had come up with a list of books, fantasy novels famous for the beautiful maps created just for them—Tolkien's The Lord of the Rings; Le Guin's Earthsea series; Lewis's The Chronicles of Narnia books; Dragt's *De brief voor de koning, The Letter for the King;* Pratchett's Discworld novels—and another list of maps from our real world, famous for their cartographic significance. We would painstakingly research all of them, studying them from historical, scientific, and artistic angles, and then redraw them in the opposite style. Our recreations of the fantasy maps would be rigidly detailed and precise, and our re-creations of the realistic maps would be embellished, expanded, and dreamlike, like their fictional cousins. Once complete, we planned to publish it in one giant volume. Readers would open it, expecting the same old type of atlas, but instead, they'd find previously familiar lands rendered in a completely unexpected manner, opening their imaginations to an entirely new way of looking at maps.

The idea was thrilling to us. A manifestation of the exact conversation that had consumed us for the entirety of our education and a perfect use of all of our talents. Daniel and Bear would research the novels and their invented maps' cartographers, Francis and Eve would research the historical pieces, Tam and I would lead the drawing of the re-creations—she'd tackle the fantastical re-creations of real places, and I the realistic ones of imaginary places—and Wally would supervise it all, organizing the data, tracking every measurement and line, ensuring complete accuracy and faithfulness to the originals, like he always did.

We were all convinced of the idea within the hour—except, surprisingly, for Wally.

Normally, he agreed with whatever Tam suggested, no matter how busy he already was. I think the *Dreamer's Atlas* idea was just too experimental, too strange, for him to understand. None of us thought about maps the way Tam did, but Wally especially so.

Luckily, though, they were also the closest to each other, and had known each other the longest. If anyone could convince him, it was Tam.

"Just think about it," I remember her saying to him as we all shuffled out into the nighttime snow, tipsy and a little sleepy. "We can't do it without you."

A few days later, Wally showed up to our study group carrying his usual back-breaking stack of reference texts—and one more, much smaller book.

It was a science fiction novel from the 1970s, by one of the same authors we already had on our list. I don't remember the title—something about heaven or a lathe—but Tam seemed to recognize it.

"Hey, I gave you that book," she said when he set the stack down on the table and she saw it. "In high school."

Wally picked it up and studied the cover. "I thought maybe we could draw some of the descriptions of future Portland," he said hesitantly, as if still unsure he understood it all correctly. "Some of the differences are pretty stark if you compare it to a real city map."

Tam grinned. "It's perfect," she said. "Perfect for our *Dreamer's Atlas.*"

"Our *Dreamer's Atlas,*" Wally repeated, finally smiling, too.

"He's in!" Tam cried, and the rest of us cheered.

Everything was ahead of us, and we were going to do it together. We were going to stun our colleagues, amaze the public. We were going to breathe passion and life back into cartography and make it something no one had ever seen before.

The day we graduated, all seven of us together in our caps and gowns, holding our diplomas, was one of the happiest days of my life.

I thought we were going to be friends forever. I thought nothing could tear us apart.

VIII

The room seemed quieter once Ramona finished her story. Smaller, colder. The dealer looked even more nervous than she had when Nell had entered, if it was possible.

"All this time," Nell murmured. The shop echoed softly, stealing the words. "You knew my parents—my mother—and he never told me."

"We drifted apart. Your father and I haven't spoken in decades," Ramona replied. "None of us have, until now."

"What happened?"

But Ramona just shook her head. "Please, Nell. Leave the past in the past, where it belongs. That's what your father would have wanted."

"Maybe not. He told me about the gas station map, after all."

Nell tried not to let her lie make her uncomfortable. But was it a lie? She and her father hadn't spoken in seven years, but he *had* put the map in the one place he knew she would recognize, hadn't he? Or had he merely been trying to hide it from everyone else?

"Well, he shouldn't have."

"*And* he had your card," she pressed. "So, why did he get back in contact with you again, after all these years?"

Ramona opened her mouth, but before she could speak, the thunderous crawl of a semitruck passing on the road outside startled her badly. She snapped upright, completely lost for a moment, as if she had forgotten there was traffic outside. As if she had forgotten anything at all was outside, beyond her dark, secretive little shop.

"You really have to go," she finally said, spinning back toward Nell with such a tense, panicked look in her eyes that Nell faltered.

"Okay, okay," she agreed, hands up in a gesture of surrender to mollify the older woman. She wanted to keep pushing for answers about the gas station map, but if she said any more, she worried she'd give herself away for sure. Ramona would know that it in fact hadn't been destroyed, and that she had it. "Just tell me what he wanted you to find for him, and I'll go."

Ramona looked as though she was going to refuse, but finally, she hurried back to the counter and ducked behind it. Nell heard the sound of a dial turning and a heavy safe door swinging slowly open.

The older woman stood back up at last, holding a single envelope in her hands. "This." She paused, then handed it over to Nell. "I shouldn't give it to you, but . . . once someone's gone, I know how much even the smallest tokens can mean."

Nell looked down at the package in her grip. It was a typical manila envelope, plain and common. And just like her father's portfolio, it felt light enough to likely contain only one sheet of paper. On the front, there was a short scrawl in a messy hand—she glimpsed her father's name quickly, likely a note from the seller to him.

"You really do have to go now," Ramona said quickly, before Nell could read the writing or open the flap, with a desperation bordering on terror.

"Whatever my father owed you for this," Nell started to say. "Once his accounts are transferred to me—"

"Don't worry about it," Ramona cut her off. "Consider it a gift."

Nell nodded. "Well, thank you."

"Don't thank me," Ramona said, but it didn't come out like a conversational pleasantry. More like a warning. "Just hurry. You've already been here too long."

She had gone to the door and was holding it cracked open. She gestured for Nell to tuck the envelope into her bag, and Nell obliged, hiding it away. Ramona's eyes combed the street outside like a deer scanning the woods for wolves at night, darting and desperate.

"Don't ever come back here. For your own safety," she said as Nell stepped out.

Nell shook her head. "I can't promise that." How could she, after finding out that Ramona knew both of her parents? "People say I'm even more stubborn than my father was. And you knew him well, apparently."

She expected Ramona to insist further, but instead, the thin pink line of Ramona's lips quirked into a shadow of a smile—the first one Nell had seen since she'd been there. "It wasn't a request. It was a statement of fact," Ramona said as she began to swing the door shut.

Just as the door closed, the click of the latch echoing heavily as it locked, Nell caught Ramona's last words.

"You can't find a place that doesn't exist."

What?

Nell put her hand up on instinct to shield her eyes from the sudden glare of morning light caught in the door's glass panel and then moved closer to peer inside. "Ramona?" she called softly.

You can't find a place that doesn't exist?

What could that mean? Nell knew where the shop was. She was standing right there in front of it. Of course it existed.

She knocked lightly, hoping to ask Ramona what she'd meant by that last line, but the dealer was already gone from the front of the shop.

Nell took a step back, hesitant. *She's probably just busy,* Nell thought. *Right?* But everything—Ramona's unease, the strange connection she had to Nell's mother and father, the way she'd checked the street before showing Nell out, as if afraid of something out there—was all too unnerving to ignore.

Slowly, Nell turned around and searched Doyers Street for the black Audi again, trying to look casual.

The road was empty. She let out a relieved breath. But it caught halfway in her throat as she looked farther down the way.

At the next intersection, there was a dark car parallel parked against the curb, with a person sitting inside.

Shit.

Her eyes darted to the wheel wells, to see if there was rust, but she couldn't get a clear view from where she was.

And she wasn't going to wait around to find out.

Nell turned and walked quickly down the sidewalk in the opposite direction, dodging pedestrians. She made a few random turns, and crossed and recrossed the street, heading deeper into Little Italy, until she was as sure as she could be that no one was following her, either on foot or in a car.

What had the driver looked like? She tried to remember, but the windows had been tinted, and she'd been in too much of a hurry to escape to recall.

On a whim, she ducked into a little coffee shop. There were just a handful of customers, all engrossed in their newspapers or phones, and the barista was chatting with the chef, unbothered that Nell didn't seem to want to order anything.

She slid into a seat away from the windows, then pulled the envelope Ramona had given her out of her tote bag. Her eyes jumped to the scrawl on the front she'd noticed before.

> Daniel,
> I'm sorry for the delay. It took us much longer than expected to find a copy.
> I hope this helps. Be careful.
>
> *Francis*

Francis. One of the other friends from Ramona's story.

The date at the end of the note was yesterday—just a day after her father's death.

It was too late, Ramona had said.

Nell worked her finger under the taped flap and pried it open.

As she shook the envelope gently to encourage the contents to slide out, there was a hiss of paper on paper, and a small rectangular shape glided smoothly free and landed in her hands.

It was facing backward, but she could tell it was a photograph.

PS: I found this while cleaning out my files a few years ago. I know it might bring up painful memories, but I thought you might want it anyway, Francis had written in the blank space beneath the film development shop's logo.

Nell turned it over, and gasped at the image with sudden, bittersweet surprise.

It was a picture of their family.

The three of them—her father, her mother, and Nell, no more than a toddler—standing in front of an old station wagon, the doors open, suitcases stacked on the seats, surrounded by a background of lush woods and sun. Nell was dressed in purple overalls, perched in her mother's arms, and her father had his arms around them both. Her parents were even younger than Nell was now, their faces smooth and unlined, her mother's hair as curly and wild as her own.

Nell touched her mother's face with the tip of her finger, transfixed. Everyone always said she looked just like Dr. Young, but here in the picture, she could see how similar she was to the other Dr. Young, as well. Her mother was even draped in an oversized, stretched-out cardigan, much like the ones Nell herself wore, comically huge on her petite frame, so big it looked like she'd stolen it from Nell's father. They all were grinning widely, as though at the moment the photo had been taken, they had been laughing out loud at something—her father most of all.

He did *look so happy,* she thought as she stared at him. She had seen her father happy before, of course—when she won her full scholarship to UCLA, when she graduated, when she got her internship at the NYPL—but there was always a painful undercurrent to it all. *I wish your mother were here to see this,* he'd say with a sigh sometimes, the most he'd ever say about her.

But here, in the photo, that deep wound hadn't yet been cut into him, then scarred over. Nell could practically feel the intensity of his joy through the faded gloss barrier, so trusting and uncontained. The way Ramona had described him.

"Hi, Dad," she said softly.

Finally, she set the photograph carefully down on the table and tugged the other page out of the envelope. It was just a single sheet of paper inside of a cardboard folder—an article? Perhaps Francis had been tracking down some research for her father? But what information could he have been after that he couldn't just download from the academic journal database at a library? He had worked at one of the biggest ones in the world, after all. That seemed much easier than going through a shadowy middleman like Ramona to have someone else hunt it down. Unless he hadn't wanted the search on his record?

But it wasn't an article, but rather another map, Nell saw as it came free of its folder. An old one, judging from the scuff marks and condition of the ink, and also clearly mass produced, she could tell at once from the style of the print and quality of pulp.

Why had her father been seeking yet *another* insignificant commercial map?

She studied it quickly, trying to figure out its relevance. It wasn't a highway map this time, like the Junk Box map, but rather a block plan of a single street's buildings—interiors drawn from an engineering or industrial perspective—from the early 1900s.

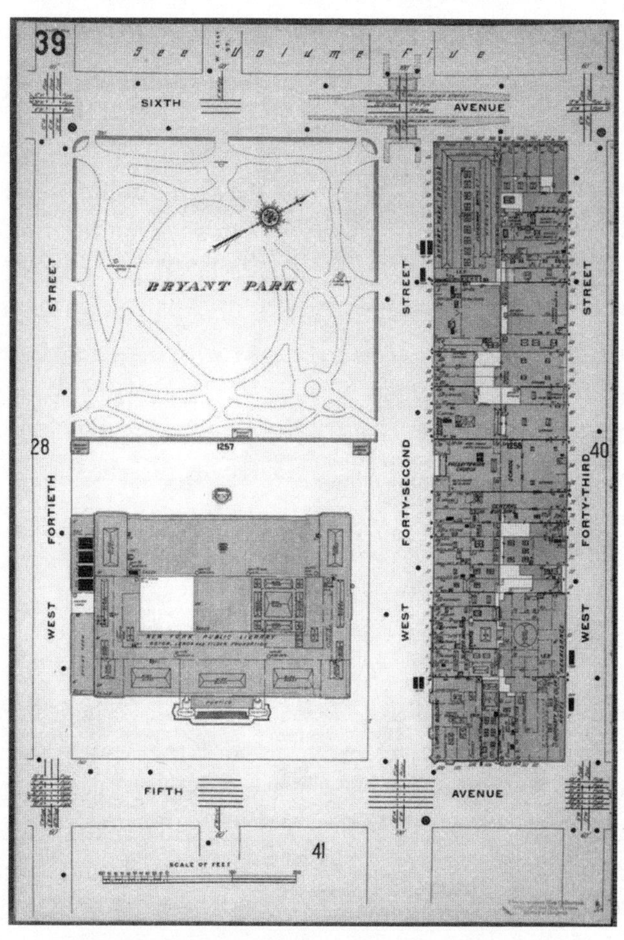

Sanborn Insurance Map from Manhattan, New York: Sanborn Map Company, 1903–1919, Vol. 4, 1910.

It's a construction diagram of the NYPL, she realized just as she caught sight of the faded stamp at the bottom of the page.

"Sanborn Insurance map?" Nell read the words softly out loud, confused.

Why on earth would her father need an outdated floor plan of the library he worked in? And what did this map have to do with the first one?

The back side of the folder the Sanborn map had come in answered her question.

On the brown cardboard, in a hastily scribbled hand, was the same symbol that she'd found on the gas station map.

An eight-point compass rose, with the letter *C* in the center.

IX

The reception was more crowded than Nell had been expecting. Someone had poured her a drink from Swann's private Scotch, and she cradled the crystal tumbler in her hands as she wandered through his home. Around her, the entire staff of the library, members of its board, and other distinguished friends and colleagues of her father talked quietly in scattered groups. The periodic clink of glass filled the air as toasts were made. They'd all been gathered there after the funeral since the late afternoon, clustered throughout the historic brownstone building.

It had been so long since Nell had been to Swann's, but it hadn't changed—it was exactly how one would imagine an old bookish type's place to be. Big windows with wooden shutters that did very little to stop the dust-swirled light from leaking in, a pipe on the desk, and books everywhere.

She'd missed it here so much.

"That was a lovely service." A soft thump on her back made her jump, then smile. Humphrey squeezed her shoulder sympathetically. "Didn't you think?"

"It was, actually," Nell had to agree. Despite the metaphorical trampled bones Dr. Young had left in his wake, there had been no theatrics. No ruined researchers sneakily distributing letters to show how mercilessly competitive he had been, no museum directors appearing to demand apologies. And Nell had managed to keep her mouth shut as well. Not a single scoff or bitter eye roll as others sang his praises from the pulpit. Not even when she'd gone up to his coffin to say goodbye.

He had looked so much older than she remembered. So much smaller, and lonelier. She had tried to take his hand for a moment before she realized it.

But it was too late now—and always would be.

"Nell, there you are," Swann called, and Nell spotted his tall, thin form as he appeared from the crowd.

"Swann." She waved him over. "This is my boss, Humphrey Turan. This is Swann, the director of the NYPL's Map Division."

"Why hello," Humphrey replied, returning Swann's handshake.

"Good to meet you. I've heard so much about Classic," Swann said politely.

Humphrey chuckled. "Well, Nell must have been being charitable. Our shop's little maps aren't quite as fancy as the ones in your library."

Nell tried not to grimace as they talked. She was touched that Humphrey had insisted on coming to the funeral for her, but also embarrassed that he had—and ashamed of that embarrassment. But there he was, joking to the head of the NYPL's Map Division about how the more weathered you could make a map seem, the more customers would like it, and which antique-looking doodles—skeleton keys, made-up languages, fake fading—made sales jump.

"Well, I'll let you two catch up," Humphrey said at last, finally noticing her discomfort. He smiled apologetically at her. "Must be some hors d'oeuvres somewhere."

"Thank you again for coming," Swann said to Humphrey as he drifted off, before turning back to Nell with an admonishing quirk of his brow.

"I know," she sighed. "I'm sorry."

"He cares about you a lot. In my book, that means more than how historically accurate his work is." He touched his glass against her own, the same outrageously expensive Scotch inside his as well. "I'm glad someone was able to look out for you all those years that I couldn't."

Humbled, Nell returned the toast. She tried to take a sip, but all she managed was one luxurious sniff. It was hard to actually bring the rim to her lips—she felt strange drinking something that was probably worth her annual salary at Classic.

"So, where's Felix?" Swann continued.

"Who knows. Probably at some swanky Haberson function," she

replied, and tried to ignore the sudden lurch of butterflies in her stomach.

Swann sighed. "I'd just thought, since you finally saw him again after so long, maybe you'd invite him."

"Not a chance," she lied. "That was seven years ago. It's long over."

Was it? She was sure he was not actually going to come, but all day, she'd debated whether or not to send him a message to see if he'd watched the security video yet. She really did want to know if he had—but she wasn't sure that was the only reason she wanted to talk to him. And even more than that, she didn't want *him* to think there was another reason.

Swann smiled, a little sadly. "Well, I'm glad *you're* here," he said. He raised his glass again to her.

"Albert Wilson Swann, if you toast again without me, I'm going to have to take more of your precious Scotch," a familiar voice called from behind them.

"Hurry up, then. To Dr. Young." Swann smiled, his arm waiting in the air.

"Ms. Pérez Montilla," Nell squeaked, all at once nervous again. She should have known it was Irene by her manner of address alone. She couldn't think of anyone except the chair of the NYPL who could call Swann by his full name. To her, and everyone else in the Map Division, Swann was always Swann. Even her father had called him Swann, after decades of friendship.

"I told you, please, call me Irene," Irene said, and bent slightly to give Nell a hug. "And let me introduce Claire Marie Roche, a member of the board," she added, gesturing to the equally glamorous woman now standing on their left.

"Charmed," Claire replied.

"Um, hello." Nell resisted the urge to tug on the hem of her own plain dress. The church had been cold, and she'd put on her work cardigan during the service, but why hadn't she taken off the stretched, faded old thing when they'd come into Swann's house?

"And this is Wolff Erickson, and Julian Leuprecht, also from the board, Pete Vance from the Smithsonian, and Dr. Nozomi Ito from Stanford . . . ," Irene added as another group approached the circle, followed by even more people.

The names and titles just kept coming, each one more intimidating than the last, but the final one surprised her most of all.

"And this is Dr. Francis Bowden," Irene finished, indicating the newest man to join the group. "Of Harvard University's Department of Conservation Studies."

Francis.

The same name as the man in Ramona's story—and the same name that had been on the envelope to her father. The one with the photograph of her family, and the second, equally baffling map of the library inside.

"Hello," Nell said, studying him as they shook hands. He was the right age—not more than a year or two older than her father—with dark brown skin that contrasted warmly with his short silver beard. He had an inch or two on even the tallest guests, but there was something very closed and wary about his manner. It was very like Ramona's had been, Nell realized.

Francis seemed nervous.

"I'm very sorry for your loss," he replied to her, voice low.

"Thank you," she said.

"It means so much that you all came to say goodbye to Dr. Young," Swann added.

"He truly was a force," Wolff agreed, to a round of nods. "May we all be so passionate. Law pays the bills, and for my own little collection, but if my collection could also be my life . . ."

"If only." Julian toasted the circle. "Hedge funds aren't much of an adventure either. I complain so much, my husband is begging me to quit, despite the money." He sighed. "In a way, I imagine it almost might have been a dream for Dr. Young, to work until the very last second. But if I were to expire at my desk—"

"Julian," Claire admonished, gesturing to Nell. "That's ghastly."

Nell smiled. "That was actually my first thought, too. That he went doing something he loved." She looked between them as she said it, curious if any of the others had also started to wonder if there was more to her father's passing than simply old age. Her gaze landed on Francis, who looked quickly away.

Clearly he thinks so, she thought.

"I actually just heard the police are now considering Dr. Young's death as suspicious, and connected to the burglary the day after," Wolff began—and then gasped, horrified. "I'm so sorry!" he said to Nell. "We've been meeting so often these past few days, sometimes I forget we're not in the boardroom still, discussing library business. I truly didn't mean to gossip about your father at his own funeral."

"I'm glad to know the police are looking into it," Nell said.

"Lieutenant Cabe came by the library to update us this morning," Irene explained to her and Swann. "I told him you two were already at the church preparing for the funeral. I'm sure he's going to call you tomorrow."

Nell nodded. She couldn't decide if that was a good thing or a bad thing.

Of course, the more the police dug, the greater the chance they'd figure out who robbed the library and possibly murdered her father, which was justice she desperately wanted. But it also meant that they might figure out that he'd had the gas station highway map with him at the time of his death and begin trying to find out where it had gone.

She didn't like that at all. Not until she'd figured out why it was at the center of all of this herself.

"Nell, if you'll excuse me and Swann for a bit," Irene said, oblivious to her fretting. "An old donor and his family just arrived, and we should go greet them."

"Of course," Nell agreed.

The group was quiet as Irene and Swann departed, and then yet another toast was made to Dr. Young. Nell raised her glass and lowered it without drinking again. She wondered how anyone was supposed to remain upright by the end of one of these events.

"It will be impossible to replace him," Wolff finally said.

Nell sighed. The sparkling crowd in front of her, all of whom were so incredibly wealthy that they more floated above the cartography industry than walked through it, likely had no idea about the day-to-day business of the library—and especially not a long-ago scandal of a lowly intern. They might not even know that she had once worked for the NYPL or been a cartographer in her own right at all. But still, the comment stung.

"So true," Pete agreed. "Both for the library's sake and for mine."

"Was he helping you curate a set?" Nell asked.

"The final touches on a personal collection," Pete replied. "Dr. Young could track a map down like no one I've ever seen."

"A veritable hound after a fox," Julian proclaimed, which drew yet another toast.

"If only he was interested in the General Drafting hunt," Wolff said.

"Not this again," Claire sighed, bored.

Wolff, Pete, and Julian chuckled, but Nell felt her stomach drop through the floor.

How did people like *this*, people who had drivers and butlers and spent their weekdays at ski resorts and their weekends at operas and art galas, know about a map like *that*?

"The what?" Nozomi asked, looking baffled.

"Oh, it's just a little hunt for an old highway road map of New York State that some of the board members play in their spare time. A silly story," Pete said to Nozomi.

Nell managed a smile. "A good one though?" she asked.

"Depends on who you ask," Julian replied. "I find it entertaining, although some of the other collectors take it too seriously. My friend Olivia especially, but she's always been competitive."

"It's such nonsense." Claire took a long drink. "This secret game."

"Claire refuses to play," Wolff said to Nell, winking. "She finds the whole thing embarrassing."

"It is embarrassing. No one with a shred of respect for their reputation has ever even heard of it, besides the two of them and some of their drinking buddies," Claire replied.

"That's not true," Julian said. "You can find other amateur collectors who are after it online. There's definitely a bit of a cult following. Small, but fervent."

"'Cult following,'" Claire repeated, with mock horror. "There are far better maps to spend one's money on."

"Like?"

"Literally any other American map from the same era!" she cried. "In the early 1900s, Rand McNally was still producing beautiful collector's atlases and giant murals, before the whole industry became obsessed with convenience and affordability."

"Blame that on the automobile," Nozomi replied. "The Model T was invented then, wasn't it? Suddenly, everyone could travel much farther than ever before in a single day. They would have needed a new kind of map for that."

"That was exactly General Drafting's business plan," Pete said, pleased at the chance to show off. "They didn't have the resources the bigger companies did, but they knew that lugging an expensive tabletop atlas everywhere wasn't going to satisfy drivers. They were the ones who invented the concept of the cheap, folding driving maps we all used for decades. I still even have some in my glove compartment, even though we all just use our phones now." He smirked at Wolff. "Don't worry, I don't have the General Drafting edition in question in there. I looked."

"Good to know," Wolff replied. "Now I won't have to break in to your car to check."

They laughed, but there was a mercenary undercurrent to the joke that made Nell shiver. She glanced around the circle nervously as they all toasted again. Now, everyone looked a lot less friendly. And a lot more suspicious.

Suddenly, Nell realized that Francis was no longer standing with their group. He'd disappeared as soon as the gas station map had come up.

"This sounds like an intense game," she finally said.

"It is," Pete agreed. "Some players can be quite obsessed. A little frightening. I'm honestly not even sure why the map has become such a valued specimen. I just like to win."

"I'm actually not sure either," Wolff admitted. "I just know that it's worth a *lot* of money, and is very, very rare. Whoever finds one will have bragging rights for life—and a target on their back from the Cartographers."

Nell managed to strangle a gasp. If her stomach had already fallen through the floor, it was in the basement now.

That name, again.

And Wolff had not said it like he believed they were just an industry rumor.

He'd said it like they were real—very real.

"Who are the Cartographers?" she asked.

"No one knows," Julian answered. "But out of everyone playing the game, they seem to be the richest by far. And the most dedicated. Too dedicated."

"You can't mean an *actual* target, though," Nozomi said to Wolff.

"Well." Wolff paused, suddenly uncomfortable. "I have friends who say they've been threatened. And sometimes, other collectors just . . . vanish. Quit the game all at once, drop off the face of the earth. Even—"

"It's gossip," Pete interrupted. "Just other players trying to spook the rest of us."

The others laughed. Nell joined in weakly.

"Actually, I heard from a curator at Sterling House that part of the reason the map's become so rare is that years ago, when the game must have started, someone went around *destroying* every copy of it they found," Julian added.

"Destroying?" Nell cried. Immediately, images from the inter-institution database, with all the vanished copies, and the scorched remains of the old General Drafting building that had burned down, flashed into her mind.

"It's an old map, and so cheaply made," Claire replied. "It seems more likely most of the copies were lost to the elements over time or tossed into the trash in favor of an updated edition, and someone's trying to romanticize it."

"Then it should hold true for all copies, but if you search for any other year, they turn up in droves. It's only the 1930 edition that's become so rare," Julian replied.

"Maybe it had something to do with the lawsuit," Wolff said. "I looked into it once, when I thought I was on a hot trail—we have some great paralegals who can chase anything down. There was a court case around the same time as the edition we're all after was published, about copyright infringement. General Drafting lost, or settled, or something. The suit just disappeared. After that, their fortunes declined."

"Copyright infringement," Nell repeated. Had General Drafting been stealing data? she wondered. Or had data been stolen from them?

"Perhaps someone was trying to force scarcity?" Nozomi offered. "Remove a bunch of the remaining copies to increase the value?"

"That was my initial assumption, but the pruning appears to have been so extreme that not a single map has been seen for decades, by even the most dedicated hunters," Wolff said. "Almost like whoever did it wasn't attempting to drive up the price, but rather trying to completely eradicate the map."

Julian sighed. "I've mostly given up. But a die-hard few are holding out hope there might be a single one left somewhere."

Mine, Nell thought with a chill.

She needed to tell Swann what she'd just heard. That some of the wealthiest figures in the amateur collecting field were playing a secret game for millionaires with the very map that someone had robbed the NYPL for. The map that they might have . . . *done something* to her father for.

The map they might now do something to her for.

"So? Interested in joining the hunt?" Pete was asking Nell now. His tone was playful, but there was a hint of suspicion threaded through it.

"She's Dr. Young's daughter. She would never stoop to play such a stupendously classless game, just as he wouldn't either," Claire said, with an air of finality. "Now, someone tell us a charming, respectable story about him."

Nell tried to listen as Nozomi launched into a humorous anecdote, but all she could think about was her father's leather portfolio, hidden among the wreckage of his silent office. The map inside that he had placed there in secret before he died. The map that so many people, and more importantly, the dangerous Cartographers, desperately wanted.

She raised her glass, before the rest of the guests noticed her discomfort.

"To Dr. Young," Wolff said when he saw her gesture, and the rest of the circle copied.

Nell finally took the smallest of sips—delicate, musky heat tingled on her lips. Probably a month's pay right there.

"Please excuse me," she said, and turned to make her way through the crowd, eager to escape. A stream of condolences and raised glasses greeted her, and she returned each with a smile, but kept moving. She was looking for one person in particular.

"Francis," she said.

Dr. Francis Bowden was standing in the corner near a bookcase, apart from the rest of the party—and seemed to have been talking to Humphrey, of all people, who had just disappeared across the room to refresh his drink. Francis looked up when she called to him, startled.

"Nell," he finally replied. "How are you? These things can be a little overwhelming."

"I'm fine, thank you," she said, joining him in the corner. "You knew my father well?"

"We spoke at many of the same conferences these last few years," he answered.

"I meant before. Long before. And me, too—isn't that right?"

The shadows across Francis's face deepened.

"I'm sorry, but it's getting late, and—"

"Yesterday I went to Ramona Wu's shop, and she gave me a package that was meant for my father," Nell interrupted. "Your name was on it." She pressed on as he withdrew even further. "Why would my father want an old insurance map of the library?"

Francis didn't say anything for a long moment. He glanced around the room, with the same cautious look that Ramona had worn.

"You should stop looking into it," he murmured.

"Ramona said that, too. Practically kicked me out of her shop," she said. "Why? I don't understand."

"You should keep it that way. You're already in over your head—and you've been careless."

"Excuse me?"

"Two visits to the NYPL in two days. Research into General Drafting Corporation. The false interinstitution catalog entry you made. And that trip to Ramona's."

Nell stared at him, stunned. The bright, busy room suddenly felt cold, sinister. "Have you been . . . following me?"

"Only to warn you," Francis said.

Nell fumbled for a response. She tried not to think of the black car that haunted the streets outside, always lurking. The hunger she'd seen in the board members' eyes moments ago. The fear in Ramona's, and now Francis's.

"How was the Sanborn map supposed to help him?" she asked again, but Francis withdrew from her rapidly—he was looking not at her anymore, but just behind.

"Nell, there you are," Irene said. "I'm sorry to interrupt, but I have to give another interview about the burglary over at the library. I was hoping to speak to you before I go."

"Of course," Nell replied. She looked pointedly at Francis. "I'll be right back," she said, and followed Irene away to a spot beside Swann's big bay window.

"How are you doing?" Irene asked.

"I'm all right," Nell replied. She paused. "How . . . is the library?"

Irene sighed. Even beneath her expertly applied makeup, Nell could see her exhaustion. "The media won't let up. And now that this might not have just been a burglary and the tragic death of one of our guards, but *also* a premeditated crime against one of our most cherished scholars—" She took a breath. "That's what I wanted to talk to you about. Something he said to me a long time ago."

"My father?" Nell asked.

Irene nodded. "The day he was hired, we had the most unsettling conversation. At the end of our meeting, just before he walked out, he told me that if something strange ever happened to him, I should suspect foul play. He refused to explain himself further, and after that, everything was fine. He worked here for decades without incident, and never brought it up again. I had forgotten about it, until the break-in." She leaned closer. "Lieutenant Cabe told me that his investigators finished going over your father's phone log for the last few months, to see if there might be anything there. Did you know he tried to call you that night, just before he died?"

Nell's eyes widened in surprise. "No," she said. She could hardly believe it. She was certain the last time they'd spoken was the day she was fired. "Are you sure? I would definitely have noticed a missed call from his number."

"At night, the new phone system shuts down, and all calls in and out are automatically routed through the front guard desk. Your father's went that far, but it seems he hung up before Henry went back to the desk from his rounds and was able to put it through." She looked at Nell. "So, he didn't try to reach out in any other way?"

Nell shook her head, still struggling to believe it.

Irene sighed. "I'm sorry. All of this is so strange. If only we knew what he'd wanted to tell you."

Nell took a breath. This was her chance.

"Actually, I think that I might be onto something. I've been going through his personal things, talking to some of his old friends . . . I might be able to figure out what he was working on." She paused. "I think it might have been the reason the library was burgled."

Irene stared at her, stunned. "What is it?"

Nell swallowed. She'd definitely made a start, but it wasn't enough to tell the illustrious chair of the NYPL what the map actually was—a cheap old thing that could barely be classified as a map compared to the countless historical treasures on the walls of the library—without anything concrete to prove it. She'd made the mistake of showing a discovery too early once in her life. She wasn't going to make it again.

"I'm not sure yet," she said. "But as soon as I am, I'll bring it to you."

Irene smiled, wavering between surprise and relief. "I'd be indebted to you. The entire library would." She considered something before continuing. "You still have a very loyal friend there, you know. He's stormed my office every morning and afternoon with impassioned speech after speech about how brilliant you are, and what a mistake it was for us to lose you."

"Swann is too kind," Nell laughed politely.

"Well, between his tireless campaign and now this revelation, I'm convinced. I know I can't make up for what happened all those years ago, but I do hope that you'll allow me to at least try. Senior researcher, perhaps? Assistant director of conservation?"

Nell held back a gasp.

Swann had done it.

He had managed to sway Irene just enough to give her an opening.

Everything she wanted—her reputation, her job, her library, her *life*—within reach again. If there was anyone with enough power to force the academic community to accept her back into the fold, to give her a fighting chance to prove herself again and restore her name, it was the chair of the NYPL.

"I promise I'll figure out what my father was working on," Nell finally said, fists clenched in determination.

Irene nodded, pleased. "This was supposed to be a surprise, but the board has been planning on renaming a portion of our collection after Dr. Young for some time. It'll be a bittersweet honor now, but I think it's even more important that we do it."

Nell gasped. "That's incredible." Someone in her family would have a collection in the *New York Public Library* named in their honor. It made her dizzy to imagine. And, despite their history, she had to admit her father deserved it. No other scholar in recent memory had brought in the priceless maps he had.

Irene smiled. "I'm glad you think so. The invitations are being sent today. There will be a small ceremony at the library on Sunday night, where we'll unveil the dedication." Her expression grew solemn again. "The police will be there, just for safety's sake. That might be the perfect time to inform them of Dr. Young's possible significant project as a potential motive for the crimes and let them take over from there."

"That's just two days from now," Nell replied, alarmed. Barely enough time to even conduct an ink analysis on an incoming exhibit specimen, let alone to complete the kind of research she'd require to be fully confident she had the map Irene needed, and why.

Irene grimaced slightly. "I'm afraid if we wait any longer, we could look suspicious, which is the *last thing* we want for the library, after everything that's already happened."

Nell fought down her fluttering panic and managed to nod. "I understand," she said.

"I'm glad. But I know how you feel. If possible, I'd so much rather have one of our own"—Nell thrilled secretly at the phrase *our own* including her again after so long—"solve this part of the puzzle. Someone who knows and loves maps the way Dr. Young did."

"I won't let you down," Nell replied.

Irene smiled again and glanced at her watch. "Thank you for your help, Nell. I look forward to seeing you Sunday—and to welcoming you back to the library properly, I hope."

As Nell stood by the window, watching Irene rush through the front door and flag down her driver, she crossed her arms and held her breath to stop herself from bursting into hysterical laughter in the middle of her father's funeral reception.

She was so close.

So close to getting back everything he had taken from her.

The deadline seemed impossible, but if anything, she was even more determined now. She would not let this second chance slip through her fingers.

A blur of motion caught her attention, and Nell glanced up to see Francis heading out of the main party and down the hall.

"Francis," Nell called.

But when he saw her, his pace only quickened.

"Wait!"

Nell dashed after him, ducking between guests as she made for the same hallway. She was sure she knew the house better than he did—he must not have realized that the corridor he was heading down dead-ended in Swann's large study, which had no exit. He'd end up cornered, with no excuse not to speak with her. After her conversation with Irene, she would not let him leave without getting her answers.

She rounded the corner in time to see Francis reach the study door. He had his drink in one hand and a small paper of some sort in the other, and used his shoulder to push it open.

"Francis, please!"

Francis didn't stop. He nudged the door closed after him as he entered, obscuring her view into the room, but it didn't matter. She was right on his heels and reached the door a moment later.

She threw open the door and leapt into the study. She would make him talk to her, somehow. Maybe she could offer him something from her father's personal collection, any map he wanted. Harvard would kill for a piece from Dr. Young's holdings. "I just want to—"

But the rest of her sentence died on her lips.

Nell took a few steps into the room, but it was no use. The study was large, but square and open, with nowhere to hide.

It didn't make any sense.

There wasn't another room to go into, or a back exit, or even a closet, and all the windows had bars on them. There was nowhere Francis could have gone. And yet, the study was empty aside from her.

He'd vanished into thin air.

X

Jimmy's Corner was as quiet as it usually was, even for a bar on Friday night in midtown. It was one of the reasons Felix liked this place so much. Back when he was an intern at the library, he and Nell used to come here all the time after work to unwind. The bar became their go-to hangout: comfortable, cheap, and totally unfrequented by any of the other employees, despite being just around the corner from the library.

He'd stopped coming after he'd been fired and had broken up with Nell, afraid of the memories, but tonight, he hadn't been able to stay away. He'd spent the first hour of Dr. Young's service pacing his Haberson luxury corporate apartment, unsure of what he felt, and the second hour roaming the streets, trying to ignore the guilt as the miles grew longer. He was completely within his rights to have declined Nell's invitation, he told himself. It would be impossible to expect him to still have warm feelings about the man who'd fired him and tanked his reputation. Or his daughter, who'd gotten them sucked into the mess in the first place.

Right?

Without realizing it, suddenly Felix was ducking under the old blue awning at the entrance to Jimmy's Corner and pushing the door open, bracing for a blast of warm, humid air from within, just like he always had.

Some places you didn't need a map for, he sighed wistfully.

He moved slowly into the cramped space, his eyes adjusting to the dim light. Everything looked mostly the same—a bar that was more glorified hallway than anything else, crammed with vintage pictures and twinkling string lights. The huge, crowded collage of photos patrons had taken of themselves while hanging out there was still spread across one wall, and an army of framed black-and-white shots of Muhammad

Ali, an old friend of the owner, and other famous boxers, midfight, still on the other. There was room for none of it, and all of it, and more.

He hadn't known how much he'd loved this place until he saw it again.

Taking a table alone seemed rude, even though there were plenty to spare. As he neared the bar counter, still half-immersed in his thoughts—they had stools now, not chairs, when had they changed that?—his eyes passed over a woman sitting midway down the row. She was short, with a crop of unruly brown hair, and her cardigan draped around her like an oversized blanket, nearly swallowing her small frame—

He froze.

"Tonight got to you too, did it?" Nell asked.

"I'm sorry," he said, his hands up, already backing away. "I can go."

"No. It's okay." She patted the stool beside her guardedly, as if unsure what she wanted either. "Sit."

Felix smiled ruefully at himself. He should have known. Of course this bar was the most likely place she would end up tonight, too. Some habits were hard to break.

Because it had been unconscious habit, and not a purposeful choice, that he had come here, hadn't it? He just hadn't been thinking as he wandered. Or had he been thinking entirely too much?

Whichever the case, it was too late now.

"Escaped the funeral early?" he asked, sliding onto the stool beside her the way one might sidle up to a venomous snake.

"I stayed for the whole service, and at least an hour of the reception after," she replied, but there was no defensive barb in her voice. For her to have even gone for one minute of it was already far more than she owed, and she knew that Felix knew it. "Swann's there now, holding court. The good Scotch is out."

"Ah," he said, envious. "I hope you got some."

"Oh, I did." She smiled. "He wishes you could have been there tonight."

"Yeah, sorry." Felix grimaced. "I just thought it would be best if I didn't go."

Nell picked up her glass. "No apology needed. I get it. Better than anyone."

He ordered a beer for himself, and they took a few awkward sips in silence. At least they were talking—not fighting—this time, he thought, heartened.

Felix turned on his stool to face her. Ainsley had said at her presentation that the news Haberson had won the contract to take over security for the library wasn't public yet, but he could tell Nell about the security video, since she'd been the one to give it to him.

"I watched it," he said. "The footage from the robbery."

"And?" Nell asked, her eyes suddenly laser-like in their focus, like how they'd been every time they'd started a new project together.

"I went over everything three times. Cross-referenced every camera and speaker, and went through every line of data." He sighed uneasily. "The police are right. It's inconclusive."

She frowned. "What *does* it show?"

Felix pulled his phone out. "Better if you just watch."

Nell gave him a curious look, and then leaned in as he hit play.

As the video rolled, he tried not to notice, but he could feel the light touch of air on his cheek each time she breathed. Saw her flinch as the guard went down, disappearing into the dark shadows on the floor. He could smell the faint floral trace of her shampoo—it was the same one she'd used back when they'd been together. He'd always loved the scent of it.

The clip ended, and Felix pulled back abruptly, before Nell noticed how close they'd been sitting.

"I don't get it," she said. "I can't see how the burglar got in or out of the Map Division. But the only way there is through the lobby."

"I know," he agreed. "That's why the cops aren't able to do anything useful with it."

"And you couldn't find anything more about how he covered his tracks?" she asked. "Like, I don't know, hidden in the code, or however it works?"

Felix shook his head. "I tried everything I could think of. There's just nothing. No gaps in the film, no looped footage, no tampering, nothing. It's just . . . inconclusive." He looked down at his phone. "But after having seen this and considering those prices we found—whatever's going on, it's sophisticated. This could be very dangerous, Nell. I really think you should tell the police sooner rather than later."

"I will, I will," Nell replied.

"When?" he urged, a familiar tone slipping into his voice. With a Young, unless you agreed on a firm date to stop working on something, "soon" meant "when I'm satisfied." It had taken him years, and no shortage of last-minute arguments the night before a paper at UCLA or the NYPL was due, to learn this lesson—but the stakes were much higher this time. And so was the danger.

She smiled, and he wondered which old project of theirs she was remembering. "Actually, the day the library was burgled, Irene Pérez Montilla told me she thought Dr. Young was secretly working on a big project just before he passed away. Something that would help the library secure extra funding, due to its rarity or prestige. I offered to look through his personal things for her while the library did the same with his office, to buy myself some time to figure out if it really was this map. I'm supposed to meet her on Sunday, to tell her what I managed to find."

Felix scooted closer. "Nell, if you just show her the prices we found, and tell her about the strange disappearances of all the other copies from the interinstitutional database, that would at least be enough to convince her the map is important, and worth protecting. She might even—"

"She did," Nell said. "Practically offered it to me at the funeral, if I can deliver."

"Your old job?"

Nell nodded.

"Nell, that's *great* . . ." Felix started to say, but the words petered out when he saw her expression. Despite the good news, she looked as lost as she had the day of the Junk Box Incident. Confused, desperate. Vulnerable. A stab of sympathy in his chest caught him by surprise.

"I know it is. And I want it. More than anything. But I also wish I could figure more out before I have to turn it all over to her and the police, and let them take over," she replied. "He was my father, you know? I just want to know *why*."

"I understand," he said softly.

She sighed. "It feels over, before it even began."

He nodded. But that was a good thing, wasn't it? One last favor for old, kind Swann, she'd said. Then they could go back to living their own lives. To never seeing each other again.

It was better that way. Wasn't it?

To his astonishment, his hand was suddenly up, signaling the bartender to send them another round.

What was he *doing*? he cried inwardly.

Nell opened her mouth to say something, equally stunned, but the bartender was already pouring.

He waited tensely for her reaction as two fresh glasses thudded down in front of them. She'd been too late to cancel his order, but she could still get up and walk out anyway. No one could make Nell do something she didn't want to do.

It was going to be bad, no matter what. He just didn't know if it was going to be awkward excuses and false apologies about it getting late sort of bad, or laugh in his face sort of bad.

At last, she picked up her drink.

"Uh, thanks," she managed.

They clinked rims, and Felix took his time with the beer, not sure what he should say. Nell was clearly feeling the same way. She wet her lips, only pretending to drink, so she could seem occupied.

The charade gave them a few seconds of acceptable silence, but eventually he was going to have to set his glass back down on the counter and come up with more conversation.

"Well, I still have two days until I have to meet Irene," she finally said. "I can at least keep working on it until then."

Felix was about to argue about the potential danger again—but then she took a sip. A real one.

"Well, how did it go with Ramona?" he asked, encouraged.

Nell turned to him slowly on her stool, and he was surprised at the expression on her face. She was so lost in the question that all of her guardedness had temporarily fallen away.

"It was the strangest thing," she said. "She recognized me immediately when I came in. She said—she said that she'd known my father since his college days. And my mother, too."

"What?" Felix cried. "Ramona Wu and your father, *and mother,* were old friends?"

"And a couple others, all from their university days. There were seven of them in total," Nell answered. "I couldn't believe it either."

"Did she tell you anything useful about the map?"

"No," she said. "I didn't let on that I actually have it, given what we found online, but she didn't want to tell me anything anyway. She was terrified, Felix. She kept trying to get me out of her shop, and then told me not to come back."

"Well, I guess she wasn't trying to sell it for your father, then," Felix said.

Nell shook her head. "The opposite. He wanted her help to *find* a map, using her shadowy network. I think she ended up sourcing it from one of their other friends from back then."

"Why do you say that?"

She dug through her tote bag and held up a large manila envelope.

"He was at the funeral," Nell said, pointing at a name, *Francis,* at the end of a note scribbled across the front of it.

"Today?" Felix asked, surprised.

Nell nodded. "I tried to talk to him, but he was just as afraid as Ramona. When I pressed him, he practically ran away. I chased him down the hall toward Swann's study." She paused, as if what she was going to say next was impossible. "Only when I got there, he was gone. Just, poof. Gone."

Felix frowned, confused. He'd been to Swann's only once or twice with Nell to have dinner, back when they were still interns at the library, but he didn't remember there being a way out to the street from the study.

"Yeah, exactly," she said, reading his expression. "I must have missed something. Maybe Swann did some renovations since I've been gone, and there was another door somewhere I didn't notice. There were so many people there, all trying to talk to me." She sighed. "But Francis definitely knows something. I just don't know what."

"We'll figure it out," Felix said.

We, he realized too late. He'd said *we*.

"Yeah." Nell toyed with her glass, too deep in thought to notice.

He relaxed. He let his gaze follow hers, where it had wandered out the front window to watch passersby. Beyond the sidewalk, the intersection ahead was full of idling cars, all waiting for the light to turn green for them. At first, it seemed like too many lanes of vehicles, but then Felix realized that the far right one was not in fact a lane, but a line of cars parallel parked along the curb, nearly fading into the evening background.

Then Felix saw Nell's eyes catch on one car in particular against the curb. It was at the front of the line of parked cars, the first one before the intersection. It was black, and Felix wouldn't have noticed it if Nell hadn't been so fixated. Its headlights were off , but the car was on. The exhaust from its tailpipe was barely visible in the coolish night air.

The longer he watched her, the more the hairs on the back of his neck stood up. *Why was she staring so intently?*

"Nell? Is everything okay?" he asked.

"Everything's fine," she said abruptly. Ahead, the traffic light turned green. A fraction of a second later, the first cars began to roll into the intersection. Red flashes flickered off as row after row of brake lights went out, and gas pedals were gently pressed. The drone of asphalt beneath tires began to pick up. "It's nothing."

Felix eyed her suspiciously. "You look spooked."

"I just . . ." She paused. "This is going to sound silly, but it's almost like that car is . . . following me."

Felix glanced at the slowly accelerating vehicles, his eyes jumping between them. The car that had been parked was moving now, halfway into the intersection, having pulled quickly into the right lane as soon as the light had turned green. "Which one? The black one?"

"I've seen it a couple times this week. Outside the library, near Ramona's, and now here, at the bar."

"You're sure it's the same one?"

He could see the tension in her shoulders as they inched up closer to her ears, as if she was about to let go of something she had wanted to tell him but had been holding back. She hesitated.

"Nell . . ."

Somewhere in the traffic, someone honked, startling them both.

"No," she said. The black car turned and disappeared down the street. "It's the break-in. I'm just jumpy."

"No, you're not! If you really think you're being followed, after everything we just talked about—"

"Let it go, Felix," she insisted. "Seriously."

"But . . ."

"You know I'm going to keep working on this no matter what," she said. "Either help me or don't, but don't argue with me."

He recognized the expression on her face. He could tell Nell was so upset, if she said one more word, she'd burst into tears, which she hated doing. Instead, she grabbed her glass and fiercely downed the rest of her beer. Felix sighed, relenting, and slid her what was left of his, and she downed that too, sputtering.

"It's just been a weird couple of days," she said once she'd recovered. "I was so angry at him, I never wanted to see him again, but even so, you don't really think about . . ." She reached for the glass again, and then gave up, remembering it was empty. "And now here I am, trying to follow his trail, hoping I can finally understand him, except the more I uncover, the more confusing it gets." She groaned, frustrated, and balled up her napkin. "What was he going to *do* with this stupid map, if not sell it? Why did he keep it all this time, then?"

Felix nodded desperately. He wanted to say something, anything, to help comfort her. His hand had drifted up from the bar on its own as she spoke, reaching for her. They both realized it was resting on her back at the same moment they realized she'd also leaned into his chest, curling into the hug.

"Can I see the other map? The one from Francis?" he asked quickly, his cheeks burning, as they leapt apart.

Nell cleared her throat and busied herself with opening the envelope, trying to look focused. She handed the map over without looking at him.

"Hey, this is the library," he said when he recognized the building on the page.

"Yeah," she replied. "It's an old insurance diagram from the early 1900s. They used them to assess a building's risk and determine what to charge them for flood and fire coverage—what each wall was made of, how close they were to other buildings. So many places were built from wood back then, it was a risk." She sighed. "So now I have *two* long-out-of-date, useless maps, and no answers."

Felix was still staring at it, thinking. "Sanborn," he muttered as he reread the title in the legend. "Wait a minute."

"What?"

But he was already holding up his phone again. "You know the rare book and maps fair they hold here in New York every year?"

"Rare book and maps fair? You mean the annual New York International Antiquarian Book Fair, at the Park Avenue Armory?"

He chuckled at her enthusiasm. "Yeah, that one."

"It was my whole life," Nell said, smiling a little, too. "I mean, my whole *old* life. My father and I went every year as soon as I had learned to walk."

"I know. You were the one to first take me, when we moved to New York from UCLA."

For a moment, the memory of that day hung sweetly in the air between them—he could remember how excited she was to show him everything, and how amazed he had been at the incredible artifacts they had there, that he was allowed to see and touch them all. But after a moment, the dark history of what happened after began to creep in.

Felix rushed on, before the bitterness of the Junk Box Incident could settle on them. "One of Haberson's other branches is working on a searchable digitization project of historical texts, and they were going to have a demonstration at the fair this weekend," he said. "I have a friend in that department, so I was going to go help, but they pulled out of the event for scheduling reasons, and we canceled our booth." He found the email he'd been searching for at last. "But now I remember noticing on my ticket that the central exhibit this year is a Sanborn maps collection."

"Seriously?" Nell gasped, nearly bouncing off her stool.

He turned the phone to her. "See for yourself."

Nell stared at the screen. "Historical preservationists from Pennsylvania State University will give the keynote lecture on the value of Sanborn maps from a genealogical, urban planning, and political perspective on the first day of the fair," she read. "Felix, this is it!"

He couldn't fight down the grin that had spread across his face. "It's tomorrow, which is really short notice, but—"

"No, it's perfect!" she said. "I'm sure Swann has a complimentary ticket, like every year. He can just transfer it to me for the day!"

Felix abruptly swallowed the next thing he'd been about to say.

He'd been assuming she wanted to go to the fair together, like old times. He felt the blush creep up under his collar.

"Well, maybe you can't get Francis to talk to you, but if you show the map he'd intended for Dr. Young to the preservationists, maybe they can tell you why it's significant," he finally said, as casually as possible. "Maybe even better than Francis can."

"Maybe it's where Francis got the map in the first place," Nell replied, her eyes still fixed on his screen.

"What do you mean?" he asked.

"Look," she said, pointing at the first scholar in the list of Penn State preservationists.

"Dr. Eve C. Moore?" Felix read.

Nell looked back at him. "One of the other friends in Ramona's story—along with her and Francis—was named Eve."

XI

The Park Avenue Armory towered before Nell, a great redbrick behemoth that took up the entire block between Sixty-Sixth and Sixty-Seventh Streets. It had originally been built to function as storage for the Seventh New York Militia Regiment back in 1880, also known as the Silk Stocking Regiment, because so many of its members were from aristocratic families, but as long as Nell had known it, it had been the site of the annual New York International Antiquarian Book Fair—the biggest and most exciting holiday in her and her father's little household. The first time Nell attended, she'd been no more than a kindergartner, her tiny hand completely engulfed in her father's as he led her slowly around the booths, pointing at especially rare or old specimens and explaining how the fair worked in hushed tones. All her life, they'd barely marked birthdays, her father almost always forgot Christmas, and they never participated in Thanksgiving, Halloween, or Easter at all—but every year, they would put on their finest clothes and set out for three excruciatingly long days in the dark pits of the Gothic Revival building, peering closely through magnifying glasses under protectively dimmed light at dusty manuscripts and rare texts and maps until she thought she might go blind.

How she had cherished those trips.

Nell pushed away the memory fiercely and tugged on the hem of her ill-fitting blazer. She'd worn it in the hope of looking more professional, but now she worried that she looked even more out of place.

Or perhaps that was only her looking for an excuse to back out.

No, she told herself. Her heart beat quicker. Her father's event at the NYPL, when she needed to tell Irene what she'd found, was tomorrow night. She didn't have time to lose her nerve now.

It was almost as strange and painful to be standing outside the armory, about to enter the annual rare books and manuscripts fair after all this time, as it was to stand outside the NYPL a few days ago, about to enter the Map Division again. When she'd been fired from the library and summarily banished from the cartography field, that excommunication had also included industry events like this. She'd known the day she stumbled out of the NYPL's huge wooden doors for the last time what would happen if she ever did try to mingle again—at the first mention of her name, researchers would be late for meetings, dealers would suddenly have customers to see, specimens would all become on reserve and no longer available for sale or perusal. She'd seen it happen before to other fallen scholars. Nell had even, regrettably, avoided those people herself, the way her father and Swann had gently instructed her to do, for her own professional protection. She'd never imagined then that one day she'd be on the receiving end.

But maybe that all could change, she thought desperately.

With one last nervous tug of her blazer, Nell scampered up the steps and into the armory. Hopefully, she'd changed enough in seven years and the exhibits would be so engrossing that no one would look too closely and recognize her if she kept her head down.

A burst of cool, stale air hit her as soon as she was inside, and Nell sank wistfully into it. It was the smell of ancient pages, of time, of her very soul, if souls could have smells, she thought. She blinked, waiting for her eyes to adjust to the soft light, and then retreated to a dark corner of the lobby so as not to attract too much attention. Cautiously, she let her gaze drift, absorbing the ornamental woodwork, the marble, the stained glass that filled the interior.

Ahead, she could see the entrance to the armory's drill hall, where the exhibition itself was held. It was over fifty-five thousand square feet—the largest unobstructed space of its kind in New York, her father had once told her.

That was a lot of area to cover to find the Sanborn exhibit, if she didn't get moving. If she missed the preservationists' keynote speech and they left the stage, within minutes they could be anywhere inside the fair, pulled this way and that by other researchers seeking an interview or collaboration, and she'd never find this Eve.

And there was also the potential danger of being spotted by someone who knew who she was. Wolff and Pete had already seemed suspicious of her at the funeral, and Francis had been reluctant to speak to her at all—what if the Cartographers knew the Sanborn map she now had was also somehow connected to the General Drafting map, and saw her here?

Nell pushed away the sudden image in her mind of the lurking black car and ducked into the drill hall.

Eyes down, she reminded herself. It had been so long since she'd been among such treasures as these. If she allowed even the most errant glance at the wrong booth, she'd catch sight of something exquisite and be unable to keep going until she'd gone over and examined it. And from there she'd spot something else, and then something else, and it wouldn't be long until someone recognized her and the whole plan would be blown. *Don't think about all the maps you're passing,* she repeated. All the beautiful, rare, historic, priceless maps, all around her. She knew the *Dili Tu,* the rarest map from Song dynasty China, would be on display somewhere. And the precious first state of the *Ratzen Plan,* a colonial-era map of the city. And a stunning Johannes de Laet *Americas* fourteen-map atlas . . .

Don't think about them. Her head spun. *Just think about the one your father had.*

The one that would get her back into this world if she played her cards right.

Nell turned left, away from the booths and toward the main area of the hall, where she knew a podium would be set up for the scheduled presentations. A smattering of applause made her speed up until she was walking as quickly as she could without drawing attention to herself.

Her phone buzzed, and she saw Lieutenant Cabe's name on the screen—probably calling to update her on her father's case or ask more questions. She sent the call to voicemail and shoved the phone back into her purse. She'd call him back later—judging by the clapping, the keynote must just have finished. She had to hurry.

Nell reached the edge of the audience just as a tall, older woman with dark skin and black braids streaked with gray stepped away from the microphone, and with the three other similarly aged men and women behind her, gave a small wave before turning toward the exhibits.

Dr. Eve Moore. Nell had stared at Eve's picture on Penn State's faculty website for several minutes before leaving her apartment, committing her face to memory so she could find her once inside.

The crowd began to disperse, and Nell made her way carefully through, avoiding eye contact.

It was now or never. Eve was about to disappear into another booth, where she'd be locked in conversation with the dealer for who knew how long, and Nell would attract too much attention lurking at the edges, waiting for her to exit.

"Excuse me, Dr. Moore?" Nell asked.

Eve turned around, scanning the crowd to see who was calling to her.

"I'm sorry, I have an interview in a few minutes, but I'll be able to give you a quote later if you'll still be around," she said, assuming Nell was a graduate student.

Nell put out her hand. "Actually, I'm not here for a class. I have a question about a Sanborn map in my own personal collection." That was such a strange thing to say, but she supposed it was true now. She had two maps of the same geographical region from the same historical period. Technically, that was the start of a collection—however ridiculous the specimens were. "The person who gave it to me said it was special, but I don't understand what that meant."

"Special? Interesting." Eve's face brightened with curiosity. She returned the handshake. Around them, the crowd streamed toward some other booth that must have just opened, and Nell had to nudge closer to her in order not to be gently bumped by passing shoulders. "Was it a private sale or an auction? Who was the original owner?" Eve asked.

"You, actually, I think," Nell answered.

Eve stared at her, confused. "I help curate the Penn State collection, but that's owned by the university. I don't . . ."

"I know it's been a long time," Nell said. "My name is Nell Young."

Eve's entire demeanor changed. The easy, professional smile had dropped off her face, and her eyes were wide and searching, as if stunned.

"I'm sorry to surprise you like this," Nell added, more softly.

"No, no," Eve replied. She reached out and clasped Nell's hand. "It's just so good to see you. Goodness, how you've grown." Her brow furrowed as she gained control of herself again. "I'm so sorry about your father."

"Thank you," Nell said. She went out on a limb. "I'm grateful that you tried to help him. With the Sanborn map, I mean."

It worked. She studied Nell suspiciously. "You found it in his things?"

Nell shook her head. "I went to see Ramona. She gave it to me."

"You did? I'm surprised you found her shop."

Nell paused, perplexed. Eve was the second person who had said something strange about Ramona's shop. "My father had her business card. It wasn't too difficult."

Eve hesitated, as if deciding about something. "Yes," she finally said. "Well. She's always been cautious."

The conference was still streaming around them, hundreds of people alone in their section, and hundreds more beyond that. Eve looked as eager to escape the crowd as Nell felt. Did she also know about the Cartographers and their connection to the other map—the General Drafting one?

"Let's go to my booth," Eve said, gesturing down another aisle. "We can talk in private there."

They slipped away toward the booth in the center of the fair. Nell was nervous that it would be even more crowded than the hall, but although there were plenty of visitors, the Sanborn exhibit was so large that it was easy for them to find a secluded corner. Eve settled them at a small examination table in the back. All around them, detailed floor plans from the collection hung in frames against a black background—a million rooms within the room they were in.

As Nell pulled the envelope the Sanborn map was in out of her father's portfolio, the photograph Francis had included with it fluttered free and landed on the far side of the table. Eve stared at it for a long moment before handing it back to Nell, smiling.

"I remember this," she said. "That was the day after we all graduated from our Ph.D. program."

"You took this photo?" Nell asked.

"No," Eve replied. "Wally did. He was always carrying that fancy camera around. Spent more time looking at everything through that lens than through his eyes—we used to tease him endlessly about it. But it was just how he was. He liked precision, detail. Photographs were just another kind of measurement, he said. Proof that things were real."

"Like your friendship?"

Eve didn't look at her. "Among other things."

Nell was about to press her for more, but Eve had turned to the Sanborn map. Even though it had come with the photograph, which proved that the map could have come only from Francis, she still expected the woman to study it carefully first—double-check the paper and the ink, compare its individual aging signs to the notes Penn State must have for each specimen—but Eve barely had to glance at it before she was sure.

"Yes," she pronounced. "This is the one I loaned to Francis, to give to your father."

Nell watched her as she picked the map up, to put it back in its folder and envelope. As she did so, her eyes passed over the little compass rose sketch on the back of the cardboard—and lingered.

"I didn't see that before," she finally said.

"Do you know what it means?" Nell asked, hopeful.

Slowly, Eve nodded. "It's a symbol for a group called the Cartographers."

The Cartographers.

Ramona's and Francis's warnings rang in Nell's ears as her mind raced.

The mark was on both maps—the back corner of the gas station map and the folder of the Sanborn. Was it because the Cartographers had owned the gas station map before her father had found it, and this Sanborn map before Eve had loaned it out? Were they much closer on her heels than she'd thought?

"Is it . . . a threat?" she asked.

To her surprise, Eve smiled. "A threat? Not at all. It's more like a greeting."

"A greeting?" Nell paused. "From whom?"

"Francis."

Nell took a step back, alarmed. "Francis is a Cartographer?"

Eve nodded. "So am I," she said. "The Cartographers were us. All seven of us."

Nell stared, stunned.

"It was what we called ourselves, back then," Eve continued. "Like a little club. Your mother made it up."

"My mother?"

"Yes—and Wally. They invented it sometime in their freshman year, long before I met them all, along with this little symbol. They put it on everything we worked on. Hid it on the backs of our essay pages or in the corners of our drafts. It was cheesy, but we all loved it. We were so young."

Everything Nell had found out about the Cartographers seemed exactly the opposite of what Eve was saying. How could it be the same group to which her parents had belonged?

"But the Cartographers . . ." She hesitated.

"Broke into the NYPL?" Eve finished for her.

Nell looked up to see the older woman staring evenly at her.

"And attacked your father?"

"How do you know that?" she asked.

"Because it's true," Eve said. "Or rather, partially true."

She looked at the Sanborn map again, and Nell waited for her to continue.

"After the fire that summer, there was no group anymore," Eve finally said. "We didn't see each other, didn't talk. That was how your father wanted it—that was how we all wanted it, really. We thought we had to put it behind us to survive the grief of losing your mother. But Wally couldn't."

"Wally couldn't?" Nell repeated.

"He was the one who found the map. He and Tam."

"You mean the Sanborn? Or the gas station map?" she asked.

Even before Eve's tense gaze met her own, Nell could see the panic flare in her body. "What do you know about that?" she asked.

"Not much," Nell lied. "Ramona told me it was destroyed a long time ago."

Eve grimaced. "It was dangerous, that thing. Cursed. Everyone who touched it got hurt." Her eyes drifted back to the compass rose symbol. "And it's still not over."

Eve

The morning after the party, Wally was the only one not hungover, of course, so it was decided that he would drive the first car, with Tam, Daniel, and me. Francis, when he woke up, would drive the second, with Bear and Romi.

This was May of 1990. You were just two or three years old then, Nell, born in the middle of our Ph.D.s. Wally, Bear, Francis, Romi, and I had been there at City Hall, overdressed and excited, clutching bouquets and cheering as your parents kissed for the first time as husband and wife, and then just a few years later, we all were gathered the same way in the waiting room at the hospital, nervously pacing in front of the vending machines while your mother labored in the delivery wing with your father by her side.

At the time, even being as tight knit as we were, and for so many years already, I remember worrying a baby would change the closeness of our group. The magic of it. We had been a little society of seven for so long. But somehow, you made it even stronger. You changed us all from friends to family.

We got on the road early, Wally going exactly the speed limit, with me in the passenger seat to help navigate and Tam and Daniel in the back with you, in your car seat. That party, the night before, where we had practically closed down the bar, was because we had all just graduated from our Ph.D. program at the University of Wisconsin. The celebration had run late into the night, and I had been so drunk I was still dizzy if I stood up too fast. I wasn't a big drinker then—later that summer, I would learn to hold my liquor, we all would, but at the time I could only stomach a glass or two of champagne—but Daniel kept ordering bottle after bottle from the bar and passing it around to the rest of us. We were all so giddy, none of us could say no to him, even after the fifth bottle.

That was how he was then. So generous, and so full of joy, all the time. Daniel could get anyone to smile, no matter what else was happening. Even when he was angry, he was still happy. When I think of your father now, that's the way I like to remember him.

"Can you believe it's really over?" Wally asked as we drove, flicking the turn signal to change lanes on the sleepy early morning highway. He seemed even more quiet and pensive than usual.

"Don't you mean, can't you believe it's all finally *starting*?" Tam replied, her energy not dimmed in the slightest by lack of sleep. She was the only one who could ever bring Wally back from one of his moods. Out the window, late spring was in full bloom, weeds and bushes and trees bursting with color, practically swallowing the highway. Calling to us, urging us on.

"I can't believe we made it, either," I admitted. "That we actually graduated."

"That's because the whole night is still fuzzy for you," Tam teased. "You look a little green."

We'd all spent what felt like a lifetime at the University of Wisconsin. For the earliest friends of our group, who met freshman year, it was even longer—more than a decade. We'd gone from children to adults, from students to scholars. Tam and Daniel had gotten married, and had you there, and it seemed Romi and Francis weren't far behind them. It was hard to fully accept that we were driving away possibly forever, that we wouldn't be back in our graduate student apartments later that evening, cooking together as someone had a far too loud party next door, like always. That before the day was done, we'd no longer be in Wisconsin, able to pop into Professor Johansson's office at a moment's notice to ask a question, but rather almost a thousand miles away, somewhere in upstate New York. Even as I'd submitted my dissertation, completed my defense, and picked up my cap and gown from the university bookstore—none of it felt real until I was sitting in that rickety folding chair and finally heard my name called. Only when I crossed the stage to shake hands with the dean and take my fountain pen did everything finally crystallize.

They had made one for each of us, to commemorate our time at the university. I was supposed to be looking at Wally, who was holding his camera in the front row to get a shot of each of us as it was our turn, but I couldn't stop staring at my pen. It was glazed deep red, one side bearing the University of Wisconsin's insignia in white and the other carved with my name and degree in gold cursive:

Eve Catherine Moore
Doctorate of Philosophy in Cartography and Geography

"When is breakfast?" Daniel asked suddenly, waking up for just a moment and then falling right back into sleep before any of us could answer. Tam and I laughed, and he smiled faintly at the sound, already snoring again.

He'd been a lot more grounded about the whole event, as always. When his name was called, he gamely shook the dean's hand, took his pen, and looked right at Wally with a big, obedient grin as Wally clicked the shutter and Tam gave him a pleased thumbs-up for actually doing what he was supposed to do, instead of staring awestruck at the gift.

To me, and the rest of us, those pens felt like the entire world. But to Daniel, it was no different than something to scribble with. By the next day his was already lost and forgotten. He probably would have accidentally thrown away his and Tam's marriage license five minutes after the ceremony if Wally hadn't snatched it away and placed it safely in its cardboard folder for them as they kissed outside the courthouse.

"You won't miss it, even a little?" Wally asked Tam, after Daniel's snoring had quieted. "After twelve years there?"

"Of course I'll miss it," Tam said. "But Bear was right. Our best hope of finishing our *Dreamer's Atlas* is to get away from the university, where there will be no distractions. No temptations to pop into the graduate lounge to catch up with friends, no guilt that we're not adjuncting some of the Geography 101 classes for a little bit of extra money, no spending way too much time that we could be working at the quad . . ."

"We can completely immerse ourselves," I added. "The *Dreamer's Atlas* is too important for anything less."

This made Wally smile. It had taken the longest to get him on board, but once Tam had convinced him, Wally had become the *most* excited about our project of us all. He'd drafted the entire proposal within a month, given out copies for each of us to review, and hadn't rested until he'd coached Daniel through his speech to Professor Johansson to win his support. When we received word that the university was going to approve us, he was so happy, I was sure I'd seen a few tears glimmering in his eyes as we'd all cheered and danced.

"You're right," Wally agreed then, looking determined anew. I tried not to smile as the car accidentally sped up just 1 mph. He'd never let himself speed outright—you were in the car, and he was even more protective of you than of Tam, if you can believe it, the most cautious, devoted uncle I have ever seen—but the look on his face was of pure exhilaration.

We could not let anything get in our way. Not teaching, not parties, not jobs. We would stop at nothing to make our *Dreamer's Atlas* succeed.

"I'm always right," Tam said, laughing. I glanced to the back seat to jokingly agree with her and saw that she had her graduation fountain pen out—and was carving up its glossy crimson shaft with the point of a pocketknife.

"What are you doing?" I gasped.

Tam held it out to me and smiled, before you saw that she had finished and laughed excitedly, reaching for it. On the side of its smooth, lacquered body, over her name, she'd etched our little compass rose with a *C* in its center.

"Nelly wants to be a Cartographer, too," she teased as she gave it to you.

"She'll be the best one of us," Wally replied, grinning through the rearview mirror.

The drive took sixteen hours total, including a lunch break and four stops for gas, and by the time Daniel, at the end of our car's third driving shift, pulled the car up the long driveway, the tires crunching over gravel, to the house we would be living in for the summer, it was already growing dark.

We clambered out of the car, our legs wobbly and necks stiff, relieved to be on solid ground. Tam chased after you as you wandered, but the rest of us stood in front of the car, staring up at the house.

"I didn't realize it was going to be this big," Wally said, a little intimidated.

Bear had told us it belonged to his parents, or his grandparents, or something. Some old family relic. While Wally was the one who had prepared our proposal for the project, Daniel the one to persuade Professor Johansson to help us push it through the department for approval, and Francis the one who had applied for loans and access to all the maps we'd need, the whole idea to get away from Madison in the first place to work on the project had been Bear's. It had come up sometime during the last semester, once we found out we'd been approved. Originally, Tam and Daniel had planned to stay on campus and teach over the summer to make a little extra money, and Francis and Romi were going to travel. I was considering a short internship abroad, in London. Then in the fall, we'd all meet back up and begin our project.

But the closer we got to graduation, the more nervous Bear had grown. He hated it when any of us left, for any length of time. As if even a temporary separation would threaten the group—or cause us to forget him, perhaps. I don't know why he always worried so much. Francis once told me it was because Bear thought he wasn't as good as the rest of us—he worked a little slower, had fewer articles accepted for publication, and was always broke. He was at the University of Wisconsin on a combination of small scholarships and mostly loans, I'd heard once. None of us ever made him feel bad about any of those things—we loved him the same as we loved every one of us. We were happy to chip in a little more so he could join us at restaurants or traveling exhibits. But still, he always worried. So, when faced with the possibility of nearly all of us leaving for an entire summer, he became almost hysterical. He cooked up a plan to start on our project in earnest, right after graduation, rather than waiting until fall. He brought up the idea of running off to this remote house to work until we'd emerged victorious, like the scholar cartographers of old used to do. Taken with how romantic the idea seemed, and how excited we were for the *Dreamer's Atlas*, it didn't take much convincing. It would be like an academic retreat, free of distractions and excuses.

He'd told us it was a normal-sized place for the area, but if that was true, every house in the area was an absolute mansion. We continued to stare, bemused. Two stories, six bedrooms, an attic, a basement, and acres of land. It creaked in the wind, and curtains fluttered from an open window overhead, beckoning.

Finally, Wally raised his camera and took a picture of it, then jokingly whispered, "Ghosts show up on film."

It was true, though. The day before, I'd been packing the last of my things before I had to be back on campus for the graduation ceremony. I came across the photos we'd taken a year ago, at Bear's birthday party. We'd gone to an old-time speakeasy, with fake lanterns for lights and an ancient, clacking cash register where the bartender rang everyone up and then served them their drinks in teacups, the way they'd used to. That night, we'd all gotten even more drunk than we'd just done at the graduation party. So drunk, hardly anyone could remember most of the festivities. All we had were Wally's photos, in which we were all grinning maniacally, eyes wide and dreamy. Except for mine. I'm smiling like the rest of them, but my eyes don't look happy. They look nervous. Guilty.

But I hadn't kissed Francis that night, in the end. I stopped myself just in time. Blamed it on the wine. And Francis had drunk so much, he was still tipsy even the next morning. He spent the whole day in the bathroom, and when he emerged at last at dusk to eat the plain soup Romi had made him, he looked like he didn't remember anything at all from the entire week.

I ended up tearing the photos up instead of packing them. I had almost wrecked everything—this was my second chance. I felt so relieved, so light and free, that I finally drank again at the graduation party. It was the first time I'd truly enjoyed myself in a long time.

"Ah, come on," Tam said, appearing behind us then, carrying you. "It's the perfect kind of place to work on a project about the history of maps. And the windows are big and bright, and there's that back deck that looks out over a little wooded area . . ." She smiled as she pointed. "Just imagine all of us out there sitting around a small fire in the pit, reminiscing about Wisconsin or talking about our *Dreamer's Atlas*, and letting Nell look at the stars."

We stared at it again, trying to see it anew.

"Big," you finally said, and we all laughed.

"It is big," Tam replied to you, winking in agreement.

Somewhere, a bird started its evening call, and everyone looked west, hoping to see it. The breeze fluttered through Tam's hair as she turned, brown curls catching the light, turning gold.

"Hold still," Wally grinned, raising his camera again to frame her in the shot.

She smiled at him, but before Wally could press the shutter, Daniel came crashing through, and scooped the both of you up in his arms as you squealed with joy. "Cheese!" he cried.

Wally took the picture.

"Perfect," he said.

There were so many secrets waiting for us, traps lying in wait, even then. But I don't think anyone but me saw that first one.

I had always wondered, from the very first day I'd met him and Tam, if Wally wasn't secretly in love with her. The way he clung to her, how they'd been inseparable since grade school, and the quiet, suppressed panic I saw in his eyes every time Tam was charming someone else in the geography department or at some academic conference, as if he was terrified that every new friend we accepted into our circle would take part of her away from him.

I imagined I understood better than anyone, after all. Wanting something to be true that never could be, and *not* wanting it to be true even more, because of what it would cost.

They were friends, best friends, and would be for life. That was what Wally believed. And he loved Daniel like a brother too, and you even more, Nell. Wally had spent so long repressing his real feelings for Tam, I think he didn't even know they were there. They were like a phantom limb to him—a thing he'd convinced himself wasn't real, even though he could still sense its ghost.

"Hey, why don't we make a fire tonight?" I asked, picking up Tam's previous suggestion. I was thinking of the other car, of having something nice ready to surprise Francis, Romi, and Bear with when they arrived. Bear could be a lot to handle when he was excited—especially for someone as reserved and serious as Francis. "We passed a grocery store on the way in—we could grill up dinner and then sit around the pit enjoying the fire while we eat."

Talk turned to getting the trunk unpacked as quickly as possible so we could all dash back to the last town before the drive had given way to woods and the house, a little place about five miles away called Rockland, for supplies. Tam and I cleared out the cobwebs while Daniel and Wally brought in our books from the trunk and our suitcases strapped to the roof, and then we all piled back into the car.

In the Rockland Grocer and Butcher, Tam pushed you in the cart while Wally picked out all the ingredients we'd need for the side dishes, and I was in charge of Daniel, who would stand in front of the meat section for hours if unsupervised, examining cuts like he knew anything about cooking in the slightest. I gave him a little bit of time, but he still wasn't done when Wally and Tam finished their part. They came over and leaned impatiently on the cart as we all waited, trying to keep you entertained.

Eventually, you started to become fussy. "Okay, give him ten more minutes. If he's not finished by then, just leave him here in the store and we'll drive home without him," Tam said, taking you from the cart. Wally, as he often did, pulled out a handful of bills from his wallet to cover the groceries, since it was such a small expense for him.

"Where are you all going?" I asked as he handed me the money.

"Wally and I saw a little antiques shop next door on the way in," Tam answered. "Almost every one of them has a musty old books and atlases section."

"It's going to be junk," I said.

"Probably," she replied. She gestured to Daniel, who was still staring at the meat and paying us no mind. "But it's going to be better than this."

"We have to get enough for the others, too," he mused to himself, without looking away from the selection. "That's seven plus a little extra for Nell."

"I can't believe how late they are," I said. "You know how much Francis hates being late anywhere."

"If Daniel finishes choosing dinner this century, we can beat them back. Take all the big bedrooms first and leave them the smaller ones!" Tam grinned as she and Wally turned away to head for the antiques shop.

"Did you look upstairs? Even the smallest bedroom is bigger than the biggest one in the graduate housing complex," Wally said, pushing the door open for her.

They went off together with you, leaving me to hold the cart while Daniel finally began piling pounds and pounds of steak and ribs into it. I managed to get him away from the meat, through the checkout line, and out to the car, where we loaded the groceries into the trunk. We sat waiting with the engine on for a few minutes, but Tam, Wally, and you were still in the shop.

"Now we're waiting on them," Daniel sighed, already restless.

"It's your own fault," I said. "They probably figure I'm still trying to drag you away from the steaks, and you haven't even picked one yet."

We laughed, and then Daniel turned to me suddenly, a mischievous grin on his face. He lowered his window and put his hand on the steering wheel, over the horn.

"Tam!" he shouted, and the horn blared noisily, startling the entire parking lot. "Come on, Tam! We've been waiting for *hours* already!"

"You're terrible!" I cried as the door to the antiques shop flew open, and they came tumbling out as the pedestrians in the parking lot chuckled at them, Wally looking embarrassed at all the attention, and Tam and you laughing at his joke.

"We were in there for not even ten minutes," Wally grumbled as he slid into the back seat, his cheeks red, and busied himself with helping Tam fasten you into your car seat. "You always take forever."

"Oh, it was funny," Tam said to him, and leaned forward to lovingly muss up Daniel's hair.

"Was it all junk?" I asked as Daniel started to reverse the car out of the parking spot.

"Yeah," Wally said. "Just old knickknacks and broken furniture."

"It wasn't a total waste of time," Tam replied, holding out something small and folded for us to see. I took it from her before she slid back into her seat and turned it over to see the front. "We did find something."

It was the gas station map.

As I stared at it, listening to Tam and Wally describe the shop—how friendly the old owner had been to them and Nell, telling them about where around town to get various supplies for the house if needed, and how the map had been only a dollar, and that even though it was junk, they felt like it would be rude not to take it after all her help—I felt the faintest sense of unease. Just a tendril of dread, down deep, starting to curl.

But I ignored it. We were all exhausted from the drive and eager to get back to the house. Too excited by what lay ahead.

I should have paid more attention.

XII

Eve finally broke off from her story, as if she couldn't bear to continue. She looked down at the Sanborn map on the table again, seeming to lose herself in it. Nell gave her a few moments, hoping Eve would say something, but the preservationist didn't offer any more.

Nell realized that if what Eve had said was true, then she'd been wrong about the gas station map. It didn't belong to the NYPL—it had only been hidden there. It hadn't come from an uncatalogued donor. It belonged to her father. Because her mother and Wally had found it, decades ago.

Whatever happened, whatever all of this was about, wasn't about the library at all. It was about them.

"That house," Nell finally said. "Is that where the fire was?"

It had to be. She knew that the accident had happened the summer she'd turned three, and she knew that it had happened in upstate New York, where her family had been renting a house. She just hadn't known that there had been other people there, her father had never said that, but he never said anything about it. The rest of the details of Eve's story all matched perfectly.

"Yes and no," Eve said.

"What does that mean?" Nell insisted, desperate. "The house we lived in burned down. I have the scars. It happened there—it had to have."

Eve sighed. "It did. It just started long before."

The chills down her back were like knives. Was this why her father had always refused to talk about her mother? Because there was more to it than just the grief? "Are you trying to tell me that her death wasn't an accident?"

Eve shook her head again, this time more forcefully. "No, it was an accident. A terrible, terrible accident. She died saving you."

She seemed to be telling the truth. Nell watched Eve for a moment, surprised at her grief. Nell's father had always kept his locked down deep, and Nell, as much as she wished her mother hadn't died, did not remember her mother the way that Eve and her father did. Nell's sadness was more of a bitterness, a longing, for something she would never have the chance to miss as much as they did.

It made her think of what Eve had said about how much Wally had loved her mother, too.

"Eve. Were my mother and Wally—"

"*No,*" Eve replied vehemently. "Your mother loved your father more than anything. She never would have betrayed him. And neither would have Wally." She sighed. "But after he lost her, it drove him to madness. He just couldn't let go."

"You're saying Wally's the one behind all of this? That he's the one acting as the Cartographers?"

Eve nodded. "It couldn't be anyone else." She looked at Nell. "He's still searching for a copy of the gas station map."

"But if there are none left . . . ," Nell began.

"It doesn't matter," she said. "Wally never will believe it. It's the only thing he has left."

"The only thing he has left?" Nell scoffed, surprised. "What about what I have left? I'm the one who lost my mother. My father lost his wife."

"I'm so sorry, I didn't mean it like that," Eve replied quickly. "I can't imagine your or Daniel's pain." Her gaze drifted down again, heavy. "But as terrible a loss as it was, at least you still had each other. Wally had nothing. Nothing but the memory of that map."

Nell waited for a moment, until she'd gathered herself. "How can I find him?" she asked.

"You can't," Eve answered. "After your mother died, he disappeared. None of us heard from him again. No one knows where he is."

"Except maybe my father," Nell said.

Eve looked spooked enough to run.

Nell backed off, searching for a new angle. Eve might not know how to find Wally, but Nell knew what he was after. And the Sanborn map was somehow connected to it—otherwise why would her father have spent his last few days desperately contacting his old friends, trying to obtain a copy?

"What's so special about this Sanborn map, then?" she asked.

"It's rare," Eve allowed. "A seventh edition."

"Why is the seventh edition so rare?" she asked.

"Your father wouldn't want—"

"I know, I know," Nell replied, frustrated. It had been the same with Ramona. She could get them talking a little about the past, but the more she tried to get them to open up in detail about the present, about anything that could somehow be related to the secret surrounding the gas station map, they'd clam up. And Francis had been even worse.

An idea occurred to her suddenly, as she fretted.

"Tell me, and I'll drop it," Nell offered. That was what all three of them wanted her to do, wasn't it? And the tactic had worked on Ramona, just enough to get her to give Nell the Sanborn.

Eve studied her, sizing up the truth of that claim. "Prove it," she said at last. "Give the Sanborn map back to me."

Nell hesitated. She didn't want to give up her only clue. But if Eve would tell her why her father had wanted it so badly, maybe she wouldn't need it anymore.

And she still had the gas station map. The one that really mattered.

At last, Nell gently eased the map a little closer to Eve, so it was in front of her instead of between them both.

"Why is the seventh edition so rare?" she repeated softly.

Eve took a breath. "Because it was discovered to be inaccurate," she finally replied. "Remember, these maps were used by insurance underwriters to determine the risk of damage or complete destruction of a given building due to accidental fire or flood, in order to charge the landlords the right premium. Precision was of the utmost importance. Once the inaccuracy was discovered here, the eighth edition was rushed out, and most of the seventh editions were probably trashed, to prevent confusion."

"Inaccuracy? Like the measurements were off?" Nell tried.

"No," Eve said. "Like a phantom settlement."

"A phantom settlement?" Nell repeated.

"You must have a specialization in ancient maps," Eve said, smiling. "Just like your mother."

"How did you guess?" Nell asked.

"Because phantom settlements are a very modern cartographic issue," she replied. "They do occasionally occur in ancient maps, but they've mostly been labeled as errors in those cases, although some of that is up for debate."

At the far end of the booth, someone had come to peruse the gallery of Sanborn maps hanging beneath the lights, startling Nell. Eve waited until they'd moved on before she continued.

"In any case, this concept wouldn't have come up in your ancient-era research because in those times, most people couldn't read, let alone copy something as sophisticated as a map."

Nell nodded. It was the curse of a doctoral degree—one's specialized knowledge was incredibly deep, but narrow. She and Felix had delighted endlessly in teaching each other things from their respective concentrations, amazed at how different every era or every country's maps could be from each other. "How modern?" she asked.

"Just within the last hundred or two hundred years," Eve replied. She looked at the Sanborn map on the table before them again. "Once the general public had largely become educated, and mapmaking was no longer an arcane art, but a rather commonplace business. Too commonplace, in fact. These days, a cartographer can work for months and months to survey an area and produce a map, only to have all that hard-earned data simply stolen by a competitor."

"There are laws protecting intellectual property against that kind of fraud," Nell said.

"Of course. But this is the border between art and science. Two painters can sit before their easels facing the same subject, and their creations will turn out completely distinct. A map is not a painting, though. A map must depict only what is *there*—the truth—precisely and without interpretation. Thus, if two maps are both perfectly accurate, how would you actually prove that someone had stolen your work to make their own?"

Nell started to speak, and then paused. "I don't know," she finally admitted. The threat had simply never been an issue for any of the cartographers in her era. "Kind of a paradox."

"Very," Eve agreed. "But someone finally figured out a loophole. No one knows who first came up with the solution to protect the original creators, but it was genius. Hide a lie inside the truth."

"A trap," Nell said.

"Exactly," Eve replied. "A phantom settlement."

"If whatever you planted ever appeared on someone else's map, you'd know they had stolen from you, instead of done the work themselves," she mused. "It *is* genius."

"The trick is hiding it well enough. An incorrect altitude on a minor mountain, a misspelling of a small body of water, a slight bend in an out-of-the-way river that's actually straight. In small-scale maps, which depict buildings and floor plans, we tend to refer to these phantom settlements, these secrets, as just that: trap rooms."

Nell couldn't help smiling despite the somber reason for their meeting. Ancient maps had always held more prestige and wonder for her, but she had to admit that there was still some magic in modern maps, too. How many times had she opened a tourist guide to some city or another while traveling, and glanced right over some cartographer's little secret just like this, without ever knowing?

Their gazes both drifted back to the Sanborn map.

She was about to ask where the secret was on it, but all of a sudden, Eve looked as though she was about to cry. "I'm sorry," she laughed, embarrassed. "I should be comforting you."

"It's really all right," Nell smiled.

"It's so good to see you again—even under such sad circumstances. I'm just a little overwhelmed. I wasn't expecting . . ." Eve wiped her eyes and searched for something to distract her from the moment, so she wouldn't begin weeping again. "I'll be right back, I need to get a transport envelope and some padding."

As she went to the other side of the exhibit where a few storage cabinets had been set up, Nell took her last chance to study the map as much as she could. Her eyes roamed over every line and label. She examined the streets, then the buildings, checking each one carefully before finally finding herself in the NYPL all over again, this time on the page instead of the world. She went hall by hall, noting each window and wall, until at last she ended up in the room she knew best.

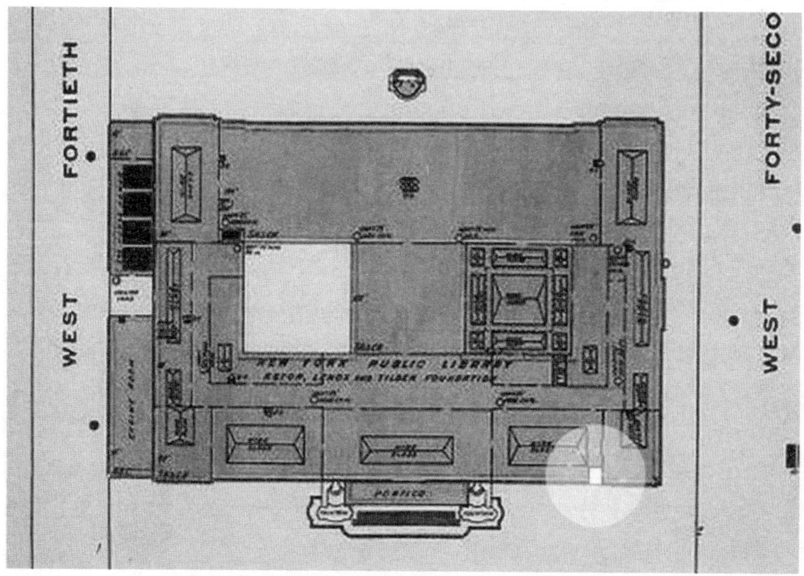

Excerpt, Sanborn Insurance Map from Manhattan

Suddenly, there it was.

The secret.

There was a false room in the Map Division.

It was tiny and unobtrusive, no bigger than a closet. She hadn't noticed before, when trying to take in the entire city block the map covered as a whole and not knowing what to look for, but it was clear now. During the production of this seventh edition, some draftsman had inserted a little nonexistent space right in her old stomping grounds.

It definitely wasn't there in real life, Nell knew. Where the false room had been hidden on the page was a smooth wall in the main reading room.

Why would her father want a map of the building where he worked, where he was murdered, with an intentional error on it in the very same office?

She didn't know yet—but then an idea came to her.

Was this the connection between the two maps?

Everything else was similar about them. They were both old, both out of print, and very rare, despite their seeming lack of value. The gas station map was just bigger, covering nearly the entire state of New York and its neighbors—so its secret would have to be bigger.

Like a whole building, or a street.

Or maybe, an entire town.

A phantom settlement, like Eve had said.

"I'm sure you're very busy," a voice startled her, and Nell looked up to see Eve reentering the booth, packing materials in hand. "But would you like to get lunch, or a coffee? It's been so long, there's so much I want to ask you. Where you went to school, where you're working now . . ."

Nell tried to turn her grimace into a polite smile as she imagined telling Eve about the Junk Box Incident and Classic.

"That would be wonderful—" she began.

But before she could finish her sentence, a face she had not expected to see appeared in the background, far over Eve's shoulder.

What was *Lieutenant Cabe* doing at the fair?

Did he know about the Sanborn map, somehow?

She didn't know—but she didn't have time to find out. He clearly was following some clue, and if he saw her here after she'd ducked his call, if he wasn't already suspicious of her, he would be.

And she did not have time to explain her way out of it.

"And I wish I could, but I have to go," she said, scrambling to pull off Swann's lanyard.

"Oh," Eve replied, surprised at the sudden turn. In the distance, Nell watched Lieutenant Cabe do a slow turn, searching the crowd. "I'm sorry, I didn't mean to—"

"No, it's not you," Nell said. She tried to see which way Lieutenant Cabe was breaking without being too obvious, so she could dash in the other direction. "Maybe some other time? I don't have a card, but I can look you up on Penn State's website."

Eve nodded, still bewildered. "Of course. Are you sure everything's okay, though?"

Lieutenant Cabe's eyes passed over Nell—and then jerked back to the massive exhibit, darting between its visitors.

She had to get out of here before he could confirm he'd seen her.

"Everything's fine. I just have to go." She was already halfway out of the booth. A cluster of scholars cut the lieutenant off for a moment, obscuring his line of sight, and she saw her chance. "Thank you so much for your help, Eve."

Nell struggled to keep the phone pressed to her ear as she dodged her way out of the Armory and onto the sidewalk of Park Avenue. A couple of taxis were waiting at the curb, and she dove for the first one even though she couldn't afford it. A cab ride would be a faster getaway from Lieutenant Cabe than walking all the way to the subway.

"Swann!" she said when he finally came on the line. "I may have figured it out!"

"Figured what out?" Swann asked, surprised.

The taxi set off toward Chinatown as Nell struggled with her seat belt. "The Cartographers," she said. "It's not an old story after all. They're *real* collectors—but you won't believe who founded the group."

Midtown rolled by out the window as she relayed everything Eve had said about her parents and their friends, copyright traps, and the Sanborn map.

"All this time, he never told me," Swann finally said. His voice was caught between disbelief and sadness. "Although I suppose if this Wally is really that dangerous, he was safer not revealing his old affiliation to anyone. Even me."

"I'm sure he was just trying to protect you," Nell replied.

Swann sighed. "Still. I could have helped him."

"You're helping now," she said.

He cleared his throat, and Nell heard his chair squeak over the line as he sat up straighter. "I'm with you all the way, my dear. So, this Sanborn map." His tone became a little brighter, more curious. "A little secret of our own, right under our noses! What are the chances? I never would have guessed the Sanborn line contained any phantom settlements at all."

"You're *sure* there's not a room there in the library, and never was," Nell confirmed.

"You'd know just as well as me, but yes," Swann replied. "There's definitely nothing there. No secret room, no door, nothing. It's just the wall where the glass bookcases are. And on the other side is the bank of smaller printers—no space in between for even a broom closet."

"That's what I thought," Nell said. "Now I just have to find the phantom settlement on the gas station map."

"But why would that be important?"

"I don't know, but maybe finding it will tell me. Maybe the name of whatever the secret error is will be a clue. Or maybe something is hidden there, where the copyright trap is supposed to be."

"Hidden?" Swann repeated. "Like buried treasure?"

Nell laughed, mostly to ameliorate the strange looks her driver was giving her through the rearview mirror. "Well, I'm on my way to find out."

"What do you mean?" he asked, just as the cab stopped. Nell looked out to see that she was at Pell and Bowery, the intersection before Ramona's shop.

"Thank you for the rush," she said as she stuffed a bunch of bills through the slot in the window and scrambled out onto the curb before the driver could give her a receipt.

"Are you in a cab?"

"I was," Nell replied. The midday glare sparkled off everything—car trims, metal shelves inside the dim sum restaurants, food carts, stop signs. She scoured the street for any suspicious cars or people, but nothing seemed out of place—just the usual bustle of Chinatown during lunchtime. "I'm going to Ramona Wu's again."

"*Ramona Wu,*" Swann said, as though she'd invoked a curse. "She wasn't very helpful the first time."

"Well, she did give me Francis's envelope for my father," Nell said, rather than telling him she'd actually fled the book fair because she'd been running from Lieutenant Cabe. "And if she knows I've now also tracked down Francis and Eve and figured out that there's a trap room on the Sanborn map . . . maybe I can make her tell me where the one on the gas station map is," Nell said as she hurried to the corner and crossed the intersection as the pedestrian sign flashed.

"Good luck," Swann said. "And take care. I can't imagine what going into her lair must be like."

"Actually, it's . . ." Nell trailed off. The sensation of twinkling sconces and books upon books upon books piled everywhere, covered in a thin golden layer of dust, just begging to be explored, came to her again. *Actually, it's beautiful—even more beautiful than the library,* she wanted to say, but there was no way Swann would believe her. "It's not as bad as you'd think," she finally finished. "Call you soon."

She hung up and turned onto Doyers Street, walking so fast she was almost jogging.

It was his insurance, Ramona had said when she'd asked what the Sanborn map was, Nell recalled as she hurried. She still couldn't figure out what that meant. How was an inaccurate map any kind of insurance? How did having it help her father?

Nell passed Nom Wah Tea Parlor and looked up, her nerves steeled. She didn't have all the answers, but at least she had the right questions now. She wouldn't let the dealer intimidate her into leaving this time. She'd stand her ground and demand that Ramona answer her, no matter what. She would—

At the entrance to Ramona's shop, Nell froze.

Because there was no shop.

What?

Had she taken a wrong turn? Nell glanced back, but she was definitely on Doyers Street, just past Nom Wah Tea Parlor and across from the post office, exactly where she'd been just two days ago, when she'd come to Ramona's shop the first time.

But there was definitely no shop here.

"What . . . ," she murmured, stunned.

It was not just that the shop had closed or moved—the door locked and the window darkened, or boarded up—the shop just *wasn't there.* Instead a smooth, old concrete wall abutted Nom Wah Tea Parlor on one side and a Western Union bank on the other.

It was as if Ramona's shop had never been there at all.

You can't find a place that doesn't exist.

That was the last thing Ramona had said to her.

"This can't be happening," Nell stammered. "It doesn't make sense."

She had just been here. *Been inside.* She had spoken to Ramona and taken the Sanborn map from her. She still had the photo of her family that had come with it in her bag—proof that it had all been real.

With shaking hands, she pulled out her phone, and typed RW Rare Maps into HabSearch. There *had* to be some explanation. A commercial listing for her company, with contact information, or something.

As the results loaded, Nell began to scroll, slowly at first, then faster and faster. Finally, when she reached the end, she let the hand holding her phone fall to her side as she stared at the old concrete wall again, lost.

HabSearch had plenty of articles about the dealer, opinion pieces about her shady reputation and reports of suspicious sales she'd made, but just one listing for her business, as Ramona worked alone, and thus had only one shop.

It had been marked as closed for *years*—with no address listed.

XIII

It had started raining in the late afternoon, and the subways were a mess of slick platforms and humid cars by the time Felix left home. As he stood under the awning on the sidewalk, his shirt still a little damp from the drizzle that had caught him as he'd run from the station, he checked his watch and grimaced.

His heart was hammering so nervously, he wondered if it was audible outside his chest.

The buzzer on the building's entry panel sounded in response to his call, snarling urgently several times before he shoved the door open to make it stop.

This was too much, he thought as he hurried up the stairs. He was overdoing it. This was something he definitely could have let Nell tell him about on the phone, or at the library, or even at another bar. He definitely had not needed to suggest going all the way back over to her apartment again to ask what she'd learned at the New York International Antiquarian Book Fair. Ahead, he could hear her scrabbling at her lock, probably already halfway through whatever she wanted to tell him, as impatient as ever.

"Come on! I have so much to ask you about modern era copyright. You won't believe what—" Nell called through her open doorway, almost before he'd even reached the landing of her floor, but she trailed off as she caught sight of him.

Her eyes drifted down, to the umbrella he had in one hand and the giant paper bag in his other, the Thai restaurant's order receipt still stapled crookedly to the top.

"Oh."

Felix sighed, embarrassed.

And he also definitely had not needed to bring dinner.

• • • •

"I still can't believe it," Felix said at last, after listening to Nell's story about Ramona's missing shop. He was looking at his phone, having found the same baffling information in his cloaked search as she had on the public HabSearch—that the dealer's shop had actually been closed for years, and there was no record of an address anywhere—especially not at the location Nell described. "And you're sure the wall wasn't new, right? Like she'd had the shopfront plastered over?"

"No, it was grimy and graffitied, like it had been there forever," she replied, flustered. "There has to be an explanation. I must have gotten something wrong, even though I don't know how that's possible."

Felix set his plate on the coffee table and leaned back into the couch cushions, trying to put all the pieces together in his mind, but Nell moved in the opposite direction, hopping up and returning to the bigger table in the kitchen, where the gas station map lay, fully unfurled. She waited, her arms crossed, clearly believing she didn't look as intense as she always did. She was practically levitating, she was so excited.

"Okay, okay," He laughed, rolling out of his seat.

The night was going a lot better than he'd even dared hope. It was almost just like the old times.

At first, it had taken a Herculean effort to get her to sit down and have some food before they examined the map for whatever she wanted to show him, but Felix had managed to convince her she had to catch him up on the book fair first, and they might as well do that over the meal. It had taken her all of three minutes to eat her pad kee mao, seemingly in one single forkful, as she talked. The only way he'd been able to drag the dinner out to ten minutes so he didn't get a stomachache was by putting bite after bite from his own plate onto hers to try, until the heat from the chilis finally registered.

"This is good," she'd said after his fourth or fifth offering, noticing at last. She reached to open the bottle of white wine he'd also brought. "Really good."

"It's from a little lunch spot by work," Felix had replied, smiling. He remembered well how much she liked Thai food, the spicier the better. They'd gone out for it or cooked it at least once a week when they'd lived together. "Office favorite."

But the food was long gone now. And Nell was so impatient she was shifting from foot to foot beside the map. "Bring our glasses," she said as Felix sidestepped the coffee table on his way to her, and he obediently grabbed them both by their stems.

"So," he said, looking down at the all-too-familiar piece of paper. "Setting aside whatever happened with Ramona's shop, you weren't able to ask her to confirm Eve's story, but you think there's a phantom settlement on this map."

"There has to be," she said. "After telling me about how they all came together after so long to get this one to my father . . ."

"Where was the one on the Sanborn copy?" he asked.

"Actually, it was in the Map Division." She smiled. "There was a little room drawn where there definitely wasn't one in real life."

Felix arched a brow. "What are the odds," he mused.

She shrugged. "It is funny. But you and I both know that main reading room. It's a perfect square."

"Yeah. But if that's the connection, why would a harmless inaccuracy make this one so valuable, and not the Sanborn?" he asked, gesturing at the gas station map.

"I don't know," Nell said, but the glint in her eye hadn't diminished in the slightest. "But maybe figuring out where the phantom settlement is on it might tell us."

They looked down again and studied the baffling artifact in silence. Slowly, Felix's eyes drifted back over to Nell, who was twirling a strand of her curls the way she always did when deep in thought. He'd been watching her do it for a long time already, he realized, lost in the familiar, comforting motion.

"What are you thinking?" he asked, before she noticed.

"Eve denied it, but I still can't shake the feeling that this all had something to do with my mother's death," she finally admitted.

Felix frowned. "It was an accident, wasn't it? The fire?"

"That's what my father always said, and the newspapers and the old police report. And Eve insisted it was, too. But then why will none of them talk about it? All seven of them were there that summer, in that same house upstate. Why are they all so afraid of this map? And why does this Wally guy want it back so badly? Enough to do these terrible things?"

"Well, there's only one way to find out," Felix said. "If there really *is* a phantom settlement on this map, maybe it'll tell us something."

Nell grinned. She scooted over a little more and carefully angled the map so that it was shared between them. Together, they leaned over it.

"We're going to have to do this the old-school way," Felix said, suddenly realizing how big the page actually was. It wasn't wall-size, but it was still much bigger and more detailed than he'd remembered. It covered all of New York State, and some of Connecticut, Massachusetts, Vermont, and Pennsylvania, a dense web of highways and county roads and mountains and rivers, dotted with a million places in between.

"They really spoil you at Haberson, don't they?" Nell teased.

He smiled sheepishly, because she was right. If only he could just scan this into his Haberson Map. All he'd have to do was run a search, and they'd be finished. It had been a long time since he'd worked like this, completely on paper.

But Nell looked unfazed. "The fastest way will be to go grid square by grid square. One of us will read out every marked town and road, and the other person will check each name against the index," she said, pointing to the staggering list of towns. "If there's really a phantom settlement, eventually we should come across something plotted here that isn't on the list, because it's not a real place."

"Eventually," Felix said, still a little overwhelmed.

"I know," she replied. She put a tentative hand on his arm—he tried to ignore the tiny thrill in his chest at the feeling of her fingers on his sleeve. "We can do this. It'll be like old times. All-nighter research binges."

"We were kids then," he laughed, but he was already lifting the top corner of the page and hunching over, so he could see the index while keeping the map mostly flat for her. "Ready?"

Nell nodded, and looked at the first grid square. "Damascus. Cochecton."

"All listed."

"Fosterdale. Bethel. Kauneonga Lake."

"All listed, too."

They worked like that for nearly half an hour, moving swiftly through the grid, falling into old shorthand and remembering how to almost anticipate each other's next thought. Felix worked well with his team at Haberson, but there was something different about the work when it was all on computers. This was more intimate, more connected.

"Livingston Manor?"

"Listed."

The wine bottle was long empty by now. He had no idea what time it was. They'd reached section M12, and were almost 80 percent done with the map. They were searching the Catskills area in upstate New York, exploring a huge green diamond of rural landscape and scattered towns. His eyes were exhausted from squinting at the tiny words, but part of him hoped they'd never actually find this phantom settlement—so that they could go on investigating, together.

"Roscoe," Nell said, pointing at a tiny dot hovering just south of the diagonal line dividing the mountains, along a red ribbon of Highway 17.

"Listed."

She glanced up at him for a second. "Rockland," she said softly. The next dot along County Road 206. That was where the fire had happened, Felix knew. The name of the town where the house had been where her mother died.

"It's listed," he said, urging her on before she could dwell.

Her finger trailed north. Just before the protected forest lands, another tiny white dot waited right at the intersection of County Road 206 and Beaverkill Valley Road.

"Agloe," she said.

Felix scanned the list obediently—

"Wait," he muttered.

He couldn't find it.

"What was that name?"

"Agloe," Nell repeated. "A-G-L-O-E."

He checked the list again.

It wasn't there.

Nell was hovering even closer to him now, breathless. "Felix," she said.

"It's not there." He looked up and tilted the paper more, so she could see the index better. "There's no town by that name."

But there it was, on the map.

A town named Agloe, where no town was supposed to be.

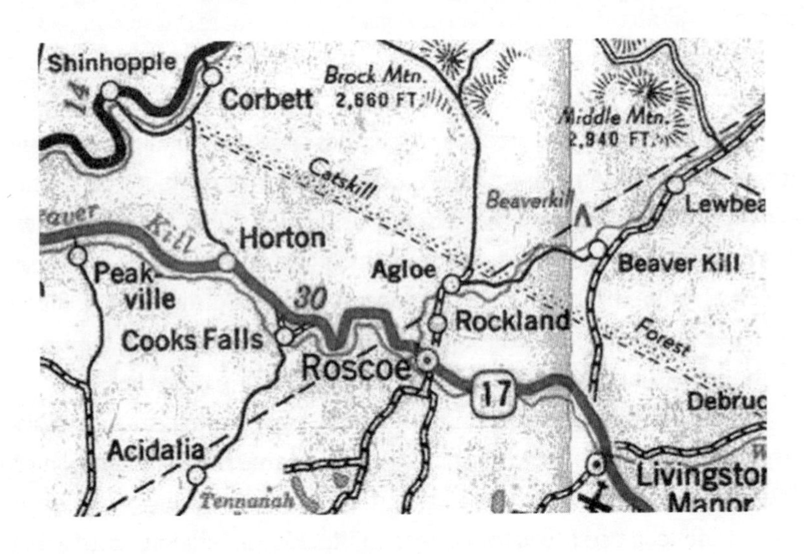

Excerpt, General Drafting Corporation highway map of New York State

They found it.

They really found it.

They stared at the nonexistent place for a few more seconds.

Gently, Nell put her finger over the little white dot, as if she could feel it.

This was the reason Dr. Young had kept this map, all these years, Felix thought. This little phantom town was the secret hidden on it.

"Felix," Nell said. Her voice was barely a whisper.

He knew what she was looking at.

It was not five miles from where Nell's mother had died.

Rockland was the last town, *real* town, that one would pass through going north before they reached Agloe.

Could that be right? How was it possible?

"What does this mean?" she asked. "That over thirty years ago, my father, and mother, and I . . . we lived *just a few minutes* from Agloe?"

The desperation in her eyes—the need to understand, for him to help her do it—reached right inside and gripped Felix by the heart. He barely resisted the urge to pull her into another hug.

"He tried to call me, Irene said," Nell finally stammered. "The night he died."

Felix blinked. "What?"

She touched the map hesitantly again. "It had to be about this."

Felix didn't know what to say, but it didn't matter. She was up, pacing now. "You don't want to take a midnight road trip, do you?" she asked. "It would only take a couple hours to get there. If we left now, we could be back in time for a late breakfast."

Felix frowned. "There wouldn't be anything there, because it's not a real place. It's just countryside."

"I know. But don't you want to go anyway? Just to be sure?"

"Nell. Wally broke into the library because of this map, and possibly killed your father, there's that car you keep seeing, and now Ramona's one *more* missing person to add to this list." He looked back at the map. "The last thing you want to do is head out to some rural field in the middle of the night without a plan. You need the police's help."

"But they'll just—"

"Okay, well then you need the library's help, at the very least," he compromised, before she could continue. "Even if this map didn't originally belong to the NYPL, they can still take it as a private donation from your father, through you."

"But what if Wally goes after Irene, then?" Nell asked. "He already got to my father."

"This time, he won't be able to get in," Felix replied, suddenly feeling hopeful. "The press release hasn't gone out yet, but after the break-in, the library board agreed to let Haberson take over database and inventory security there."

"What!" Nell gasped.

He was grinning now, thrilled to be able to give her some good news for once. "It's great, isn't it?"

"Yes—I mean, I don't know," she fumbled. "The library definitely does need better security, but . . . a tech company? It's like the exact opposite of what the library is all about."

"Come on, it's not like that," he said. "Yes, Haberson is huge, but it's a good company. More data will always benefit us, but it'll help the NYPL, too. Ainsley Simmons herself has been in constant communication with the police since the day of the break-in, and we're helping them search for the burglar using our tech—it'll only be a matter of time before it finds Wally. And until then, the library will be impenetrable. Every map and book will be backed up a dozen times, the archives better organized, and all inventory tagged with microscopic chips, trackable to the millimeter."

Nell made a face at that last part. She was even more old-fashioned than her father when it came to technology. He used to tease her constantly about it.

"Bottom line, the library will be safe," Felix repeated. "And so will this map, if you let the library have it."

Nell sighed and ran her hands through her hair.

"Plus, this is your last night with it anyway," he said. "You're still going to meet Irene tomorrow, right?"

Nell nodded—with far less enthusiasm than he'd been hoping for.

"Irene will keep her word," he continued, trying to remind her of how much she missed her old job. "You could be back in those halls in no time. The library needs a Young in it!"

It was working. Nell was smiling now, despite not wanting to. He could see how excited she was, and how conflicted. How badly she wanted both things at the same time. "You know me." She sighed, frustrated.

"Yep." He shook his head affectionately. "Can never let anything go."

Especially this.

It had hung over her life for seven long years—even more than that, if he now considered the way it had shadowed her entire childhood, unbeknownst to them. How much more would she let it take?

"I just wish . . ." She sighed again. "I'm so close, *so close*. If I could just get there, I'm sure it would finally explain things with my dad. About why he did what he did to us that day, when I accidentally found it the first time. About why he was always the way he was, even. The way our relationship was."

"I get it. I do. But maybe some things are worth more," Felix replied.

"Like what?" she asked.

"The future," he said, and then closed his mouth suddenly, shocked that it had slipped out.

She stared at him, surprised too.

"Like your job back," he raced on, before she could say anything. "I just meant, this map already ruined things during the Junk Box Incident, and it seems like all of Dr. Young's friends want to keep the past in the past, as well. If you let the library and the police take over, you might not get *all* the answers about this map, but maybe what you could get instead would be better. Not to mention safer."

Felix held his breath as he watched Nell weigh the choices, trying to see which way she would go.

For a moment, it looked like she might actually allow the library to take possession of the map. But then her expression darkened again, and she was lost in the inescapable grip of her own determination. She'd wanted these answers for so long, she couldn't quit before she had them—no matter the cost.

His heart sank.

She wasn't going to let go. She couldn't.

"Nell, I'm sorry," he began. "I know how much—"

"You're right," Nell said suddenly, her eyes defiant. "I've given up enough of my life to this map already. I'm going to give it to Irene tomorrow. I'm going to tell her and Lieutenant Cabe everything I've found out."

"Good," Felix replied, relieved. The word came out a little too earnestly, and he winced. He hadn't meant for it to sound so vulnerable.

He tried to come up with a quip to distract her before she could tease him about it, but Nell let the moment go.

"Thank you for helping me find the phantom settlement, at least," she said instead, gesturing to the map. "For all your help, really."

"Of course," he replied.

"I guess, that means . . ." She took a long breath. "I'm done."

He nodded slowly. "It's over."

They stood there for a few more seconds, suddenly purposeless. The silence was comfortable at first, but it began to grow awkward the longer it lasted.

Felix tried to think of something to bring up that would let them keep talking, but every idea seemed like a blatant stalling tactic. It would be painfully obvious what he was trying to do.

But to his surprise, Nell stalled for them both.

"You know, the reason I'm supposed to meet Irene in the first place," she began. "The board is dedicating part of a collection to Dr. Young, to commemorate the work he did for the library. The celebration is tomorrow night."

"Seriously?" Felix asked. "That's a huge honor."

She managed a smile for her father. "Swann put your name on the guest list again—if you want to come. I think he'd really like to see you, after such a long time."

"It has been a long time," he echoed.

"He'd love to hear about your new career at Haberson."

"Hey, I really do miss the library," he said.

He had become truly happy at Haberson, but he'd never forgotten the NYPL either. The excitement of walking those halls, the visiting scholars they'd gotten to meet, the *maps* they'd gotten to see. Those beautiful, priceless maps. And doing it all together.

"The old times," he finished.

"It was good while it lasted," she said.

While it lasted.

He looked down. "Yeah."

"But hey, no big deal." Nell was backtracking now. She'd misread his expression and was already trying to downplay the invitation, bringing up all the reasons he didn't need to attend, that everyone would understand, that he'd already done enough and she didn't expect him to—

"I'll be there," he replied.

Nell studied him guardedly. "You will?"

His stomach flipped.

"Sure."

Now there was a playful edge to her smile. "For Swann, right?" she joked.

Felix struggled not to blush, and failed. Was she needling him because she was trying to tell him there was no way they'd ever get back together? Or was it for precisely the *opposite* reason—because, despite their disastrous first reunion a few days ago, she also had felt a spark between them again?

Because no matter how strongly he'd tried to hide it, Felix was sure his feelings were obvious by now.

"Well, that's great," Nell continued. "Swann will be thrilled to talk to you, and I can give Irene the map and tell her what I know, and . . ."

"Nell . . ." He trailed off as she glanced up.

This was a bad idea.

Maybe it would be different this time.

No, it wouldn't, the wary half of his heart warned in response, but he couldn't help it. It had been seven years, and they both had changed, hadn't they? They both knew what they'd lost. Their work and their relationship had always been twisted up in each other, which at first had seemed romantic and passionate, but after the Junk Box Incident, Felix had realized what a liability it was.

But maybe if they tried again, they wouldn't make the same mistake.

This was a really *bad idea.*

The nervous waterfall rush in his ears drowned out the thought. Nell was looking at him not quite full on now, as if suddenly able to read his mind. Or perhaps his body was telegraphing what he was thinking, as obvious as if it were a map, and she was an expert at that. She'd had years of reading this one, after all.

He waited, but she didn't turn away. She didn't make some excuse to run to the bathroom or rush to open the door for him. Felix felt his armpits growing damp with anxiety, his heart flailing desperately in his chest until he was light-headed.

Don't do it.

Tomorrow would be proof he was right. That she could choose the future over the past, him over the map, and they could make it work this time. He'd go to her father's event and see her hand the man's last project to Irene and finally be free of it, with his own eyes.

Don't do it.

Tomorrow they could start over.

Don't—

He grabbed her into the kiss.

XIV

Nell hung up the phone and went back to staring at the clock, willing it to skip the ten minutes it had left and jump to five o'clock already.

She was still technically on bereavement leave until tomorrow, but she'd been dreading the mountain of orders at work she knew would be waiting for her and had decided to duck into Classic a day early to make a start—Sundays were always slow. And she'd also needed a reason to get out of her apartment before she wore a hole in the floor from her impatient pacing. Tonight couldn't come soon enough.

But she hadn't expected Humphrey to be there, too.

She thought he was going to send her back home, but instead, he gave a cry of relief and invited her in. The power was out, he'd explained. And the copier was broken, and the plumbing was clogged. And . . .

They'd spent the day on the phone with repair technicians, every new call uncovering another problem. The place was falling apart. Nell couldn't understand why they didn't just move to another office, but Humphrey waved her off whenever she tried to bring it up. "I have my reasons," he'd say, and that was the end of it.

Nell looked at the clock again, and sighed.

"I don't think I've ever seen you this impatient for anything," Humphrey said then as he came out of his office, startling her.

"It's a big deal," she replied. "My father's past with me notwithstanding, he deserves it."

Humphrey smiled. "Then you'd be proud, not anxious. You have a date."

"What?" Nell cried.

"Nice try," he laughed. "I have four sisters."

The memory of last night rushed over Nell again, sending her pulse racing. She'd steeled herself when Humphrey had asked her how she'd been holding up, hoping she looked as grumpy as usual, but he'd seen right through her. "Look at you!" he'd hooted. "Who is this mystery Prince Charming?"

Nell had vehemently denied it, but Humphrey couldn't be convinced. He'd spent the rest of the afternoon humming various love songs, as jubilant as if she were getting married.

"I'm trying not to let my imagination blow it out of proportion," Nell finally allowed.

"Hey." He pointed at the clock above them. "It's five o'clock."

Finally! She jumped up as Humphrey disappeared toward the printer room, chuckling to himself. She fixed her hair, cursing its unruliness, and then shoved everything from her desk back into her bag. Makeup, keys, phone—and her father's portfolio.

She glanced over her monitor to make sure Humphrey was still around the corner, and then slowly held the portfolio up in front of her.

This was it. She touched the warm, supple leather. As hard as it was for her to let go, this was the end of her investigation. All she had to do was turn over the map to Irene, let the police take over looking for Wally, and put the whole thing from her mind. After all, she'd have plenty to concentrate on in its place: negotiating the terms of her return to work at the library, giving her notice here at Classic, and reclaiming her life and her career.

And her relationship with Felix.

A grin had crept onto her lips yet again, she realized, and she desperately forced it down before Humphrey returned.

Poor Humphrey. Even though Classic was not the right place for her, she still owed him so much. He'd given her a job when no one else would and tolerated her endless complaining about their products for seven long years. Maybe she could work something out with Swann to send him scans of some of the library's maps he didn't already have in his inventory, to spare him the expensive licensing fees. That was the least she could do—she'd have to think of more.

It was still hard to believe that after tonight, she might no longer be just a design technician for knockoff art. And all she had to do was the easiest thing in the world—nothing. Just hand over the gas station highway map. The Agloe map, as she'd started thinking of it now that she knew its secret.

Her gaze drifted down to her desk—where she realized she'd been doing it again. Doodling little fragments of the Agloe map on her drafting paper throughout the day, as if by instinct. Like it was a part of her, a map she'd created herself and knew by heart, rather than something she'd found.

If only she'd had more time. Not just to figure out the mystery behind it, but also to have been able to draw the whole thing herself. A copy just for her. She craved that almost as much as she craved the answers to her questions, for some reason. To trace every line and road onto her own paper, with her own hand, to draft every town, *especially* Agloe . . .

No. She had to let go.

Even if what she was letting go of was the very thing that sparked the Junk Box Incident. Even if she'd just found the phantom settlement on it. And even if she was closer to understanding the whole mystery, and maybe her father, than she'd been in her entire life. So close she could almost taste it.

She knew what she had to do.

"Nell?" Humphrey called, startling her.

Quickly, Nell crumpled the draft paper, threw it in the trash, and shoved the portfolio into her bag. As she hurried, she took one of the stiff white Classic envelopes they used to mail smaller customer maps and jammed it into the middle of her towering in-box, so her desk was completely clear.

"You're still here?" he asked as he came back around the corner, holding an armful of freshly printed budget reports.

"I'm leaving now," she said, standing up and hefting her bag onto her shoulder.

"Well, have fun. And be careful."

Be careful? Nell cocked her head.

"Sorry," he chuckled. "I listened to my dad say it to every one of those four sisters every time they left the house. Just slipped out."

She smiled. "I'll be fine. It's the New York Public Library, not an underground club or something."

But even as she said it, a chill crept up her spine. She probably would be safer at an underground club. No one there would be after a rare inaccurate map mysteriously worth millions.

"You look great, kid," Humphrey added, and Nell glanced up to see him smiling at her—he must have thought Nell was nervous about her outfit or makeup.

"Thanks," she managed, and adjusted her bag. The top of the leather portfolio peeked back at her.

"I'll lock up, you get going!" He arched a brow comically. "Just kiss the guy first, as soon as you see him. Skip over the boring conversation part."

"*Goodbye,* Humphrey," she shouted over his laughter as she headed downstairs.

She'd been able to pretend she wasn't before, but now she definitely *was* nervous.

Could she and Felix really make it work this time?

The subway couldn't arrive fast enough. When the train finally screeched into the station, Nell had her nose pressed to the doors before they slid open.

What would it be like? To be with Felix again at the library, maybe even arm in arm, just as before. The butterflies that by now were permanent tenants in her stomach roused again, causing another grin to tug at her lips. Swann would be so happy.

Who was she kidding? *She* would be so happy.

Nell jumped off the train at Grand Central and made her way up through the rush-hour crowds in the station into the evening light at street level. As she turned onto Fifth Avenue, and the silhouette of the two stone lions and imposing columns that marked the front of the library came into view, she found herself clutching her bag tighter to her shoulder, searching again for the black car. Was that it there, at the end of the street? Or turning left? Or was she jumping at shadows? Felix was right, having Haberson's security systems in the library now made it a safer place. But she still couldn't shake the discomfort she felt over Haberson's specialists scanning every single inch of every map and atlas in its priceless collections, and then breaking down their intangible artistry into some kind of data code, a bunch of ones and zeros, as if *that* could mean more than the original. It just felt wrong, somehow. Like giving something up. Not the maps themselves, but the magic of them. The feel of their paper, and the richness of their ink. Some things just couldn't translate perfectly into data.

Her father would have agreed.

With a deep breath, Nell ascended the steps. At the doors, a docent bowed politely and checked her name off the guest list. "Right this way," he said, as a waiter swooped in with a tray of champagne glasses and a stack of programs.

"Thank you," Nell meant to reply, but the words escaped her as she entered.

Inside, the lobby of the New York Public Library was positively glittering. White marble glistened warmly everywhere, and the balustrades shined like gold. Overhead, they'd lowered the lighting to a soft yellow glow to evoke a sense of old times and ancient artifacts—she'd seen the tactic before at auctions and opera houses. Everyone was in tuxedos and gowns, hair swept gracefully up, jewelry sparkling on long necks and delicate wrists. The melody of a piano reached her over the quiet murmur of conversation and clinking glasses. And all around them, suspended on razor-thin cables in a large circle, hung a dazzling array of priceless, awe-inspiring maps.

Swann smiled when they spotted each other, and he made his way to her through the crowd milling near the entrance. "Nell! You're here." His eyes were misty, a tangle of pride and sadness, an observation that made her pull him into a protective hug.

"It's beautiful," she whispered to him as she let go.

"You really mean it?" he asked.

Nell knew her father would have found the whole thing cheesy and ridiculous, and she would have thought she'd feel the same as well, but standing there now, she couldn't argue that the dramatic mood did give the library an irresistible atmosphere. She felt like she was about to be let into a secret vault to hunt for lost treasures.

Or be *hunted,* she thought.

"I do," she smiled. "He would have loved it."

Swann hugged her again. "I'm so glad. You look lovely."

"No, I don't," she said. She was in the same simple black sheath she'd worn for her father's funeral, because it was the only black dress she owned. That day it had seemed practical, and she'd had an excuse not to look very put together. Today, and especially compared to the rest of the guests' stunning attire, she worried she just looked frumpy. She tried not to think about the sharp, perfectly tailored tuxedo Felix was going to show up wearing.

"You always look lovely," Swann admonished, like a proud, stubborn uncle, and then stepped closer. "Where's Felix?"

"On his way, I think."

Swann tried to hide the grin that threatened at the corners of his lips, but Nell saw it.

"Don't get too excited," she said, and he clucked his tongue at her. "I mean it. I'm not sure of anything yet."

"But this is a good start."

This time, Nell allowed the tiniest of hopeful nods.

Swann's grin got the better of him at that. "Well, come find me when he does arrive. I haven't seen him in so long." He raised his glass. "And thank you for being here tonight."

"I'd do anything for you," she said, like she always did. "You know that."

"We all do," a familiar voice said, and Nell turned to see the chair of the library approaching. Irene was in an elegant blue silk dress, and the hem fluttered like ripples on a lake as she leaned over to kiss the air just beside Nell's cheek.

"Hello, Ms. Pérez Montilla," Nell said, before she could stop herself.

"Nell! For the last time, it's Irene." She waved off a few approaching board members, who obediently blended back into the crowd to let them talk. "I'm very glad you're here."

"Come find me later, Nell," Swann said to her. "I have something to give you—a gift, of sorts."

"A gift?" she asked, surprised.

But Swann just gave her shoulder an encouraging squeeze and made an excuse about refilling his drink as he dashed off—to give Irene some privacy to make Nell an offer of employment if the conversation went well, Nell knew.

Here we go, she thought, her pulse racing. *It's now or never.*

"I hope you've been enjoying the event so far," Irene said.

"I am. Thank you for the honor," Nell replied, and realized that this time, she actually meant it. Someone in her family would have their name forever on a collection at the Map Division of the *New York Public Library.*

"It was the best way I could think of to thank him for a lifetime of passion and service to the library," Irene said. She leaned slightly closer, her voice dropping, and glanced knowingly at Nell. "Although I do hope to be able to honor a second Young as well."

Nell's heart skipped.

This was what she wanted, wasn't it? To let it go and get her job back. Not to beg for more time or to pretend she hadn't figured anything out yet.

Not to keep investigating.

Before she could stop herself, the words were tumbling out.

"I've had a chance to look into some of my father's things, and . . ."

Irene perked up. "Did you find something, Dr. Young?"

Hearing her title from Irene's lips thrilled her. It had been so long since anyone had called her that. She was not even sure Humphrey, bless him, remembered she'd earned a doctorate.

"Well . . . ," Nell faltered.

"Would you like to be in research? Or special collections? Name a position—it's yours."

Nell tried to find the words, but she could barely breathe.

Just tell her.

Irene had all but handed her an employment contract. The library was just inches away from her grasp once more.

Tell her and let it go.

"So, what did you find?" Irene asked.

"I—"

But this map had become so much more than that. She still wanted the library—but she wanted her answers *more.*

"I didn't find anything," she finally said.

Irene blinked, surprised. The hopeful expression on her face tumbled. "That's—that's a shame," she managed.

"I'm sorry," Nell rushed on guiltily. "I really tried, and I can always keep looking, but—"

"No, no," Irene insisted. She was deeply disappointed, struggling to pull herself back together and find the composed public face she needed to host the event. She'd been counting on Nell even more than she'd realized, Nell could see. "I am so grateful for everything you've done already. Really, I should never have asked you for this. It must have been so difficult. I feel terrible."

"Please, I really did want to help. I just . . . ," Nell began.

Then, over Irene's shoulder, she noticed a face that startled her into silence.

Francis Bowden.

After avoiding her so desperately at the funeral, what was he doing here?

"Francis," Irene said, having turned around to see who Nell was staring at. "I thought you were back at Harvard already."

Francis said something about how he had to return tomorrow but wanted to pay his respects as he reached out to shake Irene's hand. His voice was low and hurried just like before, and he looked like a trapped animal, despite his size.

"I need to talk to you," Nell said before he could escape.

He looked at her sharply, but there was nothing for him to do but agree. He couldn't simply run away from Irene the way he'd run away from Nell after the funeral without raising eyebrows.

"I didn't mean to interrupt," he finally said.

Irene politely waved off his apology. "I need to make my rounds anyway. The race for donors never ends." She gave Nell a polite, but crestfallen, smile. "Please enjoy the event."

Francis watched Irene float away like a shipwrecked man watching the last life raft disappear.

"Why are you here?" Nell said, before he could make up an excuse. "After refusing to tell me anything at the funeral."

"To keep an eye out for you," he said.

"I doubt that," she replied. "You won't even speak to me."

"Speaking to you and keeping an eye out for you are different things." He lowered his voice further. "I owe it to your father."

"That's what Ramona and Eve keep saying, too—but he's gone. I'm the one here now."

At the mention of Ramona and Eve, Francis's expression clouded further, but Nell stepped closer, refusing to give up. "And I know more than you think."

"Come," he finally said. "Not here in the middle of the room."

Nell followed him closely, afraid to let him vanish like he did last time, as he led them to the far end of the lobby, where the crowd was more scattered.

"I meant it when I said that you should drop this," he repeated once they'd stopped.

"You don't understand," she started.

"No, *you* don't." He glanced around. "Do you have any idea how dangerous all of this is? Or who else could be here tonight?"

"You mean Wally?" she cut in. Francis blinked, surprised. "I told you. I know more than you think, Francis. Too much for you to keep ignoring me."

Francis sighed. "Trust me, whatever it is that you think you've stumbled onto, you have no idea. There's so much more that—"

"I know about the phantom settlement," she interrupted. "I know about Agloe."

She expected Francis to either tell her she was wrong yet again, or turn around and run away like the last time.

But instead, his entire face changed.

The room around them seemed to contract, voices receding into the background, as he edged closer. He was no longer glaring tensely at her. Instead, he seemed to be trying to shield her with his body, blocking her from view. As if to protect her from something.

Did he really think Wally was here? In the middle of a giant, public party? There was security everywhere, including Haberson's systems now. There was no way for anyone—even someone as brazen and dangerous as they all seemed to think Wally was—to try anything tonight. Nowhere for him to hide.

"I'm impressed," Francis said, after a long, silent moment. When he spoke again, his voice was so much softer. "Which one of them did you wrestle it out of? Ramona or Eve? They both doted on you so much when you were a baby. Couldn't keep them away."

"Neither of them," she said. "I put it together myself."

Francis looked down, as if he might be ill. He removed his glasses to clean them on the silk handkerchief from his pocket. His hand was shaking, Nell saw.

"Please, just tell me," she begged. "Why is the map so important, for something so common and practically worthless? Why did it destroy your friendship? Why is Wally still looking for it, after all this time?"

And what does a phantom settlement have to do with my mother's death, if anything? she wanted to ask.

"I can't," Francis whispered. "I promised your father. We all did."

"I'll go public," Nell challenged him, desperate.

"You wouldn't," he said.

"I will, unless you tell me."

"That would be the worst possible thing you—"

"I'm a Young," she said defiantly. "You knew two of them well enough to know I won't give up either."

Francis grimaced.

"Tell me," she urged. "Why is a little mistake on a map so important?"

His voice was barely audible. "It's because it's not a mistake."

"Fine, I misspoke," Nell said, conceding the point. Eve had said that phantom settlements were placed deliberately, just in secret. "It's a copyright trap, not a mistake."

Francis shook his head. "That's not what I mean."

A smattering of applause and a nearby toast drew their attention for a moment, and Nell leaned in. "Are you talking about the copyright infringement lawsuit?" she asked.

"That's what started it," he allowed. "Even though General Drafting had been the first to realize that driving maps were the future of mapmaking and made early deals with national gas station chains to supply its maps to anyone who stopped to fill up their tank, automobile ownership just kept increasing, and the demand for this kind of map skyrocketed. The profits were too much for the bigger companies to ignore. They wanted in on the market too, and would stop at nothing to get it."

"General Drafting suspected that the bigger companies were stealing their data?" Nell asked.

"Yes," he said. "They were convinced that Rand McNally and H.M. Gousha were simply copying their maps instead of conducting their own land surveys, so they could catch up and put out their own editions faster. General Drafting was desperate, and at a loss as to how to prove it."

Hide a lie inside the truth, Eve had said.

"Agloe," Nell prompted.

Francis nodded. "The founder, Otto G. Lindberg, and his assistant Ernest Alpers, invented and hid, within their map, an entire town that didn't exist. They placed it deep in the Catskills, at the empty intersection of two deserted roads, and told no one. It's a combination of their initials—A-G-L-O-E—Wally was the one who figured that out."

Nell nodded, seeing it was true. "What happened then?"

"Soon after General Drafting's map was released, someone saw a draft of Rand McNally's own edition of the same area, about to go to print—and Lindberg and Alpers were stunned to find Agloe on their rival's map in the same place. Their copyright trap had worked. Lindberg and Alpers called their lawyers and told them to file the suit, ready to accuse Rand McNally of stealing their data instead of conducting their own research, because Agloe wasn't real. Then, wanting to waste no time gathering evidence, they hired a photographer and drove out to that empty county road intersection in the wild Catskills where they'd planted their phantom settlement, ready to claim their victory."

Nell waited, expecting him to continue, but Francis fell silent.

"What happened?" she finally asked.

"The case was filed, but then it disappeared just as quickly. Dropped, or settled. The files were hidden, records erased."

She blinked. "That's . . . that's it? That's the end of your story?"

But Francis shook his head. "That's the beginning."

Nell watched her father's old friend intently, struggling to understand what he was saying. He seemed to be trying to figure something out about her as well, based on her reaction.

"You didn't go there, did you," he said. "To Agloe." It wasn't so much a question as a statement of fact.

She paused. "Well, no," she admitted. "I had wanted to when I figured it out, but it was already dark, almost midnight. The drive would have taken hours. But it's just a phantom settlement. There would have been nothing there but a road, or a field, anyway."

Francis nodded slowly. "That is how the place appears to most people, yes."

"What? What do you mean, 'most people'?"

"Locals who know the area well or any travelers passing through using the GPS in their phones to navigate," he replied. "Basically, anyone *not* using a copy of the 1930 highway map that Tam and Wally found—which is almost everyone."

Nell stared at him, confused, her suspicion rising. "I think I understand even less now," she said.

"Before the internet, rumors didn't get passed around as quickly as they do now, and little drive-through towns don't normally get much attention to begin with," Francis continued. "But eventually, and despite Wally's desperate, obsessive attempts to crush any mention of the map, cartography enthusiasts started realizing that there was rare, scattered chatter about a little town in that same area of the Catskills, by the same name—Agloe. Some said they were sure they'd passed that place as they'd driven through on their holidays, seen it from the road as clear as day, and the rest, including longtime residents of nearby towns, insisted that there was nothing but an empty field when they drove by every day, as it had always been."

"*What?*"

"The only difference, for those of us who knew what was going on, was that some people had driven by Agloe using a map to navigate, and others drove those roads by heart."

"No," Nell said.

"Yes," Francis replied. "This is why the map is so valuable. Precious beyond measure."

It was nonsense. A huge hoax.

That was not how maps worked.

She could hardly believe the words even as she said them.

"You're telling me . . ."

It sounded ridiculous.

"You're telling me that the reason this map is so special . . . is that if you have a hard copy of this old piece of paper that shows Agloe on it . . ."

Francis nodded.

The party swirled around them, innocent and unconcerned, as he confessed.

"If you have the map, the town will *appear* to you," he said. "You can *go there*."

Francis

Eve may have told you that your mother and Wally found the map, but she didn't tell you what happened after, because she wasn't there that morning. She was still asleep—almost the entire house was. Only Daniel and I were awake. We were the first ones they told.

The night before, Romi, Bear, and I pulled up to the house after dusk had already fallen. By the time we got the car unloaded and dragged our bags in, everyone from the first group was already cooking. Daniel and Wally were on the back deck attempting to work the grill, shouting conversation through the open door while Eve tossed a huge salad and watched the vegetables on the stove and Tam chased you around the coffee table. When you saw us, you screamed with glee, and Bear heaved all his bags onto me to scoop you up for a hug.

"You're so late!" Eve cried over the rumble of the stove. "We were about to eat without you!"

"We come bearing gifts to make up for it," Romi said, and held up the case of wine in her arms.

Eve came to retrieve the box immediately, eager, overhelpful, saying how Romi didn't have to carry that, she could take it, and how kind it was to buy it for us. Romi smiled back, as bemused as ever as to why the longer they knew each other, Eve only seemed to get *more* shy around her, rather than less. If anything, Eve should have felt freer to come out of her shell with her, Romi often said, since they were so alike.

She didn't know about the almost kiss. And I pretended I didn't, either.

"Franny boy!" Daniel called. "Get out here! Does this look medium-rare to you?"

I sprang for the back door and immediately turned their propane down, and then Tam came out, you still in Bear's arms, and turned it back up, plus more. "None of you know how to grill," she laughed. "Go get the plates and cutlery ready."

All of us were in such a jovial mood—still loopy from the party the night before, drained from the long drive, and happy to be all together again, in a new place, with our new project—I remember the energy of that night. The possibility, the excitement. It was like we could all feel that something momentous was about to happen, even then. We just didn't know what it was.

Eventually, Daniel and Wally wrestled control of the grill back from Tam, determined to prove themselves, and I went inside to help Romi and Eve finish up some side dishes and collect you and Bear. Tam, happy for the break, was sitting at the table already drinking some of the wine and laughing about something when we all came back out onto the deck.

"It was just a dollar!" she was saying.

"We're supposed to be saving every penny!" Daniel returned, laughing just as hard. "That's why we're all the way out here, away from the temptations of the city!"

"What's all this now?" Bear asked, already nervous he'd been left out of something.

"It turns out that our beloved geniuses Tam and Wally are no better cartographers than we are," Daniel said.

"One single dollar!" Tam shouted, waving something over her head, and they all laughed again.

Daniel was teasing her, it turned out, because she and Wally had been talked into buying some little piece of junk from an antiques store because the owner had been so friendly. I took it from her as they continued to joke, opening it up.

He was right. It was an old road map—a worthless little thing. Faded, tattered, out of date, and something we likely could have found in the glove compartment of any old truck sleeping in a retired couple's garage.

"It's more than half a century old," Daniel guffawed, so loud that Wally almost dropped the tongs by accident.

"That's the great thing about places like this," Tam fired back. "Nothing changes, so the map's probably still completely accurate!"

This earned her much laughter and a toast from all of us. Then something happened to the grill's fire, and Daniel bent down beside Wally, their faces far too close to the flames, investigating the issue.

"Here, take it, before they burn themselves to death," I gasped, and tossed the map at Tam so I could pull them both back by their collars. Tam scooted over so Romi, Eve, and Bear could sit down, and they began pouring the wine.

"What about here?" Romi asked, looking at the half-refolded thing. "Where we are now?"

"I bet we can find it," Tam said.

Wally had given Daniel and me the tongs and gone over to the table, now bored with the grill, and held Tam's glass for her as she used both hands to lay the paper flat on the table. "What are we doing?" he asked, taking a sip.

"Finding where we are on *our* map," Tam smiled. She emphasized the word *our*, as if the little scrap was actually precious and the rest of us just couldn't see it, which drew a round of chuckles. Wally grinned, and drank more of her wine. "Okay, what did we drive up? Interstate 17?"

"Yeah, to County Road 206," I called.

Tam put her finger on the page and traced one of the snaking lines. "Hey, there's Rockland," she announced triumphantly, pointing at a tiny white dot. "That's the last town we all passed before reaching this house," she said. "Where we got the groceries."

"Where we got the wine, too," Romi added.

"So that's been here for at least sixty years, then," Wally said, shrugging.

"And this house is just past the town, so we're what, five miles north?"

"No more than that, for sure," Eve agreed.

We all watched vaguely in between sips of wine as Tam continued to trace her finger up the 206 past Morton Hill Road, where our new home was nestled into a little grove just before the land fully turned into the wild Catskills.

"Wally," she said suddenly, and he looked down at the map, to where she was pointing.

Right in between both places, there was another dot along County Road 206.

A little town called Agloe.

"Do you remember another town between this house and Rockland?" she asked him.

"No," he said, brow furrowed. "Just fields. We would have seen it out the car window if there was."

"That's what I thought," she replied. "Daniel!" she called to him, but he'd been able to hear over the grill, and shook his head.

"We didn't see anything either," I added. "Nothing after Rockland. Just a few miles of grass and road, and then the turnoff for this house."

Tam frowned and looked at the map again. "Huh. Well, this map's got another little town marked there."

"What's it called?" Wally asked, peering closer.

"Agloe," she read. "A-G-L-O-E."

Daniel, who was now leaning over all of us to see as well, snorted and then returned to the grill to flip a steak. "Strange name. But it's got to be an error. None of us saw anything, and it'd be kind of hard to miss a whole town out here in the middle of nowhere."

"It's a phantom settlement, probably," Eve offered. "It was a big thing when they were still doing surveys by hand."

"Should have hid it better," I said.

"Better than out here, in all this countryside? It was probably even less populated than it is now."

Romi shrugged. "We found it, didn't we?"

"I don't even know if the map's worth the one dollar the shopkeeper charged you," Bear laughed.

"Hey, it's still not totally worthless," Tam protested. "We could still use it as kindling. We're making a fire in the pit tonight, right?"

In response, Daniel grinned at her like he did when he was about to surprise one of us with something. Beside Tam at the table, I could see a smile starting to creep over Eve's face as well as she tried to play it cool—they were in on something together they'd planned at the grocery store. Then Daniel reached into the paper grocery bag on the bench next to the grill and pulled out a bag of marshmallows, a box of graham crackers, and a few bars of chocolate. "You bet we are," he said. "A fire *and* s'mores!"

"I knew I married you for a reason!" Tam crowed, and jumped on his back and kissed his face until they were silly dancing around the deck, ignoring Wally's protests not to bump the table with all the wine on it while the map was still spread out there. I laughed, and so did the rest of us. In the ruckus, Romi put her arms around me and squeezed me, too. Out of the corner of my eye, I saw Eve blush sheepishly and then busy herself with tending to you, boosting you onto the bench so you could join in the fun.

I slept fitfully, and the next morning got up much earlier than usual. Romi and I had lived in our own apartment off campus for years, just like Daniel and Tam, and hadn't shared with roommates since undergrad. I wasn't used to the new house, I told myself. To having everyone else so close by, only a door away. Some of those doors closer than others.

Romi, however, was still fast asleep, tangled up in the blankets. I crept out of bed as quietly as possible and eased myself down the creaky wooden stairs to get started on making a pot of coffee. The house was dead silent, except for the faint whistle of the breeze through the trees outside, but the sunlight streaming in everywhere was beautiful. In the bright morning, the house didn't seem quite as gigantic and ridiculous as it had the night before, although it was still far too large for our needs. I padded slowly around the living room, enjoying the view of the woods through each window.

"Do you know how to work this?" a voice asked softly, and I jumped. But it was not Eve.

"Tam," I breathed. "You scared me."

"Sorry," she whispered. She was in the kitchen, already dressed in jeans and one of Daniel's big T-shirts, holding a metal shape. "I've never seen a coffee maker like this."

"It's a pour-over," I said, coming over and taking it from her. "I used to have one."

"Oh good, are we making coffee?" another tired voice asked, and the stairs creaked again as Wally appeared at the foot of them, trying to work his head through the neck hole of a Henley shirt.

"Not yet," I said from the pantry, and they both looked at me, dismayed. "There aren't any coffee grounds."

"We forgot to buy any in Rockland yesterday," Tam groaned. "Bear and Daniel are going to be zombies without coffee."

"I can go," Wally offered. "It's just down the road."

"Thanks," Tam said, at the same moment that a little burst of high-pitched giggles echoed from upstairs.

"I think Nell's awake," I said, as a heavier set of footsteps began to thud faintly—Daniel, most likely, going to get you and bring you downstairs, before you woke everyone else up.

I thought Tam would go to the landing to meet him, but instead, she grinned mischievously, and jumped toward the counter, where both sets of car keys were resting on a jumble of other papers and junk—gas and grocery receipts, napkins, spare change, and that silly little gas station map.

"This is Daniel's morning to watch her," she said, snatching the entire bundle for lack of time. "If he tries to hand her off to you, don't let him! Tell him Wally and I will be back in thirty minutes."

"Let Wally drive, he won't speed," I said, shooing them out the door to the long driveway, where the cars waited, their windshields dotted with pollen from the trees.

"Did she just run out to avoid toddler breakfast duty?" Daniel asked behind me as the sound of one of the engines shuddering to life rumbled in. I turned to see him holding you, his hair still standing straight up.

"She said it was your day," I said, wagging a finger at him.

"What!" He pretended to be affronted, gasping dramatically, which made you laugh. "How about some eggs, Nelly?"

Daniel cooked you an egg and a little bit of bacon while I assembled your high chair, to be helpful. Overhead, we heard the others stir a few times, but still none of them had woken up by the time we got you settled at the table and Daniel had cut your food into a bunch of little bites.

"I hope they remembered to buy cream and sugar," I said at the same moment that a sudden crunch of tires on pebbles made us all look to the door.

"Just in time," Daniel started as the door clicked open. "Everyone's still asleep!"

But we both fell silent as Tam and Wally lurched into the room.

"Daniel," Tam gasped. "Francis."

They came in at a dead run, the car engine still idling outside. Tam was in front of Wally, and he was just behind her, almost as if he were chasing her in. Their eyes were wild and huge, flashing with an emotion I couldn't quite read. Awe, or disbelief, or exhilaration.

"What's going on?" Daniel asked, half out of his seat, unsure of whether to be panicked or excited. "Are you okay?"

"We're okay," Tam managed. She crossed the kitchen in two steps and grabbed him by the arm. "Come on. You have to see this."

"Tam," Wally said, his voice tight. At the time, I thought it was because he was simply afraid. That he hadn't wanted to tell us quite yet only because he didn't fully understand what was going on. Not because he had wanted to keep it a secret, under his control.

Tam could not hear his feeble protests. She was electrified, like a live, leaping wire. "Come on."

Daniel and I stumbled after her, Daniel carrying you, and Wally trailing all of us, your breakfast still half-finished at the table, the coffee still unmade. She shoved all of us into the back seat and forced Wally again behind the wheel before throwing herself into the front beside him.

"So, same road as always, right?" she was saying frantically as Wally turned south onto County Road 206, heading for Rockland again, and we began to pick up speed. The old station wagon rumbled over the asphalt, the grass turning from individual blades into a blur of green, as she talked. "Nothing but field."

"Right," Daniel agreed, humoring her, trying to figure out where this was going.

The sun grew brighter as Wally drove, casting everything pale pink instead of gray. Tam alternated between urging him to go faster and trying to explain to us what was going on.

"I had everything in my lap," she was saying, pointing to the bundle of junk she'd grabbed from the counter before leaving the first time with Wally. Beside me, you were bouncing excitedly in your car seat at the prospect of a field trip. "The other set of car keys, receipts, and this." She held up the gas station map.

"Tam," Wally said again, even weaker this time.

She unfolded it and spread it across the steering wheel, so she and Wally were both looking at it. "On the way back from the store, as we were talking, I realized that we were passing right through the same area where we'd found that little phantom settlement on this map the night before. 'Where had that place been, along this road?' I asked Wally. 'Which tree or patch of weeds had it accidentally marked as an entire town?' We laughed about it, and before I knew it, I was holding the map out like this for both of us, so we could see where exactly this town was *supposed* to be, and what it really was instead. What if the spot was a huge bush of poison ivy? Or a cow standing in its corral? I thought being able to tell everyone what it was would make another funny story for tonight."

Suddenly, the car began to slow. Wally, his lips pressed together and his eyes on the paper, flicked on the hazard lights. We edged toward the shoulder of the road.

"I know how this is going to sound—I know!" she cried, anticipating our wary stares. "But if you open this map, and you follow it instead of the road . . ."

She kept it splayed open and pointed out the window as the car finally stopped. Her expression was so full of amazement. So *alive*. I felt like I could see straight down into her soul through her eyes.

"Just *look*."

We looked, expecting to see just pure, unbroken field.

But this time, somehow, just in front of our car—where I'm certain there had been nothing before, or we would have noticed it, it being the only thing we'd seen for miles—there was a tall, thick, wooden pole jutting straight out from the grass, with a big metal sign affixed to it. And just past it, a small turnoff that continued as a dirt road.

"Huh?" I murmured, before I could stop myself. "That wasn't here before."

Wally turned off the car, and everyone got out.

"Was it?" Daniel asked, looking at Wally, since they'd come up in the same car yesterday. He looked as baffled as I felt. "Did we just not see it because we were tired?"

Slowly, Wally shook his head.

I stepped forward and inspected the sign. The nails were long rusted, and there was a fine layer of grime on the face of the metal itself that clearly indicated it hadn't somehow been put up in the single day we'd been at the house.

It was old. It had been there all this time. And it also definitely had not been.

And the name on the sign matched the name on the map.

Welcome to Agloe
Home of the famous Beaverkill Fishing Lodge!

Slowly, we turned to peer beyond the sign, out across the field behind it.

"What the . . . ," Daniel murmured, transfixed.

"I told you," Tam said, breathless. "I told you."

Nell, I know how all this sounds, but I swear it's true.

The town is real—if you have the map that shows the way. Your mother and Wally discovered it.

And it killed her.

XV

Nell stared at Francis in shock for several seconds, unable to feel anything at all.

Then she did.

Anger.

"What is this?" she asked, stabbing a finger at him. That was her family he was making up nonsense about. Her *mother.* "I don't know what your game is, but it's rude, and weird, and cruel. It's *cruel.* Did my father put you up to this? Is this some kind of last prank from beyond the grave, to ruin my life one more time?"

But Francis wasn't laughing.

"Is it?" she snapped, startling a passing party guest. *"Is it?"*

They stared at each other for several seconds, one steely-eyed with determination, the other still trying to process what sounded like complete nonsense.

Was he trying to scare her? Or trick her? His big reveal was something out of a fantasy novel. A bedtime story for children. An absolute embarrassment to the cartography field, at the very least. Why he thought Nell would buy it she had no idea, but one thing was for sure—if she was going to ask anyone else for help, it was not going to be Francis.

"Fine. Screw this," she said. "I don't know what your game is, but I don't care. I'm going back to Irene, to tell her I found the map in my father's things like I should have done on the very first—"

Francis's gaze snapped back to her instantly. Every hint of fear and hesitation that had been there before was utterly gone. There was only grim, absolute focus.

"What?" he asked.

Shit, Nell thought.

She'd been so careful so far. Until now, no one but Swann and Felix knew that she had the map—but she'd just slipped.

He'd stepped even closer to her. "Nell."

She could see a thousand questions in his eyes.

"Where is it?" was all he asked.

"It's in a safe place."

He didn't look convinced. "Is it at your home?"

"Yes," Nell lied.

"It's not safe there."

"It's in the safest place I've got."

Francis was staring at her tote bag now, almost as if mesmerized. She could practically feel the leather portfolio inside as if it were on fire.

He didn't believe the map was hidden at her home at all, Nell realized.

Well, he was right.

Was he going to . . . try to take her bag from her?

Her eyes darted around the crowded room, but no one was looking at them. She searched for Swann, or Irene, or even Felix, but it was just a sea of unfamiliar, glittering faces, all lost in their own conversations.

"Listen to me," he said, voice so low she could barely hear him. "This is very important. We've been searching for a long time, to be certain—your father's map, the one you now have, is the last copy in existence. And as long as you have it in your possession, you're in serious danger. You need to give it to me. Now."

"Right," she replied. "Just hand over the most valuable thing I might ever have worked on, the thing that might get me my job here back again, because you say so."

"Please trust me. Look at what happened to your father."

"How do I know you didn't do that yourself?" she asked, but from the flash of pain that immediately clouded his expression, she knew it wasn't true. He'd been the one trying to get her father the Sanborn map. He'd been trying to help him, somehow.

"Nell," he began, but shut his mouth quickly as someone walked up behind her.

"Felix," Nell said as she turned, relieved. He was in a custom, perfectly tailored tux, shoes shining, and looked incredible—like a diplomat or a movie star. "Finally! I'm glad you're here."

"Give it to me now," Francis murmured tensely. "For your own good."

"You know what," Nell said, moving farther from him and closer to Felix. "I think I know what's for my own good."

"I need to talk to you," Felix said to her.

"Please," Francis repeated. "It's not safe." He took a step closer to her, and she moved back again. She could see in the strain of his expression that he was desperate not to lose her, but like at the funeral, he wouldn't talk openly about the map now that someone else had joined the conversation.

"All of this is ridiculous," she said, and he flinched, his eyes begging her not to reveal anything to Felix. "You're embarrassing. I can't believe my father was mixed up in whatever this is. A joke. A scam."

"Nell—" Francis said, frantic, warning, at the same time that Felix said her name, too.

"You won't believe what he told me," she said to Felix, raising her voice slightly over Francis's whispered protests. "He said that Agloe is a real place. Like an actual, physical place, that we can go to with the map, like"—she sneered as she said the last word—"*magic*."

"Nell."

She finally realized that Felix wasn't the same as when she'd seen him the night before. He was much quieter now. Colder. He seemed to have not even registered the utter ridiculousness of what she'd just said, in fact.

"I just passed Irene Pérez Montilla on the way in," he continued once she'd gone silent.

It took her a moment to change gears.

"What?" Nell asked.

"She told me she'd just come from chatting with you, and that I could find you near the hanging Ratzer piece. She looked upset, so I asked her if she'd had a chance to talk to you about Dr. Young's map yet. 'There was no map,' she said."

Oh no.

"You didn't tell her, did you?"

Nell bit her lip to keep from cursing. "I can explain."

"You were never going to do it."

"I just need a little more time," she pleaded.

But the hope had already gone out of his eyes.

"Come on," she said. "You couldn't honestly have expected me to turn it all over without—"

"I did," Felix replied. "Because you promised you would. I trusted you."

Nell cringed. "I'm sorry, Felix, but this is important."

"And I'm not?" he asked.

But he didn't look angry. He just looked sad.

"I thought it was going to be different this time. That we were going to do things together. But here we are, again. I've done everything you've asked to help you, but you're doing whatever you want, without telling me what's going on, without stopping to think if it might hurt me. Expecting me to simply fall in line."

He was talking about the Junk Box Incident now, she knew.

"That's not fair." Her throat was uncomfortably tight. "There was no way I could have known my father was going to turn on us like that, back then."

"But you didn't have to fight him on it. To push him that far."

"Of course I did. He was wrong—look how wrong!"

"He was the senior curator of the Map Division. We were *interns*."

"So I was supposed to let him lie? To embarrass me in front of all of our colleagues?"

She was lining up her argument—she would win this, she would make him see—but Felix didn't have any fight left in him.

"Maybe this is my fault, for believing it could be different this time." He sighed. "I'm done talking about the past. And the present."

Nell felt sick. "What does that mean?"

"It means I'm done. One last favor, you said. For Swann. I think I've more than fulfilled that obligation."

Nell gulped, trying to fight the lump back down into her chest. Her breath was starting to hiccup. Dimly, she was aware that Francis was still there, lurking somewhere behind her, too afraid to step farther away in case he lost track of her, but she didn't care.

She had to convince Felix that she hadn't meant to hurt him. That it wasn't like that—that she had not chosen the map over him, *again.* She had to convince him to stay.

"I'm so close to figuring this out, Felix. I have to, *we* have to—"

That was the wrong thing to say.

"No," he replied. "There's no 'we' anymore."

Nell was clenching the strap of her tote bag so hard she was afraid it was going to dissolve in her hand.

"This isn't your job. It hasn't been for a long time. Just let it go."

"Don't tell me what to do!" she snapped, a little too loudly.

A couple of guests nearby glanced over, but Felix didn't raise his voice back. "I'm serious, Nell. This isn't a game. And it's dangerous. Crimes have been committed. People have *died.* Just tell the police about the map, and—"

"You know I can't," she argued, quieter again, but no less upset. "If I do that, they'll say it's evidence, and it'll get processed and put into closed-case evidence warehouse purgatory, and I'll never see it again."

"Who cares if they file it away, if you get your job back?"

"Because then I won't be any better than him!" Nell hissed. "He spent his whole life trying to do something with this map, but failing, and I'm *so close* to figuring it all out. To doing whatever he couldn't with it!"

Felix might have laughed or sighed. It came out as a dry, static cough. "Unbelievable. All these years, and you still can't let it go. You could have everything you want back, but you'd rather throw it all away just to beat him. To prove you were right."

"What do you know?" she asked. "You're not even in maps anymore. You sold out."

"*I* sold out?" he snapped, furious.

Nell grinned angrily even as she winced. She'd finally gotten under his skin and hit a nerve.

"I work at a good company, helping create technology that will make people's lives better," he retorted. "I'm bringing mapmaking into the future. *I* respect cartography. *You're* the one who's sold out by making knockoff trash at Classic for people who want a cheap piece of shit to hang over their fireplace so they look cultured!"

The air between them hung silent for several seconds as they both stared at each other, stunned. Guests toasted and admired the hanging collection all around the lobby, oblivious.

Finally, a weak laugh escaped from Nell's throat. Her eyes stung. "Well, now that I know how you *really* feel . . ."

She watched him crumple before her. His eyes closed, and his hand found the bridge of his nose and pinched, the way it always did when he was ashamed. "I'm sorry. I didn't mean that."

"Of course you did," she said. She blinked rapidly, refusing to cry. Her lips tried to smile—she would not let him know how much he'd hurt her.

"Nell, please. That was wrong. It's not your fault this whole industry was so stupidly terrified of your father. I'm just so, so tired of—"

"No, you were right. We clearly shouldn't work together, so we won't. Good luck at your amazing, respectable job. I can do this on my own, like I should have in the first place," she said fiercely.

"*Nell*—"

She turned and ran through the crowd.

She didn't know where she was going. Only that she had to keep moving, as fast as she could. Her eyes were filling with tears, and more than once she bumped into another shoulder far too hard as she hurried, too upset to call out a proper apology. Champagne sloshed, close to spilling out of delicate flutes, and people gasped, but she didn't slow. A hot splash on her cheek from her eyes startled her—and drove her on even faster.

"Nell!" Behind her, she could hear Francis's panicked voice calling for her. She cut left, around a cluster of guests making a toast, and nearly ran into Swann.

"Oh! My dear, what's wrong?" he cried, seeing her face as they nearly collided, but Nell couldn't explain. She choked out some kind of an apology, and Swann tried to take her hand, but she was already gone, lost in the crowd again, and he couldn't keep up.

At last, the short hallway leading to the Map Division appeared before her, beckoning. She'd thought she was running for the front of the library, for the exit, but of course she'd come here instead. The one place she'd felt safer and more at home than anywhere, once. She tumbled free of the outer ring of stragglers, her shoes clattering on the marble floor, and threw herself against the door, heaving it open and then slamming it behind her. Away from everything she'd ruined.

Her second shot with Felix. Her investigation of the map. Her chance of joining the library again.

Her *life.*

As the door clicked shut, Nell let out a long, shaky breath, and crumpled into the protective heap of her cardigan over her dress, wrapping it around herself as tightly as it would go. She probably looked even more small and childish than usual, but for once, she didn't care. She wanted only to disappear into one of the pockets and never come out.

All of that searching, and she still had nothing to show for it. She still had no idea why the map was so valuable, or why her father had destroyed her life over it. Because the only explanation she'd been able to track down, Francis's story, turned out to be the most nonsensical scam she'd ever heard.

She'd failed.

Again.

Dimly, she was aware that the music outside in the lobby had stopped, but she was too upset to care.

She didn't know if she was more angry or more humiliated. Did everyone think she was as gullible as Francis clearly thought she was? Had she never been a good cartographer at all, and everything she thought she'd achieved until her exile had been only because she was her father's daughter, held up by his reputation?

If you have the map, the town will appear *to you,* Francis had said. *You can* go *there.*

Like magic.

She sneered at the thought through her tears, disgusted.

A loud sound startled her, a shout perhaps, and Nell looked up. Someone was yelling in the lobby—many someones. Whatever had happened was causing a huge commotion. *A fire?* she briefly worried, but the exhibits automatically would have gone into lockdown to preserve the specimens. *An accident?* Francis had said that coming here was dangerous. Her heart began to beat faster.

Could it be . . .

All of a sudden, the emergency alarm began to clang.

The door to the Map Division slammed open as the room was pitched into a flashing red and white kaleidoscope of light, causing Nell to jump at the sudden glare.

"Nell!" Swann cried, rushing for her. "There you are!"

"What's going on?" she shouted back. His eyes were wide and terrified—she had never seen him like this. Not even after the break-in. "Is someone trying to rob the library again?"

"It's the police," he said. He grabbed her as if to shield her from something with his own frail body. The alarms wailed, deafening. "One of the donors went looking for Irene, and they found her in her office. She's, she's—"

Nell thought she was going to faint.

"She's been murdered."

"*NYPD!*" a loudspeaker in the lobby blared suddenly. The squeak of so many pairs of shoes on the marble floor pierced through the moments in between the alarm's repeating scream. "*Everyone stay where you are! No one leaves this building!*"

"We have to get you out of here," Swann said.

Nell blinked, still in shock. "Why?"

His grip on her arm grew even tighter, more desperate. "I heard one of the officers as they came in—you're the prime suspect, Nell."

What?

Swann went to the door, urging her to follow him, but she couldn't make her feet cooperate. "How . . ."

"I don't know! Maybe you were the last person the other guests saw speaking to her. But Lieutenant Cabe was here before the event even started. I saw him parked down the street in a black undercover car—"

"A black car?" she gasped. "That car has been following me for *days!*"

Swann looked horrified. "Maybe someone put an idea in their

heads, to throw suspicion on to you. Told them that you'd come back after all this time, right after your father died, and then the break-in happened just after—"

Nell faltered.

It was Wally who had cast suspicion on her, somehow. It had to be—who else knew that the Agloe map even existed?

He was here.

Swann was right, they had to run, but where could they go? There was only one door out of the room, and the hallway led right back to the lobby, where the NYPD was swarming. She'd be spotted for sure. Everyone knew who she was.

Including Wally.

"Nell. Oh my God."

He was no longer looking at her, but just over her shoulder, at the back wall of the room.

"Look."

Just then, the door to the Map Division burst open again right next to Swann, and Nell braced, expecting the police, but it wasn't officers. *Felix?* she hoped—but it was Francis, with two other people following him. Too much was happening for her to think clearly. Irene, the police, Swann panicking, the blaring alarm.

"Nell!" Francis called. He was lunging for her. "Look out!"

Swann was shouting for her to run too, but Nell could hardly move. Faintly, she realized that she was standing near the place on Eve's Sanborn map where its drafter had long, long ago hidden his secret little room in the floor plan.

Something blurred in the corner of her vision as she turned. A shifting, an opening. A door appearing in the wall where there should have been nothing but smooth paint.

Suddenly, someone else was standing behind her.

Finally, Nell did open her mouth to scream—but no sound came out before the blow.

Then the world went dark.

III

The Town

XVI

The office was utterly silent except for the occasional click of Felix's mouse, and the quiet, electric hum of the gargantuan Haberson server housed in the cold room right on the other side of the wall. It had bothered him on his first day there, burrowing into his skull, that soft but relentless whining drone. But then on his lunch break, he'd gotten the engineer on shift to badge him into the room, a vast, cavernous cube that felt more like science fiction than reality, and he sat with the unfathomable beast for a whole hour in the dim light, staring at its myriad blinking lights and circulatory system of wires, listening to it breathe. It was where the mighty Haberson Map lived, he'd realized as he watched it think. His map.

After that, the sound didn't bother Felix anymore. By the end of the next day, he could no longer even hear it, as if it had become a part of him. But he knew it was there, present and comforting, behind the scenes. The same way no one thought it was strange that they couldn't hear their own heartbeat.

Tonight, though, he craved that conscious, inescapable sound again—if only to distract him. But in the late-night quiet, his mind kept drifting back to Nell, and what she was doing now. She was probably still at the library, the event winding down. Maybe in Swann's office with him, sipping more of his very fine Scotch—the same one that Dr. Young also used to keep in the cupboard behind his desk. The first time Felix had tasted it had been the day Nell convinced her father and Swann to hire him with her as an intern at the NYPL. The second had been a few months after that, when he'd successfully defended his dissertation at the end of that final semester and received his Ph.D. in cartography. He had always imagined the third time would be when he and Nell showed the two old men the ring that he would have someday picked out with her, on her finger.

Well.

And despite not wanting to be, he was still curious about the Agloe map. Especially about what Francis's outlandish claim, that the phantom settlement on it was *real,* actually meant.

Felix shook his head. It had been nonsense. He must have misunderstood what Nell had been trying to tell him. He had to admit, he'd been so upset in the moment, he'd hardly been listening.

But it didn't matter. Tomorrow, he was sure Irene would call Nell to invite her back to the library and tell her she knew about the map—or what Felix had accidentally revealed before realizing Nell hadn't kept her promise to him. Nell would have no choice but to admit it then and accept some much needed help and security.

She'd probably hate him forever, and he'd never see her again, but seven years ago, he'd already assumed that was how things would go. If it wasn't meant to be between them, at least this way she'd finally be free of her father's damned shadow and back at the library. *And* safe.

He had his own map to worry about, anyway. A far better one. A map that not even all the esteem and scholarly power of the NYPL's preeminent Map Division could give him. This was the entire *world,* in one single map. It was going to revolutionize the field of cartography. Hell, it was going to revolutionize every field—shipping and logistics, tourism, weather, agriculture, location-based games people played on their phones, even crime. It was going to be perfect. That was the entire reason William had hired Felix and formed his team to develop the Haberson, after all.

"What makes a perfect map?" *had been* William's first and only question to Felix during his interview.

"A perfect map?" Felix remembered repeating, a sense of dire panic setting in as he clutched the phone and paced his apartment in his pajamas while William Haberson, *the* William Haberson, CEO of the most incredible, pioneering company in the world, waited patiently for his answer. Such a thing wasn't real—couldn't be real—had been the only thought scrambling through his mind. "What do you mean, 'a perfect map'?" he'd asked, frantic.

"What does the phrase mean to you?" William had replied impassively.

When Felix realized he wasn't going to get more from the man, he'd tried to guess. He could not fail—it had already been six months since he'd been fired from the library, and he'd heard back about none of the hundreds of job applications he'd sent, cursed by the Junk Box scandal. This was not only the best, most incredible mapmaking job he'd ever have the chance to interview for—it was likely also the *only* one. "Accurate? Diverse? Historical? Beautiful, even?"

"Are you asking me or telling me?"

"Purpose," Felix had said then. It was something he'd heard Dr. Young say often in the library, whenever he was lecturing new researchers about their collection. "That would be what I'd start with first. Nothing else matters about a map unless you know its purpose. What it's trying to tell you."

"And how do you know its purpose?"

"By figuring out its secrets," he replied, desperately parroting more of Nell's father's sayings. "Every map has them, but you can only know them by knowing what the mapmaker had intended when they first put pen to paper."

The line had hung in silence for ten excruciatingly long seconds—so long Felix worried that William had simply hung up on him, the ghost vanished, the interview over.

"Interesting," he'd finally said instead. He paused again, and Felix tried not to faint from the horror that he'd humiliated himself with overly romantic scholarly nonsense in front of the savviest tech mind in the industry. But then William added: "That was not the answer I was expecting, by far, but I think I like it."

In the next breath, he asked Felix to start on Monday, and just like that, Felix's life had changed. No more exile. No more grieving for the field of his passion. He was working with maps again—the most powerful one of all.

If only it had worked out as well for Nell.

Instead, she'd gotten Classic.

Felix stood up with a frustrated sigh and walked over to the window.

The Haberson building was deep downtown, but it was one of the tallest skyscrapers in Manhattan. And within it, his and Naomi and Priya's office was so high, sequestered in the private, secure-access upper levels of Haberson where William haunted, pedestrians far below just appeared as tiny dots, and cars as tiny rectangles. Sometimes, when he stared too long at the view, it started to look a little like the simulations HabWalk and HabDrive were running over in their department. Almost like he could be looking at a map of the world rather than the world itself.

He tried not to gaze toward where he knew the NYPL sat along Fifth Avenue to the north and fixated instead on the dark sea amid all the nighttime lights that was Central Park.

He wondered how William got into the building unseen by the rest of his thousands of employees, on the days that he was here. Maybe he had his own secret entrance and elevator. Or maybe he just lived here, and never left, like a true ghost.

Should he text Nell, to apologize? Felix was still hurt by what she'd done, but he also felt terrible about how he'd handled it. Or would that just draw him back into things?

He'd spent seven years feeling bitter that she'd chosen the map over their relationship the first time, unable to let go, and it had cost him so much to hope that this time around, it could be different. He didn't know if he was a bigger fool for having fallen for that hope, or for having cut and run again as soon as he realized their second chance at a fairy tale wasn't going to go exactly the way he'd dreamed.

He wished everything could be as clear as it was on the Haberson servers, within their minute calculations.

"Well, aren't you just the poster boy for hard work," a voice called from the doorway. "Didn't you have a party or something tonight?"

Felix jumped and turned around. "Oh, hey," he said, nodding at Naomi and Priya as they came from the darkness of the hall into the office. He'd shrugged off his tuxedo jacket and left it on the coatrack, but he was still in the crisp white shirt and black slacks. "I left early."

Naomi was studying him suspiciously. "Wasn't tonight the event at the library that you were taking your girlfriend to?" she asked.

He groaned, regretting telling them a little about Nell over the last few days. "Not my girlfriend," he said. "And I just wanted to familiarize myself with the new NYPL part of the server a little more, now that our team is set up there and the scans are starting to come in. We're already up to a hundred thousand."

Naomi and Priya both stared flatly, unconvinced.

"Why are *you two* here on a Sunday night?" he asked, hoping to deflect.

"We're not really," Naomi said. "Priya was having dinner with my wife, Charlotte, and me down the street at Trinity Place. We decided to swing by so she could pick up her dry cleaning."

Priya held up a set of hangers with clothes wrapped in plastic that had been draped over the back of her chair as evidence. "We would have invited you if we knew you weren't at your party."

Felix nodded.

"Are you sure you're okay?" Naomi asked.

"Yeah," he said, so unconvincingly that they all laughed. "Sorry. Just got a lot going on right now."

"You want to talk about it?" Priya asked, propping herself on the side of his desk.

"I was just thinking," he began, slowly spinning in his chair. "Once we have our copies of all the library's maps—"

Naomi threw up her hands. "It's always work with you!"

"I know, I know." He shrugged helplessly.

"Look, Felix," she said after they'd finished chuckling at him. "I have to go—we left Charlotte in the lobby since visitors aren't allowed outside of business hours. You should go home, too."

"I will." He sighed.

"I mean it," she replied, rolling her eyes at his tone. "Go do something not work-related, for once."

"Maybe go apologize to Nell for whatever reason you gave for ditching her at the event you just left," Priya suggested.

Felix groaned. "No, that's definitely over. It wasn't ever *not* over to begin with. But it's definitely over now."

"Felix." Priya sighed, throwing up her arms.

"I don't know," he said, and sighed too. "It's all a mess. There's too much history there."

Naomi shook her head. "This is life, Felix—not a test scenario. It's never going to be perfect. You just have to go for it."

"So inspirational," he replied with mock awe, and she pretended to punch him in the arm. An alert popped up on his screen as Felix rubbed his bicep, catching his attention. "Well, next time you're all going out, let me know. I'd love to meet your wife too, Naomi. And your boyfriend, Priya," he said.

"I'll bring him if you also bring Nell," Priya winked.

He grimaced. "Touché." He glanced at the alert out of the corner of his eye again, trying to see if it was actually an emergency, or if it could wait a moment. "I think I really need to move forward with my life. I'm doing my best to forget about all of that."

Naomi shook her head, sighing, and turned to head toward the door. "There's not a map for this, Felix. If you keep waiting around until you have one, you're going to lose her for good."

But Felix was no longer listening. And neither was Priya, it seemed.

"Hey," she said, her eyes on the screen as well. The alert had flagged part of the NYPL system.

Just then, everyone's phones dinged, and the giant flatscreen overhead turned on.

"Is that the library on the news?" Naomi asked, pointing.

"Again?" Felix sighed, as the door to their office opened abruptly, startling them all.

"William," Naomi said. "What are you doing here on a weekend?"

But William didn't answer the question. "I just got the alert," he replied, his gaze snapping quickly between all of them to make sure they were already aware of it.

"Oh my God," Priya murmured. She turned her phone toward Felix, but she didn't have to—he was already staring at his own.

"The chair of the NYPL has been *murdered*?" he cried.

XVII

The ticking called gently to her, like a beacon in the darkness. Nell wanted to turn her head toward the sound, but when she tried, nothing happened. Her eyelids felt as heavy as stone. But the ticking kept calling. A calm, even click that pulled her closer to waking inch by inch if she focused on it. Its steady rhythm gradually made her aware of her nose, her fingertips, the rise and fall of her chest, the pillow behind her head. And the pain.

Oh, the pain.

"Don't try to sit up," someone said to her. "Francis! *Francis!* She's awake!"

It was Swann. Familiar hands softly pressed her shoulders back down.

"Welcome back, Nell," Francis's measured voice replied as it drew closer. She felt a light touch on her forehead and realized that he was checking under a fold of fabric—a handkerchief pressed there. "You really gave us a scare."

"How is she? How are you?" Swann asked, the last question directed at her. Nell tried to muster a response, but it came out as a groan.

"The bleeding's stopped, and the swelling isn't bad. I think she'll be all right."

"She's going to be all right?" Swann asked, deliriously happy.

Hands were back at the handkerchief, taking away the old wrap and replacing it with fresh material, propping up her head a little. She instantly knew that it was Francis again, not Felix.

Felix was not there. He hadn't come back to find her after the fight.

"Do you remember what happened?" Francis asked her softly.

Nell's eyes finally opened. The room was a fog of blurry streaks and dim lighting. She was reclined on a couch, a cushion under her head. Faintly, she recognized the tall shape and circular face of a grandfather clock in the background—the ticking that had been calling to her—but not much else. Swann and Francis hovered in front of her, crouching by the armrest, and two more blurry shapes floated behind them.

"Nell, thank goodness," one of them said, and Nell's eyes focused enough to recognize Eve's face, and Ramona's beside it. "I thought we were too late."

"How . . ." Nell managed to whisper. Had they also been at the event? Had they come to try to help Francis dissuade her as well?

The attack came back to her in snatches, then. The fight with Felix, running into the Map Division to hide, the sound of the alarms, Swann telling her the police had stormed in, Irene's murder, and clutching her tote bag to her in terror as something—*someone*—overwhelmed her.

Her tote bag.

"My . . . my . . . ," she whispered. Her fingers grasped uselessly at her shoulder, where the bag's straps should have been.

"Oh, my dear, it's gone," Swann said. "Stolen."

No. Nell's head fell back against the cushion. *No.* Her eyes burned, hot and wet.

Her father's portfolio. Her precious, only belonging of her mother's that she owned. And the photograph that Francis had sent her father of the three of them that she'd been keeping inside of it—the only one she'd ever seen of her whole family together.

Gone.

The tears prickled as they slid down her cheeks.

"I'm so sorry," Swann said gently. He was crying a little as well now, not for the portfolio, but for her, at how close he'd come to losing her.

"It was Wally, wasn't it?" Nell finally whispered.

"You saw him?" he asked.

Nell shook her head. She had sensed a vague shadow of a man and felt his iron grip on her arm as she tipped off balance, but it had all happened too fast. "But it had to be him," she managed to choke out before her eyes grew hot and flooded again.

Eve nodded. "There's no one else but us who knows how to do what he did."

Knows how to do what? Nell wondered through the tears.

The rest of the room beyond them finally swam into focus. It was small, with the same fabric pattern on the couch and the same green paint on the walls, the same lights that she was used to, but somehow everything was also unfamiliar.

"Where are we?" she asked.

Swann looked at Francis hesitantly. "Ah," he began, haltingly, as if he didn't entirely believe what he was saying. "Well, we're in . . . the Map Division."

Nell looked around again. It *did* look like the Map Division, but it couldn't be. She knew the place inside and out—there was no room like this. She tried to sit up fully, but a wave of dizziness so strong it made her queasy forced her to lie back down.

"Nell! You need rest!" Swann cried, reaching to steady her.

"I don't know this room," she said. "My head—"

"It's not your head," Francis cut her off gently.

Slowly, he reached his hand back, and Eve handed him a single sheet of paper. He gave it to Nell.

It took her a moment to see through the dizziness what she was looking at.

"This is the Sanborn map of the library you tried to give my father," Nell said. "The one I gave back to Eve at the book fair."

Eve nodded. "I brought it tonight, just in case we needed it."

Francis pointed, and her eyes drifted down the page, to the room Eve had shown her leading off from the main reading room in the Map Division. A room where in reality there wasn't one, she well knew.

"If you have the map . . . you can go there," Francis had whispered to her.

They were inside of it.

Inside of a room that didn't exist.

Nell looked up at him, thunderstruck.

"It's also how I disappeared on you the first time," he said.

"Apparently, my home is quite historical," Swann added, dazed. "Historical enough that there are several old maps of it from earlier centuries still in existence. Someone drew a secret room into it at some point."

"A phantom settlement," she said.

"Yes," Francis said.

"Because they're real. *Real* real," she stammered.

"Yes."

She looked past him, to Ramona. "Your shop . . . I went there the first time using the map my father had drawn on your business card . . ." She swallowed. "That's why I couldn't find it again."

Ramona nodded. "I just wish we could have gotten the Sanborn to him in time." She closed her eyes and gave a shaky sigh. "I don't know how your father realized that Wally suspected he still had the Agloe map all this time and had come back to take it, but when he called me to ask me to find a Sanborn, I knew it had to be the truth. Wally was never going to really give up."

"It was his escape route," Nell said, finally understanding. "If Wally came for him in the library . . ."

Ramona nodded again. "Although it's clear now that Wally found a seventh edition Sanborn of his own at some point. It was how he got into the library the first time—all three times."

Dr. Young's murder, the break-in, and tonight.

"Where's Wally now?" Nell asked.

Francis sighed. "Who knows. He pulled you into the room here, but he didn't realize that Swann, or all of us, would be with you. You dropped your bag as you fell, and he took it and ran before we could stop him." Francis pointed at another door in the wall, one that must lead outside, onto the street.

"You should have gone after him," she said.

"You were bleeding, and unconscious," Eve said softly. "You're our little Nell. We couldn't leave you."

Something passed through the three of them—Francis, Ramona, and Eve—in the silence. They were standing a little bit apart from each other, at a distance strangers would keep—which perhaps they were, after all these years—but the longer they talked, the more the stiffness of their shoulders and the tenseness in their faces began to slowly ebb. There was an undercurrent to their fear now that Nell could just barely see. They were still clearly afraid, but the heart of it, the soil the seed of the fear had grown from, was made of something more like guilt, or shame.

And love, maybe. Trampled and withered.

As she watched them, Nell thought she was finally, truly beginning to understand why things had always been so difficult between her father and her. Why he had seemed to both love her and push her away at the same time.

It was because the closer she got to him, the closer she got to uncovering this secret.

And then when she finally did, that terrible day, the fight they'd had over the Junk Box hadn't been what she'd believed it to be—the cruel retaliation of a powerful, selfish man who didn't want his daughter to someday eclipse his reputation. His reaction was not because she'd stumbled onto simple treasure, but something very dangerous. A curse that had stolen her mother and plagued her father for most of his adult life, and the entirety of hers, as well.

He had not been trying to ruin her, but rather to protect her from Wally, in his own clumsy, rough way. And she had been too stubborn to listen.

But the most important question still remained.

She couldn't say it out loud. Not yet.

She was almost afraid to even *think* it, as if just the hope alone could dispel its possibility.

"What happened after my mother and Wally found the town?" Nell asked instead.

Francis, Ramona, and Eve all looked down again, and the distance between them grew once more.

Nell waited, resolute. She finally knew the truth about Agloe. There was no reason for them to hide the rest of the secrets from her anymore.

At last, Eve looked up, and cleared her throat.

Eve

Everything fell apart, is what happened. Slowly at first, and then all at once, before any of us could stop it.

That first morning, I was awoken by a commotion in the kitchen. I sat up in bed, listening as several voices echoed from downstairs, frantic, excited. Then the door slammed and a spray of gravel pattered across the driveway as tires peeled out.

I dressed quickly and scooted out to the landing, where Bear was poking his head out of his room.

"Did you hear that?" he asked.

Romi and Francis's door opened, too. "Francis?" she called. He must not have been inside with her.

No one answered. Perplexed, we all made our way down and stared at the strange stillness. A half-eaten egg on a plate and a bunch of empty chairs—your high chair included.

"Do you think something happened to Nell?" I asked. "And they rushed to a hospital?"

"No," Bear said. "I couldn't make out much, but I definitely heard Tam say, 'you have to see this,' right before they left."

"'You have to see this?'" Romi repeated, curious. She glanced out the windows, where dappled morning sun was coming in through the trees from the forest beyond. "What could there be to see out here?"

"Maybe some wildlife?" I offered. "Maybe they found some deer—a mother and fawn?"

"I want to see that, too!" Bear smiled.

"I want eggs," Romi replied, and went to the stove. "Anyone else?"

Bear did. I handled the toast, for something to do. I tried to make conversation, but Bear was still too drowsy, and Romi was concentrating on the stove, so everything fell flat until I finally mentioned our *Dreamer's Atlas* after we'd finished eating.

"Let's get it set up!" Romi cried. She was already scanning the living room, figuring out the best way to change the area from lounge to cartography studio.

"You know Tam's just going to argue with you if you do it your way," Bear said with a laugh, carrying plates to the sink.

"She can try." Romi winked at him. "But they took all the good bedrooms because we were late, so fair is fair."

We got to work, pushing furniture to the walls and dragging over the big kitchen table. We scavenged the desks from our bedrooms to serve as research stations and positioned all the lamps where we'd need them for detail work. Then we unpacked the maps we'd brought, poring over each one excitedly. It wasn't until a car rumbled up the driveway that we realized it was already early afternoon.

"Where have you all been?" Romi asked as Tam, Wally, Francis, and Daniel, carrying you, came into the living room. "It's past lunch!"

"Did you bring any, by any chance?" Bear asked.

"Forget lunch," Daniel said. His voice sounded the same as when they'd all left—exhilarated, confused. I was closest—he threw a set of car keys to me. "Follow us."

"What's going on?" Romi asked.

"You won't believe it unless you see it," Tam said.

"Try us," Bear grinned, feeding off their energy. All of them, except Wally, were practically vibrating with excitement. "What did you find, guys?"

"I don't know if . . . ," Wally murmured, and then fell silent.

Somehow, despite the volume of our conversation, Tam heard him. She put a hand on his shoulder. "The glory is Wally's. Couldn't have done it without him."

"I . . ." He trailed off.

"Come on, Wally," Bear said teasingly. "No point fighting it."

Tam gave his shoulder another reassuring squeeze, and Wally sighed, acquiescing. He knew it was true. Whatever belonged to one of us, belonged to all seven of us.

Especially Tam.

"A town," he said at last.

At that, the rest of them jumped in over him, interrupting each other. Bear, Romi, and I listened in stunned silence. They told us they'd found a town, but not just any town . . . a hidden place, just a few minutes down the road. So invisible that you could drive or walk by every day for your entire life and never know it was there, accessible only if you had the key.

You can imagine our reactions.

"That," Romi finally said, "is the biggest load of bull I've ever heard."

It sounded like something out of a children's fantasy novel.

At first, I thought maybe that was it, that it was a game for you Tam had made up on the drive home from wherever they'd been. Some off-the-cuff legend about a magical kingdom right around the corner that might keep you entertained during the day and give us easy material from which to make up bedtime stories at night. That was certainly how you were taking it—you were clapping your hands as Daniel shifted you from arm to arm, singing about "Mommy's town"—but the longer Tam talked, pacing the living room so intensely I was afraid she was going to knock something over, it was clear this wasn't something she'd made up for you. Or us.

My second guess had been that this was supposed to be a preproject brainstorming experiment, to loosen us up and get us into the creative flow. But she, our most ambitious, dedicated cartographer in the group, hadn't even *noticed* that we'd gotten started on the *Dreamer's Atlas*. I could see the confusion clouding Romi's and Bear's expressions as well.

Tam was describing this town like it was a *real* place. Streetlights, gas stations, restaurants, houses with picket fences and manicured gardens. Not the kind of thing you'd put in a children's bedtime story, or an intellectual exercise for our project, at all.

"Hurry," Daniel said, heading for the cars again. "We're going to drive side by side, with the windows open, so you can see."

"See what?" Bear asked, already following him as Romi and I ran after.

Tam held something up as Wally, Daniel, and you got into their car, and I struggled to unlock ours. "This," she grinned.

It was that damned gas station map.

I drove, with Bear and Romi in the back and Francis up front with me—he was riding with us to help with this strange operation, since he knew what was going on—and we eased down the deserted county road as slowly as possible, so we could be tire to tire with Wally.

"I am totally confused," Bear said.

"Seriously. An imaginary town?" Romi added.

"Just trust me," Francis said to me, ignoring them as they chattered, with such earnestness in his voice that it made my heart flutter, despite my not wanting it to. "Look there."

Tam had spread the map across their dashboard, so that Wally could see it as he drove, and I could just barely make it out as well. She put her finger on the road where we were and began tracing slowly, checking to make sure we were both watching.

"Are we talking about that error she found the night before?" I asked, struggling to keep us as close as possible without swiping their car. "Francis, we all just drove up yesterday, and there was nothing—"

"What the *hell*?" Romi swore, at the same moment that I almost crashed into them.

After we'd all parked on the shoulder, cars mercifully undamaged, we scrambled out to stand beside the others. To stare down the dirt road at an entire town I *knew* had not been there yesterday.

"How is this possible?" Bear stammered at last.

"Is it safe?" I asked. "Did you take Nell in—"

"It's safe," Tam said. "I promise. Wally and I explored it first, before we brought the others." She bounced you on her hip. "You want to go on another adventure, Nelly?" she cooed.

And we did. We went on an adventure.

I can't properly describe it to you even now, Nell. Agloe defies explanation. It's impossible to convey just how remarkable it was, because anything I say will make it sound like just a town. And it was just a town—but it was a town that *didn't exist*. Or rather, it didn't exist anywhere but within the map. How could that be possible? And yet, it was.

That day, we spent a few hours in Agloe, tentatively peeking into a few buildings, trying to understand how it was all possible.

It was an eerie place. Full, but empty. There were houses and buildings, but no furniture, no occupants. Gardens and parks, but no pedestrians strolling through. A gas station with a functioning pump, but no cars, other than our own. In the diner, there wasn't any food or sign the grill had ever been used, but somehow, the utilities and appliances worked. The stove had gas, the lights had electricity. Water ran from the sinks. It was like the whole place had been set up, ready for something, but then lost, or forgotten.

There's so much we could tell you about that town. And we will—but that isn't the point. The point is what it did to all of us.

We didn't realize how long we'd been there until the sun started to set. That spooked us—it had seemed safe so far, but can you imagine being inside a huge, fully built, completely deserted town like that at night? We sped back down the dirt road that led out of Agloe and to County Road 206 as fast as we could. As I drove, wheel to wheel with Wally, for a moment I worried that somehow we wouldn't be able to leave. That the road would end without meeting back up with the real world, and we'd be trapped inside forever. We all did—everyone's eyes were as desperately locked onto that little scrap of old paper as mine.

But the map showed us the way out, just as it had shown us the way in. I don't think Tam folded it back up until we were all the way to the house, on familiar ground again.

We stumbled up the porch as quickly as we could, eager to get out of the dark.

"I'm starving," Bear said, as we all realized we hadn't eaten since breakfast. "Let's get dinner going."

"Let's get *drinks* going," Francis replied. "I'm going to need a lot more than dinner after that."

But when we made it inside, conversation stilled.

"I totally forgot," I said.

"The *Dreamer's Atlas,*" Romi added. "We got it all set up."

We all looked across the kitchen, to the assembled workspace in the living room. To where our project, once an all-consuming passion, sat utterly forgotten.

Slowly, I went over and picked up the first map I'd started working on before Tam and the others had come back to get us. It was the Franklin, loaned to Romi by the Madison Geography Society for our project, one of the most valuable in our fledgling collection.

Except now, it seemed so . . . insignificant.

The entire *Dreamer's Atlas* did.

How *could* it be important, after what we'd just discovered? How could we simply go back to working on mundane, ordinary maps, when we now knew about the secret this one held? How could we marvel at the invented places on the literary maps, nothing more than figments of imagination, when we knew there was a place like Agloe?

"Someone get the wine," Tam said then. When I turned to her, I was surprised to see not the same confusion that was on everyone else's face, but instead a fierce clarity—the same expression she always got when she was on the verge of a breakthrough back in Wisconsin.

"What are you thinking?" Wally asked, hesitant.

"You'll see." She grinned. "But we're going to need to get really drunk first."

I'm sure you can imagine what Tam had realized.

We decided to change our *Dreamer's Atlas* project. It would no longer be about reversing the styles of fictional and historical maps so they mirrored each other, to evoke a sense of wonder and magic about cartography—rather, it would be about Agloe. About how it was possible that it existed, how there could be two places at once in the same geography.

We would produce only two maps now, but they would be the two most important maps in existence. One would be of the known world, the one that everyone could see and experience, and the other would be of Agloe.

And then we would show the world both places.

We were dizzy with the possibilities. We believed that by finishing our reenvisioned project, a whole new understanding of how maps worked, and their relation to the world, would open up to us. Our ambitions in the first place had been to revolutionize cartography—but how silly that grand idea seemed now that we'd found Agloe. How little we'd truly known about maps, only just hours ago. How little *everyone* knew, really.

Because as far as we could tell, no one else had ever found, or published, anything even remotely like this.

The day after we found Agloe, as Tam and Romi were brainstorming how to begin our project again from scratch, Francis and Daniel drove to the nearest college, the State University of New York at New Paltz, about an hour and a half away, where they used the catalog system to call for every book and academic journal that might be relevant—but there wasn't a single mention of anything like this, anywhere. There were plenty of articles about psychogeography, and the concept of phantom settlements, from artistic and legal perspectives, but nothing about phantom settlements being *real*.

No one else knew about Agloe.

No one that was still alive, anyway.

While Francis and Daniel were at the college, Wally took the other car to do some research on the original makers of the map, General Drafting Corporation. They'd been incredibly productive in the early 1900s, the era from which our map had come, but by the time we'd stumbled onto our copy, their profits had been in decline for some time. The founder and his closest drafters—the ones who had made our edition—had all died decades before, and those running the company now seemed to have no connection to them, and knew nothing about the secret within their work, either. In fact, they seemed only concerned with revenue and were considering selling what remained of General Drafting to some big sightseeing guide conglomerate, where their work would dissolve into the existing structure.

"They told me all about the founder, Otto G. Lindberg, his top cartographer Ernest Alpers, and gave me a tour of the whole drafting room and the archives," Wally told us when he'd gotten back from

General Drafting's sole remaining office in New Jersey. On the table, he'd spread out a huge pile of their maps and put them in order—General Drafting didn't have backstock for every year for such a cheap, disposable product line, but Wally had brought back at least half of them. "I begged them to let me buy these as souvenirs. They were so tickled that anyone could be such a fan, they just gave them to me for free. If you look"—he opened each one, until there was no room left on the table—"Agloe doesn't appear on any of them but our 1930 edition."

Daniel studied the assortment of useless General Drafting maps in front of us. "And they didn't have any more copies for that year?"

Wally shook his head. "None, and I poked around for an hour. The oldest I was able to find in their files was this 1941." He held up one, badly aged. "The office, believe it or not, is an old Tudor-style castle some wealthy family built in the early 1900s. Pretty neat looking, but terrible for conservation and storage. Their basement was a mess—humid in summer, drafty in winter. It would be hard for old paper to stand up to that."

"What about the old lawsuit Francis found in the county logs?" I asked. "Did you ask them about it?"

"Yeah, but I didn't get anywhere," Wally replied. "The secretary said she always assumed that since there are no files from the case, the founder, Lindberg, must have settled and had the records sealed as part of that agreement, to protect General Drafting's reputation. Except business never really bounced back after that."

"Or . . . ," Tam said.

Wally nodded. "Or they took the loss because they were trying to protect this place. No matter the cost."

"So, even if the founder knew he'd created Agloe, if they worked that hard to keep it hidden, we really might be the only ones who know about it *now*," Daniel mused. "We really could do this. To show the world. We really could be the first, with our new *Dreamer's Atlas*."

"We really could," Tam said, leaning close to the fire we'd made that night in the pit, so she could speak to us over the top of your drowsy head.

"We just have to keep it a secret," Wally echoed, his gaze far away. "Our secret."

We could do that, I thought. This was the biggest discovery any of us would ever make—that anyone in the entire cartography industry would ever make. I couldn't imagine any of us doing something to jeopardize that.

And we didn't. As you know now, Nell, there isn't anyone else out there who knows that Agloe exists but us. We did keep it a secret.

We just didn't know that it would also be keeping all of ours.

I don't know how it happened—isn't that what everyone who betrays someone says? But I don't know how it happened. I just know why. If we had never found Agloe, if we had all never gone inside . . .

But we did find it, and we did go inside.

And suddenly, there was somewhere I could hide my secret. Not just a glance that someone might notice, a whisper someone might hear, or a risky stolen moment that someone might stumble upon, but an entire town. I could bury it down deep there, where it would never be found.

Work began in earnest on our new *Dreamer's Atlas*. Every spare moment that we weren't sleeping, we were working on our masterpiece, with even more fervor than we'd already had. It used to amaze me back at the university how much our ideas could grab hold of us, but our studies had been nothing compared to this.

Even though everything about our project was now different, the way that we worked didn't change at all, as if we were fated for it. Tam and Romi, our artists, would be responsible for drawing our two new maps of the same, but not same, area—Romi, with her exacting hand and lines more steady than a compass and protractor, would lead the drafting of the real-world version of the Sullivan County and Catskills territory, and Tam, with her boundless creativity and artistic eye, would lead the drafting of Agloe. The next time we went into our mysterious phantom settlement, they took over an empty ice cream parlor off the central square and made it our headquarters, where they spread out notes across the bare counters and taped up dozens of preliminary sketches on the huge front window, so they could use the light to quickly trace revisions.

Daniel, our goof, always throwing curveballs to make us think deeper, and Bear, forever game to be included in his adventures, were tasked with gathering the references and research Romi would need to conceptualize her map—so she could make it as real and accurate as possible, while still allowing for the possibility that Tam's map could exist therein. In their efforts to understand how the town worked, and how it was connected to the real world, if at all, the two of them became obsessed with experimenting on a cluster of six vacant houses and a small diner in a single neighborhood block they claimed for themselves. Daniel dug up power lines, Bear tried to follow telephone poles. They brought groceries and pans and plates from Rockland and made lunch at the diner for the rest of the group. They took us on boat rides from the vacant boat rental shop on Beaverkill River, which ran through the town. The rest of us were still so unnerved by the sheer impossibility of it all, I don't know how much we really enjoyed it, but you loved it, Nell. It was the perfect summer adventure for a kid. Your laughter would ring out across that empty place, echoing off every window and roof.

And last but not least, Wally, our details genius, was consumed with the research he'd started on General Drafting, obsessed with tracking down every single reference he could find to every single article, to ensure that we truly were the only ones who knew about Agloe.

That left Francis and me, our group's usual surveyors, to handle exactly that, so that Tam would be able to draw her map of the town.

It was overwhelming, to say the least. Before, we'd had perfect references—London was going to be drawn like Discworld's Ankh-Morpork, the neighborhoods of New York City like the islands of Earthsea, and Narnia like Cassini's 1744 map of France—we could compare one paper map to another paper map, and tweak the scale and style to make them match. But while Daniel and Bear, when they were not experimenting, could pull data from historical maps of the Rockland area for Romi, Agloe was entirely new to us. The place would have to be walked and measured from scratch, if Tam would have any hope of rendering it well.

With a whole team, it can take weeks to survey a town, and Francis and I were only two. Even so, no one noticed that we took far longer than we should have to complete each neighborhood.

Ever since that almost-disastrous night last year, I'd been ashamed to be around Romi, but I'd sworn outright never to be alone with Francis. It was easy enough with such a large group, and I thought it was the most respectful thing I could do, even though neither of them would ever know I was doing it. So, the first time Tam insisted we do the survey work, I refused. Even more than not wanting to break my private vow, I was terrified that although I'd shoved my feelings down deep, and would rather have died than act on them, Francis would be able to sense them anyway, and then might remember that night, and everything would be ruined. I would lose him, and all of the others. I finally understood why Bear was always so desperate to keep us all happy. He and I were the last ones in, and the easiest to discard, if we threatened the harmony of the rest.

But Tam was insistent. And no one could ever say no to her.

"Please," she begged, graph paper in her hands, pencils tucked behind both ears, pushing us out of the ice cream shop as the bell jangled.

"We need the data if we're going to get anywhere," Romi agreed. "Francis is a good surveyor, but he can't see the forest for the trees, sometimes."

Neither could she.

Our first day out, I barely said anything, I was so nervous I might trigger a hazy recollection of that horrible, alcohol-soaked night. Francis was so fascinated with the town, I don't think he noticed how quiet I was. But by the second day, it was obvious. He tried to get me to talk, and when he got nothing more than one-word answers, he spent the whole time talking instead, to fill the uncomfortable silence. He was funny, very funny. His humor was almost as sharp as Daniel's then, although you wouldn't know it now. By the third day, I finally talked, and Francis didn't bring up Bear's old party, to my immense relief. By the end of the week, I was finally convinced that he really didn't remember at all.

Who noticed the printing factory first, I don't remember. But we turned a corner in the shopping district off Main Street, and both of us laughed out loud at the sight, caught by surprise.

It looked just like the one where we'd celebrated Bear's birthday—the old printer and bindery downtown that had been fashionably renovated into a speakeasy.

"Wow," he said, reaching for the door. "What are the odds."

Inside, it looked just like every other place in Agloe. Clean, lit, and empty. Francis began exploring, opening every cabinet, while I tried to take notes about the basic dimensions and location, like we were supposed to be doing.

"Look!" he yelled from the next room.

I came around the corner and gasped as I saw what he was pointing at—a hulking old-fashioned printing press. Just like the one that had been at Bear's party. Or perhaps all old-fashioned printing presses look the same.

But it was even in the same place as it had been at the speakeasy, not in the center of the room but rather in a far, darkened corner—where Francis and I had found ourselves huddled near the end of that night, our backs against its bulky frame, shielded from view while the rest of the party continued obliviously on the other side. Where I leaned in to him, and almost destroyed everything, and then saved it again in the nick of time.

I watched Francis nervously as he looked at it. Did he remember now? Did he know? But he seemed mostly proud he'd found an actual object in Agloe—whereas almost every other building and house was unfurnished. Not confused, not guilty. I breathed a sigh of relief.

"Do you think General Drafting's founder and his assistant brought it?" he asked. "That's why it's here, when so little else is?"

"Maybe," I allowed. It was an offset press, with a rubber roller to transfer images—ancient technology by today's standards, but right for its time.

Later, the more we explored, we found small hints that there had been other groups there before us, in addition to the two men who had mysteriously or accidentally created this place. An old empty rucksack with a tag from the 1960s, a broken doorknob in one of the cafés. Probably tourists, or teenagers, who had once owned a copy of this same map back when they were in print, and wandered in and became trapped, not understanding what was happening.

Or perhaps they did understand—but they turned on each other before they could reveal this secret to the world.

It seemed to have gone that way for Otto G. Lindberg and Ernest Alpers, after all. And would slowly happen to us, too.

But that printing press was the very first sign we found that anyone else had been here ever before—and also the most important one, by far.

Francis crossed his arms. "What do you think they were planning to do with it?"

I could imagine a couple of possibilities, all of them tantalizing. Were they hoping to print more copies of their Agloe map? Or experiment with adding more secrets to other maps? But I didn't say any of them.

"I don't know, but we should go. We have a lot of neighborhood still to cover," I replied instead. Even if Francis didn't remember what had happened, I still wanted us out of there. We could tell the others about it, and come back later all together, when it would be safer to spend more time there. When Francis and I wouldn't be alone.

"Yeah," he agreed, but he was still examining the machine. "Too bad there isn't paper," he sighed.

"Why do you want paper?" I asked.

"Because then we could have a speakeasy here, in Agloe," he joked. "One Daily News, hot off the presses!" He cried out the undercover drink name like the bartender-disguised-as-a-draftsman had, pulling a lever. His impression was so spot on, we both burst out laughing. I don't know why it was so funny, but we couldn't stop.

"I can't believe I almost—" I started to say as I wiped my eyes, and then choked the sentence off, horrified.

Francis and I stared at each other, both of us frozen in the silence.

"Kissed me?" he asked.

He did remember.

"No," I said. I took a step back. "Let's forget it. Let's just go."

He was looking down now, at his hands. They clenched nervously, his fingers twisted into knots.

"I don't understand," he finally said, so softly. The openness of it stopped me cold. "Nothing happened, but I feel so bad about it. I don't know what's wrong with me."

"Nothing's wrong with you," I said, coming back over to him. He looked so upset, like he might start ripping his hair out, or burst into sobs. I just wanted to stop him from spiraling. The shame wasn't his, but mine. I wanted to take it from him. "You had nothing to do with it—it was my fault. I was so drunk. We all were so drunk. It didn't mean anything."

"Then why can't I stop thinking about it?" he asked. "Why can't I stop thinking about you?"

We were standing too close, I realized. Much too close. He was so near I could feel the warmth of his breath on my forehead. See the flecks of amber in his dark brown eyes.

The kiss was so hard and sudden, our teeth bumped, but I hardly noticed. Everything was on fire—my face, my skin, my insides. I was gasping, about to either faint or explode. We were against a wall, and then I was on the floor, Francis against me. We almost tore his shirt, we moved so desperately. I pulled him to me.

The town was big, but I still clamped my hand over my mouth, and he put his over mine, to hide my cries at the end.

I wish I could say that was the only time. But it wasn't.

We betrayed Romi again, and again, for the entire summer. Every spare moment we could find together, we drove the blade of our secret deeper.

I became sick with the guilt. I had trouble eating, lost weight. Even Daniel, who wouldn't notice a new hairstyle if a person had cut their whole head off, asked me if I was all right. And even still, I kept begging Francis to meet me, in darkened corners of that town. I had spent so long denying what I felt for him, and kept doing it still, in the world out there, every time we all went back. Agloe was the only place it was real.

We were so caught up in our secret, we didn't see what was happening to everyone else around us. Not until it was too late.

XVIII

Somewhere outside the room, in the Map Division, the shouts of a police officer running by reached them, and Nell jumped, startled out of the story.

"Don't worry," Ramona assured her. "They won't find us. Without a map, it's just a wall to them. There's no way in."

Eve seemed to shrink even further at the sound of Ramona's voice, unable to look at her.

"What's past is past. We all lost something," Ramona said, but she didn't look at Eve or Francis either. "Besides, we all were at fault. I have just as much to regret as you."

"Felix!" Swann said then, his memory sparked by Ramona's words, and he patted his pockets frantically. "I've been sitting here watching over you with such terror that I didn't even think to call him! Does my phone even work here, where we are?" His bony hand yanked his phone from his blazer at last. "I can't believe I forgot—"

"No, don't," Nell interrupted sharply, and grimaced at the throb of pain across her forehead that doing so caused.

"You don't . . . want me to call him?" Swann asked, surprised. "You don't want him to know?"

"I don't want to see him," she answered. And he certainly didn't want to see her either, she thought bitterly.

He studied her, puzzled. "But you were hurt, Nell. Attacked!"

"No, Swann," she repeated, as firmly as she could manage with her pounding head. "Please, just don't."

Swann watched her for a long moment. "That's why you were upset. Something happened," he said at last. "Again."

"Again," Nell agreed, sighing.

He looked down. "I'm very sorry about that."

Nell winced as another wave of pain rolled through. The waves were fainter each time, but they still sent her reeling—almost as much as thinking about how badly she'd ruined things with Felix did. "We don't have time for that now."

Swann finally nodded, agreeing to let the conversation go. He took a small envelope from his jacket pocket. "Well, there's something I need to give you. That gift I mentioned."

She took it from him. "It's from my father," Nell murmured when she saw Swann's name in his handwriting. The others leaned in as well, surprised. "But how?"

"I found it in my library mailbox just before the unveiling event earlier tonight. With everything that's happened, I hadn't gone to check it since . . . He must have put it there just before . . ." He swallowed hard.

Nell put a hand on his arm. "You didn't open it yet," she said gently.

His smile was sad. "I thought we'd do it together."

They both looked back to the letter. Slowly, Nell worked the flap free.

Swann,

I'm going to say something very uncharacteristic, so save this letter, because it'll be the only time: I'm sorry.

I'm sorry for being such a boorish bastard, for antagonizing our researchers over every project and article, for always voting so obstinately on every department motion. But most of all, I'm sorry for hurting you and Nell. But I promise you, everything I've done—every single thing—was to protect her.

She is the most important thing to me in the world.

I'm going to call her tonight. I'm going to tell her everything.

But if something happens to me first, I'll need your help. I need you to destroy the map from the Junk Box Incident. I know, I know. But I don't have time to explain. You know where it is, that old spot. Take it and tear it to shreds as quickly as you can. It's the only way to keep Nell safe.

And give this to her. I know it isn't much, but it's the only picture of her mother I kept.

Tell her I love her, Swann. That I always have.

Thank you, old friend, and I love you, too.

Daniel

Nell didn't realize she'd been crying until a tear landed on her knuckle, dangerously close to the letter. She glanced up quickly, at the dimly glowing chandelier in the ceiling of their imaginary, not-imaginary room, until it was no longer blurry. She knew she probably looked silly, but she didn't care. They were her father's last words to Swann, and to her, in a way. She was terrified of getting the page wet and making the ink run.

"I'm sorry, my dear," Swann said, equally teary. "I don't know why he wrote to me instead of you."

"You know me, and so did he," Nell said. "If this letter had shown up on my doorstep with no explanation right before he died, I would have thrown it away out of spite."

Swann wiped his eyes, chuckling. "He could be wise, at times. But if only I'd found it sooner. I could have spared you all this danger."

"I'm glad you didn't," she said. She would have been safer without the Agloe map, but she also never would have had the chance to finally understand what this had all been about—and to maybe forgive her father.

Swann smiled again and scooted closer to her. At last, Nell pulled out the photograph.

"That's the road to Agloe," Ramona said, surprised. "The first day that Tam and Wally brought all of us there."

Nell glanced at the back, where someone had long ago written *Tam, Daniel, Nell, Francis, Romi, Eve, Bear* and then turned it over again to study the picture. Everyone was posed in a row in the caption's order, in the middle of a dirt road, some smiling, some still looking dazed. Wally, she assumed, was the invisible one behind the camera. Off to the side, two cars, both with their doors flung wide open, were parked crookedly. And just behind them, Nell could barely make out the unfocused shape of buildings on the horizon—a town.

She gasped as her eyes reached the seventh, last face in line.

"That's Bear," Eve confirmed, pointing.

Nell stared. She could not believe it.

"We have to go," she said, struggling to sit up. "You can tell me what happened next on the way, Francis."

"What? Why?" Swann asked. "The police are very likely still looking for you! And who knows where Wally is!"

"All the more reason not to wait!"

"But it doesn't matter," Francis replied, cutting her off gently. He could clearly see what she was thinking. "You can't get to Agloe without the map. There won't be anything there but a field."

"But we do have the Agloe map," Nell said.

Swann shook his head. "It's gone, remember?"

Nell swung her legs over the couch. The last lingering wave of nausea crested—she closed her eyes and held her breath until it passed. Her head was finally clear.

"No, it's not," she said.

"Your bag was stolen in the attack," Swann said patiently. "Everything that was in it—your wallet, your phone, the portfolio . . . all stolen. Wally has the map now."

Nell's feet found her shoes. "No, he doesn't."

The rest of them faltered, confused.

She rose to a full stand, shaky, and then firm. She turned to them. "Because the Agloe map wasn't in the portfolio."

"I don't understand," Francis said.

As he, Ramona, Eve, and Swann stared at Nell, stunned, she looked back to the photo again. At the last face in the line of friends, grinning even more broadly than the others, so unexpected and yet so familiar at the same time.

"I hid it," she said.

"Where, my dear?" Swann asked.

She still could not believe it. But all of it made sense now—how much Bear had cared for her, in the others' stories. How he had helped her when almost no one else would, reputations be damned.

She turned the photo around so Swann could see it.

"At Classic," she said.

Bear was Humphrey.

Francis

The weeks dragged, each one more strange. It seemed like that summer passed in an instant, a surreal, horrible blur that could have been just a single day, and also never ended.

The day the Sullivan County Government Center was burgled, the house woke up to yet another argument between Tam and Romi. Romi had made a good start on the real-world map, enough that Tam was ready to begin drafting her version of the same area, but almost immediately, the two of them had butted heads. Romi wanted Tam to do what she'd done on her map—render Agloe precisely, as accurately as possible—because she believed that would be the only way to understand how it worked. But Tam wanted to start experimenting right away. We'd told everyone about the printing press when we'd found it, and she wanted to use it for her version. What better way to understand what General Drafting's founder had been doing? Who cared if it wouldn't match Romi's aesthetic? Romi argued that the variables were too great, that the significance of our project would lie in comparing the two places, not contrasting them. But Tam's imagination couldn't be stopped.

"They're just notes! You have your own scratch paper, too!" Tam was shouting when I came stumbling down the stairs that morning, still in my pajamas.

"But I'm not hiding the map they go with!" Romi shouted back.

"I'm not hiding a map, either! And I'm definitely not the one snooping through your things!"

They were squared off in the living room, and Daniel, Eve, and Bear were trying to run interference. Daniel, especially, looked at his wit's end—I knew how he felt. The strain on Romi from their constant arguments was probably the same as that on Tam. Some nights, after everyone had gone to bed and just he and I were outside by the fire, he'd confess he was starting to feel a little desperate about this place.

That it might be tearing us apart rather than bringing us closer together, the way our project was supposed to. That he had to do something, before it spiraled out of control.

I ached to tell him about what was happening with Eve. I came close many times. But Daniel had always been so carefree before, even during finals—I had never seen him like this. I didn't want to add even more strain by asking him to carry my guilt with me.

"If you're not hiding anything, why are you accusing me of snooping, then?" Romi cried.

"Please, don't shout," Wally begged from the kitchen, where he was distracting you from the argument by letting you make a mess with a box of Cheerios.

"What's going on?" I asked, before they could start again.

It turned out Tam had come downstairs to see Romi going through her notes—not notes they shared from their drafts at the ice cream parlor, but notes Romi had taken from the printing factory, without Tam knowing. Tam had sworn to us that she only went there for inspiration and wouldn't actually use the printing press for her map unless we all agreed, but Romi was convinced Tam was already working on a draft in secret. She couldn't shake the feeling she was being lied to, she whispered to me so many nights as we got ready for bed.

She was right. She just didn't know that the betrayal was coming from me.

"Everyone, listen," Eve interrupted, pointing. The television had been on in the corner amid all this.

"—arrived at the Government Center today, where all legislative archives for the county are kept, to find the building had been broken into overnight. There were no injuries, but damage to some of the glass displays in the public hall have been reported, and it appears that some items from the Local Sullivan County History exhibit are missing."

"The place was robbed?" Bear asked.

Onscreen, a montage of photos from the municipal building—the jimmied front door, shards of glass on the tile floor, yellow police tape—rotated. "Detectives have not named a suspect, but are working with county officials to . . ."

Daniel studied the screen. "Hey, Wally," he called. "Isn't that where you went last week?"

Wally appeared, holding you in one arm and the cereal box in the other. "Yeah," he confirmed. "I'm glad no one was hurt."

"What were you doing there?" Tam asked, surprised.

"Looking up administrative records for the county. I wanted to see if anyone had ever logged Agloe as a location for a residence or business," he answered. "Don't worry, there was nothing. No addresses, no tax files."

"Do you remember the exhibit mentioned?" I asked.

Wally shrugged. "Only junk. Old photographs of the first settled dairy farms, stamps from the post office. The kind of stuff those places always have."

A junk shop had our Agloe map, I was about to say. But the reporter had shifted stories, and a burst of festive music for some outdoor fair began playing.

Tam turned to Romi again. "I'll show you my notes anytime," she said. "I'll show you anything you want. But please ask me first."

Romi sighed. "I'm sorry. This is all just—a lot."

"Why don't we finish breakfast and go to the town together?" I suggested, before Romi could consider her nagging suspicion further. Before she might realize that it wasn't Agloe causing her to feel the way she did, but me.

But Wally didn't come with us that day. He had an appointment at the university in New Paltz again, to review more of the journal loans he'd requested. If we all had our own angles of obsession with Agloe, Wally's was definitely all about its secrecy from the rest of the world. He was fascinated with how utterly devoid of mention such a phenomenon was in any of the industry literature and research, and how completely oblivious the entire county and surrounding lands seemed to be to its existence.

At least, that's what I thought he was thinking, at the time.

I didn't start to put it together until a few weeks after that, when Bear discovered that Daniel had also been lying to everyone.

• • • •

We had just come back from Agloe, six adults plus you unwisely crammed into one car since Wally had the other, but County Road 206 was never busy, so the chance of an accident was low.

Everyone was exhausted and hoping that Wally had beat us home and started dinner. When we saw the other car in the driveway, we let out a weak, rejoicing cry. Romi and I carried the group's papers and drafts up the steps to the door, while Eve helped Tam and Daniel coax you out of the car.

"I'll be right back," Bear said, jogging down the driveway. "Going to check the mail."

"He's becoming obsessed with the mail," Romi said to me as we knocked, waiting for Wally to let us in.

"It's his family's house," I shrugged, though it was true, Bear seemed to check the mail more and more often the longer we were there—sometimes more than once a day, as if he'd forgotten he'd already looked, or couldn't help himself—but I didn't think much of it. I had far worse things to worry about. "He probably feels responsible to maintain it while we're all here."

"It's kind of weird such an out-of-the-way vacation house that no one regularly lives in gets so much mail in the first place, isn't it?" she asked. She raised her voice as Bear started back toward the house, flipping through the envelopes he'd gathered. "Anything good?"

Bear shrugged. "Just ads!" he yelled back.

"There all of you are," Wally said behind us, opening the door. "It's getting late."

"Please tell me you started dinner," Tam said to him as she, you, Daniel, and Eve joined us on the porch.

But Wally wasn't looking at us anymore. "Bear, what's wrong?" he asked.

Bear had stalled right before the steps. He was staring down at the pile in his hands—whatever letter was on top had caught his eye.

"Bear?" Romi echoed.

Bear finally looked up. He lifted the envelope and turned it toward us. "What's this?" he asked.

I could barely make out the wording on the front in the dying light.

Professor Johansson
University of Wisconsin
Science Hall, Room 346
550 N Park St
Madison, WI 53706

And in the upper left corner where the return address, to *this* house, was written—Daniel's name was there as the sender.

Tam turned to him. We all did.

"Did you . . . ," she tried to say.

Daniel had told Professor Johansson about the town.

"But why?" Wally asked.

"I thought he could help!" he cried. "The further we get with this project, the more we disagree! You've found nothing in any of the research out there, Bear and I can't make sense of the town from the inside, Francis and Eve aren't even halfway done surveying, and Romi and Tam are fighting over Tam's map so much, she can't even start!" He threw up his hands. "Professor Johansson was our advisor for every paper. Our mentor! Who else can we trust, if not him?"

Before, we'd each done things like this a thousand times—taken the lead on various parts of projects, made a change to an article without consulting the rest. But it was because back then, we could all trust that the choices we were making were for the good of us all. Now, everything felt like a secret, so every revelation felt like a betrayal.

Daniel admitted everything as we all argued—he'd written the letter and dropped it off at the post office when it was his turn to make our grocery run. He swore it was the only one he'd sent, and that he was going to tell us what Professor Johansson advised the moment he received a reply—but no amount of confession was enough for us. Even though the person Daniel had turned to was our beloved professor, Daniel had gone behind our backs and tried to let someone else in on our secret.

"But it doesn't matter! It didn't even get there," Daniel finally said, snatching the envelope from Bear. "Look!"

There was a big red blot beside the stamp that read INSUFFICIENT POSTAGE—the letter had never been delivered and had returned here.

But the damage had already been done.

"I don't need this," Daniel finally said, turning away from us. "Come on, Nelly. Let's get you something to eat." He scooped you up and stomped through the door.

Wally started after him, the raw fury of Daniel's betrayal still smoldering in his eyes, but Tam stopped him.

"Let me," she said.

"But it's not fair," Wally said. "He can't—"

"Just give me a minute."

She followed Daniel, despite Wally's protests. He stood on the porch fuming, so upset he wasn't able to even speak as we hesitantly tried to comfort him. We were all angry, but it was hitting Wally the hardest by far. Maybe because he was the one who was the most nervous about our ability to keep Agloe a secret until we'd finished our project—or maybe because Tam seemed to have taken Daniel's side in this, even though he was in the wrong.

By the time we all finally went in, Tam was alone with you in the kitchen, getting out the plates for the dinner Wally had started. Daniel was already gone, hiding upstairs to brood.

Dinner was horrible—a tense, silent affair with Wally seething, Tam hurt by Daniel but playing peacemaker for the good of the group, and the rest of us caught somewhere in the middle. By midnight, Daniel still hadn't come downstairs, and Wally still hadn't mellowed. When I finally went to bed, Wally was the last one in the living room, glaring stonily out one of the windows into the night. I was dreading tomorrow.

But Tam must have talked some sense into Daniel overnight, because the next morning, he came downstairs once the rest of us—save Wally—had gathered for breakfast, looking repentant. He apologized again and promised he wouldn't send another letter. Romi suggested that I take over Daniel's turns to make grocery runs for the group to help rebuild some of the lost trust, and he agreed.

"Wally will be happy to hear this," Tam said, glancing back toward the stairs. "Hey, Wally!" she cried. "Daniel has something he'd like to say to you."

But the upstairs remained silent.

"Do you think he could still be that mad?" Romi asked.

Tam handed Bear the spoon she'd been feeding you breakfast with, but I stood up.

"Let me go," I offered. "Impartial party."

Upstairs, Wally's door was closed. I knocked, but I didn't hear him stir. I knocked again.

"Okay, I'm alone, I'm coming in," I said, and pushed the door open, but the room was empty.

Wally was gone. He'd left before any of us had even woken up—off to do more of his mysterious research, alone.

I thought he just needed a day to cool off, but things stayed that way for weeks. In fact, the more time we all spent in Agloe, it seemed that Wally spent even *less*. He was gone more often, and for longer each time, and had become even more brusque about what exactly he was researching, whenever someone did ask. He just insisted that it was important, and we leave him to it.

We let him carry on. He was always our fail-safe, for every project. We believed that whatever angle he was working, it would be important to the *Dreamer's Atlas*.

But as for Eve and me, we put a stop to things after Bear found Daniel's letter. The shame of our affair was already hollowing us out—every errant glance was a cut, every accidental touch a knife to the gut—and being surprised by Daniel's betrayal woke us up. We finally realized the monstrousness of what we were doing, and the pain we were going to cause everyone if they found out. Especially Romi.

In a way, it was a relief. We wanted each other as much as we wanted it to be over. To no longer want each other. To be free. We'd been searching for a reason, and Daniel's mistake seemed perfect.

To make it easier, I offered to take even more errand duties. In addition to Daniel's turns for grocery runs, I also adopted Eve's, which meant we could spend more time apart. She'd continue surveying, and I'd spend more time away from Agloe, being responsible for three people's worth of chores in Rockland.

I enjoyed it more than I thought I would. At first, every minute I spent outside Agloe when the others were there was so nerve-racking, I could hardly breathe. I was panicked at what I might miss. But each time, it became a little easier. Maybe I started to see just how consumed we were by that place. How isolated and secretive we'd become. The clerks at the grocery store started to greet me by name, and I didn't realize how nice it was to talk about something other than that cursed map until I was already doing it.

But Agloe wouldn't let me go that easily.

One Tuesday when I walked into the Rockland Grocer, a list of snacks and booze dangling from my grip, I heard someone calling me from behind the registers.

"Nice to see you, Rose," I replied. "Been busy?"

"You wouldn't believe," Rose said. "Happens every summer. I've been trying to catch that friend of yours all week. The one always with the camera."

"Wally?" I asked, surprised.

"He's got some mail but hasn't been in to pick it up. You're all still in that same house, aren't you? Could you take it to him?"

"Sure," I said, following her over to the back corner. Even though there was a proper post office in Rockland, many of the locals kept mailboxes at the grocer, because it was so convenient. "I didn't know he had a box here."

Rose nodded. "Stopped by and opened it the first week you all came to town. Normally he's in almost every day to check, but I must have missed him the past couple days, and I'm taking a trip to see my sister and her kid over in Scranton."

"That'll be nice," I said.

Rose sighed. "Normally would be, but I'm going because they need help around the house. There was an incident at the high school where her husband cleans. Someone broke in at night, and he fell wrong and fractured his leg trying to stop the guy."

"How horrible!" I replied. "Was it a student prank gone wrong?"

"They're saying it might have been a robbery, actually," Rose said, shaking her head.

"A robbery? At a high school? I can't imagine what they'd want to take."

"Me either," she replied. "But they heard from the principal that the geography section in the library had been pawed through."

I couldn't shake the prickling sensation creeping up the back of my neck.

"The geography section?" I repeated.

"I know, so strange. But thank goodness Jeremy's all right, and that I can get the time off to go over there for a little bit."

"Yes, thank goodness," I echoed, but my mind was far away. I was thinking back to a few weeks ago, when Eve had noticed that strange story on television, about the burglary at the Sullivan County Government Center.

And now this.

"Anyway, I'm the only one authorized to handle the mail here, so they'll lock up this counter until I get back," Rose was saying, sorting through a pile. "And your Wally seems like such a serious fellow—I wouldn't want him to be upset at having to wait a week."

"That's very kind of you," I managed.

She handed me a couple of envelopes and then marked them off as delivered in her book. "Well now he'll be happy," she pronounced. "Thanks for your help."

"No problem at all," I said. I was deadly curious now about what sort of mail Wally might be receiving, but I didn't want to look nosy in front of her. I tucked the little bundle into my pocket and waved our grocery list at her. "You have a safe trip," I said.

Once I got back to the car, I took the envelopes from my pocket. I didn't recognize the handwriting on any of them, but they were all from local addresses. So, Wally wasn't writing to Professor Johansson or anyone else at our university, then. I wouldn't have suspected that of him anyway—of all of us, he was by far the most dedicated to maintaining the secrecy of the impossible town.

But then why didn't he have these letters sent to the house? Why would he need to hide them from us?

Two of the envelopes were well sealed, but the third had weak adhesive, the entire flap practically dangling free. I couldn't resist.

I didn't understand at first.

The note inside was made out to the Cartographers. It was very short. Only a few lines—more like a list. A man's name, an address, a phone number, a couple of dates for the coming week, and a short description at the bottom.

"Not sure what year you're looking for, but it's the right maker. Fair condition. Some fading along the folds from use, and a little tear in section A5. Found it in my uncle's old car last week after he passed away. My wife and I will be at the house until evening most days helping clean it out, come by anytime."

At first, I didn't know what to do—if I should confront Wally alone and ask him what was going on, or if I should tell the group first. I didn't want to accuse him of something if I was simply mistaken, but I couldn't shake the feeling that something bad might be going on.

In the end, I split the difference. I decided to tell Eve first, to see what she thought.

I should have gone to Romi, I know. But Eve was the one who had noticed the news story that first day, and I was already so used to keeping secrets with her.

Or maybe that was an excuse. Maybe I was looking for a reason to be near her again.

The next day, Wally still hadn't returned to the house yet, and I wanted to figure out what was going on before he did. When we got to Agloe and went out to survey another neighborhood for Tam and Romi, I showed the letter to Eve.

"Are you sure it was him, in Scranton?" she asked when she'd finished reading.

"No," I said. "But who else would want something in the geography section of a high school library?"

"He has been gone for days now," Eve allowed. "But this letter makes it sound like he's trying to buy another copy of our map. Not steal it."

"Maybe not everyone will sell," I said.

We were standing in a part of Agloe we hadn't surveyed before, one of the outermost neighborhoods, farthest away from where the others were working.

"Hey," Eve said, pointing. "That's Wally's, isn't it?"

On the ground beside the door of one of the buildings, there was a little roll of film half-buried in the grass.

It had to be—none of the rest of us had a camera.

"I think he's been in here," I said, bending to pick it up. The roll was dusty, as if it had been forgotten there for some time. "A lot."

We looked up slowly. Like most of the structures in Agloe, the building was a simple, modest commercial construction. A single story, a basic roof, with a few small windows along the walls and one main door.

As Eve and I were surveyors, our domain within the town was always changing, different every day, but the others all needed more fixed workstations. I had suspected for a while that—the same way Tam and Romi had taken over the ice cream parlor and the printing factory, and Daniel and Bear had taken over their experimental neighborhood block—Wally had adopted a small place for himself, too. Somewhere he could store his research and think in peace. He'd always needed quiet when conducting his final reviews of our projects, to ensure every single number and measurement was exact.

Maybe that was why none of us had tried very hard to seek him out on the days that he was with us in Agloe—we knew he needed his space and silence. Or maybe that was an excuse. Maybe each of us were so caught up in our little parts that we didn't want to be distracted by the others' troubles so clearly brewing around us, and so we left it until it was too late.

We hesitated, studying the door.

"Are you sure?" Eve asked. "It feels . . . wrong, somehow."

I knew what she meant. I felt the same way.

But that was all the more reason to go in.

"If he's got nothing to hide, then he's got no reason to be angry," I said. "We could even do our survey of his building now, when we won't be interrupting him while he's inside, trying to work," I added, to seem more optimistic about Wally's innocence than I felt.

Eve didn't look convinced either, but she nodded.

Slowly, I eased the door open.

From the outside, the place had reminded me of a small-town library at first—but as I looked at what Wally had done with the interior, and the way the silence hung oppressively around us, the building didn't really look like a library at all.

It looked more like a vault.

There, organized and labeled and catalogued on what had once been bare shelves, were copies of the same map Wally and Tam had found by accident, the very first day we came to Rockland.

Not just a handful, but hundreds of them. *Thousands*, even.

Thousands of maps of Agloe.

"Oh my God," Eve finally said.

What had it cost him to do this? How much money? Or how many sins?

"We have to tell them," I said. "How far this has gone. What he's doing."

"How did we miss this?" Eve asked. "How did we not see?"

"Maybe we would have, if we hadn't been so caught up in us," I replied.

Eve grimaced, ashamed.

My gut twisted. "I'm sorry. I didn't mean it like that. I'm just as much to blame. More, even. I'm the one betraying someone."

"No, you aren't," Eve said. "I'm just as guilty." She took a breath and let it out shakily. "I'm trying, Francis. I really am."

"Me too," I sighed.

The silence lingered a moment too long.

"Let's go get the others," Eve said, looking away from me. "Before Wally comes back."

"He's been gone three days." I shrugged. "It gets longer and longer every time."

"Still," she replied. "We've seen enough to share our concerns with everyone. Better sooner rather than later."

What she said made sense. We did need to tell the others. But the knowledge that we were in a place that there was no urgent reason to leave was starting to become too hard to ignore.

"We should go," Eve whispered again, the same way she had at the very beginning, the day our affair started.

"We should," I said.

But neither of us moved, at first.

And then finally we did.

But it wasn't toward the door. It was toward each other.

"We can't keep doing this," she said. Her face was buried in my neck. "This has to be the last time."

"Yes," I agreed, in between breaths as we kissed. "This is closure."

"Closure," she repeated. "For good."

Really, it was selfish, but that's the excuse we gave ourselves. The last time we'd cheated together, we hadn't known it was the last time, that it would be too difficult to hide after that and so we'd simply have to cut it off without warning and hope it would stick. I told myself that was why it had been so hard—because we hadn't known it was the end until it was already past us. That if we did it only once more, promising it was the last, it would work this time.

I had just ripped off Eve's dress and pressed her to me, her skin hot against mine, when the door opened again.

We were doomed from the start. The question was never if, but when.

"Hurry," I begged her as she raced to get dressed again, cursing, but her dress was tangled with her bra, the sleeves and straps all twisted up, and she couldn't put it on without pulling them apart first. She scrambled frantically with the fabric, and I ran around the corner toward the door, to stall whoever was entering.

Please don't let it be Romi, I prayed. *Please let it be Daniel.* He was my best friend and would never believe I could do what I was doing. He wouldn't even know to suspect it. Maybe I could stall him long enough or convince him that he wasn't seeing what he was seeing . . .

But it wasn't either of them.

"Francis!"

I scrambled to a halt in front of Wally.

He gasped. "What are you doing here?" He looked like a puppy who'd been caught pooping on the rug, his eyes huge and terrified. He would have realized I probably looked the same, if he'd been any less surprised. "What's wrong with your shirt?"

"What are *you* doing here?" I asked, tugging on the hem, hoping I'd yanked my top more into place. "You said you were going to be on the road all day. How did you even get into Agloe by yourself?" Even through the haze of my adrenaline, I managed to notice what he was carrying. Car keys and papers, and *another* copy of our Agloe map. "Is that . . . "

I shouldn't have said it. I was trying to keep Wally distracted, but the words had the opposite effect. They replaced his confusion at finding me there with panic. He jerked his belongings to his chest guiltily. "It's not what you think." He pushed past me, desperate to escape.

Right toward where Eve was still struggling to cover herself.

"Wait," I begged, giving chase.

"Leave it, Francis," he said, running faster now. "You don't understand."

"No, you don't understand," I cried. "Wally, *stop*!"

Then Eve screamed.

I came around the corner to find her still huddled there. Mostly dressed, but not completely. Not enough to hide what we'd been doing.

Wally stared at us in openmouthed shock, unable to believe what he was seeing. His shoulders slumped, and his hands went loose, almost spilling everything he was holding across the floor.

He looked so horrified, so *hurt*. As if we'd betrayed him just as much as we'd been betraying Romi.

Maybe he was right.

"Wally," I said weakly.

I thought he was going to run. To expose us to Romi, and the rest of the group. It was what we deserved.

But instead, he stared at his hands. At the map he was holding. Merely the latest one he'd found—or stolen, perhaps.

"You keep my secret, and I'll keep yours," he finally said.

XIX

"Felix. Felix."

Felix blinked hard, trying to clear his eyes, but the screen continued to swim in front of him, a blur of out-of-focus words. "I'm fine."

He prepared to keep arguing—to say that he wasn't in shock, he didn't need to go home, that what he needed was to keep digging until he understood what was going on—but he didn't have to. A faint thud by his elbow made him look over.

"Thought you might need this," William said, gesturing to the coffee mug. "I made a fresh pot."

"Thank you," Felix said gratefully, and drank as much as he could of the steaming brew while William sipped his more slowly. The office door opened again, and Naomi came back in carrying a pizza. It was almost midnight, but Felix's stomach barely grumbled at the sight of the white-and-red-checkered cardboard box.

The story of Irene's murder was all over the news now. Priya had put a live feed from a local television station up on the big screen, which was currently showing a mess of police cars, ambulances, and people in sparkling attire all huddled together on the steps between the two gigantic lion sculptures. They all looked shell-shocked, both terrified to be there but also unable to make themselves leave, even though they'd likely already been cleared by the police. Ainsley had arrived at the library too now and was answering questions about how Haberson's library security would share everything they had with law enforcement, would spare no expense, and would not rest until justice had been served.

And somewhere inside, there was a paramedic team with a stretcher, draping a body bag over Irene Pérez Montilla's lifeless body.

Felix shivered. He had just been there, he had *just* seen her.

So had Nell.

"Police finished another sweep and have confirmed again there are no other victims," Priya said to him then, seeing his expression. Her meaning was clear. *Nell and Swann were safe, wherever they were.*

Felix nodded and glanced at his phone again, which sat silent on his desk. He'd been frantic, in those first moments after hearing the news, that Nell might have been with Irene when she was murdered, finally doing what he'd implored her to do all along, and had been attacked as well. It had taken all three of them to calm him down enough to tell him that the police were leaning heavily on Haberson for information about the event as they investigated, and that Haberson security had assured Ainsley, who then assured William, that there was only *one* victim.

He was still desperate to call Nell—but she and Swann were probably still giving their statements to police, and even more than that, he didn't want to do it in front of his coworkers and boss. He wanted to talk to her alone, so he could apologize for starting the fight they'd had and could comfort her, let her cry or scream or be angry or afraid. None of that was possible hunched over a cell phone in the middle of his crowded office.

Besides, the best thing he could do now to make up for being such an ass to Nell—and to help her—was to focus on solving Irene's murder.

As soon as he left, even if it was four in the morning, he'd call her or go over to her apartment. He'd sleep outside the door if he had to, until she had rested enough and woken up. Then he'd apologize and tell her everything he, Naomi, and Priya would have dug up tonight on Wally.

Because it had to be Wally. Even if Felix had no idea what Francis had meant by his nonsensical claim that Agloe was real, all three of Dr. Young's friends were deathly afraid of the same person. That had to count for something.

"This is the third incident at the NYPL in a week," Naomi said with a sigh, mystified. "And the most brazen of all. If only our security system was fully installed."

"It was scheduled to take another week, but it will be done by tomorrow, I promise," William said. "But at least we already finished affixing every piece of their inventory with our micro RFID tags." He frowned as he looked at his tablet. "And it seems that nothing was taken this time, again. We don't have our own movement data from the first murder, or the first break-in, of course, but if we accept the library's security data from those two events, nothing was stolen either of those times, too."

"Out of everything so far, that part is the most confusing to me," Naomi said. "Now not one, but two scholars have been killed there, and the building has been broken in to three separate times—*what* the hell could this burglar be after?"

You wouldn't believe it even if I told you, Felix thought. None of them would.

"You look troubled, Felix," William said to him then, noticing his expression. The Haberson Map dinged on his tablet with another update before Felix could answer.

"And how could they be leaving no trace every time?" Priya asked, turning back to Naomi.

Another update came through as Naomi and Priya continued to debate the strange crimes, and then another, until they all looked to William, waiting for him to pass along the information. But he was just staring at his tablet, his eyes glued to the screen. He'd been silent for a very long time, Felix realized.

"William?" Priya prompted softly.

Felix couldn't read William's expression at first, until he finally looked up from his tablet.

"What is it?" Naomi asked.

"It's done," William said. "The Haberson Map found the burglar."

"That's great!" Felix cried, spinning toward his own screen, where the map was also open.

But William didn't look happy.

"I'm sorry, Felix," he finally said.

"Why?" Felix asked. Warily, he clicked on the Haberson Map, but William was already reading aloud.

"According to the algorithm, the map has designated Dr. Helen Young as the primary suspect in Dr. Daniel Young's case, as well as the attempted burglary of the library the day after, and the murder of Irene Pérez Montilla tonight."

WHAT?

"What the hell?" Felix gasped, unable to stop himself.

It wasn't true.

He turned away from his computer, his hands scrambling across his desk for his phone.

It couldn't be.

He had to call her. Warn her.

You can't warn her, she's about to become a suspect, he thought as he continued to scramble anyway, unable to stop.

"Felix, what are you doing?" Naomi asked nervously.

He shouldn't do this, he knew. The Haberson Map automatically updated Ainsley's team and the police—a warrant could be out for Nell's arrest in no time. But he didn't want to warn her because she was a criminal. He wanted to warn her because she *wasn't.*

His hand was already moving, unable to resist.

<Nell, this is an emergency. You're about to be named a suspect.>

He sent the message, then fired off another immediately.

<This has to be a setup. You have to tell the police about Wally, before he uses this to find you.>

He hesitated, but then at last added:

<I'm so sorry about earlier. Please let me know you're okay.>

After he sent the third message, he looked up at William, who was studying him intently, as if watching Felix could help him understand what was going on better than even his own tablet.

"The Haberson Map is wrong," Felix said.

"Felix . . ." Naomi hesitated. "I can't imagine how you must feel, but the amount of data the map has, the places it can pull from and the probabilities it can run . . ."

"It's wrong this time," he insisted. "I can explain."

"I think first, you need to call the police," William replied. "At the very least to tell them you just messaged her. The Haberson Map has already pushed its search results to them—they're going to be looking for her. If they find your communication in her cell records before you disclose it, you could become a person of interest in the case."

"That's ridiculous!" Felix said, even though he knew William was right. "I had nothing to do with this!"

"I know. But they don't. And if it's true that you were trying to rekindle your relationship, it could come across as suspicious," William continued, as diplomatically as he could.

"And you both worked at the library before," Priya added. "They could argue that you both would have known the Map Division's pre-Haberson security systems inside and out."

"You have a great job now, but they could argue that if she was still bitter about her termination all those years ago, and you had recently gotten back together . . ."

"No." Felix groaned. "Stop. Just stop."

He was becoming more desperate by the minute. The truth was that in the right light, Nell *did* seem horribly suspicious. But he knew it couldn't be true. He'd seen the confusion on her face the first night he'd gone to her apartment and seen the Agloe map—it was as intense as his own. He'd heard no trace of dishonesty in her voice each time they'd met after that, as her findings became more and more strange. She was as lost and innocent in all of this as he was.

And now, with a target on her back, she was in even *more* danger than she had been before. If the police arrested her, Wally would know exactly where she was, and where the map was. If he could break in to the New York Public Library, could he break in to a court room, or a prison? Could he have been the one to cast suspicion on her in the first place?

"Felix . . . ," Naomi began.

"It cannot be true," he murmured. He looked up at her. "I know Nell, Naomi. I know her."

William cleared his throat gently. "Sometimes, people can be not what they seem."

Felix shook his head, refusing to believe it. His phone buzzed in his hand at the same moment, catching his attention. "Look," he said, relieved. "That's her now."

But when he held up the screen, the notification wasn't a reply from Nell. It was an alert that his messages had been kicked back to him, a little red *X* next to each one, indicating they hadn't been delivered to her phone, because it was unreachable.

Huh?

Had Nell . . . had she . . .

Had she blocked his number to avoid him?

There's no "we" anymore, he'd said to her, in the heat of the moment. He'd wanted out of everything—her investigation, her obsession with the map, her life.

You got what you asked for.

Hadn't he?

"Did she reply?" Naomi asked.

He shook his head, the dread at the pit of his stomach growing.

"I'm sorry, Felix," William finally said. "But I think we should call the police now. For your own sake."

Felix shook his head in frustration. "If she's not answering, it's not because she's guilty. It's because she's in danger *herself* now. She's the target."

"That's what the map is saying," William said.

"No," he replied. "I mean, she's not the burglar. She's who the burglar is after."

"What?" Priya cried.

"Why, Felix?" William asked. "Tell us what's going on."

Felix grimaced nervously. Nell would probably kill him for revealing what he knew, but he didn't see any other choice anymore.

"It's because of a map," he finally said.

Naomi rolled her eyes gently at him. Every crime had been centered around the Map Division, after all. "But *which one*? Because during every one of these crimes, not a single thing has been taken out of the library." She pointed at her computer. "Even more than that, if you reorder our database so their inventory goes by value, not one of the top fifty biggest specimens was even *touched* tonight. The Buell, or anything from the Ford Collection, or Cassini's *Carte de France* . . . not so much as a jostle of their cases. It doesn't add up. Not a single item is missing."

"The map the burglar's after is not in the collection," Felix replied.

All three of them looked up at that. Naomi and Priya looked surprised, and William was studying him curiously.

"Because Nell has it."

Romi

The last days of August descended on us like a summer storm, dark and heavy. Tam spent almost all of her time in the printing factory. It was so swelteringly hot inside my ice cream parlor, the big window would fog up—and outside, the air was so muggy and mosquito-filled, even you didn't want to play, Nell. We all worked with a feverishness that matched the cloying weather, coming back from Agloe each day parched and exhausted, our clothes streaked with salt from sweating. As miserable as we were, the intensity of our work only increased. We could feel the end of summer bearing down on us, just weeks left, and we were desperate to finish our project before we were supposed to be back at the University of Wisconsin to triumphantly show off our creation.

The stress of our deadline only made things worse between Tam and me. The two maps of our *Dreamer's Atlas* could not have been more different, in every way. Mine was nearly finished, each measurement double-checked and drafted in pencil, ready to be inked, but Tam's map was still a chaotic concept, fragments laid down and then erased, and then laid down and erased again. She said she couldn't explain what was blocking her, but whenever I asked to see her drafts, she refused. She insisted she was on the verge of understanding, and then everything would work itself out from there, if only I could give her a little more time. If only I could trust her.

But trust was becoming our rarest commodity—for all seven of us.

Eve had become even more shy and distant than she'd been before we left campus, Bear seemed sick with worry over something, although he refused to tell any of us what it was, and Daniel was still tense after admitting that he'd tried to send Professor Johansson a letter, unsure if he had truly been forgiven or not. So far, our instructor hadn't written to us or called the house—I couldn't even remember the last time I'd heard the sole, old phone in the corner of the living room ring—but we still weren't sure if we could trust that Daniel had told the truth, that he'd really only attempted to send that one letter. That there hadn't been others. The last time Tam and I had gone to the pharmacy in Rockland, she'd called the university to see if she could feel out the situation, but the department secretary said Professor Johansson wasn't in and had hardly been in that summer. We took some comfort in that, trying to believe that perhaps it had been only that one letter, or even if there had been another, maybe Professor Johansson hadn't checked his faculty mailbox yet, if he'd barely stopped by—but there was no way to know.

And Wally was gone even *more* often, if that could be possible. He was not at the house or in Agloe with us more days than he was—and when he was there, he seemed agitated, lost in thought. A haunted, pursued look clung to him, which he couldn't shake, even when you tried to draw him out of his brooding and into a game, Nell. Like he couldn't wait to get back on the road, conducting his mysterious, essential research.

But to me the strangest change was that he'd somehow convinced Francis, of all people, to go with him on these excursions.

Perhaps they were searching for a specific piece of data, I figured at first. Perhaps Francis needed some historical context for the area, for his and Eve's survey. Sullivan County had once been part of neighboring Ulster County until the early 1800s, when it was split off—maybe he wanted to go through even older records for the land, to find what previous colonial settlements might have been there, or perhaps the Indigenous tribe that had lived on the land before the colonists took it, the Esopus, had ever mentioned anything strange about the hills in their history. He was nearly as detailed in his work as Wally and always liked to do things himself, if he could.

But when I asked him about it, Francis was brusque. He refused to talk about it and made up some excuse to leave dinner early. By the time I got up to the room, he was already asleep, or faking it, and when I woke up the next morning, he was already gone again with Wally.

Something was going on with him, I could tell, but I couldn't figure out what it was. We'd been together for a decade by that point—I'd seen him stressed out, angry, or sad plenty of times. But I'd never known him to be withdrawn. Yet somehow, there was now a huge gulf between us, one that I couldn't bridge, no matter what I tried to do.

"Has Daniel ever been distant?" I finally asked Tam one day when she'd come to see my progress at the ice cream parlor, in a rare moment that we weren't fighting over her own. We hardly ever talked anymore, not about anything but our impossible project, but I was desperate.

"What do you mean?" she asked, looking up from my notes.

"Become secretive," I said, fumbling. "That's not it. It's not like it's something specific—Francis just seems aloof, and tense, all the time. Has Daniel ever been like that?"

As soon as I asked, I felt foolish. Daniel was never any of those things. He wore his heart on his sleeve, as the saying goes. You could always tell what Daniel was thinking, even before he could.

But to my surprise, Tam smiled. "Actually, yes," she said. "There was one time. It went on for a couple of weeks. I couldn't draw him out of it, or get him to talk about it, no matter what."

"What did you do?" I asked, my hope buoyed. If they'd survived it, perhaps so could we, I thought.

"Nothing," she said.

"Then what changed?"

Her smile had grown into a full-fledged grin by that point. "He proposed."

It felt so good to laugh, after so long. We laughed and laughed until our cheeks hurt, and we could hardly breathe.

"Do you really think so?" I finally asked, wiping my eyes. "We've been together forever, but it doesn't seem like the right time. None of us have thought about anything but this town for months now. I can't remember the last time we even went on a date."

"Maybe I shouldn't have said anything," Tam replied, backtracking. "We're coming to the end of our sabbatical, and maybe he's stressed out. I just meant, there isn't necessarily always a bad reason for things."

"You're right," I agreed. "It's probably not a proposal, but I should go easier on him. This project has been hard on all of us."

"It has," Tam said. "But you never know. It is almost over, and maybe he's looking forward. To what comes after this."

The idea was so unexpected, and so wonderful, I was afraid to get my hopes up. But despite my best efforts, the excitement still caught me. For the rest of the week, while I waited for Francis and Wally to return, I felt lighter and more tender toward everyone than I had in a long time. Tam and I didn't argue as much, and I didn't feel as trapped, as claustrophobic, inside of empty, mysterious Agloe as before. Little accidents like burning dinner on the stove barely bothered me, and even bad news seemed less dire.

That is, until I was tidying up our bedroom one evening and found a little scribbled note. It was in Francis's pocket, but the words were in Wally's handwriting: *Abram's Books and Stationery. Closes 5 P.M.*

Doubt flickered in my mind as I stood there, staring at it.

Why would someone need to know not when a shop opened, but when it *closed*?

The next morning, I asked around at the grocery store and the antiques shop in Rockland if there was a bookstore called Abram's nearby, but no one had heard of it. Eventually, I ended up at the bank of phone books in the post office, combing each one for that name. Finally, a few towns over, I found it.

The owner picked up on the tenth or eleventh ring, right before I gave up. He apologized for the delay—the local police were there, asking him questions, he said.

His shop had been robbed a few days ago.

Someone had broken in during the middle of the night and rifled through the travel section.

"I know what they were after," he said to me. "But we've been out of stock of road maps for months, ever since this run on them started. Doesn't matter which company, or which area. Can't keep them on the shelves."

"'This run on them'?" I repeated, confused and full of dread.

"It's all the antiques hunters are talking about these days. Some mysterious collector is willing to pay big money." He sighed. "What could make a little thing like that so popular? I just hope I can afford a better security system, in case this happens again."

I hung up with shaking hands. Outside, Bear, Eve, Tam, Daniel, and you were waiting in the car, ready to take us all to Agloe, but I couldn't bring myself to move.

The door opened, and Tam poked her head in. "It still hasn't arrived?" she asked when she spotted me by the pay phones on the wall. That had been my excuse to stop in here—that my parents had mailed me a book, and I needed to pick it up.

"The highway is going to get busy if we don't get moving. It's going to get harder to make the turn onto that road unseen," Bear said from behind her.

"You all go ahead today," I said to them. "I need to go to the library. Do a little research of my own."

The Rockland Library was not large by any means, but what it lacked in reference texts, it made up for in local newspapers—hundreds of them, every day for every edition in the county and its surrounding neighbors, all stored in rolling drawers. I spent the entire day there, desperate to disprove my growing suspicions.

What I found made my blood run cold.

There had been more robberies over that summer. Many more.

A string of break-ins across the whole county, and even farther than that. Schools, travel agencies, local museums, gas stations, long-term storage facilities, car junkyards, even some houses. To an outsider, there would have appeared to be no connection between them—but to someone like me, who knew what the burglar might have been looking for, the pattern stood out as bright as day.

Someone was hunting copies of the same map we'd found.

And I was terrified that it was Wally—and maybe even Francis.

The library's newspapers weren't available to be loaned out the way books were, so I made photocopies of every single article I found about the break-ins. I walked back to the house, all five miles, and spread everything out on the living room table, like some kind of horrible exhibit.

I didn't really have much of a plan, other than simply to get the truth. Part of me still didn't fully believe it or didn't want to. I held out hope that there would be some explanation that would magically make it all better. That I'd been mistaken, and it was all just a huge, weird coincidence. That none of this was really Wally. Or if it was, that we could convince him to stop, before something truly terrible happened.

Of course, it was already far too late. By that point, news of Wally's fervent collecting had spread all over the East Coast, through the amateur hobbyist network. He'd spent months seeking out copies, honestly or otherwise, but now, invitations and offers came to him, to that post box he kept in Rockland. News spread quickly about the kind of money this strange, obsessive collector who called himself part of the Cartographers would pay for a copy of such a seemingly worthless little map—or even a rumor about one. He'd created a web of eager, oblivious informers, everyone from retired schoolteachers to mischievous teenagers to antique-book sellers, and was using them to scour the countryside for every last copy of the Agloe map, so that he could have them all.

But at the time, overwhelmed by the evidence I'd only started to find, and the phone call I'd had with the bookstore owner, I scarcely had the first inklings of how far it had really gone. None of us really knew just how deep this obsession of his really went. We didn't know what he was truly capable of.

The car from Agloe reached home first. I heard you laughing as someone carried you up the front steps, Nell, and then Tam was through the door, calling for me.

"Romi, we're so sorry! We went back to the Rockland Library to pick you up, but they said you'd left two hours ago!" Tam apologized as she came into the living room and spotted me.

"You should have waited, it's way too hot to walk," Bear said, with you on his shoulders. Eve and Daniel were behind him, lugging our research books back inside, and he let you down to run to your mother so he could help them.

Finally, as the bustle settled down, they all noticed everything spread out on the table.

"What's going on?" Tam asked.

"Sit," I said. "And wait."

"What are we waiting for?" Bear asked.

"Just sit," I repeated. "It can't be long now."

It wasn't. Just a few minutes passed in uncomfortable silence before we all heard Wally's car crunching up the gravel driveway. Then the engine faded out, and doors slammed, and the scrape of a key echoed in the lock.

"We're back," Francis called from the door.

I could see that the others wanted to call out to them, but I fixed them all with a glare.

Francis and Wally drew closer, footsteps going from mudroom to kitchen to where we were waiting for them in the living room.

"There you all are," Francis said, at the same moment that he realized something strange was going on. "Guys?"

In the meantime, Wally's eyes had drifted to me and then to the table behind me, where all the photocopies waited. "What's this?" he asked.

"You tell me," I said.

Francis and Wally looked at each other and then back at me. Finally, they both came up to the table and began to look through the articles.

Only a few seconds passed before I saw their faces shift from confusion to something else.

Panic, I thought. Or guilt.

"I can explain," Francis said.

"Okay, that's it. What is going on?" Tam asked, and went to snatch up a bunch of the papers. "What are these . . ."

But she trailed off as she read them.

That made Daniel get up, and Bear, too. Eve hung back nervously, waiting for one of them to pass her some of the pages.

Tam finally looked up. You took the paper she'd been holding and pretended to read it, blessedly oblivious to what it actually said. She was too stunned, too confused, to even try to get it back from you.

"Wally, what's going on?" she asked. Her voice was so quiet and sad. He looked wounded by the sound of it. "Were all of these . . . were they all you?"

"We're not criminals," Wally said.

"Really?" I cried. "Then what do you call it? You're just doing it for fun?"

"No," Francis insisted, aghast, but I was too angry to stop.

"Or to make yourself feel tough? Or for money? Or—"

"I owe it to Wally, okay?" he finally shouted. "It's only a favor!"

"A favor? What kind of a favor could he possibly have done for you that would be worth you *committing crimes*?" I shouted.

"I'm trying to protect the town," Wally stammered. "Our project depends on it staying a secret until we finish. I thought if I gathered as many as I could find—"

"Gathered?" I repeated mockingly. "You call this 'gathering'? I don't think that's what your victims would call it!"

"No one even *cares* about these maps," he tried to argue, but I cut him off, still yelling.

"You're breaking in to people's businesses and homes, Wally!"

"But we're not taking their valuables! We leave everything else!"

"Are you kidding me right now? You could go to jail. And now you've drawn Francis into it!"

"It was his choice!" he cried, his voice cracking slightly at such volume. Wally had seen the rest of us argue plenty, especially toward the end of any major project, but he was always a bystander, always waiting on the sideline for our tempers to die down before he offered up any of his suggestions. He wasn't used to the anger being aimed directly at him.

I knew I could make him crumble.

"If he owes you, it doesn't sound like his choice!" I snapped back. "It sounds like you coerced him into this! Are you trying to blackmail him, Wally?"

"No," Wally pleaded, shaking his head. "It wasn't like that!"

"What was it like, then? What do you think you have on him that would be worth this?"

"Romi, please," Francis said, his voice tense, desperate. "Just leave it."

"I'm not leaving it. I want to know what the hell is going on!"

Wally was cowering before me, miserable, terrified. I had grabbed his arm, clutching so tight his skin was turning white under my fingers, so he couldn't get away from me. "Please. Francis doesn't have to come anymore," he tried to promise me, but I shouted over him.

"It's too late! You already dragged him into this. I want to know why!"

"I just . . . I saw something I shouldn't have!"

"Romi, *stop*!" Francis yelled, looking panicked.

I slapped Wally in the face. "What did you see, Wally?"

"Romi, stop!" Tam shouted, horrified.

But I did it again. "What did you see?" I slapped him a third time, so hard the others cried out. "What could be so horrible that he would agree to—"

"He cheated on you," Wally moaned, his eyes wild. He looked like he was going to faint. The words lingered as he repeated them, like a horrible, unconscious chant. "He cheated on you."

The whole room went silent at that.

Everyone stared at everyone else in abject shock.

It couldn't be.

"But . . . how?" I finally whispered.

It sounded so unfathomable to me. I couldn't even imagine it was true, let alone believe it.

"With who?"

And then, Eve burst into huge, heaving sobs.

The motel was dingy, but it was better than the house. Anything was better than that house.

At the little table in my room, I repacked my things into my suitcase more carefully, now that there was time.

The first thing I'd done, after nearly blacking out from the shock, was sprint upstairs, while Daniel shouted at Wally and Francis for what each of them had done, Bear tried to calm everyone down, and Eve continued to cry. I didn't know where you were, Nell, but I hoped that Tam had taken you outside, so you didn't have to see all of it. I tore everything of Francis's out of the dresser drawers and threw it over the banister and down the stairs into the middle of the living room, for the rest of them to see. Then I changed my mind and pulled out my own suitcase and started packing that.

I probably could have convinced the group to throw Francis and Eve out that night, but I didn't want to stay, anyway. I couldn't sleep in the same bed where I'd been sleeping with him that whole summer—not until the sheets had been stripped and washed, or better yet, thrown out like trash.

I just wanted to escape. To get away from all the lies and secrets, away from the house, away from the town.

While everyone else continued to interrogate Wally, I forced Francis to drive me to Rockland and drop me off at a motel there. I didn't know if I could bear to be near him, but it was also the cruelest thing I could think to make him do, in the moment. I yelled at him for half the drive, demanding he tell me everything, every disgusting, shameful detail, then refused to speak at all for the rest, no matter what he said or asked me, and then yanked my suitcase out of the back seat and left him begging me for forgiveness in the parking lot without saying goodbye. When he tried to follow me into the lobby, I screamed at him so loudly that the clerk told him she'd call the police if he didn't leave me alone. Francis left, tears streaming down his face, and the clerk gave me what she said was the best room they had.

"If that bastard comes in here again, I'll say you already checked out," she told me, patting my hand sympathetically as she handed me the key.

I still could hardly wrap my mind around it. That the whole summer, Francis and Eve had been sleeping together, right under my nose. Every day he'd gone to Agloe to be with her, and then the same night, crawled into bed right next to me, turning me into a fool, over and over.

I thought I was going to be sick.

And the worst part of all—even worse than Francis's betrayal, somehow—was that Wally had known about it.

He had known all this time, and instead of telling me the truth, he'd held them hostage and used their secret to his advantage.

He'd betrayed me, too.

I heard someone on the stairs outside then, and held my breath as I waited to see if they would pass by down the corridor or stop at my door. If Tam had come to try to comfort me, or Eve to apologize, I didn't know what I'd do. I was terrified I might try to throw them over the banister outside, the way I had Francis's clothes back at the house—or even worse, break down crying. I would not let Francis know how much he'd hurt me. I would not crumble.

The footsteps crested the landing, and then, after a long moment, there was a knock. My eyes were so hot, burning like acid, I could barely see. I willed the tears not to fall.

"Romi?" Bear asked softly, through the door.

I waited at least five minutes, but he didn't go away.

"It's just me."

Finally, I undid the lock and chain. "What do you want?" I asked.

Bear put a hand out, offering a hug if I wanted it—but I just stared, afraid to touch him. If I accepted his kindness, my rage was going to turn to agony instead, and I didn't think I could survive that.

"I don't need comforting."

He shrugged gently but didn't move. When I glanced up again, I saw that his eyes were wet and shimmering as well. The realization that everything might be over was hitting him like a wave, dragging him under. There was no way Francis, Eve, and I could ever be in the same room again—Bear couldn't endure the pain it would cause to force us to remain, but he also couldn't endure the loss if any of us left.

At least, that's what I thought his tears were about.

"I can't just forgive them for this, Bear."

"I know," he said helplessly.

"It's over. I don't ever want to go back."

I said it in anger, without thinking, but as soon as I did, I realized I meant it. I wanted to be free of the map, free of the town. I didn't ever want to go back.

But I did. Just one time.

I should have listened to myself.

Bear was on the verge of breaking down, grinding his big fists into his eyes, as if he could rub out his emotions the same way he could the tears. He went on so long, I grabbed his hands before he hurt himself.

"There's something I need to tell you," he finally said.

I gritted my teeth. "What else did Francis do?"

But Bear shook his head. "Not Francis," he whispered. "Me."

The last words came out so softly, I could hardly hear them at all.

"I need your help."

I was just so full of hate. I wanted to punish Francis and Eve, but they were already punishing themselves so much, drowning themselves in their shame. Francis already knew I would break up with him, and Eve already knew that the rest of the group would never trust her or let her stay, either—any cruel thing I said wouldn't be enough. They could barely feel even the faintest heat of my rage from within the inferno of their guilt.

But I couldn't let it go. I needed someone to pay, I realized. Even if it couldn't be Francis. I needed to hurt someone the way I'd been hurt.

And Bear gave me the perfect opportunity.

XX

The light under the front awning of Classic's building was out, and in the darkness, Nell had to find the keyhole mostly by touch. Her own keys were gone, having been in her tote bag, but she knew that Humphrey always kept a spare set buried in the flowerpot with yellow roses on the stoop.

Behind her, Swann, Francis, Ramona, and Eve waited nervously, all scanning the silent street.

She could still hardly believe that they'd actually made it all the way to Classic without being caught—or how they'd done it.

The police had stayed for hours, combing every inch of the NYPL, especially the Map Division. They'd walked the room a hundred times, stalking right by on the other side of the door that was only there to Nell and the rest, so close it made her jump every time, even though they could never get in. Sirens wailed endlessly from the front entrance.

When the commotion had finally died down enough that Francis thought they could make a break for it, they followed Ramona to the other door on the opposite side of their hidden room. She opened it a crack, and when the coast was clear, flung it open and hurried them out. Nell stumbled. The rush of the night breeze on her skin, the darkness of the late hour, and the glare of streetlights pressed in, startling her all over again.

Somehow, impossibly, they were standing on the sidewalk outside the library, back in the regular world.

Ramona folded up the Sanborn map and handed it to Eve, and the door they'd just come through was gone. Only the silent, impassive exterior stone wall of the NYPL stared back at them, as if they'd simply phased through it.

"Unbelievable . . . ," Swann stammered, still staring at the side of the library.

A taxi honked as it passed, seeing potential customers, and Nell jumped at the sound. Francis waved it tensely on.

"Come on," he'd said. Farther down, too far to make out their features, there were still some guests lingering at the main entrance in between the two giant lion statues, giving interviews to a swarm of news crews. "My car's around the corner."

The drive had taken hardly any time at the late hour. Once they reached President Street, Francis parked across the way instead of in Classic's parking lot and killed the engine and lights. They all waited for a few minutes before climbing out, to see if anything moved in the dark. Lieutenant Cabe's black undercover police car tailing them—or Wally, perhaps. By now, he'd have gone through Nell's bag and realized that the Agloe map wasn't inside. He was probably already out there somewhere, searching for her again.

All the more reason to get away from the library before he returned, and to get away from Classic with the map, before he guessed that might be where she would go next.

"I still can't believe it," Swann whispered then, as Nell brushed the dirt from the flowerpot off the key. He looked slightly sick with disbelief that the most valuable map any of them had ever come across was currently stuffed somewhere on Nell's disorganized desk upstairs, completely unprotected. That of all the places the wayward daughter of scholarly royalty could have hidden something of such immense worth, she'd chosen the junk pile of a shoddy, knockoff home decor shop in Brooklyn.

Just before Nell had left her office earlier that evening to go to her father's event at the library, she'd taken the Agloe map out of her portfolio, put it in a plain Classic envelope normally reserved for customers' orders, and hid it in the middle of her in-box's huge stack of projects.

"I know," Nell whispered back. "But it worked for my father for decades at the library." A needle in a haystack of junk. If she hadn't stumbled upon the Junk Box down in the uncatalogued storage basement completely by accident, the map might have stayed buried there forever, safe from Wally.

"Well, let's keep up our good luck," Ramona said. "Classic might be an unlikely hiding place, but Wally has always been very thorough. Bear would do everything he could to stop him if he showed up, but . . ."

The possibility of Humphrey upstairs, hurt and alone, seized Nell's heart. As quietly as possible, she wiggled the key into its lock and let them inside the darkened building.

They crept across the small ground-floor lobby and up the stairs without turning on a light, in case the glare might attract attention. At the landing, Nell led them over to the door to Classic. The chipped lettering on its glass face glinted dully as they crowded in front of it.

CLASSIC MAPS AND ATLASES™
WE CAN MAKE ANY MAP!

"I've never been to your office," Swann said softly.

"That's my fault," Nell replied. Even now, with everything that had happened, and knowing who Humphrey really was, she still felt a twinge of embarrassment that Swann, the Director of Collections for the Map Division of the New York Public Library, as well as a professor from Harvard and a preservationist from Penn State, were about to see the type of maps she'd been working on the last seven years, and the life she'd been living since her expulsion from the library. "I kind of wish you didn't have to come inside now."

He put a hand on her arm. "You have nothing to be ashamed of," he said.

She fed the second key on the ring into the lock, but it was already unlocked.

"Are we too late?" Eve whispered.

Francis peered in first, then shook his head. "It doesn't look ransacked."

They stepped inside, leaving the door cracked in case they needed to make a hasty escape. Classic's office was high enough compared to the bodega, the laundromat, and the row of sagging three-story apartments surrounding it that the moonlight came in through the windows. The pale glow spilled over the silent, cluttered place, a faint blue.

"Here," Nell whispered, hurrying over. "My desk."

She watched Swann take it in and then looked at it herself, trying to see it without all its history. It was smaller than her old place at the NYPL, not much more than a little table jammed next to a radiator, with an old computer and a towering pile of paper that had clearly begun in her in-box but had grown to completely overtake half her workspace. Underneath, she could barely see the hint of her huge tablet of grid paper, where she added her flourishes to the map reproductions assigned to her.

Swann picked up the top package from the stack. "Frederik de Wit 1654 Dutch Maritime Atlas: fake creases, water fade, add sea monster version?" he murmured, reading the project title on the envelope.

"Pirate ships are one thing, but you should see my sea monsters." She shrugged. "You wouldn't believe how many people want a kraken on their Ptolemy or their Waldseemüller."

Swann stifled a chuckle—but there was no haughty disdain, no affront at the inaccuracy, in his eyes as he looked at her work. Just love. He touched the little sea monster on the draft affectionately.

Nell found that she was smiling too, to her surprise. For the first time in her life, Classic's maps only felt sort of funny, not humiliating. They'd just learned about a secret town and maps to places that didn't exist. What were a few giant squids or some manual crumpling for age effect on a harmless bit of paper that would make someone happy? Their customers were going to look at her artfully exaggerated product in their living room and feel the same sense of wonder and possibility and adventure that she felt when she looked upon any map in the library's collection—was that really so bad?

Nell scooted closer and began to sift through the towering jumble of paper with him. "I hid it here before I left—shoved it right into the middle of the mess."

"What does it look like?" Swann asked, as the others joined to help.

"It's a plain white Classic envelope," she said. "No writing on the front."

Please still be here, she prayed as she dug through envelope after envelope, package after package.

"I don't see any with no writing," Swann replied tensely.

"Keep looking," she said. "It has to be here."

Please don't let Wally have found it.

Then suddenly, halfway through the mountain of paper, she pulled a thin, plain white piece of mail from the rest.

Her heart fluttered.

The Agloe map.

It was still safe.

"I've got it," she said.

Carefully, she slid her finger under the flap to open the envelope and took out her father's map.

The others all drew back a step at the sight of it, both horrified and mesmerized.

"I never thought I'd see it again," Ramona said.

"I hoped I wouldn't," Eve added.

Francis was the first one to come forward. He looked at it intently in Nell's hands, but made no move to touch it. "But I still don't understand how Daniel ended up with it. That night, the fire, we lost them all."

"It was Tam," Ramona said.

Tell me, Nell was about to say, but there was a gasp behind them.

"Stop right there!" a voice shouted.

Swann banged against the desk as he startled, nearly toppling it and himself, and Nell spun around, holding her keyboard like a weapon.

"Humphrey!" she cried.

"Nell!" Humphrey gasped, relieved. He dropped the umbrella he'd been brandishing and rushed out of his office to her. Behind him, Nell could see his phone on his desk, off the hook—he was still leaving messages for repair technicians, even hours later. "Thank goodness! I thought we were being robbed."

But he fell silent as he saw Francis, Ramona, and Eve standing behind her in the semidarkness.

"Nell, what . . ."

"She knows," Ramona said, cutting him off. "Bear."

Slowly, Humphrey looked back to Nell.

Her eyes suddenly stung. She tried to speak. "Humphrey . . . everything you did for me, all these years . . ."

"It was nothing," he said.

"But I was so ungrateful. Every day—"

He cut her off, shaking his head. "Every day with you was a treasure, Nelly."

He opened his arms, and she fell into his huge embrace.

"But why didn't you tell me?" she asked when she finally pulled back.

"Your father forbid us to," Humphrey answered. He looked down. "When you and he left Rockland, we all went our separate ways. At first, it was just too painful to see each other. When I finally moved back to my family on Long Island, I reached out to Daniel, to ask to see you two again—he was so afraid that you'd remember things, if we stayed in touch. He was your father, and I was only a friend, even as much as I loved you like my own niece. I did as he asked and kept my distance." He sighed. "But after what happened at the library, how badly he'd hurt you . . . I couldn't just stand there and do nothing. And you were an adult now. I thought if I could keep the past secret, since the two of you weren't speaking anymore, it might be all right. I might be able to help you without betraying my promise to him."

"Well," Nell murmured. She put her hand on his arm again. "I'm glad."

Humphrey smiled, and shrugged. Then he noticed the cut Francis had been dabbing at earlier on the side of Nell's head and the ugly bruise beginning to bloom beneath it.

"Oh my God, what happened?" he cried, puffing up like he always did whenever he could tell she was upset, all shoulders and chest—*like a big old bear,* she'd always thought to herself. If only she'd known how true it was.

Everything, Nell wanted to say. She didn't even know where to start.

"I hid the map here," she said instead.

"What map?"

"*The* map," Ramona said. "Daniel had it, all this time."

Nell held it up so he could see it in the dim room. Humphrey stared at it in shock. He looked at Nell again, and then back at Ramona, until Ramona finally nodded.

"But how . . . ," he started.

He took a step back from it, as though it might hurt him, and then looked at the others.

"I swear I never said anything," he said to them. "I didn't even know it still existed! I never—"

"We believe you, Bear," Francis said. He shrugged. "Nell's a Young. It was foolish to think we were going to be able to hide this forever."

Despite still recovering from his shock, the words brought a faint, proud smile to Humphrey's lips. "You were always going to be the best one of the bunch, if you ask me. You blow them both out of the water."

"Humphrey, please," Nell replied, a little flush rising to her cheeks. "And don't you start, either," she said to Swann, who was nodding in agreement with Humphrey.

"All right, my dear," Swann replied placatingly. His gaze fell to the map in her hands. "So, what now?"

Nell ran her hand tentatively over the faded cover.

"Are you sure you want to go?" Eve asked her, as gently as she could. "All this time . . ."

"The whole place may be burned down by now," Francis added grimly. "There might not even be anything left."

Nell knew what they were trying to warn her about. That even if they could evade Wally and make it to the phantom settlement, all they would find in Agloe of her mother was ash, if even that. It had been decades, and the blaze had been strong enough to burn the whole town to nothing.

But something still didn't add up. Something she'd realized when she'd come to in the hidden room in the NYPL, when she finally realized Francis had been telling the truth that Agloe was real, and was still trying to puzzle out.

She was a Young—she could not let go until she'd pursued something all the way to the end.

She had to be certain.

"Tell me how you know for sure," Nell finally said to them. "How you know she's really gone. I need to hear the rest of the story. I need to hear about the day of the fire."

In response, Humphrey hung his head, ashamed.

"It was my fault," he told her softly.

"It was all of our faults," Eve said. "We all went into the town. We all were responsible for what happened that summer."

Humphrey shook his head. "Maybe. But my lie was what sent Wally over the edge that day. I'm the reason there was a fire." He looked down. "The reason Tam died."

Nell stared at him. "How?" she managed to say.

Her boss wrung his hands. His nickname was obvious in the slope of his broad shoulders, the way his dark hair drooped over his eyes as he slouched.

"First, let me give you something," he said. He went back into his office, where he opened his desk drawer and took out a small lockbox. Not the one they used for petty cash during the day—she had never seen this one before. It had been shoved far back in his mess, covered in old receipts and who knew what else. He fished around in his pocket for his key ring and unlocked the little rusted lock.

"This is for you," he said when he came back.

It was a fountain pen, a deep crimson lacquered shaft with a gold head and a white University of Wisconsin logo.

"This is the one from Eve's story," Nell said, realization dawning. She turned to Humphrey. "The one my mother made me."

He nodded.

She smiled as she took it, and her fingers felt the roughness of an uneven texture along the side of it. It took her a moment to get the angle right so that the scratches would catch the light, but she already knew what they would form anyway.

A simple, slightly jagged eight-point compass rose, with a *C* in the center.

Her mother's symbol for the Cartographers.

"I guess the map wasn't the only thing we thought was lost in the fire," Ramona said at last.

Humphrey nodded. "I managed to save it. I just couldn't bear that Nell might not have anything of Tam's, once she grew up."

Nell ran her finger slowly over the etched markings again, entranced.

"I wanted to give it to you so much sooner, but I had promised your father—" He sighed. "So, I decided I'd give it to you when you finally quit working for me."

Nell smiled. "I was never going to quit working for you, Humphrey. Not really."

Humphrey smiled back, a little sadly. "Yes, you were—your father's ridiculous scandal be damned. You're too talented to stay at Classic forever. I wouldn't have let you."

Nell rolled her eyes at him in mock frustration the way she always did, hoping it hid the sudden hot, wet prickle in them from the rest of the group. She took the cap off the pen and ran its nib along the back of her hand. The ink came out dark and rich like oil against her skin, even after all this time.

"I had it restored," he added. "I clean the piston and refill the cartridge every few years."

"Thank you, Humphrey."

But Humphrey shook his head. "Please don't." His broad, heavy shoulders sagged even farther. "It doesn't even begin to make up for what I did."

Nell put a hand on his shoulder. She knew him so well—even when she hadn't realized it. After everything he'd done for her, both as a kind older brother type when she was a child, and professionally and financially as her boss at Classic, she couldn't believe he was guilty of something as truly terrible as he thought he was. "Whatever you lied about that night, I'm sure it can't be as bad as you think."

Humphrey's despair only seemed to deepen at her words.

"It wasn't just that night. I'd been lying to them all for the whole summer," he finally said.

He looked up at her at last, his eyes big and deep, and welling with shame. But before he could start his story, Francis cleared his throat, interrupting them.

"You'll have to tell Nell on the way to Agloe," he said.

Nell turned to him, surprised. "What?"

But Francis wasn't looking at her. He was leaning against the wall, peering out one of the windows nervously. "We have company. The police are surrounding the building."

Lieutenant Cabe! His officers must have run her records and figured out where she worked after they found no sign of her at the library or her apartment. "We have to get out of here," she said.

Just then, a storm of flashing red-and-blue lights and the keening wail of sirens overwhelmed the office.

"How?" Swann asked. "There's only the front door and the fire escape, but that ladder would put you right down in front of their cars!"

"Helen Young!" a megaphone boomed. "This is the police. We have you surrounded!"

They all leapt into action, ducking away from the windows. Humphrey ran for his office, and Nell spun around, scanning the room for any possibility. Could she use the big vent in the bathroom to escape? Or should she hide in the closet? Or maybe go to the roof? And then what?

The sirens peaked. "Come out with your hands up!"

The sound of paper rustling startled her, and she turned around.

"Here," Humphrey said, coming back out of his office. He held up the single sheet he'd pulled out from a notebook that had been in his office. "This will get us out."

It was another map—a zoning diagram of Crown Heights from the 1970s done in a city planner's clean, shaded lines, with Classic and its adjoining buildings visible.

"These other stairs will take us straight out to the back, where there will be a parking lot," he said, pointing at their office.

"Perfect," Ramona said, grabbing the page from him and hurrying them all toward the door.

"Stairs?" Nell started to ask—she knew there was no second set of stairs leading out from their building—and then she understood.

Sure enough, as they all spilled out onto the landing outside the office, there wasn't just one stairway this time, but two—another on the opposite side of the landing, leading down in the other direction, away from the front door, where the police were currently swarming and about to batter it down.

"What the . . . ," Swann murmured, his eyes wide with disbelief, as the crush of wood splintering made them all jump.

"Police!" the megaphone blared, and the front door downstairs splintered further under another kick.

"Let's go!" Ramona shouted, starting down the stairs only they could use.

"You next," Humphrey said to Nell, gesturing quickly for her to follow. "We'll cover you from the back."

Nell lurched down the stairs. "All this time," she managed to say, "I complained about this office so much, begged you to let us move—"

Even amid the panic, he found a smile for her as they ran. "I told you there was a reason we stayed in this god-awful building, Nelly."

Bear

Yes, when we found Agloe, we all began keeping secrets. But mine was different, Nell. I'd been lying to everyone since the day we arrived in Rockland. Since even before that—before we'd even graduated and left Wisconsin.

I told everyone the house we were living in belonged to my parents and sat vacant most summers. That it was waiting for us to move in and continue working on our project. But that wasn't true. The house didn't belong to my parents. It didn't belong to anyone in my family at all. It was a rental. Our last semester, I saw a travel agency ad offering vacation cabins and had gotten an idea.

I only wanted to keep all of us together. Tam and Wally were so brilliant, Daniel so driven, Romi and Francis so meticulous, and Eve so well connected in the industry, I was sure that despite our grand plans, if we drifted apart over the break, we'd never come back again. I figured, we just had to get started on our project, and the rest would take care of itself. But I needed to take the first step for us. A harmless lie, I thought.

Because they all knew how broke I was. They never would have agreed if they'd known that the cabin wasn't free—that in fact, not only had I paid for it, but I'd spent every last penny to do it.

It sounds so stupid now. But I was young, and desperate. My friends felt as much like my family as my real family, except that there was always the chance I could lose them. My relatives all still lived in the same town on Long Island, but Tam, Daniel, Wally, Romi, Francis, and Eve were different. They were from all over, brought together at university, and never intended to stay there forever. They would get offers for prestigious jobs and be gone. We'd try to stay in touch, but the years would grow long, and it wouldn't be the same.

And, I'd always been poor. Always stretching my budget until I got my next measly paycheck from tutoring or waiting tables. When you have barely any money anyway, having none at all didn't seem that different.

What was one summer?

I did have a plan, at first. I had just enough for the deposit, and I'd intended to get a side job in Rockland while we finished our project, and use that money to pay the rent. Then once the *Dreamer's Atlas* was finished and we'd gone back to Wisconsin to submit it for publication, I could go back to teaching undergraduate geography classes or tutor freshmen, and no one would ever be the wiser.

But then Tam and Wally discovered Agloe, and everything fell apart. We spent all day, every day consumed by it. There was no time for a part-time job, so I couldn't make any money. What I owed compounded with every payment I missed.

The evening before the big fight, when we all learned Francis had been cheating on Romi, it was my turn to cook dinner. I'd planned a feast—Romi had been in such a wonderful mood lately, and I wanted to do anything I could to keep it that way. When she and Tam were working well together, everything in our group was working well together.

We left Agloe, and the rest of them dropped me off at home to get started and carried on to Rockland to replenish our wine supply. I was dicing onions, garlic, tomatoes, and mushrooms for spaghetti when I heard their car pull back in.

"That was fast," I said, opening the door.

But it wasn't our old Volkswagen.

And it wasn't them.

It was a much newer, sleeker car, with tinted windows. Two middle-aged men I'd never seen before were in the front seats, in dark, conservative suits.

Debt collectors from the vacation rental company.

"Humphrey Turan?" the first one asked as they climbed out of the car.

"Sorry," I said, stepping back through the door.

The men moved calmly up the drive. "Mr. Turan, stop."

The screen door banged shut, and I reached for the solid one behind it. "The stove is on, I have to go."

"We've been trying to reach you, but you haven't returned any of our messages, via mail or phone," the first man continued as the slab of wood slammed closed between us, ignoring my excuse entirely. "You've left us no choice but to come in person."

I knew it was true. The rental company had started with the mail, sending me threatening letter after threatening letter, but when that hadn't worked, the calls had begun. After a few weeks, I was so exhausted from leaping up at the first ring to grab the phone before anyone else, I'd secretly unplugged the cord. Even then, I'd known it was only a matter of time before they'd start showing up in person—but somehow it was still a surprise that it was finally, finally happening.

"This is serious, Mr. Turan," the other said.

This was it. They'd come to evict us.

"You have to open the door," the first man added, knocking again.

I turned the lock and put my head against the wood. I thought that maybe if I waited long enough, they'd get tired and go.

"We're not going anywhere," the first continued, in an almost bored, expectant way—they probably went through this every time. "Not until you talk to us."

My eyes slid to the window. In the falling light, I could still make out the lazy curve of the highway, up which Daniel would be driving the rest of them, wine in tow. Back here, where they were expecting to find dinner waiting.

Instead, they were going to see the debt collectors' car and their ominous silhouettes lurking at our door, threatening to throw us out. They would know how much trouble I was in, and how far I'd gone to hide it.

Or, even worse, maybe the men *would* leave before the others returned—but then they'd come back. Because men like these always came back. And if they did when we were all in Agloe, they might let themselves inside the house. I didn't really know the laws, but as delinquent on the rent as I was, the place might not even be mine anymore, contractually. It was one thing if I was physically inside, but if all they had to do was show up when the house was empty . . . the owner probably had even already given them a key, by now.

And if they did go inside, if they saw our notes, what we'd been working on . . .

If they tried to reach Agloe on their own, or told the rental company about their findings, if the news got out . . .

I had no plan, but I had to say something to buy some time. I opened the wooden door just a crack. "Give me a week," I said.

The two men looked at each other, then back at me.

"Please," I begged. "If I talk to you in good faith like this, don't you have to give me at least one extension?"

"Your account is already incredibly past due," the first man said.

But the second finally shrugged. "How much will you be able to contribute toward your debt, after this week?"

"All of it," I promised, even though I had no idea how.

They both arched their brows in surprise. "All of it?" one repeated.

I nodded. "I just need a week."

The first man still looked incredulous, but the other took pity on me. "One week," he said. "We'll come back next Monday."

"Thank you. Thank you." I closed the door again as fast as I could.

My heart was pounding as I ran back to the kitchen, just in time to save the sauce from bubbling over. I raced to finish boiling the pasta and stir the sauce as I listened to their car ease down the road—and then, a few minutes later, heard the one Daniel had been driving pull up and sigh into silence. Doors slammed, bottles clinked, and tired, familiar voices mumbled as the gravel crunched.

"Bear?" Tam's voice floated in from the mudroom.

"In here," I called back.

As they came into the kitchen, and the scent of the spaghetti sauce and my homemade garlic bread enveloped them, I watched the strain melt off all their faces.

"It smells incredible," Eve said, smiling.

"Wow, Bear," Romi agreed. Their eyes roamed the still-steaming platters I'd set out on the counter. "This looks so good!"

"Let's eat while it's hot!" Daniel cried.

The room swelled with laughter. I passed out plates, and Tam opened the wine. If things had tentatively been going better lately, that night felt downright magical. Everyone was joking, helping serve each other across the counter, and playfully stealing bites off someone else's plate. Daniel poured far too much to drink for everyone, and we finished it all, and then drank more. Even Eve was laughing, more relaxed than I'd seen her in a long time. The only thing that would have made it better was if Wally and Francis had been there, but I knew they'd be back from their latest trip and rejoin us soon. I would cook again, and I would figure out something to save us from my horrible secret. If I just worked hard enough, I could keep this feeling going forever.

Because that, right then, was all I'd wanted. That moment was the reason I'd ruined my life to rent the house. Not for the *Dreamer's Atlas*. Not for that godforsaken gas station map. And especially, especially not for Agloe. I did it *for* us. For us to be together, the way we'd always been. It was the only thing that mattered.

Twice, I was so overcome, I had to pretend I'd gotten a little sauce in my eye when Tam noticed me tearing up.

I wish I could say it was happiness that had been welling in me. It was, but it was also fear. I had one week to come up with thousands of dollars, or it would all be over.

I thought it was hopeless—but then the next night, we found out what Wally had been doing all summer. That he'd been buying up or stealing every single copy of our map he could find, in an effort to control them all. That by that point, rumors of his obsession had spread far and wide among amateur collectors and antiques hunters, all desperate to make a quick buck on a piece of junk. And that most of all, he must have had hundreds, or maybe even thousands, of that map lying around somewhere.

And suddenly, even amid the despair of Francis's and Eve's betrayal, and Romi's anguish, I had an idea.

A terrible, dishonest one.

But I didn't see any other way. I didn't have a choice.

• • • •

Romi knew where Wally kept the maps he'd found or stolen, she said when I went to her motel. Francis had confessed everything to her in the car on the way there, desperate that she might forgive him.

"He said Wally calls it the vault," she whispered.

I had barely dared hope that I might be able to convince her to tell me where in Agloe that was—but Romi offered me much more than that.

"I don't understand," I said. "You were so mad at Wally for betraying you when he found Francis. But isn't stealing a map from him the same thing?"

Romi almost smiled. It made her look even more sad than before. "Exactly," she said.

Morning dawned somberly at the house. Since Francis and Eve had betrayed Romi, it was Romi's right to choose first whether or not she wanted to remain part of the project. Tam, Daniel, and I took her to Agloe so she could gather up her research until she'd decided, and Francis and Eve stayed home to watch you and keep an eye on Wally.

After we finished taking everything out of the ice cream parlor, I kept Tam and Daniel occupied helping me load the car while Romi took a walk alone—to clear her head and think, we'd decided she should say. They believed her. They had no reason not to.

It seemed to take her a long time to reach the vault. Or perhaps that was just my nerves.

After dropping off Tam and Daniel at the house at dusk, I drove Romi back to the motel. We sat there a long time in the dark in the car, neither of us able to get out.

"I wish there was some way . . . ," I said, but I knew it could never be. I could never ask Romi to forgive Francis or Eve, so we could all stay together.

She sighed. "I know."

She reached into her purse and pulled out one of Wally's maps.

She'd chosen one that was well-preserved but unremarkable, no unique marks or wear, like we'd discussed. One hopefully Wally would not be able to recognize as one he'd already found.

"He had thousands," she confessed. "Even for Wally, with all his records, there's no way he's going to miss only one—or be able to tell."

I tried to convince myself that my plan was harmless. It wasn't even really stealing, because Wally would still get his map back, in the end. He cared about that far more than he cared about money.

"Let's make the call," she said.

Upstairs in her room, Romi dialed the shop she'd rung the day before, the one whose name she'd found on a note in Francis's pocket, which had led to the unraveling of his and Wally's secrets in the first place. Abram's Books and Stationery.

I pretended to be a customer. I said I'd been cleaning out my garage and came across some old maps, and heard his shop had the best text and art antiques section in the area.

The man wasn't interested—his shop had just been broken in to, he told me. All his funds were going into repairs. He shrugged off my attempts to set up a meeting until I finally mentioned exactly what map it was that I wanted to sell.

Romi knew he'd already heard of this strange collector called the Cartographers, and what kind of maps they were looking for.

And just how much they would pay for a copy.

"I had a friend take a look, and she said one of these might be worth something," I continued, feigning ignorance. I described the Agloe map we'd stolen from Wally in detail. "She told me there's a buyer out there willing to pay good money for it—is it you and your shop?"

The man was so relieved at this stroke of luck, he didn't consider we might be suspicious. All he could think about was the money.

"That's right," he lied, straight to us. "If you've got the right edition, it can be worth quite a bit. Thousands, at least. Abram's Books and Stationery would be glad to help."

I asked for exactly as much as I owed on the house. Not a penny more.

Even after complaining about how tight money was, the man didn't hesitate in the slightest. He knew how much Wally would be willing to pay—it was far more than what he would be paying me.

"The shop's not open until we can get the plate glass window fixed, but I'd be happy to meet you somewhere else?"

I didn't think I could take one of the cars for long enough to drive out to him without the others noticing my absence, but I could easily fake a stomach bug and stay home. I gave him the address to our house in Rockland and told him to meet me there the next day at noon, when everyone else would be in Agloe.

The man hung up quickly, excited. I felt ill, and hopeful, all at once.

"Thank you," I said to Romi.

"I did it for myself," she replied. "Even if the rest of them will never know it."

"I'm so sorry," I murmured again, for probably the hundredth time.

Romi shrugged, the way she did when she didn't want to talk about something anymore because she didn't want to lose her composure. I never understood how she was always able to keep everything locked down so deep, but I respected it. I never would have had the courage to pull off what we'd just done without her.

"What are you going to do now?" I asked instead.

"There's a weekend bus that runs to Manhattan every Saturday," she mused. "I think I'll catch that, and then get a flight from there."

"To Wisconsin?"

She shook her head. "I don't know. Just anywhere but here."

I didn't know if she meant Rockland, or Agloe. I guess it didn't really matter.

The next day, Wally left to continue his research over at the University of New Paltz—this time with Tam, who would make sure that he didn't steal anything else, and would come back home before nightfall. Daniel, you, Francis, and Eve went to Agloe in the other car, to keep working. If Romi didn't want to continue as part of our project anyway, was it worth exiling them from it as well? Would they try to beat us to the punch and publish early? we worried.

As for me, I waited in bed and listened to the car rumble away. Tam had made me a mug of tea before she and Wally left, and I drank all of it out of guilt.

I was so disgusted with myself, for not being able to ask them for help to pay down my debt. If I'd had the courage to do that, none of this would have happened. But shame is a terrible, terrible thing. It makes you lie to others, and to yourself. I had twisted things around so much that I was convinced stealing a map from Wally and then selling it back to him was different from admitting my secret, because even though it would still be Wally paying for the house in the end instead of me, if he didn't know about it, then maybe it didn't have to be true. I could keep hiding my lie the way Francis, Eve, Daniel, and Wally hadn't been able to hide theirs.

I was standing in the driveway at noon when I heard the Abram's owner's car coming up the road. The map was already in my hands. I wanted the exchange done as quickly as possible, so I didn't have to face it a moment longer than necessary. I was so impatient, I began walking toward the end of the driveway to meet him before he'd even fully turned in.

But halfway there, I stopped.

The car couldn't have been the man's—because I recognized it immediately.

It was Wally's.

"What are you doing here?" I asked him as he and Tam climbed out.

"The same thing as you," he said.

Tam's eyes were bewildered, stunned—but his were so, so cold.

He didn't even ask if I had the map. He didn't have to.

The bookstore owner had been so excited, he hadn't waited until after he'd gotten the map from me to sell it. He'd started calling around looking for the Cartographers the minute he'd hung up with me yesterday, until he'd found Wally somehow. And Wally was as eager as always at the prospect of yet another Agloe map, and incredibly curious. The amateur collectors' network had been quiet for weeks, their own search on Wally's behalf exhausted. From where had this mysterious copy suddenly appeared?

He finally got the man to admit he hadn't found it himself, but rather was about to buy it from someone else. He wouldn't reveal his source, terrified Wally was going to scoop him, until Wally agreed to pay him in advance. Wally did, of course. He wrote a check for whatever amount the man had named without protest.

And in return, the man had given him the address where he was supposed to meet me.

The address to our very house.

Tam hung back, unable to believe it was true. Wally came closer to me, until he was standing just inches away. My heart was hammering in my chest. I had never seen him so angry, ever. I was sure, in that moment, that he was going to kill me.

I had thought he might demand to know why I did it, or how I could betray him. But he didn't say any of those things. He didn't even ask me to apologize.

"Give it to me" was all he said.

Wally drove us to Agloe using the stolen map. We raced down County Road 206 and lurched into the town at a dangerous speed, the gas pedal practically against the floor. The car skidded into the main square, where Wally threw on the parking brake and then fought his way out of his seat belt. Everyone else—save Romi, who was at the motel—was running toward us, drawn by the squeal of our tires.

Wally snapped the Agloe map closed, and the dirt road disappeared behind us. Then, without another word, he climbed out of the car.

"What's wrong?" Daniel demanded as Wally slammed his door shut. But Wally just walked away from him, too, as if he wasn't there either. As he passed, he was so furious his anger radiated off him in waves, almost physically. Even as confused as they all were, it was impossible not to see how angry he was. Even you, at a safe distance in Eve's arms, shrunk back from Wally.

"What happened?" Francis repeated, prying open the back door and pulling me out as Wally continued walking away. "What the hell is going on?"

"It's bad," Tam said, still shaken.

"I'm so sorry," I finally managed, as I started to cry. I couldn't help it. "I'm so sorry."

"Wally!" Daniel shouted after him. "Where are you going?"

Wally didn't stop. He was already halfway across the park in the town square, so far I'm not sure he even heard. He kept walking.

"Wally!" Tam cried.

But he still didn't stop—even for Tam.

Francis turned back to us. "He's going to the vault," he said.

Tam looked at him. "The vault?"

"It's where he's keeping all the maps he's . . . found."

Daniel studied Wally's fading form for a moment and then looked back to me. "Bear," he said. "Did something happen with a map?"

But I couldn't answer. I was too ashamed.

"Wally said we've been doing this all wrong," Tam said for me. Even after I'd betrayed her—the whole group—she still was so kind. "He said that we've been letting the map control us, and it should be the other way around."

But Daniel could tell anyway. He knew Tam too well. "You tried to take one, didn't you?" he asked me.

Finally, I confessed everything, in halting, shuddering gasps. I swore to them that I wasn't really trying to *steal* a map—I was just trying to save myself from financial ruin and protect the town from becoming evidence in an eviction case. Even if I'd given the map to that man, who else was he going to sell it to but Wally? Who else would ever want it or pay so much?

"First me, then Francis and Eve, then Romi, and now Bear," Daniel mused.

Eve had come up to us, still holding you. "Wally thinks we've all betrayed him, and threatened the town, in our own way," she said, quietly. "Even Tam."

"How have I threatened the town?" Tam objected. "I'm the one who *discovered* it!"

"But you're the one who made him share that discovery with the rest of us in the first place."

Tam fell silent at that. She stared after where Wally had disappeared around a corner of silent, empty buildings. "You think he's going to do something drastic?" she asked.

Francis looked at her. I could see the shame of the robberies he'd helped commit on his face, the same way my own theft was etched onto mine. "Hasn't he already?"

That sent a chill through all of us.

"Come on," Tam said. "Show us the way."

We followed Francis, walking far apart from each other, as if we were all going there alone rather than together. Maybe we were. We'd all been alone for a long time. At the door to the vault, Tam knocked once, but Wally didn't answer.

"Wally, we're coming in," Tam said. She opened the door and disappeared inside.

We all waited a moment, but she didn't come out. You squirmed in Eve's arms, and she let you slide to the ground, so you could stand on your own.

"Tam?" I called as we came in but as soon as we did, I saw why she hadn't answered.

I stood next to her, looking around as the rest of the group murmured in surprise.

"It's . . . empty," I finally said.

Wally had been driving around for months on his feverish quest to collect every single copy of the map still in existence—and yet now every table, every shelf was completely bare.

Tam glanced at Francis. "I thought you and Eve said he had thousands."

"He does," Francis replied, confused.

"Where are all of them, then?" I asked.

There was a sound from deeper in the vault, something heavy being set down. Tam took another step forward. "Wally?" she called.

Following her, we moved deeper, going around the empty shelves.

"Wally, what are you doing?" Tam asked.

Wally looked up from where he was crouched, a cornered animal. In his arms was a huge pile of maps—the Agloe maps. Quickly, he dumped them into the open cardboard box in front of him, one of the boxes we'd used to help move our things here from Wisconsin.

It was full again now, though. Hundreds of his maps were already inside of the box, stacked to bursting, and even more waiting in haphazard piles around him.

"I'm going to fix this once and for all," Wally said, his voice high and tight. He stood and picked up the box, which nearly buckled under the weight of all the densely packed paper. "I've been going about this all wrong. We're never going to be able to protect this place unless we have better control over it. Today made me realize that."

"Please," I begged. "Just let me explain."

But Wally ignored me—or perhaps he was too worried about making his escape before we could stop him. He edged toward the door carrying the box, grimacing with effort.

"Where is a safer place than here to store them, though?" Tam asked, trying to get in front of him so he had to stop, but he was no longer looking at her. Daniel had scooted around to his other side, almost within arm's reach. "As long as they're in Agloe, no one but the seven of us can reach them."

"It was one of the seven of us who tried to steal one," he replied.

I took a step closer to him. I only wanted to apologize again, to throw myself upon his mercy—but Wally flinched as if I'd been reaching out to strike him.

"I wasn't—" I started to say, and then stopped as I saw what was happening.

Francis was beside me now, and Eve had also circled around as we'd argued so she was between Wally and the door. Daniel was so close to him, he could have reached out and touched him—or the box.

We were closing in on him without realizing it. Or maybe we had. We'd surrounded him like prey, and he could feel it. I could see the whites of his eyes as they darted between each of us, more and more frantic. His arms hugged the box tighter, creasing the cardboard.

We were pushing him too far.

"Who's to say someone else won't try?" Wally asked.

I scooted back a little, hoping the others would copy me, but they didn't. "I'll do anything to make this up to you, Wally," I pleaded, hoping to defuse the situation.

"It's too late." But Wally was looking at Tam as he said it, not at me.

"It was too late the day we let everyone else inside. We should never have showed them."

"What are you going to do?" Tam asked.

"What I have to," he said.

"Let's just talk about this first," Francis offered.

"I'm done talking," he replied. To the rest of us he said, "Let me go."

And then he jerked roughly away—and I saw Daniel's hand slide off his arm.

"Don't you dare," Wally said. He was trembling now, on the verge. "Get away from me. Get away from this box."

"This is not only your choice, Wally," Daniel said, his hands up in a gesture of surrender—but he didn't back away. And Eve had moved closer as Daniel kept him distracted.

No, I wanted to say. *This is only making it worse.* But they were all shouting now, so loud I couldn't hear myself even as I tried.

"Yes it is! I gathered all of these!" Wally yelled, trying to keep hold of the box with one hand and shove the rest of them back with the other.

"But that doesn't mean the town belongs only to you!"

"I found it," he hissed. "I found it with Tam. And I will protect it—even if it's from all of you."

He fought against Daniel, stumbling farther and farther back as they argued. But Francis also rushed forward, preparing to take the box from him entirely. It pitched between them, the cardboard failing. "Get back right now!"

And then it split as he turned, the maps pouring out onto the floor in a huge, messy scatter.

I gasped as everyone lunged for the chaos at once. Wally was screaming, fighting to keep them all back before they could grab a copy, but there was no way he was going to win. There were too many of us, and only one of him.

But then a strange, warm flash of light bloomed hungrily on top of the pile before any of us got there.

We all pulled back, surprised, confused.

"What . . . ," Tam murmured.

"Fire!" Daniel shouted. "He lit them on fire! He's *burning* them!"

It was true.

Wally stood over the maps, the box of matches shaking in his hands as he watched.

"What have you done?" Tam asked, horrified.

"Protected the town," he replied. "It was the only way."

"Oh no," Francis whispered, horrified. "No, no, no."

All those copies—the last ones in existence—gone.

We all watched the blaze in stunned, horrified silence as it began to spread, obliterating the maps, then creeping outward, toward the shelves and walls.

"We have to get out of here," I said, suddenly recognizing the danger we were in. The buildings in Agloe were from the 1930s, when the phantom settlement had been created, and were all made of wood. "The whole place is going to come down."

"Where's Nell?" Tam cried suddenly, spinning around.

"Oh my God," Eve gasped. "I set her down when we came in here."

Terror struck us as we heard you scream. You were somewhere in the fire, Nell.

I couldn't even move—but Tam was already gone. She threw herself straight into the blaze.

"Tam, no!" Daniel yelled, trying to chase her. "Nell! Nell!"

All of us leapt into motion after him—but at the same moment, there was a horrible whooshing sound from everywhere around us, and it seemed that all at once, the entire vault was on fire, every surface covered in dancing, licking flames. There was so much smoke, so thick and black I could hardly breathe. I had never seen fire move that fast—we were in a tinderbox. The walls were already buckling around us, the shelves collapsing, threatening to trap us beneath them. And in the middle of the room in a towering molten heap, the maps Wally had collected were blazing so brightly, they were glowing white.

We tried, but it was impossible to go forward. The fire had become a wall, cutting us off from the rest of the vault. From Tam, and from you. We were driven back, first to the door, and then to the sidewalk outside, still yelling for you and Tam.

"Get off me!" Daniel shouted, his throat raw, but the fire surged again, swallowing the building. "I have to go after them!" he kept shouting, but Francis and Eve had pinned him down so he couldn't run to his death, and I was holding Wally around the waist, clutching for dear life as he tried to drag himself back inside as well.

"This is my fault," Wally cried as he fought me. "Let me go, you have to let me go—"

Just as Francis and Eve lost control of Daniel and he lurched toward the blaze with a howl, something moved from within the flames.

"Tam!" he screamed.

And she was there—stumbling, coughing, and carrying you. You were covered in ash and there were scorch marks on your clothes, but you were alive. Your mother had somehow spared you the worst of the deadly smoke, but it had taken its toll on her. Her face was covered in black soot, streaked with lines where her tears had run down and then evaporated in the heat, and her hair was crisp and frayed. She was wheezing, barely able to breathe.

"Tam!" Daniel called, running for her as she emerged. "Tam, here!"

She cleared the doorway, one foot on the sidewalk, strong enough that I thought she might make it to his arms. And then as the roof collapsed in behind her, she fell.

Daniel lunged to catch her. Together, you all hit the ground, Daniel first, trying to cushion you against his chest from the blow, and Tam last, crumpling softly on top of you and him.

We all ran forward, to pull the three of you back from the flames—but just as we were close enough to grab hold, suddenly everything disappeared. The stoplights, the sidewalks, the little shops with their awnings.

The whole town, vanished.

We were back in the empty field, crouching in the grass, County Road 206 somewhere behind us.

And in Daniel's arms was only you, Nell.

Tam was gone.

XXI

After Felix finished talking, the silence lingered for what felt like a full minute. Naomi, Priya, and William were all staring at him, stunned.

"A folding gas station map," Priya murmured at last.

"I know," he said. "It sounds totally impossible. But it all adds up, as strange as it seems."

"And this old friend of Dr. Young's named Wally is still after the map all because . . . it has a copyright trap on it?" Naomi asked. "An Easter egg, like we sometimes put in our code? That's really what Nell's parents' friends said?"

"Yes, although I don't know why that actually makes a difference," Felix replied.

He'd told them everything he knew so far—except what Nell had said Francis revealed was the real reason the map was so valuable. Because that last part was just too unbelievable to be true. And if he had any hope of convincing William that the Haberson Map had gotten close, but was wrong, and that they needed to help Nell, he needed to give him facts. Not fantasy. "But after everything that's happened, I do believe that they really were telling the truth when they told Nell that if she kept looking into it, Wally would come after her."

"And you're positive she still has this map now?" William asked.

"No," Felix replied. "But I do know she still had it up until at least last night. I saw it with my own eyes, at her apartment. She'd been planning to give it to the chair of the library tonight, but she changed her mind." He shuddered. "And now Irene is dead."

William glanced down at his tablet as it dinged again, and he rubbed his temples. "I need to call Ainsley and tell her what you just told me, but I'll be back soon."

"What can we do?" Felix asked.

"Stay here," he said. "I'm going to have her send an officer over to take your statement."

"But—"

"Nell's not answering her phone, and you don't know where she is." William didn't allow himself to be interrupted. "The police won't like that we're about to rescind our best lead and will likely keep pursuing her anyway—the more background you can give them, the faster they're going to understand. This is your best chance of helping her."

"He's right, Felix," Naomi agreed.

Priya nodded. "We'll wait with you."

William started for the elevators, moving briskly, his phone already ringing in his hand. "Thank you. Just hang on—Ainsley will get an officer here within half an hour."

The door slid shut after him, and the office plunged into stunned silence again.

"Do you need anything?" Naomi asked Felix.

"No," he replied. "You don't have to stay, really. Is Charlotte still down there in the lobby? She must be worried."

"She's at home. As soon as the news about the murder broke, I called her," she said. "We're here for you."

Felix tried to smile, but it came out as a grimace. "I just wish there was more I could do than sit here. What if the police don't believe me?"

"We'll cross that bridge if we come to it," Priya said.

The thought did little to comfort him. Frustrated, Felix spun his chair back to his computer, where he began clicking through the server to his personal files.

"What are you doing?" Naomi asked. "How can you work at a time like this?"

Felix shook his head. "I'm not."

"Is that a security video?" Priya asked, leaning closer. "Of the library?"

"From the night of the break-in," Felix confirmed. "Nell gave it to me when she showed me the Agloe map."

That drew Naomi over to his desk as well. "And?"

"It's useless," he admitted. "But I can't just sit here and do nothing."

He'd watched it ten times that day, but that was before he knew hardly anything about the Agloe map or the old web he was now tangled up in over it. Maybe this time, something would jump out at him. Something he hadn't seen before.

It *had* to.

Then something did.

"Actually, Nell told me there was a *second* map that her father was after, right before he died," he said to Naomi and Priya as the realization came to him. "It was an old building diagram of the library where he worked. We couldn't imagine why he'd want something so random, so Nell went looking for answers."

"A building diagram of the library?" Naomi repeated, thinking. "Maybe he was looking for an old room or something? One that had been blocked off in a remodel?"

"The opposite, actually," Felix said. "It wasn't a room that had been closed off and then removed from the floor plan, but rather a room that had *never* existed, yet still showed up on paper. Its own little phantom settlement."

Priya frowned. "But again, why would a little error on a piece of paper make either of these maps so valuable?"

"I don't know. But the error on that map was in the Map Division." He took a breath. "The exact room where the burglar was searching."

Francis told me that the reason the Agloe map is so special is that . . .

He could hear Nell's voice, just as mystified as he now felt, in his mind.

"But why would a fake room matter to a break-in?" Priya mused. "You said it yourself. It wasn't bricked over—it never existed in the first place."

Felix ignored them as they debated, turning back to his computer, where the video waited for him, a big, dark, silent square.

It's because the town becomes real if you have it. You can go *there.*

He still couldn't imagine that could be true at all. But Dr. Young had risked his life to keep the Agloe map, and Francis, Ramona, and Eve had risked theirs to get him the Sanborn . . .

He clicked play, and the video began to run.

"What are we looking for?" Naomi asked, as she and Priya saw that the playback had started.

"I don't know yet," he admitted. "But I . . . have a hunch. Maybe."

He watched the burglar—Wally—comb through the Map Division again, nimble and swift, as Naomi and Priya peered over his shoulder. Priya winced as he attacked the guard and callously continued on, and Naomi groaned as the view tilted downward as always near the end, still shuddering from the damage of Wally's swing.

They watched shadows cross in and out of the frame, back and forth as Wally double-checked every shelf in the partial view, moving increasingly faster with frustration. Then, finally, he vanished the same way he had the first time, there in the periphery of the lens one moment and then gone the next, with no other alerts elsewhere in the building triggered, and the recording ended.

"Wait, that's it?" Priya asked, as surprised as Felix had been the first time he saw it. "How the hell did he get out?"

Felix sighed, desperate, and hit play again.

The black stared back at him, peaceful and still. A flash erupted as the camera's lens came to life, and the burglar was there again, darting across the room, dodging the tables, opening every cabinet. Then the camera crashed downward again.

"Felix, I know you want to help, but . . . ," Naomi tried, but he didn't look away. He scrolled back yet again and watched the familiar room as Wally darted in and out of view, studying its thick old walls, its towering double-paned, wrought-iron windows. The shelves, the desks, the tables—

Wait.

There wasn't a door there in the library.

"How—" He gasped, confused.

"What is it?" Priya asked, leaning closer. "What do you see?"

Felix pointed. There *was* a door in the back wall of the reading room in the video—even though that was impossible.

What was going on?

Felix grabbed his mouse and scrolled back on the timer, frames stuttering, this time dragging it much, *much* further back, hours before the relevant break-in section, all the way to when the security guard first began his walking rotations after hours, around nine o'clock in the evening. Felix waited on the Map Division, watching the dark screen as the guard moved down the hall, and then the room came to life, the camera triggered by his motion—

There was no door.

Felix hit pause and rubbed his eyes again, trying to clear his head.

He could still see the Map Division perfectly in his mind, even after all these years. He knew that side of the room well—he'd been in charge of dusting the display cases there every Monday morning. There was definitely *not* a door there, only the glass cabinets and a small expanse of wall they sometimes used to hang single-piece specimens belonging to no collection. A door *couldn't* be there. If one was, it would open directly into the huge bay of printers Swann had installed in the back-office archives. And Felix had just seen when the guard entered the Map Division that there wasn't one.

But somehow, during the break-in—and also on the Sanborn map Nell had—there *was*.

"Felix, what are we looking at?" Naomi asked. Neither she nor Priya knew the details of the room as well as he did. "What do you see?"

"Just watch," he said breathlessly. "One more time."

He skipped forward all the way to midnight again, to when the break-in occurred, and hit play.

He pointed at the spot on the screen where he wanted them to look. "Watch."

The room came to life the same as it had in the previous viewings of the security footage. Wally appeared, triggering the camera, and began searching the room. He had a small piece of paper in his gloved hand, Felix realized this time. A list? A diagram? *A map?* It was in one frame before Wally moved again, barely visible in the grainy night vision—

And the door was there.

The camera was hit and tilted down at the table again. Felix hit pause and jumped back in time to the security guard's first nine o'clock walking check.

There was no door.

"What the . . . ," Naomi said, seeming now to see what Felix had just found.

This didn't make sense.

Felix skipped forward to the break-in on the feed.

There was a door.

He skipped back.

There was no door.

He skipped forward.

There was a door.

How was that possible?

Romi

I wasn't there when your mother died, Nell.

I should have been, but I was still too furious at Francis and Eve for what they'd done. A whole town was not big enough to hold the three of us—there was no way I ever would have agreed to be inside it at the same time as they were. But if only I'd known what was about to happen. Maybe I could have done something. Maybe I could have stopped it.

But maybe I couldn't have.

After all, I was the one who helped set it all in motion. I was the one who stole the map for Bear.

That horrible day, I had spent the entire morning at the motel, lying on the bed staring at the ceiling, seething with anger at how I'd been wronged. But as justified as my brooding felt, by the afternoon, even I was bored with it.

My room didn't have cable for the TV or even a stack of magazines. I'd packed my clothes before fleeing the house, but I'd been in such a rush, I hadn't taken anything of mine from downstairs. And while I'd collected my research from Agloe with Tam, Daniel, and Bear, I wanted nothing to do with it. What I really wanted were the little things, still scattered around our living room. The novel I'd brought to read, my Walkman, my sketchpad.

It was getting close to dinner, but I knew how late the group always stayed in Agloe. Only Bear would be at the house, since he'd pretended to be sick. I wouldn't have to see Francis, Eve, or Wally at all. If there was ever a good time to go, it was then.

And, I'm ashamed to admit, I was curious if Bear had managed to sell the map. I wanted to know I'd succeeded in stealing something from Wally, the way he'd stolen the truth from me. I wanted Bear to tell me how the deal had gone.

It was five miles, but I'd already done the walk once, the day I'd found evidence of all of Wally's robberies at the Rockland Library. I could do it again. The sun was low enough in the sky that it wasn't too hot, and I liked listening to the crickets in the grass along the side of the road. I could always ask Bear to plug in the disconnected phone to call a taxi back to the motel. He could just unplug it again right after.

But when I got to the house, Bear wasn't there. And neither was either car.

I still had my key, so I let myself in. "Bear?" I called hesitantly. Had he gone somewhere else with the buyer? I wondered.

It took me half an hour to find the rest of my stuff, as well as our old maps—the ones we'd originally intended to use for the *Dreamer's Atlas*. Daniel had done most of the tracking down, especially for the maps in the fantasy novels, but some of the historical ones—a Franklin, a Calisteri, and a Dutch Visscher of New York—had been loaned to us for the project in my name. I didn't want to leave my reputation in the others' hands, if they were late returning them.

I stood at the door with the bundle in my arms, stalling. I was torn between waiting to see if Bear might come back so I could talk to him and leaving before the others returned.

I finally decided to write Bear a note and make my escape. But as I tore paper off the pad on the refrigerator, I heard a set of tires on the driveway. And then another.

Both cars were home.

"Shit," I cursed.

It was too late to escape unseen, but perhaps if I rushed out the door and kept going, I could get past them all before they'd gotten out of their seats. If I walked far enough down the road, they'd have to leave me alone eventually.

But when I got outside, my resolve crumbled into confusion.

"Wally?" I gasped.

They were all slowly climbing from the cars, but he was the one I saw first.

And there was something very wrong with him.

There was something wrong with all of them.

I couldn't make sense of what I was seeing. They were all dirty, their clothes covered in something dark, and moving like zombies. Even though their eyes were glazed with shock, I could see the streaks down their faces through the grime. They had been crying—all of them—it looked as though they'd been crying for a hundred years, until they were no more than husks of themselves.

"What happened?" I asked, running down the porch steps. Bear was also with them, somehow, even though they'd left him behind that morning.

"Romi," Francis whispered in surprise, his voice so hoarse it cracked.

He collapsed into me, halfway between an embrace and a faint. Even as angry as I still was at him, I let my belongings slide to the ground and put my arms around his waist to hold him up, instead of shoving him away from me—everything was so off, it was terrifying, and I couldn't think straight. The world felt suspended, like we were frozen in time, or had gone outside of it, where old history didn't exist. Something far worse did.

"Where's Tam?" I asked, when I realized what was different, who was missing. "Francis, where's Tam?"

"We have to burn the house" was all he said.

The sheriff, police, and fire department showed up, eventually. Drawn from town by the hot glow and the smoke churning over the trees, blotting out the sky. It was after midnight by then, and the horrible white beams of their headlights blinded us when they came roaring up the long driveway. As they jumped out of their vehicles, engines still on, I caught sight of Eve and Bear clinging to each other, both sobbing, and Daniel, standing at the edge of the grass, staring off into the trees. You were in his arms, although I'm not sure he could feel you there. You had been crying hysterically after the fire in Agloe, but now you were staring up at him silently, perfectly still, more like a doll than a child. Waiting endlessly, for him to come back to life. To tell you that your mother was fine. That she would be back soon. That everything would be all right.

But nothing would ever be all right again.

"All of it," Francis said softly as we stood beside each other in the dark, watching the embers of what used to be the house, orange lines traced through the pile of black char. "All gone."

"I don't want any of it back anyway," I answered numbly.

The gravel crunched, and I heard the crackle of a radio, felt the piercing halo of a flashlight pass over me.

"This was your house?" the sheriff asked gently, once he reached us.

I turned back to the ashes. I wanted to plunge myself into them.

"Yes," Francis managed. "We were renting it this summer."

"And she was inside? Tamara Young?"

I closed my eyes, so they wouldn't see my heart break.

Francis took a ragged breath. "Yes," he lied. "She was inside."

Over the next hour, the officers gathered our statements and the paramedics treated your burns, Nell, but it was already over. They would never find Tam's bones there in the ash, but it didn't matter. They already believed she had died in the house. Everything else about that night was real, after all. Our open, agonizing grief, and your desperate cries for her, the burns on your arms. And no matter how hard they searched, they would never find the place where it had truly happened. The way back there was gone forever, without a map.

They had all burned up. All of the thousands Wally had hunted down, and the very first one that Tam always kept. The one we all used to get in and out of the town together each day. The one she'd found together with Wally.

It had died with her. And so had Agloe.

As the fire department was packing up to leave, the remains of the house waterlogged and cold, the sky already brightening with dawn, the sheriff convinced us to follow them back to Rockland in our cars, where they could book us into the motel until we got back on our feet again. Just yesterday, I would have fought tooth and nail against the insult of having Francis and Eve in the same building as me, after what they'd done. Now, I didn't care at all. I didn't care about anything.

The paramedics guided Daniel into the ambulance, so your burns could be cleaned at the local hospital. I watched them close the doors, until the only part of either of you I could see was his face through the little square window on the back of the ambulance—the horrible emptiness in his eyes.

As the ambulance pulled away, I saw a flicker of movement in the trees. It was Wally, I realized. He seemed so far away, so hollowed out, that he looked more like a stone than a person, just part of the landscape. Or maybe more like a ghost.

I was so buried in my pain, I couldn't even raise my voice to tell him to get into one of the cars. But I could see that he wouldn't ever have come anyway.

"Come on, Wally," Bear finally said. Each word was such an effort, they barely made it past his lips. "We have to go."

But Wally took a step back, receding farther into the trees, disappearing.

He was going back to the field, I knew. That empty, empty field. Looking for a way back in, even though it was impossible.

We stayed in the motel for two weeks, waiting for the case to close. The firefighters combed through the rubble four times over searching for Tam's remains, until the station chief finally told them to give up. The whole house had been made of wood, which burns hotter than a house made of mixed materials, the sheriff told us when he broke the news. If a fire smoldered so long, sometimes not enough could be found to make an identification. I think he just wanted to be done with us, more than anything. Rockland was a peaceful little place, unused to such agony. We all were barely alive, barely able to even hear him, whenever he came to the motel to update us. He was a father too, he'd told us the first night—I could see how Daniel's grief haunted him. By the end, he couldn't even look Daniel in the eyes. Couldn't finish his sentences if you were in the room, whimpering helplessly. Couldn't wait to escape us.

And the whole time, Wally was barely there.

Sometimes late at night, I thought I could hear the creak of his door at the end of the walkway, but he was never inside his room when any of us went to knock. Because he was out there, trying to find a way back to Agloe.

The only time I saw him was the day they closed the case. It was late and dark, and I was sitting on a plastic chair by the motel's dirty, silent pool, staring at nothing. I heard the gate open, and then he came around the corner, on his way to his room.

He looked terrible. He was barely more than a skeleton.

"They closed the case" was all I could say.

"I don't care," he answered.

His voice was toneless, like it wasn't even coming from him, or rather, like he was very far away. He was, in a way. He was still in Agloe, even though his body was here.

"It wasn't supposed to happen like this," Wally murmured. When I looked up, his eyes were fixed on the dark, still water.

"The fire? Weren't you trying to destroy them all anyway?"

"No," he said. He raised his hands and then let them drop.

I didn't understand at first—until I did.

"You were trying to destroy all of them—but one," I said.

Wally nodded. "The town was safe from outsiders, but it wasn't safe from us. There were still thousands of chances for me to be betrayed again, no matter how carefully I tried to guard them all. I had to fix that."

He could not possibly keep track of thousands of copies. But he could keep track of just one.

"I was going to take them out and burn them safely. All of them but the original. The one Tam and I found together. But then everyone started fighting, and Nell . . . and Tam had to save her . . . and . . ."

For a moment I thought he might cry. But there was nothing left inside of him.

"I just wanted one thing," he finally said. "Daniel and Nell could have her love, all of you could have her friendship, the whole world could have her brilliance. I just wanted one thing that could be ours. That's all."

I looked down because I couldn't bear to keep looking at him.

"I'll finish it," he pronounced.

"What?"

"Our *Dreamer's Atlas*," he said. "I'll finish it for her. No matter how long it takes."

He stared at me in the dark. Determined, helpless. Alive, dead. I could see it, then. That our cursed project was the only thing sustaining him. The only thing keeping his guilt from completely consuming him. I knew he would never stop looking until he found the town again. And I knew that he would never manage to do it. Because if there was no map, there was no town.

"You don't have to do this to yourself," I whispered.

"I'm not doing this for me," he replied.

"Tam's gone, Wally." I swallowed. "Even if you could find a way back into Agloe, it doesn't matter. She's gone."

Wally turned away from me slowly, moving as if in a dream.

"Goodbye, Romi. I hope it works out for you and Francis."

Then he disappeared up the stairs and down the walkway. By the time we'd woken up the next morning, he was already gone. The desk clerk said he'd checked out at dawn.

That same morning, Daniel rented a car from the local depot. He told us he was also leaving. He would go to New York City and find a job, and never come back. He didn't care about Agloe anymore and wanted nothing to do with it.

I knew how he felt. I wanted nothing to do with it, either. None of us did, except for Wally. We had only been staying there, waiting, for you and Daniel. Once he'd gone, it took the rest of us no more than a few days to disappear as well.

Even though none of us could bear to be near each other for more than a few minutes, Daniel still knocked on each of our doors to tell us it was time, when he'd finished packing the car.

"Room for one more box?" I asked him.

"What is it?" he asked as his eyes fell on it, and he recognized Tam's handwriting. It was another of the boxes we'd originally used to move our things to the house in Rockland, and that I'd then grabbed to get my stuff out of that same house in a hurry, the night I found out about Francis and Eve. Tam had jokingly written *junk* on the side of it, because we'd packed it with all of the group's more scientific texts and tools, as opposed to her and my artistic ones. Inside, I'd put my share of the maps from our original version of the *Dreamer's Atlas* that I'd taken from the house before we burned it. The Franklin, the Calisteri, the Visscher.

"No," he said.

"They're all that's left," I said.

"I don't want them."

"Not for you," I said. "For Nell, someday. She might."

Finally, Daniel took the box and put it in the trunk. I thought the maps were probably as good as gone—that he'd throw them out as soon as he drove away—but I figured it was his choice. No university would hold unreturned loans against us after finding out about the fire and Tam's death.

"I'll miss you," he said to me.

We all hugged, and he let us say goodbye to you, but you were already dozing in your car seat. You seemed so peaceful, almost happy, for the first time in a long time. Not caught in a nightmare—just dreaming. We didn't want to wake you from it.

He drove away, and that was it. The end of the Cartographers.

That was supposed to be the last time any of us saw each other. Not because of the pain, but because we were trying to protect you, Nell.

Your father never stopped loving your mother, but he had you to take care of. I didn't know at the time why he was so afraid Wally might come after him someday—why he was so adamant about severing ties with the rest of us and all memories and research of Agloe in the hope of convincing him not to. If anything, I thought that if Wally ever resurfaced, it would be to Daniel least of all, for all the pain he'd caused him. I couldn't understand why Daniel was so sure it would be exactly the opposite.

It wasn't until much, much later—the day of the Junk Box Incident, to be exact—that I finally did.

◦ ◦ ◦ ◦

I was the next to leave. It was only Francis, Eve, and Bear left at that point—the only one I really wanted to say goodbye to was Bear, but I didn't want to run into the other two. Luckily, Bear was already waiting in the lobby, huddled in one of the dirty old armchairs.

"Weekend bus," he said sadly, when he saw me.

"If only I'd taken it earlier," I replied. "Before you'd ever asked me, before we'd had the idea . . ."

Bear wrapped me in a huge, heartbreaking hug. "I know," he whispered, his voice muffled by my hair. "I know."

It didn't make any sense—I couldn't have taken the bus unless I'd known about Francis and Eve's affair, and if I'd known about their affair, I couldn't have left without striking back, trying to wound like I'd been wounded—but it didn't matter. We were both so destroyed inside, we had gone far past needing things to make sense. We just wanted none of it to have happened. We just wanted Tam back. It wasn't fair that the town wasn't real, but her death was.

Bear helped me carry my suitcase. We waited in silence, blinking at the early sun, until the bus shuddered into the little depot with a groaning wheeze.

"Do you want me to tell Francis anything?" he asked as the driver opened the door, gave us a wave, and looked back to his clipboard.

I shook my head. Then I changed my mind.

"Tell him it doesn't matter," I said. Because it didn't.

I had thought that I could never feel anything but rage ever again, the moment I found out he'd betrayed me—but now after what we'd lost, I could hardly even remember what it felt like to be that angry. I couldn't feel anything at all but the void Tam had left in my heart. What he had done seemed like hardly anything at all, now.

"You mean . . . you forgive him?" Bear asked.

I could not even muster the will to try to explain. "Sure," I finally said.

Bear studied me for a moment and then looked back at the bus, his eyes darting to the waiting open door, as if what I'd said might mean that there was a chance, the slenderest sliver of a hope of a chance, that I could repair things with Francis. Even amid our agony, he was still Bear. Still desperate to keep as many of us together as he could.

But I shook my head again.

Even if I wasn't angry at Francis anymore, I could never go back to him—for the same reason I couldn't be near any of them again.

Because the only thing any of us would be able to think about would be what we'd all done to Tam.

The bus dropped me off in Manhattan, at Port Authority Bus Terminal.

After so many months in quiet, peaceful Rockland, and most of them spent hiding within an even quieter, more deserted town, the city was overwhelming. Lights and horns and clattering subway tracks everywhere, a crush of pedestrians and cars. I scrambled away from the streets as fast as I could. I wasn't ready to face the real world yet. I'd spent too much time in the unreal one.

I had promised myself I wouldn't work in maps anymore—but eventually, that's where I found myself again. It was what I'd studied for, what I'd trained for. I didn't have any other skills. I rented a room in some giant, faceless building where I never saw any of my neighbors and set up as a freelance graphic artist. I drew simple line maps of local neighborhoods for restaurants to print on their paper menus, to show their delivery radiuses.

It was not art. But I no longer wanted that anyway. I just wanted enough to pay for groceries and rent, and to disappear.

And I did, for years. The only reason I finally returned to our cloistered industry and became a private dealer was because I found the Lawrence Street map.

You know how this works by now, Nell, but it was a moment of discovery for me. Lawrence Street is on a page from the Brooklyn section of an old Five-Borough atlas—and only there.

When I found my way in, I was both stunned, and also not. We all had suspected that summer, on some level, that if the phantom settlement on the Agloe map was real, then it was possible that smaller phantom settlements and traps on other maps could be real, too, if only you could spot them. I'd promised Daniel never to speak to anyone from our group again, but I considered breaking that promise, to tell them what I'd discovered—but I didn't have to. When I found out where Eve was working, as a preservationist with the Sanborn collection, and looked up city copies of the zoning maps for Bear's office, I knew they'd also arrived at the same conclusion.

But that realization did little to comfort me.

Because I knew that if Eve and Bear had also figured out what I had—that there were other places out there like Agloe, hidden from the world—that wherever he was, Wally probably also had. And he could use them like we could.

And that was when I received the news about Professor Johansson's memorial at the university.

I worried I was being paranoid, when my first thought upon seeing the card was that something had happened to him, that it had not been a natural death. But I couldn't help it. I found myself combing through city records online again, this time for Madison, Wisconsin, looking at blueprints and municipal service plans of the university. I hoped I was wrong, but after everything that had happened, I feared the worst.

And then I found it.

There was a trap room in the science building at our old university, on an 1886 construction map. A utility closet that had been planned, but never built, because the classrooms had expanded in a later draft. It was one floor down from the faculty offices.

The rest was not hard to find. I knew what to look for.

It turned out that even though Wally hadn't been seen since that summer, his ghost had been haunting us all along. The private castle in New Jersey, where General Drafting Corporation had kept all their records and past editions, had been burned to the ground in yet another accidental fire some years after we all left Rockland—everything destroyed. When I asked, my clients told me rumors they'd heard within their amateur collecting circles about a private buyer somewhere, part of a group called the Cartographers, who had resurfaced after a few years of silence and would pay impossible money for some seemingly worthless map—except as hard as they tried, they couldn't find one anywhere. Perhaps I could help them locate a copy, for a split commission? And online, I saw scattered reports of threats and disappearances, and even deaths, of scholars and dealers, of hobbyist geocachers and local librarians, of museum administrators and teachers. They had happened over so many years and across so many states, that police had not been able to put the pattern together.

It was Wally. Hunting another final copy of our map—and removing anyone who might spread the word or get there first.

I didn't know if he would be waiting for us at the memorial in Madison, laying some plan to blackmail us into helping him steal something else he thought would help him get back to the town, but I didn't want to take any chances.

I decided to disappear.

I massacred my reputation on purpose. Every terrible rumor you've heard about me in the field, about how I sold counterfeit maps or couldn't provide provenance papers to private collectors, was all on purpose. I had to make it so that no one would want to come looking for me. I thought if I had no connection to the industry anymore, Wally would not see me as a target.

If he could even find me in the first place.

It wasn't Wally who eventually found me, though. It was Daniel.

He used my business card, one I'd given him a long time ago, when I'd gone underground—the same one you found after he'd died. It was a day much like the one when you came. I was alone, going through inventory, searching for more impossible places. Escape routes, hiding places I could save to use later if I needed to.

It was the day of the Junk Box Incident—but I didn't know that at the time. I only knew something terrible had happened. I could see it in his face.

How old that face was. How creased, and sad, and tired. It had been at least twenty-five years since he'd driven away from our motel with you. I had wondered, in the intervening decades, if I would even recognize any of the others if I ever passed them on the street. Grief can raze a face far worse than ten times as many years. It was one of the things that worried me about Wally the most—by that metric, I would never see him coming for me, if he ever did.

But Daniel I did recognize, somehow. Or maybe I could feel that it was him more than I could see. For the briefest moment when he'd come inside, it had felt as though two people had been there, instead of just one. That Tam was there, too.

We stared at each other in silence.

"Something happened," I said finally, studying him warily.

He nodded.

I waited for him to tell me what was going on, but he didn't say anything. I thought he was trying to find the right words, but then I realized as my heart faltered that it was because there were no words. He didn't need any. There was only one reason he would be here, so many years later.

"You still have it, don't you?" I whispered. Horrified. Amazed.

Somehow, impossibly, he did.

The last copy of the map.

Your mother had saved it at the same time she'd saved you, he told me once I'd calmed down. She'd tucked it into your clothing before she'd handed you to your father and succumbed to her wounds. He didn't find it until much later, when he was at the hospital letting the nurses examine your burns. How surprised he must have been.

Your mother managed to save the town after all, with her dying breath—and your father had decided to protect her last secret.

"And Nell found it, didn't she?" I finally asked.

He closed his eyes and nodded again.

I was dizzy, barely able to feel the ground under me, the way I'd been when I'd seen them all returning to the house, soot-stained, crying, without Tam. Despite everything we'd done to be free of that map and that place, it was going to happen all over again. "What does she know?"

"Nothing," he insisted. "She was so young. She didn't recognize it at all. Not it, and not the other maps from our old project I buried it with." He held the Agloe map out to me like it was hot, still on fire itself. "I tried to convince her it was worthless. I—"

"What did you do?"

"What I had to," he said. "But I can't keep it now. If she ever tells anyone, even in passing . . . If Wally ever catches wind of it . . ."

He held it out to me, pleading.

But instead of helping him, I took a step back.

I was just as afraid of Wally as he was—perhaps even more, because I had been the last one to see him that night at the motel. I knew he'd never give up. And I knew the only thing keeping all of us safe from him was the fact that if there was even a single remaining copy of the map out there, it was not with us.

Except it was.

"I don't understand," I finally said. "Why did you keep it in the first place?"

I couldn't figure that out, even years later. That map was the key to an impossible place, and the last thing that had belonged to Tam, but even so, it was not worth the danger, to him or to you. Not with Wally lurking out there. Daniel was the one who had said that in the first place. He was the one who left Agloe, and Rockland, first.

"That's why I came to see you," Daniel replied. "I thought out of everyone, you might understand."

He held out the map as if to say *If you help me, I'll explain.*

"You were our other artist. You know how much that place meant to her. You saw the ideas she was trying to work on."

I didn't understand what he was trying to tell me, but I also didn't want to know. I didn't want to face what I'd done that horrible summer, everything I'd lost because of it. And I didn't want to become the one who Wally would come after first, when he inevitably worked out whatever had happened that day at the NYPL between you and your father was about the Agloe map and then traced Daniel's steps thereafter to me.

"Please," Daniel begged me. "Help me. He'll never find it here."

He was so desperate. So alone.

But I couldn't.

I told him that if he gave it to me to hide, I'd burn it, just like the house. Just like he should have done that same night of the fire, the moment he realized he still had it. That was the only way he could guarantee that we—that you, Nell—could really be safe. I offered to do it right there, so I could see it with my own eyes and be sure it was gone forever.

But Daniel wouldn't hand it over on those terms. And those were the only ones I would accept.

Eventually, he left with the map and promised never to come back again. And I pretended that he did go home to destroy it, for my own sanity. There was no one who could hide it better than me, so he had no other options. I convinced myself I had done a good thing. I had forced him to do what he should have done a long time ago. As each year passed, I slowly came to believe that was really true.

But when he reached out again a few weeks ago, to beg me to help him find a way out of the library, just in case, I could no longer pretend Daniel had done it. He had kept it after all—and Wally had finally figured it out.

I could not bring myself to call Eve. But Francis picked up immediately.

Even decades later, we were still an incredible team. Archives, inventory, edition verification, manufactured loan permissions, insurance, mail. We moved fast. So fast, I thought we could save him in time.

But Wally was even faster.

When I read the news that Daniel had died, alone in his office in the library, one day before Eve's Sanborn arrived via Francis, the only thing I could hope for was that you still didn't know anything about it, Nell.

Then you showed up at my door.

XXII

Felix continued to stare at the screen in disbelief. At a door that could not be there—in the wall of the Map Division as it glowed in the freeze-frame—and yet it was.

That's how the burglar got in and out.

Through a trap room on a seventh edition map from an early twentieth-century flood and fire insurance company. From the page, and into the library.

It was real. The error on the Sanborn map was *real.*

The proof was right there on the security footage. Hiding in plain sight this whole time, if only he'd been able to notice. But who could have noticed a thing like that? It wasn't possible.

Was it?

Even with the video in front of him, he could still hardly believe it could be true. But if it somehow was real for the NYPL, and after the strange incidents with Francis at Swann's home and Ramona at her shop, then . . .

This meant that the phantom settlement on Nell's map also might be . . . real?

He couldn't make sense of it. The physics, the cartography, the architecture, the bend in reality. But one question stood out above all the others.

Did Nell know about this?

"Felix." He finally realized Naomi was shaking his shoulder gently. "Hey, Felix."

When he looked up, she and Priya were hovering at the edge of his desk, staring at him with concern.

"Are you okay?" Priya asked.

"I have to go," he said suddenly, jumping out of his chair.

"What?" Naomi asked. "Now?"

"You can't leave!" Priya insisted. "The cops are coming to talk to you! And we don't even know what we're looking at! How the *hell* is this even possible?"

"I have no idea," he said helplessly, scrambling for his keys. "But I can't wait for the police now. You saw Wally on that video. You think they're going to know how to deal with someone who can do that better than us?"

"But you can't even reach Nell!" Naomi said. "Her phone is disconnected, remember? How are you going to find her, to tell her all of this?"

That slowed him down. He'd forgotten she wasn't answering her phone. There were several places she might be, if the police hadn't caught her at the library—at home, or Swann's brownstone, or her father's darkened, closed-off apartment, or maybe even Classic—but what was he going to do? Rush between them all, back and forth through New York nighttime traffic for hours, until he finally guessed right and found her?

"Actually, I know where she's going," Felix finally said. "The only problem is, I don't know how we can get there."

"Agloe," Naomi answered, with dawning understanding.

He began to pace. "The whole point of Agloe is that it doesn't appear anywhere else but her cheap little map, so we can't refer to another one or look it up in our database . . ."

"There's not much online either," Priya confirmed. "Some old sales for possible copies like you found earlier, but nothing about its secret value—or the actual location of the town."

Felix stopped—an idea occurred to him.

"Let's set the Haberson Map to look for Agloe," he suggested.

"What?" Priya cried.

"It got close the last time, when we set it to look for the burglar!" he reasoned. "Honestly, maybe it did better than we asked—it found what we needed, rather than what we thought we wanted. Maybe if we aim it toward Agloe, it'll find Nell."

"But what more information can we input to help it search?" Naomi asked. "If only we had a scan of her map."

If only, Felix thought. He wondered what the Haberson Map would do with an impossible data point like that. In response, the map seemed to glow brighter at him from the big screen.

He closed his eyes, trying to picture Nell's map from the last time he'd seen it. When they both had been crouched over its faded old paper on the table the night before, going square by square on the grid, searching for that mysterious little place. The closest they'd been to each other in a long, long time. He remembered the faint floral scent of her hair, the sound of her shallow, focused breathing. How long it had taken, moving inch by inch across that miniature world, searching for the phantom settlement, and then how he'd been surprised when they'd gotten to—

Felix gasped suddenly.

"Maybe I can get us close enough," he said. "The phantom settlement was just down the road from a house upstate that Nell's family used to live in a long time ago." He waved off the surprised looks they gave him at that. "I don't know the house's address, but I remember that the name of the town it was within was called Rockland."

"Priya, pull our—" Naomi started to say, but Priya had already opened up the section of their server devoted to residential apps to sort through a huge address database. "There's nothing under owners or renters," she said. "But you said that house burned down, right?"

"Yeah," Felix confirmed. "It was how her mother died."

Priya was no longer in the Haberson server but logged into some kind of public records database. Overhead, the Haberson Map was following her, mirroring her search within one of its myriad frames, making guesses at additional sources from there. "If she died, there would have been a police report, and probably some local news stories . . ."

"They wouldn't list the address of the house, though," Naomi said. "For privacy reasons."

Felix knew Naomi was right. He'd looked up the obituary himself years ago, when he'd first gotten together with Nell and she'd told him the sad history. There hadn't been much, just a few mentions in local papers, but he didn't recall ever seeing an exact address.

He glanced up and saw that the Haberson Map was no longer

looking for articles on Dr. Tamara Jasper-Young—it was combing through property tax records, for some reason.

"What about real estate listing archives for the area?" he asked, suddenly realizing.

Naomi looked up at him. "What do you mean?"

"The news never gave out the address, but if the house burned all the way down, the property wouldn't really be classified as a residence anymore, would it? It would revert to being a vacant lot, or land tract, tax-wise. There must be records for that. If we look for sale listings for empty lots anytime after that summer, for addresses that went from residence to land . . ."

"I got it," Priya said.

Felix rushed over. "Show me."

Priya turned the screen toward him. "There are plenty of houses that went up for sale in Rockland, and even more tracts of available land, but there's only one that changes classification—from house to land—in that entire year." She pointed. "One sixty Spring Rain Road, Rockland, New York."

His eyes jumped across the screen as she talked, double-checking everything.

Priya was right. That was it.

"That's got to be the one," Naomi breathed.

As if to agree, the Haberson Map chimed. They all looked up to see it had accepted the same data point—a slim glowing line from their office in Manhattan snaked its way across lower New York State, toward the destination.

He was halfway there. If the Haberson Map could find the house, maybe if he took it with him, something there could lead it to Agloe, too.

Felix grabbed his phone from the desk and hugged Priya over the back of her chair. "You're a genius."

"I know," she laughed, but as he pulled away, she caught his arm, so he had to look at her. "Be careful, Felix," she said. "We don't even know who this Wally is, and he could be out there after her, too."

"I will," he promised. "Thank you both."

As he turned to leave, Naomi called out to him one more time. "This can't *really* be real, right?" she asked, looking over again at the impossible room in the NYPL still on his screen. "I mean, an entire town? How can it be real?"

"I don't know," Felix said. "But I'll tell you when I get there."

Even though he'd been awake all night, Felix never once felt his eyelids start to droop on the drive. The closer he drew to Rockland, the more nervous he became. In the east, dawn was threatening, the horizon already beginning to brighten. As he drove, winding along the quiet country roads through square after square of pastel-green-and-yellow farmland, Felix couldn't help imagining a tiny image of his car cruising along one of the thin black lines on Nell's highway map, and himself watching from above.

His phone, the Haberson Map's route on its little screen, dinged politely—he was getting close to the house's address they had found.

His pulse quickened. The old house was as close as he could get to this mysterious phantom settlement, but it was still at least a few miles away. What could he do once he reached it, to help the Haberson Map find his real target? Would this really work?

He gripped the steering wheel, anxious. It always had succeeded before. Traffic, weather, crime, practically any question he had—he could find a data stream in the Haberson Map to show him the answer. The greatest map in the world, a map that could achieve a level of accuracy and detail that was nearly unfathomable, but would it be able to explain what was actually going on this time?

Would it be able to show him the way better than a cheap, old paper version could?

A rumble of thunder startled him. Above, the deep navy clouds were curdling with the first hints of rain. Felix rolled up his window just as the gentle patter began against the roof of his car.

His phone dinged again, more urgent.

Please be there, Nell, Felix wished. *Or at least have left me a clue about how to find you.*

A moment later, the automated navigation voice advised him to turn, and then suddenly in front of him, he saw a long gravel driveway leading up from the road to the right and a rusted mailbox posted at its start. Felix eased onto the brake and guided the car off the asphalt and onto the damp path. The trees closed in overhead, unkempt. The way sloped slightly, and he took the corner slowly so as not to skid.

"You have arrived at your destination," the Haberson Map announced.

At the top of the driveway, the trees opened up into a small clearing—where a house *should* have been but was no longer.

Felix stopped the car.

"You have arrived—" his phone started to say again, before he canceled the route, and silence fell back over him again.

This was it.

The place where Nell had lived when her parents and their friends discovered the Agloe map. Where whatever happened that summer had changed them all forever.

He waited for a moment and then climbed out of the car, even though it was raining. His shoes squished in the thickening mud as he went forward, to what remained of the house.

A great, black expanse stretched before him, a mixture of fine silt much darker than the greenish-brown earth beyond, where no weeds grew. And atop it, a mound of old, forgotten ash and scarred concrete foundation.

"Where are you, Nell?" he whispered.

He was so close to her. He could feel it. She, and the town, couldn't be more than a mile or two away from him, in any direction.

He just had to find it.

Suddenly, the sound of footsteps on gravel broke the quiet patter. Felix turned quickly as a shadow emerged from the trees behind him and into the early morning gloom.

"Nell?" His heart thudded with hope.

But it wasn't Nell.

"Felix," William Haberson said.

Felix took a step back, surprised.

How did William know where he'd gone?

"You look like you've seen a ghost," William remarked, opening an umbrella. Behind his boss's form, Felix could now make out the dark outline of another company car, much farther back. He'd pulled into the driveway without noticing it parked there in the rain.

"How did you find me?" Felix asked.

"You were using the Haberson Map to navigate. We're all on the same system."

"Oh," Felix replied, feeling silly. "Right."

"I know how much Nell means to you. I figured you might not wait for the police."

Felix felt his phone buzz in his pocket, indicating a text message.

"It's Naomi and Priya," he said, seeing Naomi's name as the sender, and William nodded. He tried to skim the message quickly, without being rude.

<Felix, we're still in the office. Something weird is going on. The Haberson Map is showing that William is also where you are, at the house.>

"I'm sure they're worried about you, too," William was saying.

Felix put the phone away, already knowing what Naomi was telling him, and turned up his collar to keep the rain off. "I'm sorry I ran off. I just thought if I could find Nell . . ."

Naomi's next message came in, another urgent buzz.

"Sorry, let me just tell her everything's fine," Felix apologized, as William shrugged off the interruption, unbothered.

He swiped the screen to reply—but found himself confused by Naomi's words.

<But it's telling us that William left before you. Way before.>

"We'll figure all this out," William assured him. He studied the scorched ground. "As long as you can explain what you're doing here."

"It was supposed to be a stepping-stone," Felix replied. "Nell lost her mother here. She died saving Nell in a house fire when she was a baby. This was the house where it happened."

William was silent for a few moments, as if considering something.

"It wasn't here," he finally said.

Felix paused, confused. A prickling sensation along the back of his neck needled at him, like a tiny warning.

Naomi's messages were coming fast now, frantic. <William left before we found Nell's old Rockland address and put it into the Haberson

Map. How did he know about the house before us? How did he know where to go?>

Felix took a deep breath. Tried to ignore the feeling, tried to think. "How do you know the fire wasn't here?" he asked William.

"Nell would have come then, wouldn't she?" William answered. He gestured to the ground around them, to where their cars had stirred the mud and leaves together as they'd each crept up the long driveway. "Only two sets of tire tracks—ours. Do you think she'd drive all this way and not come to the place where her mother was last alive with her?"

Felix looked at the remains of the house again. "I guess not," he said.

But something still didn't make sense. He tried to shake off the growing unease.

<Felix, answer us. Are you okay?>

"But if Nell's mother didn't die here, then why is the house burned to ash?"

"To keep a secret," William said.

"But what secret? Nell said the fire had been an accident," Felix replied. "And her parents' friends confirmed it. How would her mother have died, then?"

"Maybe the secret isn't how," William answered. "It's where."

"Where?" Felix repeated.

The chill of sudden understanding crept over him then.

William turned back to the house. "It's like the Haberson Map. This has been the eternal struggle with our algorithm, hasn't it?" He sighed thoughtfully. "The paradox that even if our map could be perfect, every bit of data completely measurable and knowable . . . the world it represents isn't."

Felix had listened to him quote this very speech many times over the years—William drifted off into exploring this personal philosophy of his more often than not during their brainstorming meetings. *Could a perfect map only be developed for a perfect world? Or would the perfect map* make *the world within it perfect?* he'd ask.

But now, Felix heard the words with new, frightening clarity.

"But there's no such thing," he insisted. "Perfection—complete accuracy—is the goal of every map, but it's not actually . . . it's not *actually* possible, William. Even for us. Even if we could manage to make the Haberson Map completely accurate for every single data point for one instant, the world is always changing. Something will shift, and we'll be right back to square one again."

"You'd be surprised," William said. "Sometimes you just need to get something working on a miniature scale, and then everything unfolds." He turned back to the charred, rain-soaked heap in front of them and then looked beyond it, out into the woods. "The smallest thing could be the key. Like a building, for example. Or a town."

Felix's heart stuttered.

There it is, Nell had said, the night they had crouched over her coffee table, staring at her father's map, her voice full of wonder. *The phantom settlement. We found it.*

"I know you've always thought of the Haberson Map's philosophy as more of a charming intellectual exercise to push your team rather than an actual truth, but seriously consider it, Felix. Open your mind. It's already almost real," William urged.

"No, it's not."

"Sure it is. Just think of how far the field of cartography has come, these last few decades. Ignore the Haberson Map for a moment—think about how people now use even just our little city streets app on their phones while walking." William reached into his pocket and pulled out his own phone, as if to demonstrate. "They don't look at the street and check HabWalk. They walk with their eyes glued to HabWalk. They only stop when the map says they've arrived, and then they look up to see they've reached their destination." He looked back at Felix. "They're not comparing our map to the world—they're comparing the world to our map."

"William—"

But William continued, unperturbed. "And if that's true, if we could just take it one step further . . ." His eyes were distant, focused on something that wasn't there, rapt with wonder. "If we could just assimilate the final piece of data . . . our map would truly be *perfect.*"

Felix took a step back.

"All of it," he whispered. Dr. Young. Irene. Even the library security contract. "It was you. You did all of it."

But how was that possible?

"That's the wrong way," William said calmly. "We want to go south from here."

Felix looked at his car. He had to get away. As far as he could, as fast as he could.

"If you leave now, you'll miss Nell," William added, almost an afterthought. He shifted his umbrella and reached into his suit jacket to retrieve something—a photograph. He held it out to Felix.

Felix hesitated. But if William somehow really knew where Nell was, Felix couldn't leave now. He couldn't let William do the same thing to her that he'd done to everyone else in his path, standing in his way of the map.

"How did you even begin to suspect she was the one who had it?" Felix asked. "How did you know Dr. Young had owned it before that and hidden it at the library?"

In response, William simply held the photo out farther.

Finally, Felix gave up and took it. He leaned over slightly, so he could study the image without letting the rain touch it.

It was an old picture, slightly faded, one of the corners creased where it had been accidentally bent at some point. Felix lifted it up to examine it closer and froze.

But how . . .

It was an image of a couple standing in front of a packed car, on a driveway that looked just like this one. In the man's arms was a small child in a pair of purple overalls, mid-squirm. They all smiled back at him through the aging glossy paper, their eyes sparkling.

Felix recognized the man as a youthful Dr. Daniel Young.

A gust of wind slithered through the grass, and a pair of birds sheltering in the dripping trees somewhere began to sing, a rush of sound.

His gaze jumped quickly to the young woman's face. If the man was Dr. Young, that meant that she was Dr. Tamara Jasper-Young.

And that meant that the little girl in Dr. Young's arms . . . was *Nell.*

"Why do you have this?" Felix asked, voice shaking.

William looked down, to the puddle he was standing in. His shoes were already soaked to the bone, but he didn't seem to be able to feel it at all.

"William," Felix repeated. "Why do you have this picture?"

"Because I'm the one who took it," he finally said.

IV

The Cartographers

XXIII

They drove in tense silence after Ramona finished her story.

All six of them were crammed into Humphrey's old Toyota, him at the wheel, Ramona beside him, and Francis, Eve, and Swann in back—with Nell awkwardly perched half against the inside of the door and half on Swann's lap. It would have been more comfortable to be split into two groups, but with the police swarming the building, there had been no time for half of them to sneak across the street to Francis's car.

But even more than that, now that they were all back together, none of them *wanted* to be separated anymore. Wally had struck Nell's father and Irene when they were alone—there was safety in numbers, Nell hoped.

After escaping the police, who were busy breaking through the front door of Classic's building, they'd sped through the still-chaotic, crowded streets of nighttime Manhattan, up the West Street viaduct along the western edge of the island toward the Lincoln Tunnel. Nell had watched nervously as the overhead lights along the interior of the concrete tube flashed past them one after the other, the car flickering like someone was playing with a light switch, willing them to go faster.

When they emerged safely on the other side of the river, in Weehawken, New Jersey, she thought someone might say something, but it wasn't until they were clear of the urban streets and traveling north on I-95 for hours, when the buildings and cars had given way to trees and slowly brightening sunrise, that Ramona finally did.

"I'm so sorry," she said to Nell. Even as softly as she spoke, her voice seemed to echo in the car.

"It wasn't your fault," Nell replied. "It was like my father told me all along. The fire was a terrible, terrible accident."

"But we should have stopped it. We should have known where it was heading. But we did nothing."

Nell looked down. "I could say the same thing about myself."

His stubbornness and fiery temper aside, her father had been the head curator of the New York Public Library—*who* had she thought she was to believe she was going to win an argument against him, in his own office? She knew better than anyone that he would never back down, and yet she'd kept pushing, attracting more of their colleagues, backing him further into a corner. Instead of giving him a chance to let her in, she'd forced his hand. And even still, he'd protected her. He'd died to keep the map, and Wally, away from her.

What's the purpose of a map? Swann had asked her in the very beginning, when she had stumbled back into the NYPL after so long, clueless to the danger she was walking into. She had brushed it off then the same way she had a hundred times before, believing it a sentimental oversimplification. It turned out to have been true all along.

Cartography, at its heart, was about defining one's place in the world by creating charts and measurements. Nell had lived her life by that idea, that everything could be mapped according to references and thereby understood. But she could see now that she had been paying attention to the wrong references.

It was not a map alone that made a place real.

It was the people.

"Nell," Francis said softly. "Now that you know everything, we can turn around, if you want. We don't have to do this. We can do what your father wasn't strong enough to do. We can destroy the map for good, so Wally can never find it."

"No," Nell said.

She finally understood, she thought. She hoped.

"It wasn't that he was weak," she said. "It was the exact opposite. Keeping the map was the strongest thing he's ever done."

The others all looked at each other, not understanding.

"And we do have to go." She took a breath. "Because even after finally knowing everything that happened, there's *still* one last question I can't answer."

"What's that?" Swann asked.

"I think . . ." Nell trailed off. "I think she's there, somehow. I think my mother's still in Agloe."

The others shook their heads, afraid to believe it could be possible, but Nell was growing surer by the moment.

"How do you know?" Swann asked. "After hearing the whole story . . ."

"That's exactly why," Nell replied. "It was what you said, Ramona. You were right, that hiding this map meant my father was under constant threat his entire life, if Wally ever came to suspect he might have the last copy. And if there's really nothing left in the town but ash, and he wanted nothing to do with Agloe, and even more than that, wanted *Wally* to never be able to go there again . . ."

She held the map up.

"Why keep it all these years?"

She watched as the rest of them studied its cover in silence.

"No," Humphrey said, voice quavering. "He kept it because it was the last thing of your mother's."

"Or he might have been saving it for you, if it ever became safe to give it to you," Eve offered, equally hesitant.

"But why? Why save it for me, if all that's in Agloe is nothing?" Nell asked. "What if . . ."

She could see all of them struggling with the idea. They were desperate for her to be right, even as vanishingly plausible as it was.

"We want it to be true as much as you do, but we were there, Nell," Francis said. "We saw the flames. It's just not possible."

Nell looked at Ramona, who had remained silent as the rest of them argued. Nell put her hand in her pocket and clutched her mother's red Wisconsin fountain pen for courage. "You believe me, don't you?" she asked.

Ramona was lost in thought. "That same night I saw Wally come back from the field," she began, "I also saw your father. It was even later, almost turning to dawn again, when he came through the gate, you slumped over his shoulder. I was surprised, but I thought maybe walking you was the only way to get you to sleep, those days. He told me he'd gone to say goodbye. That's how I knew he was planning to leave for good the next day."

"Goodbye," Nell repeated.

"I thought he meant to the field—as close to the town as he could get. I didn't know then that he had the map. Maybe . . . maybe he meant Tam."

Ramona sighed, long and slow, as if learning how to breathe for the first time. Her eyes were filled with a new wonder.

"Maybe she's been there, all this time, the only place she could ever truly be safe."

"But why?" Humphrey asked. "Why would she have needed to stay hidden for so long? Away from Daniel, away from Nell? What could she be doing there that she couldn't do out here, with the rest of us?"

"Something she had to keep safe from Wally," Nell finally said.

Outside, a gentle rain had begun falling as they drove, misting the windshield and turning the road slick.

The patter against the roof swallowed Francis's words as he leaned forward. "Let's slow down," he said as he stared out the windshield. "We don't want to attract attention by speeding, in case he's following us."

"He already knows Nell still has the map," Humphrey replied. "Where else could she be heading but there?"

"We just have to get inside before he catches up," Francis said. "Then we'll be safe."

"And trapped," Ramona added.

Humphrey's eyes were locked grimly on the road ahead. "We're already trapped," he said. "We've all been, since we first found the town."

For a moment, no one said anything. Despite Francis's advice, Nell felt the car speed up a little more beneath them.

"It's happening all over again," Eve murmured. "Who would have thought that decades later, we'd be doing the exact same thing, in some inescapable cycle?"

Nell watched a collective shudder pass through the group.

"All of us together, going back to this same terrible place," Francis said. "We even have Nell with us."

"You've grown up so much," Eve said to her, studying her tenderly. "You look . . ."

"Just like Tam," Ramona agreed.

Almost like she was taking her mother's place, Nell could tell that she meant. A chill slipped down her back at the open fear she could see in their eyes.

"And Swann makes a fine Daniel," she said. "If everything is repeating all over again."

"It should be Felix then, not me," Swann replied.

She put her hand on his. "I'd rather be going with you."

He smiled at her. "You're really sure you don't want me to call him?" he asked.

"Very sure," she said.

She thought Swann was going to beg her to tell him what happened again, but instead he just said, "I'm sorry."

Nell sighed in response. She would not admit that she was, too.

"Just give it time," he offered. "Maybe he'll come around."

Nell shook her head. "He won't. Not after I ruined things again."

When she looked up, she realized that the faintest hint of a smile was on his lips.

"What?" she asked.

"Nothing," Swann said. "It's just, that's the first time in seven years that when I suggested you two might patch things up, you said 'he won't,' instead of 'I won't.'" He smiled. "It gives me hope it might work out after all."

"Why, because this time Felix hates me instead of me hating him?" She scoffed.

Swann shook his head. "My dear," he said, his voice gentle. "He's never hated you. It was always you standing in the way of you both."

"That's not true," Nell said.

It couldn't be. Felix was the one who left the first time. And he was the one who left again this time.

But then again, she had asked him for only a few minutes of advice the day after the break-in. It was Felix who kept coming back to her. He was the one who wandered into the same bar they always used to visit because of the memories, and then stayed. He was the one who invited himself to her apartment for dinner.

He was the one who had leaned in to kiss her that night.

No. She gritted her teeth. The idea was nonsense. She was not her father, and it was not that simple—if she would only open up and really let him in, Felix would come running back, and everything would be fine again. That made for a good story, but it wasn't real life. What was keeping them apart, what had kept them apart for seven long years, was not *just* Nell and her inability to let go of the past. It couldn't be.

"Nell—" Swann began.

But before he could continue, the old Toyota shuddered slightly on the slick road as Humphrey began to slow. The rain picked up, pelting the windshield, so thick they could hardly see through it.

"We're almost there," he said grimly.

Ramona leaned forward. "It should be right ahead."

Nell pressed her face to the streaked window, scanning for lights, or telephone poles, or roofs, anything . . .

This is it, she thought breathlessly. *The moment of truth.*

Even after everything she'd seen—Francis disappearing at Swann's home, Ramona's shop, and the room in the NYPL—part of her still couldn't believe in something as huge as an entire hidden *town.* A town that travelers drove past every day, that generations of families lived right beside for decades, unbeknownst to them all.

"Stop!" Eve said, and the car lurched into the brake. The tires rumbled as they went from road to dirt and sticks and finally came to a stop along the shoulder.

The silence lingered.

Nell looked at Humphrey. "Are we there?" she whispered.

He nodded.

She and Swann turned to each other, then out, toward the empty field.

It was bright enough that even with the rain, they could see clearly without the headlights now. Just beyond the car, the road gave way to little sprigs of green, tendrils forcing their way through the cracked asphalt, and then rapidly dissolved into a waist-high tangle of weeds.

That tangle continued for what looked like miles. No lights, no telephone poles, no roofs, no other roads. As far as they could see, there was nothing.

Ramona popped her door and stepped out into the downpour. "Come on."

They all scrambled after her, their hands over their heads.

Ramona led them, and Humphrey grabbed onto Eve, to help her across the slippery ground. Francis waved Nell and Swann on so he could bring up the rear. Slowly, warily, they moved deeper into the field.

As they went, Nell thought it seemed like they'd been walking without going anywhere. That they should have been farther than they were. As if the field kept lengthening, swallowing them up.

It felt like the whole world was off by one degree. Everything in its right place at first glance, but tilted ever so slightly.

Stop it, she told herself. *It's just a field.*

And it was. She turned around—the car was right where they had been parked along the shoulder. The road was where it had always been.

It was still just a field.

"Nell," someone said—but it wasn't one of them. "*Nell.*"

They all froze.

It was a voice she'd never expected to hear. Not then, in that place, or ever again.

Slowly, she turned toward the sound.

"Felix," she whispered.

Felix *was* there—her heart clenched—standing stiffly in the middle of the grass. Beside him was a large duffel bag, zipped closed against the rain so she couldn't see what was inside, but emblazoned with the unmistakable icy white-and-blue Haberson Global corporate logo.

And beside him was someone else.

An old man, tall and thin like Swann, but with a face that could not have been more opposite. Hard, cold, lifeless. She didn't know what he'd looked like before, when he was young, but now he looked like a ghost. A shell of a person, all the innocence and joy drained out.

And in his hand—currently pointed at Felix—was a gun.

"Hello, Nell," the man said. "It's been a long time."

Nell stared.

It was startling to see him in the flesh. The man who had once been her mother's closest friend and would have grown to become an uncle to her like Swann, too, if they had never found the town.

"Wally," she finally whispered.

Wally's face pulled into a painful grimace. "I haven't been called that in a very long time," he replied. "I left it behind when I left this place."

"Nell, Swann, he owns Haberson," Felix cried frantically to them. "He's the one who broke in. He's the one who murdered your father and Irene—"

"That's enough, Felix." Wally sighed.

"Haberson," Ramona repeated. His old friends were staring at him with a mixture of horror and pity.

"I thought there was a poetry to it," Wally said to them. "Our project was called the *Dreamer's Atlas*, and Tam was the one who had me read that book in the first place."

"What?" Nell asked.

"He named himself after a character," Ramona said through clenched teeth. "The oneirologist. It was a book about dreams." She shook her head. "It was on our dormitory shelf for years. I should have realized."

"None of you liked those stories like she did," Wally replied.

"This isn't about a book," Felix interrupted. "It's about a map. The Haberson Map."

"Enough," Wally said.

Felix flinched as Wally gestured with the gun, but he didn't look away from Nell. "Run," he pleaded.

"Yes, Nell," Swann whispered softly. He was hovering protectively, trying to slowly ease her behind him. "Run."

But Nell could only stare at Felix. "I can't leave you," she said to him.

"Yes, you can," Felix urged.

"She won't," Wally agreed. "She's just like her mother."

A flash of anger cut through her fear. "You don't get to speak of her," Nell said to him.

Wally shook his head. "I don't know what the others told you, but that night was an accident."

"You still don't see," Eve said. "Even after all this time, you still don't see."

But Wally ignored her, his gaze still locked with Nell's. "I'm sorry you never got to know her," he said. "It's my greatest regret. That's what all of this has been about. What I have spent my life trying to do. To find a way back into this place."

"At what cost?" Francis asked. "How many more have there been?"

"Sometimes we must make hard choices," Wally said.

Ramona's eyes shimmered. "Was Daniel a hard choice, too?"

"He brought it on himself," he replied. "The map is not his. It never was."

Nell looked down to follow the line of his gaze—to the Agloe map in her hands, half-hidden behind Swann.

"How did you realize that he still had it?" she asked, voice trembling. "All these years later?"

"I've known for a long time," Wally said. "Seven years, actually. It's just taken me that long to find a way to get my company into the NYPL."

Felix looked at him in horror.

"I remember how much you loved maps, too. Even as barely more than a baby," Wally continued. "When I heard about the Junk Box Incident, I knew something was wrong. You would never leave the library willingly, and your father would never damage your career like that. Unless . . ."

Nell closed her eyes.

Her father must have known what would eventually happen, that day. He had not gone to beg Ramona to hide the map out of fear, but rather certainty. And still, he had given everything to keep her safe.

"How many nights, I searched that place. Every exhibit, every archive. He was not supposed to see me any of those times." Wally sighed. "But then, he did. And I knew if I didn't act quickly, he would be forced to hide the map somewhere else—or perhaps even to tell you everything. I had to stop him before he could do it."

Nell couldn't find her voice.

"I was only trying to protect you," he said. "To finish it before you had to get involved."

When she finally opened her eyes, she saw that his free hand was out, beckoning.

"This can all be over now. Give me the map."

"Please, no one has to get hurt. Put the gun down, and we can talk," Swann urged.

But Wally pressed the muzzle closer to Felix, and Nell's heart flailed.

"Don't give it to him," Felix insisted grimly.

But she couldn't think. "It's yours," she said to Wally. She held the map up a little, trembling. "It's yours. I just . . ."

She needed to stall, to keep Wally talking, but her mind was a runaway train—speeding nearly off its tracks, too fast for her to come up with anything helpful. Her finger slipped slowly into the first fold of the paper as she turned the map over, and she caught a glimpse of a swath of countryside, delicately veined with roads.

She had been so close. So close.

"Can I do it?" Nell blurted.

The others braced, but Wally cocked his head.

"That's what you want, right? To go back to Agloe with the map?" she asked. "I want to be the one to do it, just one time."

Wally might have smiled, but it was barely a shadow of an expression. Finally, he nodded. "Your mother would have liked that," he said.

"No, Nell," Swann hissed desperately to her. "You can't lock yourself in there with him. He's got a gun, and—"

"I know," she whispered back, helpless. But Wally was too determined, too consumed. "I don't know what else to do."

She took a few steps forward, her heart racing, her shoes squelching in the mud, as Swann clung to her sleeve, continuing to plead with her. She pulled the hood of her cardigan out from her head as wide as she could, to shield the map from the rain, and then looked to Ramona.

"How do I . . . ?" she asked softly.

"Just open it," Ramona answered at last.

Nell unfolded the map and stared at the all-too-familiar lines. The sea of pale green and the roads she knew so well by now.

"Find the town," Ramona said.

Her eyes darted, searching, trailing up from New York City into Sullivan County, toward the Catskills.

"Please, Nell," Swann begged. "I can't let you do this, it's too dangerous."

"Hurry," Wally said.

She found the road they'd been on and glanced quickly north up the route, her gaze racing toward her destination.

"I have it," she whispered. "Almost there . . ."

Before she knew what was happening, Swann had lurched forward, his arms so long he didn't even need to take a step, and snatched the map from her.

Nell gasped. *He's going to rip it in half!* The last copy, their last hope of ever getting inside.

"No!" Wally roared, jerking the gun from Felix to Swann so wildly that the others all cowered. "Put the map down now!"

"Wait, just wait!" Nell pleaded, at the same time that Felix was yelling, "Don't shoot!"

She put a hand on Swann's shoulder, willing Wally not to lose control. She was so terrified, she didn't know if her knees were going to hold her.

She tried to keep her voice as even as possible. "What are you doing?" she whispered.

"What your father asked me to do," Swann said, his eyes fixed on Wally. "Protect you. If there's no map anymore, there's no danger either. There's nothing for Wally to take from you."

She edged closer to him, reaching slowly for the map. If she could get it back, everything would be all right, somehow. "But if we destroy the last copy, we can never go inside. We can never . . ."

Swann nodded grimly. "I know. But I knew your father, Nell. How much he loved you. How he would do anything to keep you safe, at any cost. He would want me to do this." His voice was quiet and tender. "*Both* of your parents would want me to."

"*Don't*," Wally threatened, frantic.

But Swann whipped the map above his head, each side of it gripped in one hand.

"Swann!" Nell shrieked.

A strange force shook her suddenly, drowning out her words in a dull boom.

Nell blinked. Everything felt strange. Her insides had been rattled. Her ears hurt.

Someone—*Felix?*—was screaming, over and over.

Swann was still holding the map over his head. But his arms were sinking, his fingers loosening their grip, as if the world was suddenly happening in slow motion.

Then she saw the red stain blooming steadily across his back.

"*No!*" she cried.

Swann collapsed backward into her, and together they sank into the grass.

"I'm sorry," Wally said. "It's the last copy. There was no other way."

The blood was hot, so hot. It was pouring into her lap, like a sickening bath. Her hands searched his chest, but she couldn't find the place where the bullet had entered.

"Call an ambulance," she said to the others, but Wally was pointing the gun at all of them now, and they could do nothing.

"William, please," Felix begged. The gun didn't waver.

"Just hang on," Nell said to Swann, digging in his pockets for his phone, but he put a palm on her scrambling hands and patted them gently.

It didn't matter. An ambulance would never arrive in time, even if she'd called it before Wally and Felix had appeared. Swann would be dead in moments.

He looked at her from somewhere far away and tried to touch her cheek. "Save . . . ," he whispered hoarsely.

Her tears splattered against his face, but his eyes were already going dull, and he didn't seem to notice.

"No." She shook her head. "I'm staying here with you. I don't give a crap about the map. I only wanted it in the first place because I wanted to get back to the library again. But what's the library without you in it?" she said to him, so the last thing running through his mind wouldn't be a burning need to tell her to run with the map, to leave him to die alone, because what he was doing wasn't important. That would be exactly something Swann would think. Even in his final moments, he would be caring about her, and not himself.

"Save . . . ," Swann repeated.

"I don't care about saving the map," she said again to him.

But Swann shook his head. He was smiling now, as impossible as it seemed.

"Go, save . . ."

And then he was gone.

"Swann," Nell whispered. She cradled his face. "Swann. Swann. Swann."

Through the haze of her grief, she saw that Felix had also fallen to his knees, where he was still hostage beside Wally, crying, too. Ramona, Francis, and Eve were clutching each other in horror, and Humphrey was hovering over Nell, larger than she'd ever seen him, looking determined to take Wally's next bullet if he dared aim at her.

But Wally was not looking at any of them at all. He was still staring at the map in Swann's absent grip, its open face becoming lightly misted with rain, its back in danger of becoming stained with the spreading red if it stayed there much longer.

"The map," he finally said. It was not a statement, but a command.

"Wally," Ramona started, stepping forward, but he stopped her with the aim of his gun.

"Not you," he said to her. "Or any of you." His gaze returned to Nell. "It's just going to be the three of us." Himself, Felix, and Nell.

"Don't you dare hurt her," Humphrey said, still hovering over Nell. "I don't care if there's a map or not, if you so much as touch a hair on her head, I'll—"

"You weren't her only beloved adopted uncle, Bear," Wally said, sneering. "The library was an accident. You know I would never hurt

Nell. Never on purpose." He glanced sidelong at Felix. "That's what Felix is for."

Nell thought she might faint from the horror of those words.

"Just the two of us," she said, her voice cracking. "Let Felix stay here."

"I'm not leaving you," Felix argued, even as he flinched as Wally brought the gun back toward him. "Never again."

She glared desperately at Felix, willing him to take it back, or make a break for it, to try to escape somehow. She had already lost Swann—she wouldn't be able to bear it if she also lost him.

But Felix just glared desperately back at her, equally determined.

"The map," Wally said to Nell. "Do it now, or I will."

There was nothing left to try. She looked at the others who had come with her, and then took the map from Swann's lifeless grip with shaking hands.

Slowly, blinking through her tears, her eyes found their way back along the winding roads to the place where they all were, in the pale green fields off County Highway 206, and moved toward the little white dot of a town that didn't exist. She read the tiny name above it. Five letters that were the answer to the greatest secret she had ever known.

AGLOE.

"Nell," Felix said then, his voice tiny.

"It has to be," Nell murmured, her eyes still locked on the map. "It has to be here . . ."

"Nell."

She looked up, and her heart almost stopped.

There was a dirt road in front of them.

XXIV

The town was like something out of a storybook.

All down Main Street, wood-paneled two-story shops lined the sidewalk, offering their wares through curtained windows above little flower beds on the sills. At the corner, there was a diner, and across from it, a gas station. A fire hydrant waited stoically at the curb.

On the lamppost just in front of Nell, at the first intersection leading to the heart of the town, a sign in the same bright green of all state tourism signs proclaimed:

Welcome to Agloe
Home of the famous Beaverkill Fishing Lodge!

"It's real," Nell whispered. "It's really real."

She stared, awestruck. At the stop sign, the intersection, the buildings beyond it. At the trees, which looked to be at least a hundred years old, with thick gnarled trunks and heavy boughs that shaded their roots.

She had thought the liminal room in the NYPL, and the phantom staircase at Classic, had been the most fantastical things she would ever see—but this was even more impossible. Moments ago, she had been standing on the side of the road in the rain, staring at an open, empty field. Then she'd taken a few steps down the muddy dirt road, and suddenly, she was inside of an entire *town*.

A town that no one else in the world but they could see.

"Wait," Felix said. "It's not raining here."

Nell looked up. Before they'd entered Agloe, they were being pelted by the downpour, so heavily the ground had turned to mud around Nell's shoes and sucked at the soles with every step. But inside the town, it was a perfect spring morning. There wasn't a single cloud in the sky.

"It was always this way," Wally answered, his voice strangely quiet.

He wasn't staring at the sky, Nell saw. He was staring at Agloe. At the place he'd been locked out of, a place almost no one else in the entire world knew existed, but he'd been convinced still did. A place he'd spent his life desperately trying to prove was real, to return to, no matter the cost. His eyes were glazed with shock.

As if he could hardly believe he had finally, *finally* made it back.

Nell wanted to run, to make a break for it and hide somewhere where he'd never find her, but she couldn't will her feet to move. For one, Wally knew the town and she didn't. As much as she was afraid of him, she was also a little afraid of Agloe. She didn't know what would happen if she got lost inside of it.

And she also couldn't leave Felix.

Despite the incredible impossibility of what was around him, Felix was still looking at Nell, rather than at the town. As if by letting her out of his sight for a single moment, he would lose her forever.

"This way," Wally finally murmured, startling her and Felix both.

"Where are we going?" Felix asked.

"To where the fire happened," Nell answered him. What else could Wally want to see but the ruins? But to her surprise, Wally shook his head.

"It's not far," he said instead. He turned and stared down one of the wide, empty streets, hypnotized. "The town isn't as big as it looks."

They went slowly, Wally lost in reverie, Felix wary, and Nell, despite the danger, utterly entranced.

She couldn't help but stare at everything as they passed. At the first intersection, there was a little café on the corner, the lights on and door open. The sign in its front window proclaimed, Coffee! in blue cursive over a little painted cup, a curlicue of steam rising from it. It looked so inviting that Nell half expected a barista to call out to them.

But there was no one inside.

It was the same with the general store at the next stoplight. There was a counter with a cash register, stacks of menus, and a few tables and chairs in the far corner. Even the lights were on.

Nell just stared.

"You see why we had to keep this place a secret?" Wally asked her, hungry, obsessive. "Why we couldn't let it go?"

He seemed to almost be encouraging her to explore, as long as she didn't try to make a break for it—he knew she wouldn't leave Felix anyway. At the diner, Nell went all the way up to the door, and when he made no move to stop her, she nervously pulled it open.

She held her breath and listened. There were no sounds coming from the back kitchen, through the thin swinging doors. No dishes being washed, no pop of oil on a pan, no clinking of dishes or cutlery. But there was a board on the wall listing weekly specials, and a pad and pencil for taking orders beside the phone, as there would have been at a real restaurant in the real world.

Everything was so full of potential—the shops waiting for customers, the traffic lights over the intersections changing from green to yellow to red—it seemed like at any moment, someone would push open the door of the convenience store across the street and walk out carrying a sandwich and a can of soda, or someone else might pull into the parking lot and head into the gas station to pay to fill up their tank.

But there was no one. There hadn't been since the night the town had swallowed her mother up, and they all believed the last map had been lost with her.

Nell waited until Wally wasn't looking and turned over the top page on the pad of paper at the hostess stand, mystified.

How was it possible?

Had Wally realized yet? she wondered as she darted back out of the diner to the street. Had he also noticed all the things that were somehow now here, that shouldn't be?

"Nell," Felix whispered to her at the next corner.

She turned to see him looking across the road, where there was a gap in the buildings. A space where there should have been something built, but instead there was just sunny, unbroken sky. The exteriors of the two shops on either side were feathered with faint black marks along their corners. And between them, a scorched floor, a foundation peeking through, and blackened walls.

Wally's vault.

There were the skeletons of shelves, some still upright, some sprawled across the ground, but they were all bare, the delicate maps they once held all burned completely in the blaze. There was nothing left. Not even bones.

Wally, however, was not looking at the vault at all.

He was staring straight ahead, down the road they were heading, every fiber of his being avoiding the ruin of ash, as if that would mean it wasn't there, and the fire had never happened. But even though he refused to look, Nell could still tell that he was in the grip of that horrible, inescapable memory. She could almost see the reflection of the flames still dancing in his eyes.

He marched them stiffly on, past more empty streets and more empty buildings. Nell caught sight of a bookshop with books in it, lonely on the shelves, and a drugstore, with an advertisement for toothpaste on a sign outside. As they passed the main square and the sunlight glinted off a large pane of glass across the park, she thought she recognized another place.

"The ice cream parlor," she said, pointing.

Wally stalled in his tracks, surprised. He looked at the ice cream parlor and then back at her. "You remember it?" he asked.

She didn't. She only knew it from Ramona's, Francis's, and Eve's stories. But she nodded anyway.

Wally seemed both saddened and pleased by that. After a moment, he let them go up to the big front window.

"All our maps used to hang here," he whispered. He touched the glass, hesitantly at first, as if he was afraid there would be nothing there. But the glass was real. He left little dots of fingerprints across its face.

As he stared, his gaze slowly unfocused, and Nell followed it, where it was fixed on something inside, on the far back wall.

Hundreds of photographs, all tacked up in a giant collage.

"Wait!" Felix cried as Nell yanked the door open with a sharp jangle of its bells, but she ignored him. After a moment, she could hear the soft sounds of his and Wally's shoes on the wood floor behind her as they followed.

She turned to Wally when she reached the wall, then back to the pictures.

"You took these, didn't you?" she asked.

He nodded.

The photographs were of all of them. The Cartographers.

There they all were, outside the house Humphrey had rented before they'd burned it down to keep the town a secret forever, around the fire pit with their marshmallows. In another, Ramona and Francis were standing outside the grocery store in Rockland, holding up a giant bottle of champagne they'd just bought. And then there were the photos that had been taken in Agloe. Humphrey doing a handstand next to the town's sign. Ramona and Tamara posing outside of the same ice cream parlor. Nell's father and mother together, sitting on a roof, looking out over their secret world at sunset.

In almost all of them, whether the photo was of one person or the whole group, Tamara was the focal point, the shining star at the center of every moment—and Wally was invisible. Watching from afar, behind the camera.

"I took that one of you, too," Wally finally said, pointing.

Nell followed the line of his finger. There was a picture of her father, her mother, and her near the center of the collage.

She pulled the photo from the wall and held it close. The three of them were in the park outside the parlor, sitting on a blanket and having a picnic. Her mother and father were eating sandwiches, and she a hot dog that her father had cut up for her, the fork still in his hand. In front of them on the blanket was a single slice of cake with three candles in it. And behind them, in the background, the unmistakable view of the town.

On the back of the photo, her father had written, in his giant, blocky scrawl: *June 1990. Happy third birthday, Nell!*

"Come on," Wally said. "We're almost there."

"We've done as you asked. This is over," Felix argued.

"Oh, it's far from over," he replied. He waved his gun, as if to say *Let's go.*

"Where are you taking us?" Nell asked, before Felix could anger Wally further.

Wally looked at her with an expression that told her she already knew the answer.

"The printing factory," she realized.

Of course. Her mother's favorite place in Agloe.

It took only a few more silent streets and a handful more silent houses to get there. Nell could see why it had taken Francis and Eve a long time to find this place on their surveys. The printing factory was small and unassuming, a little square wooden building that seemed to blend in with the scenery rather than stand out, as the two bigger vacant shops on either side of it did. Subtle, intimate. As though it would only appear to whom it wanted. As though it hid something incredible within.

At the entrance, Nell hesitated, but Wally didn't move.

"You should do it," he said. "She would have wanted you to."

Slowly, Nell put a hand on the door and pushed.

Inside, the factory reminded her of Ramona's shop, in a way. Dark, mysterious, cluttered with shelves and shelves of drafter's tools and other old-fashioned supplies. As they all stood there taking it in, she wondered if her mother's friend had subconsciously designed her impossible hideaway after this place. Nell was too nervous to wander deeper, but her eyes roamed every surface, desperate, curious. Finally, they settled on the printing press, glinting dully in the dim light. Even though Nell had heard all of the stories, her heart fluttered at the sight.

It was real. It was here.

"I knew it," Wally said, breaking the silence.

"Knew what?" she stammered.

But Wally gestured to the Haberson duffel bag in Felix's hands. "You can bring that here."

Felix hesitated, but a gentle wave of the gun forced him to comply. He handed the bag to Wally, who went to the press and set the bag on the flat expanse where a roll of paper would feed in. He slowly unzipped it. Inside was a small, sleek-looking device, like a futuristic printer, with the Haberson logo painted on the side of it. Wally tossed the bag out of the way and then pressed a button to wake the machine.

It was a portable scanner, Nell realized, as a sliding motion along the top, a mechanical arm moving across a plate of glass, caught her eye.

"Why do you have that?" she asked warily.

Next to the much larger antique contraption, it looked so strange. Too aerodynamic, too artificial. Compared to the press, which required setting paper and cranking levers by hand, all it took was a button push to make the Haberson scanner work. There was hardly any soul to it. It just copied maps—it didn't make them.

"I know you've also wondered why your father didn't destroy this map," Wally continued as he prepared the device, ignoring her question. "Why he kept it all these years, despite the terrible things that had happened here, and despite knowing I was searching for a copy."

"Because it's the last thing that belonged to my mother," Nell said. She wasn't going to tell him what she really hoped was true.

But Wally was nodding as if reading her mind anyway. A smile had crept onto his face.

"Tear it," he said, pointing at the Agloe map in her hands.

"What?" Nell and Felix gasped at the same time.

"Tear the map," Wally repeated. "Right down the middle. Then again, and again, until it's scraps."

"Are you *serious?*" Felix cried, nearly hysterical with anger. "You murdered Swann to stop him from destroying it, and now you want to—"

"We needed it then, to get into Agloe," Wally said. "Now that we're here, we don't need it anymore."

Nell clung desperately to the little folded paper. Was Wally trying to kill them?

Because if Agloe only existed on the paper, what would happen to it when the last copy was destroyed?

What would happen to them if they were inside when that happened?

"Do it," Wally commanded. His voice was soft, but the threat was clear. *Or else.*

Nell's hands fumbled as she unfolded the map again. She could see the memories flickering across Felix's terrified face as he looked at it too, this little tattered thing that was worth more than any other artifact they'd ever seen. This single sheet of printed paper that had caused them so much pain and damage in their young lives, splitting them apart, bringing them back together, splitting them apart again, and pulling them inexorably to each other one last time, here and now, but not in a way that either of them could have imagined.

How many times, after they'd both been fired, had Nell fantasized about finding this map and shredding it, she wondered. Probably about as many times as Felix had.

Now she had the chance—she was being forced to do it—and would give anything not to.

Wally held up a hand to still her for a moment. He turned slowly in a circle, his arms out, his eyes falling over every cluttered surface of the factory. As if waiting for something—or someone—to stop him.

But nothing happened.

He grinned and aimed the gun at Felix.

"Tear it," he commanded again.

Nell closed her eyes and ripped the page.

The sound struck her to the core. She shuddered, and so did Felix. She kept ripping, tearing it into quarters, then the quarters in half to eighths, and onward, until the map was no more than a bunch of tiny scraps of paper, each no larger than a puzzle piece. They slid through her fingers and fluttered to the ground like leaves in a breeze, covering the floor in a perverse autumn blanket.

She and Felix stared in stunned silence at the fragments where they lay.

It was gone.

The thing her mother had died for, and her father had given decades of his life for, and Nell had lost her career and her relationship with Felix for, even if she hadn't known it at the time.

Gone.

After a long moment, she finally looked up. Wally was still standing where he'd been, looking at the same tatters of paper—but he was still smiling.

"See?" he finally said. "I was right."

"Right about what?" Felix asked tensely.

"Right that this wasn't the last copy," Nell said, understanding.

They had destroyed the one they had with them, but the town was still there around them. They were still inside of it.

Which meant that something else was keeping them there.

Another copy.

Wally nodded. "I was right that Tam didn't die all those years ago in the fire."

"What are you saying?" Felix asked.

Wally's eyes blazed as he looked at Nell. "She's been alive, all this time. She's been here, in Agloe."

"That building was ashes. How could you know she survived?" Felix asked, incredulous, but Wally was still looking at Nell. She could tell that he knew she had also suspected it all along. That she believed he was right.

In response, Wally turned back to the printing press.

He ran his hand over the old contraption, his fingers sliding across the wood cranks, the smooth rollers, inspecting its parts as meticulously now as he must have all those years ago, when they were all deeply consumed with their reimagined version of the *Dreamer's Atlas*. Their secret project that was going to change the way the world understood maps forever.

In all of their stories, Ramona, Francis, Eve, and Humphrey always insisted that Nell's mother had never used the founder's printing press in this abandoned workshop. She had been desperate to, convinced that it had been installed here for that very reason, but tragedy had struck them before she'd reached a point in her drafts to be ready to bring the antique machine to life.

It had been sitting here for decades, ever since the day of the fire, when they were all torn back into the real world and unable to return.

And yet.

At last, Wally held his finger out, so Nell and Felix could see what was now smudged on the tip.

Ink. Freshly wet.

XXV

"I know you saw the signs, too," Wally said to Nell, continuing to stare her down.

"What signs?" Felix asked, still in disbelief. "No one has been here for over thirty years. No one . . . could have survived that long. This place is empty."

Wally ignored him. Felix hadn't heard the stories that Francis, Ramona, Eve, and Humphrey had told Nell about what Agloe had been like when they first found it—he didn't know what had been here before and what had not. To him, the town probably still did look empty.

But it wasn't, Nell knew.

It had appeared that way at first, in her initial shock. But the longer the three of them had walked, slowly making their way toward the printing factory, she had started to notice. Details that didn't match their memories, things she couldn't explain.

Her father and Humphrey knew the electricity in the town worked—but there were now lights on in buildings she knew the Cartographers hadn't used when they were here. Furniture, too. Sundries on the shelves in the general store, books on the bookstore shelves, menus in the diner.

And that notepad at the hostess stand in the diner—with something *drawn on it.*

Every time she had noticed a hidden tell inside some café or little shop, if she poked around the inside of the building, she always spotted it.

A little scrap of paper, lines carefully etched across its page.

Tiny maps, of individual buildings or streets—all from the printing press.

"Yes," Wally said, encouraging her. The ink was staining his finger. "You believe me now."

But Nell was so overcome, she couldn't speak.

Her mother really *was* alive after all.

Before Nell turned around, she knew. But even so, nothing could have prepared her to see the person standing there in the doorway when she finally did.

"Tam," Wally whispered, spellbound.

She was there.

Real.

Alive.

Tamara Jasper-Young was much older than she'd been in the photos, but the resemblance was unmistakable. She was no taller than Nell, her now-gray hair was just as unruly, and she was wrapped in a stretched-out, ratty old cardigan even more overwhelming on her frame than Nell's was on hers. In her hand was something small, a little package, and her own fingers were also dotted with ink stains and graphite dust as though she'd been interrupted midproject, still just as furiously dedicated to her craft as she had been in all the stories Nell had ever heard about her.

"It's you," Nell stammered. "It's really you."

Her mother opened her arms and pulled her into a fierce hug.

"I have waited so long for this," she whispered into Nell's hair. Nell hadn't even felt her arms move, but she was hugging her mother back, so tightly both of them could barely breathe.

"Mom," Nell finally managed.

There were so many things she needed to tell her mother, and so many more she needed to ask, but her eyes were streaming, and her throat was so painfully tight, she couldn't make it work right. All she could do was hold on.

"Nell," her mother said. "Nell, Nell, my Nell." Over and over, like a chant. "You're here. You're finally here."

"I'm sorry it took so long," she managed to say. "I didn't know. Dad never—"

"I know," Tamara replied softly. "It was the only thing we could think to do." She touched Nell's cheek. "Someday, when it was safe, he was going to tell you everything and bring you here."

Nell tried to summon the courage to tell her mother that her father was no longer alive, but the words didn't come. But it seemed that she knew anyway. After all, how else could Nell herself be in Agloe, but not also her father?

"I'm so sorry," she finally whispered.

"No, I'm sorry," Tamara said. "We had a choice to let this map become our entire lives, but you didn't."

Slowly, Nell felt her mother's grip on her loosen as the scene over Nell's shoulder registered. Tamara seemed to finally remember that there were other people in the room—and that something terrible was happening. Wally was there, and Nell, but not Nell's father. And Felix was still Wally's hostage, still fixed within the aim of his weapon.

At last, she let go of Nell.

"Wally," she murmured as she looked at him. "What have you done?"

"What I promised I would," he said. He was staring at her like she was an apparition, a spirit. "All this time, I never gave up. I knew you couldn't be gone. I've been searching for a way back in ever since."

Nell watched her mother's eyes dart between Wally, the gun, Felix, and the strange scanning machine on top of the printing press beside him.

"You can't imagine how difficult it's been to return to a place that doesn't technically exist," Wally said, as if it were a sufficient explanation. His words were slow and thick, clumsy. He had been convinced he would find her here, but to truly see her again at long last was overwhelming. "But all of it, everything I had to do to find Agloe again, has been for you."

"No, it hasn't," Tamara replied. "I didn't want you to do any of this."

"Then why did you stay?" he asked, but it wasn't really a question. "Why did you leave your husband and your daughter, and let all of your friends believe you were gone? Why did you let *me* believe it?"

He pointed to the package in her hands.

"Why did you finish your half of the *Dreamer's Atlas*?"

As one, their eyes all drifted down to follow the line of his finger. Tamara gently pulled the package to her chest, as if doing so could protect it.

When Wally finally spoke again, his voice was soft, as if coming from somewhere far away. "I didn't understand at first. The fire, and you had vanished. . . . But after a few days, while we waited for the local police to close the investigation into your death and let us all leave, I realized what had *really* happened. That you hadn't died, but were trapped inside Agloe, somehow. And I knew that if you were still inside, you would still be working on your half of the atlas. I swore that I wouldn't rest either, until I'd finished my part of it as well."

"Would that be your Haberson Map, or all the people you murdered in your search for a way back in?" Felix asked sharply.

Wally didn't bother to look at him. "I just had to find a way back in, to find you again, and the atlas could be complete. And now it can. You and I, Tam. The town can be ours."

"Oh, Wally," Tamara said. She shook her head. "It was never supposed to be ours. That's why I stayed. To stop that from happening. To stop you from going too far."

"Too far?" he asked. "This is just the beginning."

"No," Tamara said. "No more."

Wally stared at her, not understanding—or refusing to.

"You have to let it go."

Finally, Wally smiled. Nell could see in his eyes that he never would. Maybe his original goal, all those years ago, had been only to prove that Tamara hadn't died in the fire after all. To prove that he wasn't guilty of killing the person he loved most in the entire world. But the grief had festered, the years had corrupted.

For so long, the map and Tamara had been the same thing—he had believed that if he could have one, it would be the same as having the other. He had spent so long seeking the map, he had lost sight of the fact that it was simply a means to an end. It had become the end for him.

"You just have to trust me," Wally said. "You always trusted me before."

Even now, when faced with Tamara herself, Wally had become too obsessed with the thing he'd been hunting his entire life. It was more real to him than the person. He would choose the map over everything else.

"Give it to me, Tam."

Nell and Felix both froze—all Nell could think about was Swann, how he had tried to do something heroic with her copy of the map and she had lost him for it, how she had to prevent that from happening again—but Tamara's hands didn't move. Instead, she looked at Nell.

"I want her to do it," she said. "I want her to see."

Wally studied her for a long moment, then finally nodded. "Carefully," he allowed.

Nell wiped her eyes and dried her hands on her clothes, and Tamara held out the bundle that she'd been carrying. It was wrapped in plain brown paper and tied with twine, but the shape and size were unmistakable.

It could be only one thing.

"Now," Wally said to her, spellbound.

"Don't do it," Felix urged. He looked poised, ready to spring on Wally, even as Nell frantically shook her head. "Just run. Use it to get away."

"No," she insisted. "We're not leaving without you."

She was not going to live her life the way that her parents had. She was not going to choose the map over Felix or her family.

With trembling hands, Nell untied the twine, and the map unfolded.

She could not help but gasp.

It was beautiful. Breathtaking. An entirely hand-drafted, hand-colored, hand-pressed custom map of Agloe created by a single cartographer—her mother.

Nell studied it, spellbound by the artistry. She found the ice cream shop, and the park, with every tree and bush and blade of grass. The central square and the road into Agloe that connected to Main Street. The boats in the river, the printing factory. Even the welcome sign. Every single corner and building that existed in a town that couldn't exist was there. All of it perfectly, lovingly rendered, down to the smallest detail.

This was her mother's half of the *Dreamer's Atlas*. The precious thing she had given up her family and her friends to stay behind to create. She had hidden herself and her work here, in the one place she knew Wally would not be able to reach her.

In the bottom corner, the symbol of the Cartographers echoed in simple dark ink. An eight-armed compass rose, with the letter *C* in the center.

Nell touched the little shape on the page.

This was what Wally had been after, all this time.

The *true* last copy of the Agloe Map.

"What's that?" Wally asked sharply, suspicion flaring in his voice.

"The map," Tamara replied, but Wally wasn't looking at her masterpiece anymore. He was looking at Tamara's hands, Nell realized. At the wrapping she'd taken from Nell so Nell could hold the map open. There was something else inside her mother was trying to keep hidden there, she could see now, tucked within the wrinkled layers—another small bundle of paper, plain white and folded into thirds in a stack.

"It's a letter," Wally murmured, with wonder. His free hand drifted up, as if pulled by invisible strings out of his control. He reached for it. "You wrote a letter."

But Tamara took a step back. She pulled the paper slowly closer to her chest.

He stared at her, as if not understanding what she was doing.

Then, his eyes drifted to Nell. The coldness inside them made her shudder.

Tamara had been trapped in Agloe for decades, lonely and waiting, and when Wally finally managed to reach her again, she had a letter for her daughter, but nothing for him, even after all this time.

"Wally," Tamara started, but he shook his head.

"No," he said. The words came out of his mouth as though they tasted awful, like poison. "Don't you destroy it. Thirty years you saved those words. It would be a shame to waste them now."

"It's just a letter," Felix tried, hoping to draw Wally's attention, but he didn't move.

"Just a letter," he repeated softly.

Wally's gaze was still locked on Nell, but it was as though he wasn't really seeing her anymore. He seemed lost with his ghosts again, trapped in the past.

"Your mother wanted you to read it, so you're going to read it," he said. His grip on the gun tightened. "Out loud. So we *all* can hear it."

Nell could see the handwriting faintly through the thin white sheets. Hurried, half-cursive, a mess. She had to work up the courage to reach out and take the pages from Tamara.

"From . . . my father?" she finally managed to ask.

Her mother nodded gently.

"From both of us," she said.

Tamara and Daniel

August 1990
Agloe

Darling Nell,

You're asleep now, dozing in our arms as we take turns sitting with you and kissing your soft forehead. Soon it will be time to go back to the motel and rent a car bound for New York City after that. But there are still a few more hours until dawn. A few more hours we can spend together.

There is so much we want to tell you, and so little time.

If you're reading this, you know that your mother survived after all. I hope that you already knew it anyway before this letter, before you even came to Agloe, because it finally became safe to tell you everything. I hope we're all together as you hold these pages.

But no one can see the future. We certainly couldn't, when we all showed up here earlier this summer, young and innocent and wholly unprepared for what we discovered. And now that Wally has disappeared, his motel room cleaned out as though he was never there, we can't take any risks. You are too precious to us, Nell.

Until the day we can be sure that Wally is no longer a threat, we have to protect you from this secret. If you know nothing about what happened, nothing about the map or the town, you cannot be a target.

But we don't know how long it will be until that day. How long it will take the one of us on the outside to figure out what happened to Wally, or for the one of us on the inside to complete our final work.

A letter is not enough, but it may be all we have. We write it just in case.

Inside Agloe, the fire burned for days. But the building Wally had chosen to be his vault was small and simple—mercifully, the flames did not spread to the structures next door. They consumed the place where he'd hidden all of his maps and then finally flickered out.

I lay alone on the curb across the street and watched the building burn until it was ash. I was too exhausted and in too much pain to do anything else. And I'd already done the most important thing. You were safe, Nell. And so was your father. I'd managed to get you both away from the blaze—and the last map, as well.

I knew that eventually your father would find it stuffed into your clothes. I knew he'd come back as soon as he could.

I just had to figure out how to survive until then.

I decided to take shelter in the printing factory. I gathered what Romi had left behind from the ice cream parlor and brought it here. I was sure the answer was somewhere in one of our drafts, some scrap of our notes. That whole summer, she and I had argued about the direction of our Dreamer's Atlas*—Romi had insisted we could only understand the town from the outside in, but I was convinced of exactly the opposite. We had to understand it from the inside out.*

When the project had belonged to all of us, I'd tried to wait until Romi and I had agreed on a path forward before I began my part. I'd crumpled up half theories, shredded unfinished ideas, afraid to go too far without her. Without the Cartographers. But now, I had no choice—experiment or perish.

I began experimenting.

There were false starts. I was hungry, dehydrated, and impatient. My surveys of even single buildings were rushed, sloppy. But I got the hang of it in time.

I already knew Agloe existed only within its map—and so was visible only when the map was being used. It was why we had to open it and follow the road into and out of the town each time, rather than navigating by sight or memory. And when I'd folded up and hidden the map on you, Nell, I sealed the town away from you, your father, and all our friends. It disappeared because they could no longer see it on the map, because they no longer knew where the map was. They had no idea it hadn't burned up, too. And they also didn't know that I'd just barely begun my own copy of it right before that terrible day—the roughest preliminary outline of my half of the Dreamer's Atlas*—and had it here with me, inside Agloe.*

My theory, impossible as it was, had been right all this time.

A map could make things real—literally.

I realized that I could use my skills as a cartographer to save myself and the town. That if I made a map of part of the town using the printing press, I could change *Agloe with it. It would become real within its map, just like Agloe was within its own. Buildings could have furniture in them. Shops could have provisions.*

And more.

At first, I used the press only to stay alive. I mapped places onto my draft of Agloe to make what I needed to appear in the town. I drew a restaurant to get water and food, a clinic to get bandages and medicine, and a clothing store to get new, unscorched clothes. But after my basic necessities had been satisfied, after my lungs cleared and I'd started to heal, I began to realize there was something much more important to consider than simply surviving and hiding. Something that would cost everything I had left, but I didn't see any other way.

By the time your father came back, I knew what we had to do.

It was one week until your mother and I finally saw each other again, after the fire in Agloe. A week of not knowing what had happened to her, or her to me. Without the map, she was trapped inside the phantom settlement, and with everyone's eyes on me, I was trapped outside of it, trying to breathe through the grief and fear in order to take care of you. And all the while, Wally was always lurking, haunting the silent, empty countryside day and night like a vengeful spirit, searching for a way back into the town.

Even after finding the map hidden on you at the hospital and realizing I could go back after all, it took planning. Wally could not know that this map hadn't burned to ash like the rest of them. With only a single copy left, there's no telling what he'd do to obtain it. Every night, I followed him as he went back to the part of the field he knew was the entrance to Agloe, where he paced and paced for hours. I waited in the shadows, studying his routine, learning when he gave up and went home, and when he was only checking some other part of the field and would return, so I could finally slip inside unseen.

That first time, I didn't bring you with me. It was probably irresponsible, but you were exhausted every day from crying and slept like the dead, and if you had woken, Romi's room was right next door.

It wasn't that I wanted to leave you. It was that it was impossible to know what would be waiting inside Agloe. What if your mother had died in the fire, and you saw her body before I could shield you? That kind of a memory could never be erased. Or what if the fire had never burned out? What if it was still burning, engulfing the whole town? I had to face it alone first.

It was the middle of the night, but your mother was wide awake, waiting. There was no way she could have known I would finally return to Agloe that evening, no way for me to have gotten her a message from the outside, but somehow, she knew anyway. When I walked up the dirt road into the town, the map clutched desperately in my hands, she was already there on the sidewalk at the very first intersection.

I don't know how long we cried. My throat was so raw, my eyes so swollen from the salt of my tears, I could hardly even speak or see her when we finally quieted.

There was so much to tell her. The house we'd burned as a decoy, the police investigation, the agonizing days and the endless nights at the motel. The way our friends had become hollowed out. How everything had broken apart and could never be put back together again. And how Wally, in his guilt, had become even more consumed with finding and controlling this place again.

That last bit hit her especially hard.

She'd been hoping, she told me, that this tragedy might have cured Wally, somehow, rather than driving him even more deeply into his obsession. That we wouldn't have to do what she knew we needed to.

I didn't understand at first. And then when I did, I didn't want to agree.

But your mother is right.

There's no easy way to say this, Nell. But the only way to protect all of us from Wally is to make him believe that she's really gone, because that's the only way he'll also believe the town is really gone, too. And the only way we can do that is to keep her here. In Agloe.

As long as she stays, and as long as Wally believes the last copy of the map is really gone, there's no way he can reach her. She'll be safe from him—and able to save the town, too.

Because if your mother can manage to completely map Agloe from the inside out, the way she always wanted to as part of the Dreamer's Atlas, *this town—the most incredible, important discovery of our lives and in the history of cartography—can be preserved. Because even if Wally manages to find my copy of the map, there will still be one more. He won't have total control.*

In the meantime, my job will be to search for Wally in the outside world, so we know where he is and what he's up to. And, even more importantly, to keep the map she hid with you a secret, until it's safe for us to return to get her.

We know it's dangerous for me to have it, but it's the only way. If your mother keeps the map with her, she could leave Agloe whenever she wants, but she'll never know when it's safe to do so—Wally could be waiting right outside in the field for her, and she'd have no idea until it was too late.

Our only hope is that she can finish her version of the map, and I can track him before he ever begins to suspect me.

And that's why, Nell, we have to leave. To pull all this off, Wally has to be convinced that I believe your mother really died in the fire. If you and I stay and live in Rockland to be near her, it'll be too suspicious. He'll know we still have the map for certain. I have to appear like I've given up hope and moved on with my life, and yours, too. I have to take you away from here, to find a new job for me and a school for you, and raise you on my own. Just the two of us, starting over together. Pretending that Agloe no longer exists.

We know this seems cruel, for your mother to stay here, and for me to hide the truth about it from you. It is cruel. It's just that there's no other way. Nothing else will stop Wally.

We talked for hours that first night, asking if and reassuring each other that we were doing the right thing, until it was nearly dawn, and I had to go back before you woke up in the motel. I swore to your mother that I would find a way to return to Agloe at least one more time before I left Rockland for good and would bring you with me. It took until today, when the sheriff closed her case, for Wally to finally give up and disappear—but we know that he won't stay away forever. He won't be able to let go. And so, we have to set everything in motion tonight. Too soon to say goodbye, but anytime would have been too soon. It was always going to be impossible.

But your mother was always impossible to say no to, too. God help me if you turn out to have even half of her stubbornness, half of her drive and brilliance. I already have no idea how I'm going to raise you by myself, terrified I'm going to do a horrible job, but your mother is convinced we'll make it. I promised her that I would do anything in the world to protect you, no matter the cost.

And I will, Nell. I promise you that, too.

No matter what happens, whether in the end I tell you all of this or you read it, I promise that part, at least, will always be true.

It's time, Nell.

You are so beautiful, as I look at you in your father's arms. So perfect. I can hardly finish this letter because it means I have to turn away from you to do it.

We've had another week to prepare, after we came to our decision, but now that the night is finally here, it's hard to believe it. The police case is closed, the house's insurance policy has agreed to cover the accident, and our friends are just waiting for your father to leave Rockland behind before they do, too.

I'm not ready, but I have to be. The sun is threatening on the horizon here, which means dawn is flickering out there in the real world as well, and you have to be back to the motel before anyone notices. You have so much ahead of you. A whole life to live. A whole future to seize. And we have so much work to do to make sure you can.

I have to stop writing now, because it's my last chance to kiss you goodbye as many times as you'll let me, sweet Nell. How many times in just a few minutes can I tell you both that I love you? Because we have only minutes now, before I have to watch your father carry you back down that dirt road, fold the map up, and separate us for what could be months, or years, or even longer. I don't know how I'm going to survive that moment. Only that I must. That one, and all the ones after it.

I will do the only thing I can.

I will draw.

I will work on this map, to make it as perfect as possible, and wait for the day it is safe for you both to return.

You will always be our Cartographer, Nelly.

I've always believed that the purpose of a map is to bring people together. We forgot that with the one Wally and I found, but maybe I can change that. Maybe I can save things.

I hope someday, this one I will make here for you will bring us all back together again.

Love always,
Your parents

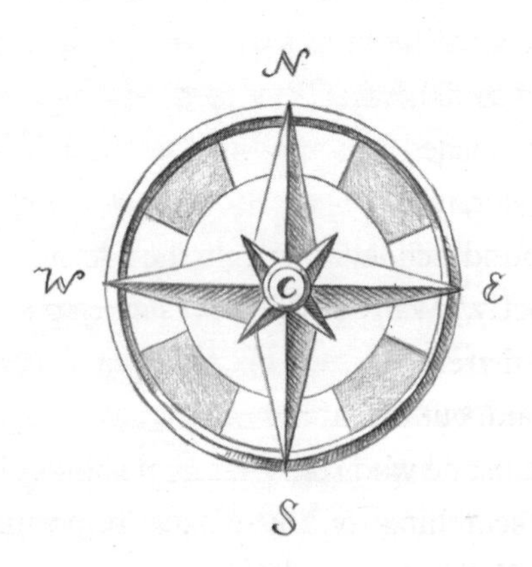

XXVI

Nell looked up from the letter at last, her eyes shimmering.

"I'm so sorry, Nell," her mother whispered.

But Nell shook her head. "I understand," she said, as her mother enfolded her into another embrace. "I understand now."

She pressed the letter to her heart as she hugged Tamara back. Even though he was gone, her father had still managed to speak to her again, to tell her everything, in the end. He'd still managed to say goodbye to her.

When they let go, Nell reached into her pocket and pulled out the fountain pen Humphrey had given her. The little etching on its side her mother had done all those years ago, next to the University of Wisconsin logo, caught the light.

"You still have it," her mother said, surprised. She was smiling, despite the grimness of the moment.

"It's yours," Nell said, holding it out.

But her mother pushed it gently back to her. "I made it for you. You're a Cartographer, too."

A small, dry sound echoed through the factory. A laugh, or the ghost of one. "Exactly," Wally said. He was staring at the pen as well. "That's right. We all are."

"No," Tamara said, but he cut her off.

"No? Who was the one who kept that name alive, all these decades? Who was the one searching for a way back in, no matter the odds?" His teeth flashed—Nell couldn't tell if it was a smile or a grimace. "Ramona, Francis, Eve, Bear. Did any of them refuse to accept that you were gone? Did any of them come looking for you?"

"That's because Daniel—"

"Yes, Daniel." Wally sneered. "Even after all this time, you still take his side. Who was the one who agreed to let you languish in solitude for decades, away from the world, away from your family, and who was the one who spent his life trying to save you from that fate? To save this place?"

"You heard the letter, Wally," Tamara replied quietly. "You know it was my idea. All of it."

For a long moment, Wally didn't say anything. He stared at her, smoldering with betrayal, his pupils so large and dark, they swallowed his pale eyes. Nell clutched her mother's map and fountain pen in one hand and the letter in the other, waiting breathlessly to see which way his reaction would go.

But Wally didn't become angry or upset. He turned back to the waiting scanner on top of the printing press and stroked its pristine surface gently, almost lovingly.

"I forgive you, Tam," he finally said. "It isn't your fault. You've been here so long, you don't know what I've spent my life trying to achieve. Let me show you. Once you see, you'll understand. You'll see I was right all along. That I still can fix everything."

"It's too late," Felix said to him. "It's been too late for a long time."

But Wally ignored him and turned back to Tamara. "Once we combine them, the *Dreamer's Atlas* will be complete. With the only copy, our map will be as close to the world as you can get. It almost *will be* the world, in a way. We can do whatever we want with it."

"You and I may have found the town, but I never wanted it to be only ours," Tamara said. "We never should have tried to keep it a secret. That was where we went wrong, all those years ago."

"Where we went wrong was trusting the others," Wally replied.

"Maps aren't meant to be secrets, Wally. They're meant to be shared," she said.

"Not this one." Slowly, his gaze slid over to Nell. "You understand what I mean."

"No, I don't," Nell started, but he quelled her argument with a tired wave of his gun.

"Yes, you do. You had every opportunity from the start to turn the map over, and you didn't. You didn't tell the police, you didn't tell Irene or the NYPL. You didn't share it with anyone, didn't let anyone help you. You didn't even tell the Cartographers, when you found them. You wanted to keep the map all for yourself."

"No," Nell insisted again, but it came out weak, barely more than a whisper.

She knew he was right. She was no better than Wally was. At any moment, she could have told any of them—Irene, Lieutenant Cabe, Ramona, Francis, Eve, Humphrey—but she'd done the exact opposite. She *had* tried to keep it a secret, even to the point of wrecking her chance at a better life at the library, and her own personal safety. And even worse, she'd forced Swann and Felix to go along with it—and it had cost Swann his life and might be about to cost Felix his.

Felix was shaking his head at her now, begging her not to listen, but Nell couldn't deny it. She could lie to herself that it was because she'd been trying to help the NYPL, or find justice for her father, but that would be all it was. A lie.

Wally's eyes bore into her, knowing.

"You've been on your own for so long, Nell. Wouldn't you like to belong somewhere?"

"I belong," she said reflexively.

"Where? At the NYPL?" he asked. "They cast you out, and now your only friend left there has died. At Classic? You'll stay there for ten more years because you don't know what else to do, and then what?" He took a small step closer to her and her mother. "I spent a *lifetime* trying to finish this map alone. But here we all are, drawn together again. That's worth something. Wouldn't you like to be part of something bigger than you are again?"

"But this isn't the way," Felix said, but Wally took another step, forcing Nell to take a tiny one back.

"Put the map on the scanner," he said to her.

"I won't," Nell argued.

She stared at her mother nervously. Wally had been her best friend for their whole young life. No one knew him better than she did—no one could stop him except her. Her mother had to know that. She had to *do* something.

"What's the purpose of a map?" Tamara asked her.

But Wally spoke first.

"Let me show you," he urged her, before Nell could answer. "The Haberson Map isn't just any map, Nell. Combined with the one you're holding, it could be even greater. Imagine a map that not only showed every corner of the world, down to the most minute detail, but would let you control it, as well. A map that would allow you to improve reality by changing its lines." He looked at her. "A map that is *perfect*."

Nell took another helpless step back.

What Wally had built wasn't a map. Maps were love letters written to times and places their makers had explored. They did not control the territory—they told its stories. But there could be no stories in Wally's Haberson Map. If he could hold this secret place captive on his server and use it to shuffle the rest of the world around on a whim, rearranging reality in whatever way he needed, that was not a story. That was not love.

Wally extended his hand, inviting.

"To bring people together," Nell finally answered her mother's question.

The hopeful excitement that had been flickering in his gaze died out at that.

Slowly, as Nell's knees nearly buckled, the gun's aim swung from Felix to Tamara.

"Wally," her mother said softly.

"Put the map on the scanner, Nell," he repeated.

"Tear it!" Felix begged her.

"She won't," Wally said. "It's the last copy. What do you think happens to a town that ceases to exist while we're in it?"

"Under the circumstances, it sounds like a bargain I might be willing to make," Nell replied through gritted teeth, even though she knew she couldn't really do it. Maybe if it was just her and Wally, and no one else, but Felix and her mother were there, too. She had already lost them both once—she was not going to let there be a second time.

Wally could see she wouldn't do it either. He didn't bother debating her. He took hold of her mother's arm so she couldn't run and pulled her closer to the gun.

"Easy," Nell pleaded. "I'm going."

She took a slow step toward the scanner on the printing press to placate him, frantically searching for a way to drag the moment out, to buy her time to think. Wally turned himself and Tamara slightly to keep her in his sights. His focus had narrowed to the map, and nothing else.

Nell risked a glance at Felix and stared for as long as she could before Wally would remember he was still there. His eyes were filled with terror, but finally, just before she had to look away, she saw a flicker of understanding pierce through his fear. Ever so slightly, he nodded to her.

"Keep going," Wally urged her, still staring at the map.

Nell took another step.

"That's it," he continued, mesmerized.

"It doesn't have to be like this, Wally," Tamara said. "Things don't have to repeat."

But he ignored her. "Your mother will understand, once we show her," he said to Nell. "Put the map on the scanner and join Haberson. Join me. You'll have access to more maps than you could in a hundred lifetimes at the NYPL. There will be no place you cannot go. Nothing we cannot do." His grip on the gun tightened. "When the scan completes, when you behold the Haberson Map at its full potential, you'll both see. You'll see this is really where you belong."

Nell didn't answer him, but she didn't have to. Wally touched the muzzle of the gun to her mother's temple.

Her resolve to drag out the walk as long as possible failed her, and Nell scrambled forward, terrified. All she could think about now was Swann, the look of shock on his face, the dimming as the light went out of his eyes. The scanner's glass pane looked blankly back at her, hungry, empty, waiting for her to put her mother's map into its frame. The mechanical arm with its lights and clamps and rollers waited to the side, ready to trap the page into the machine.

"Now," Wally said.

Nell slid the map inch by inch onto the glass, numb with panic. She needed more time.

"Press the green button," he commanded. "That's all you have to do."

Nell looked back at the scanner, frozen—but the dull click of a safety disengaging from its trigger made her own hand move.

She gasped as her finger pressed the button.

The lights on the scanner's plastic siding began to blink, its heavy mechanical arm jerking to life and lowering on its hinge so that it could carefully creep over every millimeter of her map.

"Very good," Wally said, as the arm clamped down and the cameras whirred inside, beginning their scan. "You did the right thing. You'll see."

As Nell watched the machine slowly devour her mother's final creation, she clenched the fountain pen so tightly, she could feel the little scratches forming the Cartographers' compass rose against her palm. The only thing she could think to do to stop Wally and end his long, twisted struggle was to destroy the map, but she couldn't do that without also destroying them, too.

There *had* to be another way.

As she stared desperately at the map on the scanner, something her mother had written in her letter to Nell—that she realized she could use her skills as a cartographer to save herself, and the town—triggered an old memory. A conversation she'd had with her father over and over in the library, every time he called her to his desk and let her peek at whatever priceless specimen was inside the leather portfolio that day. The words came back to her in a rush.

You're a what? he'd ask as she'd reach for the portfolio with her tiny hands, bouncing up and down excitedly.

I'm a cartographer, she'd answer. *Just like you.*

And what do cartographers do?

They make maps.

A *cartographer,* not a *Cartographer.* She had been using the word to mean its common definition, because she hadn't understood then. But the answer was there all along, in both of her parents' words.

She looked down at the pen in her hand again.

Suddenly, she knew what she had to do.

"Wally," she said, and he looked away from the scanner to her at the sound of his old name. "You're wrong, except about one thing. Where I belong."

She didn't belong at Classic or even the NYPL, as he'd said—but least of all, at Haberson Global, working with him.

She belonged somewhere else.

Wally looked puzzled at her statement, but her gaze left him and moved beyond, to the back of the printing factory. To where Felix had slowly crept away when Wally had turned the gun on her mother, forgetting about him. Felix was crouched in the corner, his hands fumbling with something small. Moments ago, a small mote of light had flared there against the dry wood, nothing more than a spot at first—but then had grown warmer, bigger, brighter, as Wally had been distracted.

Fire.

"No," Wally whispered, stunned.

Nell looked back at her mother, waiting to see what she would do.

Tamara looked at Wally.

And then she wrenched free from him in his state of shock and disappeared into the depths of the factory, toward the growing flames.

"*Tam!*" Wally screamed.

He stumbled forward a few steps after her, horrified, as the fire rushed up the walls.

But Felix had taken advantage of the moment to circle around, and he suddenly appeared again from the other side of the factory, sprinting straight for Wally. "Run, Nell!" he cried as he crashed into Wally, throwing them both to the ground.

But Nell didn't want to run. Just the opposite.

She spun back to the scanner, her eyes locked on the map as it glowed under the blue light, as Felix wrestled for control of the gun.

"Don't you dare!" Wally yelled as he fought. "Don't touch the map!"

"Get back!" Nell shouted to Felix, and Felix shouted something back to her in the scuffle. "Get as far back as possible!"

"Tam!" Wally cried again. "Nell, stop!"

Felix and Wally struggled—Felix was strong, but Wally was too, and filled with desperate rage—until the gun suddenly went flying. It discharged as it hit the ground and clattered away, a bullet ricocheting off a shelf and then embedding in a bookcase as Nell screamed and ducked.

"Get out of here, now!" Felix yelled to her. A rush of blistering air washed over them as the fire engulfed the roof. "This place is going to burn down!"

"No," Wally gasped as he struggled to his feet, his expression full of terror. He was in the grip of his memories now, replaying that horrible day as they fought over the same map again, in almost the same way, Nell knew. He lunged for her and the scanner. "No, not again. This can't happen again, I will not let it happen . . ."

Felix tackled him. "Run!"

"Hold him, Felix! And get back!"

"You can't destroy the map—you'll destroy us all! You'll destroy your *mother!*" Wally was shrieking, calling to Nell with everything he had as Felix dragged him backward.

"Farther!" Nell shouted over Wally, watching Felix manhandle him away before she turned back to the machine. It took all her strength to stop the arm of the scanner, but she leaned her shoulder into it and braced against its juddering attempts to continue copying her map.

"Nell, what are you doing!" Felix was frantic.

"Don't!" Wally yelled.

"Do it!" her mother shouted over him. She appeared from the inferno and rushed forward to grab Wally and help Felix drag him back. Wally howled, trying to hold on to Tamara so she couldn't escape him and also run toward Nell.

Nell gripped her mother's fountain pen harder in her free hand as she pushed, but she couldn't let go with her other to uncap it or the scanner would throw her back. She tilted the pen toward her and bit down on the end.

She understood now, what her mother and Wally had long ago figured out. It was why Tamara had stayed behind for decades to produce her masterpiece, and why he was obsessed with uploading it into his Haberson monstrosity and then destroying the physical version, so only his remained.

If a place existed only within a map, then it existed in every copy of that map. And so, if there was only one copy of a map left, if something changed on that sole copy, it would become true in the physical world, because it would also be true on every copy of the map—since there was only one copy.

Nell didn't have to destroy her mother's map. There was another way to save them all, and the town, from Wally's clutches.

She didn't need to remove Agloe from the map, or the world.

"Farther!" she yelled at Felix and her mother through bared teeth.

She just had to *move* it somewhere else.

"Don't!" Wally screamed. *"Don't you dare—"*

Nell pulled the tip free and spit out the cap.

XXVII

Everything was quiet.

Slowly, millimeter by millimeter, Felix opened one eye.

The town was gone.

"What?" He lurched to his feet, slipping on the wet grass. Grass, not factory floor—he was in the middle of the empty field again, one foot in a tangle of weeds, the other in a puddle. Above, the sky was overcast and heavy, the thunderstorm abating. In the distance, he could see County Road 206 slithering past, a dark gray ribbon through the green. He spun around, nearly tripping on himself, but it was true.

He was back in the real world. There was no dirt path, no shops, no houses, no factory around him.

No Agloe.

"Felix?" a voice called. *"Felix!"*

Felix turned to see two figures rushing toward him across the field.

"Naomi! Priya!" he said, startled.

"Thank goodness you're all right!" Naomi exclaimed as they reached him, and both she and Priya wrapped him in a hug.

"How—"

"We followed you!" Priya said. "You weren't answering us, and then we saw you and William start to move away from the house address, so we kept tracking your phone signal. Then all of a sudden, it just vanished!" She grabbed his arm as if to check that he was truly there. "We got in Naomi's car and took off. We've been searching everywhere—I thought we'd lost you. And then all of a sudden you just . . . appeared! Right in front of us!" she cried.

Felix rocked sideways as they let him go at last, trying to find his feet.

"What *happened?*" Naomi asked him.

He shook his head, overcome. He didn't have the words to explain.

"Felix!" another voice called. The others Nell had come with were running toward him from the far side of the field, where they'd been huddled beneath the trees.

"You're all right!" Humphrey cried, scooping him into an even fiercer embrace than his friends had. "Where are Wally and Nell?"

"Oh my God," he heard Ramona say.

They were all facing Felix, Humphrey still holding on to him after the hug, but looking past him now, staring over his shoulder in shock.

"Is . . . that . . . ," Naomi stammered.

"Is he . . . ," Priya asked.

"He's alive," Felix said. "But it's over."

On the ground just behind Felix, William Haberson—Wally—lay crumpled in the mud, hopeless at what he'd lost. He would never find the town again. Not without the map it had taken him nearly his entire lifetime to find. His eyes were glossy and distant, barely blinking, and all the fight had gone out of his body.

If Felix hadn't been there in Agloe himself, he'd hardly have been able to recognize the man.

But he would have known the woman standing beside Wally anywhere.

Even decades later, she still looked just like Nell.

"Tam?" Ramona whispered.

Tamara smiled. "Romi," she said.

Felix didn't know any of them well, but the bewildered, relieved sobs that burst out of Ramona, Francis, Eve, and Humphrey as they collapsed upon Tamara, hugging and kissing her as she cried too, made his own eyes sting. Or perhaps he was thinking of the inevitable grief Tamara would have to endure over Daniel's death. He suspected she knew that her husband was gone already, because it was Nell who had showed up in Agloe at the end, and not him, but that would not dampen the loss any, once she'd had time to face it.

He thought he knew how she must feel, in a smaller way.

He wiped his tears and looked back out to the field, where, by all laws of physics and nature, there should have been a town, but was not. Where Nell should have been but was not either.

"Was it all still there?" Francis asked at last, his gaze lost somewhere in the same field. "After all this time?"

"It was," Felix replied.

"Did Nell save it?" Eve asked.

"I . . . think so," he said.

He didn't know what Nell had done—but he did know that it had worked. She'd finally found the town, and saved him, and her mother. Just . . .

Humphrey took a small step closer to him, as if afraid to speak the words too loudly. "But where is she, then?"

Felix looked down. "I'm not sure," he managed. "Whatever she did to the map to stop Wally and let us escape, it must not have worked for her."

"She might still be there?" Eve asked. "In the town?"

"I don't know," Felix replied. "I don't even know if the town exists anymore."

Had Nell really destroyed the town, and herself with it, to save them? Or had she thought of something else in the nick of time?

He shrugged helplessly—he was crying again. All he knew was that she wasn't with them. She hadn't made it out.

And he no longer had any way to get back to her.

Naomi put a hand on his arm, comforting him. "I know how much you meant to each other. I'm sorry."

Felix tried to nod. He was sorry, and he also wasn't.

Maybe if they were both still here, standing in this field, with the town safe and Haberson no longer a threat, something could have . . . happened. Not a second chance, but a third.

But also, maybe this was the best they could ever have. Maybe it was not possible for Nell to have both maps and Felix, the same way it hadn't been possible for her parents to have maps and each other. And if that were true, then he was glad that she chose maps, in the end. They were perhaps even more a part of her life than they had been for her father, from the very day she was born, and she had been cut off from them for so long.

The grass squeaked softly behind him as Priya came around to his other side. The faint wail of sirens reached them on the breeze. "We called Ainsley when we got here. Police are on their way up from the city," she said. "They radioed ahead to the local county precinct—officers should be arriving any minute."

Felix bent down and forced Wally to sit up so he could fish his phone and tablet out of his pockets, to prevent him from deleting anything from the company servers. "Can you watch him?" he asked the rest of them. "There's something I need to do."

He saw Humphrey look across the field in response, to where he knew Swann was still lying peacefully in the grass. Felix swallowed hard against the lump rising in his throat again. He wanted to be there when the police examined Swann, to make sure his remains were treated with respect. Not splashed all over the news as a sensationalist crime report. It was the least he could do for the old man.

"I imagine the police also will have a few questions for me, too, once they're finished with Wally," Tamara said.

"How are we even going to explain it?" Ramona asked.

"And even though the last copy of the map is truly gone now, word will get out from this investigation—it's going to reignite the search among collectors," Humphrey added.

Felix smiled sadly. "I think this time, Nell's made it so that no one else has to disappear."

They all glanced down at the ruin of a man still hunched lifelessly at their feet. Haberson Global might no longer be finding missing persons, but it would no longer be creating them, either.

Finally, Francis sighed, a long, slow gust. "The truth will be good, at last. But are you sure you're going to be okay?"

"I will be," Felix said. "Let's just get him secured."

Naomi and Priya pulled their old boss to his feet, with the others' help. The sirens were growing louder as they neared.

"She's not really gone, is she?" Felix asked Tamara, once the rest of them had moved away.

Tamara turned back to him, her curly hair tossing in the breeze just like Nell's always did.

"She's a Cartographer now," she said. "Like she always wanted to be."

A Cartographer.

He liked that. It wasn't enough, but it was something to hold on to, at least. That even if Nell wasn't here with them, she was still out there, somewhere, in Agloe. It was better than the alternative. And if anyone had any idea what had happened, it would be Tamara, and she was smiling at him, not crying.

Tamara put a hand on his shoulder. "I'll go with them too, and let you have some time alone," she said, and he nodded gratefully. "Take as long as you need. We'll wait for you."

Felix went to Swann's body as she left and crouched beside him. It made his heart ache to see him up close. To see how much older he looked than the last time Felix had seen him, when he'd left the library. If only he'd gone to Dr. Young's funeral, or not stormed out of the NYPL memorial event early. Their first conversation in nearly a decade wouldn't have had to be their last, too.

He looked up. In the distance, the others were making their way through the grass back toward the road, Naomi and Priya leading as Francis and Humphrey half walked, half carried Wally between them, to where their car was still parked along the shoulder.

So much had changed in just one night.

Swann had come to help, but now would not be going back. The unconquerable Haberson Global had crumbled. Nell's mother had returned, impossibly.

And Nell herself . . .

Nell . . .

After a few moments, Felix heard the faint sound of car doors slamming closed and the sputter of an engine coming to life, so the heat could be turned on. He imagined the local police pulling up around them, lights flashing, radios blaring. Naomi on the phone with Ainsley, explaining everything. The eventual news stories breaking that William Haberson had been arrested and was responsible for countless crimes. He tried to picture what was going on back at the sleek, towering Haberson offices right now, within the company that had once seemed like his whole world and now would utterly cease to exist.

And he wondered what would happen to the Haberson Map. It was easy with maps on paper—if you tore them, or burned them, they were gone. But what about a map like that? Where did it go when you turned it off for good?

Slowly, Felix touched Swann's still, cold shoulder and told him he'd be right back. There was one other person he had to say goodbye to today, as well.

He stood and walked forward, deeper into the field, leaving the sounds of the humming engine and the others' voices behind him. He kept going, until he was alone, and all he could see was meadow and the low gray sky.

"Well, I guess that's that," he said softly. The green absorbed the sound into its myriad blades of grass and did not reply.

He toed the dirt.

There was no point in staying. Nell could not answer him now, or probably even hear him. And there was so much to do. But he couldn't make himself start the long walk back to Swann, and then back to the police to answer their thousands of questions, and then to reporters after that, and who knew what else.

He wished he and Nell had just had a little more time, or that there was some way he could see her again—but that was impossible now. She was in Agloe, wherever Agloe was, if it was anywhere at all. There was no way to get to it anymore.

But he had so much left that he needed to tell her. It was infuriating—for years, they'd had absolutely nothing to say to each other, and now all of a sudden there were a million things—but she was gone.

"Take care of yourself, Nell," he whispered at last, his throat tight.

Something he'd heard her father sometimes say on the phone to colleagues at other institutions came to him, a memory from a lifetime ago. He smiled and wondered if perhaps it was something the Cartographers used to say to each other long ago, when they'd all still been friends.

"I hope the maps are good where you are."

• • • •

Autumn at the NYPL was nothing like autumn at Haberson Global. All of Haberson's internal systems had been run by a smart computer, from the lights to the thermostat to the humidity in the air to the grocery orders for the free gourmet cafeterias, and it all adjusted with the seasons. It had never been too sweaty there in June, nor too dry in November. If the outside weather suddenly shifted, the computer would adjust, raising or lowering the temperature across the entirety of the facility so all employees remained comfortable.

But autumn at the NYPL was like being tossed from a boiling furnace into an icebox and back, a hundred times a day.

The hallways were always so frigid, icicles practically grew from the corners where the walls met the ceiling. It was all that marble, and the centuries of settling and resettling the old building had done. In the copy area, people actually held their breath when they went in to retrieve their print jobs, because the vents gushed such scalding air straight onto the machines, the smell of burnt ink pervaded the whole room.

And in Felix's office, it was practically a steam sauna.

He loosened his tie and tried to sit in his chair without letting his back touch the leather, lest he stick to it through his shirt. He'd taken to eating his lunches outside, hip propped against one of the lion statues that flanked the building while the snow swirled around him, just to relieve the flush on his skin. There was a collections meeting after this, and he wasn't sure how he was going to talk himself into putting his blazer back on for it without fainting.

It was funny how much things had changed since the spring.

William Haberson's—Wally's—trial was ongoing, and it would likely be years before everything he'd done was fully uncovered, but Haberson Global already no longer existed as a company—some of the smaller branches had been spun off or purchased by competitors, but the tech juggernaut that had previously ruled the industry was no more than a ghost, even more than Wally himself was.

Once the dust had settled, Francis retired from Harvard University to become the new chair of the NYPL. He nominated Dr. Tamara Jasper-Young to take up Swann's mantle as the new director of the Map Division, and she won by a stunned, unanimous vote. The publicity the library received from her mysterious, miraculous return to the world saw every research room and reading table packed to the brim, and its rotating exhibitions docket and invitations for joint initiatives from fellow museums and universities overbooked for years—if there had been any worry about funding for the NYPL before, it now seemed like something Francis would never have to consider again, for as long as he was in charge. Ramona, Eve, and Humphrey all returned to their jobs, but now, a week never went by without at least one of them dropping by the library for a guest lecture or a visit.

And as for Felix, he had found himself in Dr. Daniel Young's old office.

He'd upgraded the ancient computer as quickly as he could—the NYPL's first geospatial librarian needed adequate tools to do his job properly—but he'd kept the majority of the books, and most of all, the delicately painted letters that spelled out the former head curator's name and position on the door, for now at least. He liked looking at them every time he arrived in the morning and left in the evening. It made him think of both Drs. Young he'd known so well—Daniel and Nell. A good reminder of how far he'd come and who he had to thank for it, in the end.

Every time he sat in that chair, he wanted to reminisce for the entire day. But there was still that meeting he needed to put his jacket back on for despite the overenthusiastic heating system, and he'd barely gotten through the morning's stack of messages in his in-box. The sheer volume of paper would have made him furious at Haberson Global, and it was doing the same to the rest of his newly hired but very familiar team of geospatial librarian specialists, Naomi and Priya, but Felix loved these old, hallowed halls for what they were—that he could convince Francis to finally, *finally* let IT streamline all departments into one email server, and everyone still just kept sending handwritten notes anyway.

With an affectionate sigh, Felix slid the silver letter opener Dr. Young had left behind deftly into the gap in each envelope, sorting the pages into *business* and *junk*. There were still a fair number of congratulations cards coming in from old colleagues far and wide, as well as no shortage of invitations to various conferences and symposiums.

Then there was one simple white envelope, made out to Felix Kimble and bearing no return address.

He inspected it curiously and then slit it open. He was expecting mass-printed spam and almost tossed the whole thing into the junk pile, but the contents stopped him. The papers inside were old and custom-looking, and the ink on them darker and richer than what a typical office printer would produce.

Nell?

His heart leapt illogically, like it always did in the moment before he discovered whatever he'd foolishly hoped had been from her was actually mundane, and he felt a little foolish.

But when he turned the envelope over to glance at the back, his breathing quickened. Where the flap was, the sender had drawn a shape he immediately recognized.

An eight-point compass, with a small *C* in the center.

He moved too quick—the rest of the envelope tore clumsily, offering its contents.

Had she written him a goodbye letter? An explanation for why it had to be this way? *It would be* so *like her,* he thought. *Damn you, Nell.* Making yet another rash decision that affected them both and then stealing the final word.

Carefully, he reached in and pulled the note free.

After a long moment, Felix looked up, across the cluttered, book-crammed office, everything cast in pale gold as the dust motes swirled in the sunlight, and smiled.

It wasn't a letter after all, but rather an invitation.

Printed on an old-fashioned offset press.

In the next few weeks, thousands of them would go out, to every university and library and museum in existence. The greatest secret in the world of cartography would no longer be a secret. It would be shared far and wide, so many maps printed that it would be impossible for anyone to do what Wally had done again.

Agloe would be for everyone.

But for now, until the postal service delivered the others, his invitation was the first copy.

The next page had no words. Just a picture, sketched in that singular frenzied scribble that he knew so well and loved so much.

Nell had drawn him a map.

A map to somewhere new.

Acknowledgements

Acknowledgments

In writing, there are no maps except the ones you create yourself. This book would not have been possible without the people, my landmarks, below.

Thank you to Naomi Kanakia, Mike Chen, and Jillian Keenan for always being willing to talk craft, first drafts, and the labyrinth of revision, and to my mother, Lin Sue Cooney, for always believing this novel was going to get finished. It never would have without you. And thank you to my husband, Sathyaseelan Subramaniam, for your constant friendship, tireless encouragement, and love.

I'm indebted to my agents, Alexandra Machinist and Felicity Blunt, who are both very wise and endlessly patient. To my editors, Emily Krump and Emad Akhtar, for helping me find the heart of this story, and to Danielle Bartlett, Ryan Shepherd, Stephanie Vallejo, Hope Breeman, Ploy Siripant, Julia Elliott, and everyone at William Morrow and Orion who make the incredibly difficult task of turning a manuscript into a book look easy. I'm also grateful to the National Endowment for the Arts for its generous writing fellowship, and to the New York Public Library for being a place of wonder and inspiration.

Last, but not least, thank you to General Drafting Corporation for putting magic into maps. As I mentioned in the Author's Note at the beginning, this book is a work of fiction, but its seed grew from a true story. General Drafting was a real business. Agloe really was a phantom settlement its founder hid on a map to protect his copyright. And it really *did* become real—for a time.

In the early 1900s, when the automobile was still a new invention, Otto G. Lindberg's General Drafting Corporation took a risk and began to produce cheap, foldable driving maps. The two biggest mapmakers in the United States, Rand McNally and H.M. Gousha, initially ignored what they believed would be a fleeting style, and let General Drafting corner the market. But by 1930, the juggernauts had realized their mistake, and raced fiercely to catch up. Lindberg and his assistant, Ernest Alpers, were concerned that because there would be no way to prove it, any rival looking to cut corners could simply copy General Drafting's hard work instead of conducting their own measurements. Lindberg and Alpers had far less money and manpower, and desperately needed a way to protect their craft.

And that was how Agloe was born.

Some time after General Drafting published its New York State driving map with their secret town hidden on it, Rand McNally released its own version, and Lindberg spotted Agloe on their competitor's map in the exact same area. He sued, claiming he'd caught Rand McNally stealing red-handed, because he and Alpers had made up Agloe. It wasn't real.

Except it was, said Rand McNally.

Lindberg and his lawyers drove out to the deserted Catskills countryside where he'd placed Agloe on his map, ready to claim victory.

He was stunned by what he found.

There, where there should have been absolutely nothing at all, was a gas station, a general store, houses with people living in them—and an official record in Delaware County administration logs.

A town that was not supposed to exist at all somehow mysteriously did.

I first heard about General Drafting and Agloe years ago, and have remained captivated by the story ever since. I kept thinking about this impossible town, returning again and again to the idea in between other deadlines. Maps already hold so much beauty and wonder for all of us, and the real-world mystery of an imaginary town that became real was too tantalizing to let go.

The truth of what happened is just as fascinating as any fiction. It turns out that when General Drafting's map first went into circulation, residents of the area where Lindberg and Alpers had planted Agloe saw this new name on the paper and assumed the local government had established the town for them. They began re-titling businesses and revising addresses already in the general area, which then prompted county administrators to record the information. This flurry of activity attracted new residents, who then built even more buildings and named them after Agloe, too. By the time Rand McNally's cartographers traveled through on their own geographical survey, they came upon a bustling little village the residents confidently informed them was called Agloe—and so they put it on their own map as well.

This incredible town existed for decades and even became somewhat of a tourist attraction before the residents of Agloe eventually disbanded, and mapmakers, at last, removed the town from their maps. But even though now there's only an empty field left where Agloe used to be, its legend lives on.

The more accurate a map is, the more powerful we understand it to be—that is, the world is what makes the *map* real. But Otto G. Lindberg achieved something even more spectacular, even if it was by serendipity. His map made part of the *world* real, at least for a little bit, and proved that even in this day and age, there are still secrets to be discovered within the folds of their pages.

And that seems pretty magical to me.

About the Author

Peng Shepherd was born and raised in Phoenix, Arizona, where she rode horses and trained in classical ballet, and has lived in Beijing, Kuala Lumpur, London, Washington, D.C., and New York City.

Her first novel, *The Book of M*, won the 2019 Neukom Institute for Literary Arts Award for Debut Speculative Fiction and was chosen as a best book of the year by Amazon, *Elle*, Refinery29, and The Verge, as well as a best book of the summer by the *Today* show and NPR's *On Point*. A graduate of New York University's MFA program, Peng is the recipient of a 2020 fellowship from the National Endowment for the Arts, as well as the Elizabeth George Foundation's emerging writers 2016 grant.

[illegible] thor

[illegible] Arizona, where she [illegible] and has lived in Bos[illegible] and New York City [illegible] Neukom Institut[illegible] ction and was chosen [illegible] and The Verge [illegible] show and NPR's [illegible] MFA program, Peng is [illegible] tional Endowment for the [illegible] emerging writers [illegible]